IGNITED BY PASSION

NEW YORK TIMES AND USA TODAY BESTSELLING AUTHOR

BRENDA
JACKSON

IGNITED BY PASSION

ARABESQUE®

Recycling programs
for this product may
not exist in your area.

ISBN-13: 978-0-373-53438-8

IGNITED BY PASSION

Copyright © 2011 by Harlequin Enterprises S.A.

The publisher acknowledges the copyright holder of the
individual works as follows:

STONE COLD SURRENDER
Copyright © 2004 by Brenda Streater Jackson

RIDING THE STORM
Copyright © 2004 by Brenda Streater Jackson

www.kimanipress.com

Printed in U.S.A.

CONTENTS

THE WESTMORELAND FAMILY

Scott and Delane Westmoreland

John (Evelyn)

- ② Dare (Shelly) — AJ, Allison
- ③ Thorn (Tara) — Trace
- ④ Stone (Madison) — Rock
- ⑤ Storm (Jayla) — Shanna, Johanna
- ⑥ Jared (Dana) — Jaren
- ⑧ Durango (Savannah) — Sarah
- ⑨ Ian (Brooke) — Pierce, Price
- ⑪ Spencer (Chardonnay) — Russell
- ⑩ Casey (McKinnon) — Corey Martin
- ⑫ Clint (Alyssa) — Cain
- ⑬ Cole (Patrina) — Emilie, Emery

James (Sarah)

- ① Delaney (Jamal) — Ari, Arielle
- ⑦ Chase (Jessica) — Carlton Scott
- ⑭ Quade (Cheyenne) — Venus, Athena, Troy
- Reggie (Olivia)

Corey (Abbie) — Madison

THE DENVER WESTMORELAND FAMILY TREE

Raphel and Gemma Westmoreland

Stern Westmoreland (Paula Bailey)

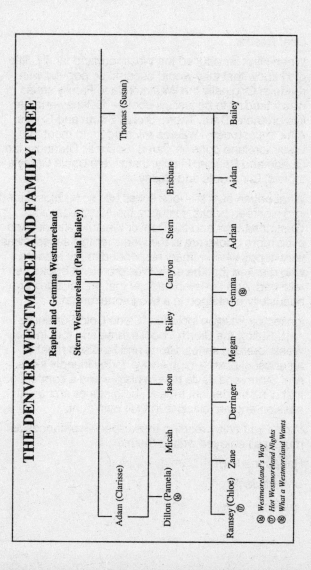

Adam (Clarisse)

Thomas (Susan)

Dillon (Pamela) ⑯

Micah   Jason   Riley   Canyon   Stern   Brisbane

Ramsey (Chloe) ⑰

Zane   Derringer   Megan   Gemma ⑱   Adrian   Aidan

Bailey

⑯ *Westmoreland's Way*
⑰ *Hot Westmoreland Nights*
⑱ *What a Westmoreland Wants*

Dear Reader,

When I first introduced the Westmoreland family, little did I know that they would become so popular with readers. Originally the Westmoreland Family series was intended to be just six books—Delaney and her five brothers, Dare, Thorn, Stone, Storm and Chase. After their stories, I wanted my readers to meet the Westmoreland cousins, Jared, Spencer, Durango, Ian, Quade and Reggie. Finally, there were Uncle Corey's triplets, Clint, Cole and Casey.

What began as a six-book series has so far blossomed into eighteen books, featuring the Atlanta-based Westmorelands and the Denver Westmorelands. And even more books are in the works for this series. I was very happy when Kimani responded to my readers, who'd asked that the early Westmoreland books be reissued. And I'm even happier that the reissues are beautifully packaged in a two-in-one format.

Ignited by Passion includes "Stone Cold Surrender" and "Riding the Storm," books three and four in the Westmoreland series. Stone and Madison meet in an unusual place—high above, in the friendly skies. And Storm and Jayla have a history and a connection that can't be denied. Indeed, both stories sizzle with passion and are classics in their own right.

I hope you enjoy reading these special romances as much as I enjoyed writing them.

Happy reading!

Brenda Jackson

STONE COLD SURRENDER

Happy is the man that findeth wisdom,
and the man that getteth understanding.
—*Proverbs* 3:13

To my husband, the love of my life and my best friend
Gerald Jackson, Sr. And to everyone who asked for
Stone's and Storm's stories, this book is for you!

Chapter 1

The woman had a death grip on his thigh. The pain was almost unbearable but her hands touching him felt so damn good.

No longer satisfied with looking at her out of the corner of his eye, Stone Westmoreland slowly glanced over to stare at the woman, studying every single element about her. She was strapped in her seat as if the plane would crash unless she grabbed hold of something. Her eyes were shut tight and her breathing was irregular and it reminded him of the breathing pattern of a woman who'd just experienced the most satisfying orgasm. Just thinking about her touch aroused him….

He leaned back in his seat as the plane leveled off in the sky and closed his own eyes. With back-to-back book deadlines, it had been a long time since he'd been with a woman and a mere touch from her had sent his libido into overdrive.

He opened his eyes and took a shaky breath, hoping the month he would spend at his cousin's ranch in Montana, getting his thoughts together for a new book, would do him some good. At thirty-three, he and Durango were only a few months apart in age and had always been close. Then there was his uncle Corey who lived not far from Durango on a ranch high up in the mountains. Corey Westmoreland was his father's youngest brother who, at fifty-four, had retired as a park ranger after over thirty years of service.

Stone had fond memories of the summers he and his one sister, four brothers and six male cousins had shared visiting Uncle Corey. They had gained a great appreciation for the outdoors, as well as for wildlife. Their uncle always took his job as a park ranger seriously and his love for the wilderness had been contagious.

The one thing that stood out in Stone's mind about his uncle was that he never planned to marry. In fact, other than the women in the family, no other woman's foot had ever touched the soil of Corey's mountain. His uncle always said it was because he was so ornery and set in his ways that marriage wasn't for him. He much preferred living the life of a bachelor.

Stone's thoughts shifted to his brothers. This time last year all of them had been happy-go-lucky, enjoying every single minute of playing the field. Then the next thing you know, Dare, the eldest, got married and less than six months later, last month to be exact, his brother Thorn was marching down the aisle. Everyone in the family began ribbing Stone, saying since he was the third Westmoreland brother he would probably be next.

And he had been quick to tell them that hell would freeze over first.

He enjoyed being a bachelor too much to fall for any type of marriage trap. And although he would be the first to admit that the women his brothers had married were the best and more than worthy of their undying love and affection, he had decided a long time ago, just like Uncle Corey, that marriage wasn't for him. Not that he considered himself ornery or set in his ways; he just did not want to be responsible for anyone other than himself. He enjoyed the freedom to come and go whenever he pleased, and being a national, award-winning, bestselling author of action-thriller novels afforded him that luxury. He traveled all over the world to do research, and whenever he did date it was on his time and no one else's. For him women were a necessity, but only at certain times, and usually it wasn't difficult to find one who agreed to an affair on his terms.

To be completely honest, Stone had no issues with the concept of marriage, he just wasn't ready to take the plunge himself. He'd made a decision long ago to remain single after watching a good friend, who was also a bestselling author, become hopelessly in love and besotted with a woman. After getting married, Mark had decided that writing was not a priority in his life anymore. His focus had switched. He much preferred spending time with his wife instead of sitting at a computer all day. It was as if Mark had become Samson who'd gotten a hair cut. Once married, he had been zapped of his identity.

The thought that he could lose his desire to write over something called love totally unnerved Stone. Since publishing his first book at twenty-three, writing had become his life and he didn't intend for that to change.

Doing so would mean losing control and the idea of losing that type of control on his life was something he couldn't handle.

Stone decided to check out the woman sitting beside him once more. Even with her eyes closed, he immediately liked what he saw. Shoulder-length dark brown hair and skin the color of dark coffee. She had a nice set of full lips and her nose was just the right fit for her face. She had long lashes and her cheeks were high. If she was wearing makeup, it was not very much. She was a natural beauty.

He glanced down at her hand, the one gripping his thigh. She was not wearing an engagement or wedding ring, which was good; and she had boarded the plane in Atlanta, which meant she either lived in the area or had come through the city to catch this connecting flight. Since they were on the same plane, unless she had another connecting flight, she was also bound for Montana.

His body tensed when he felt her grip tighten on his thigh. He inhaled deeply. If her hand moved even less than an inch, she would be clutching the most intimate part of him and he doubted she wanted to do that. Chances were she assumed her hand was gripping the armrest, so he decided he'd better let her know what was going on before he embarrassed them both.

He noticed that the sun, shining through the airplane window, hit her features at such an angle that they glowed. Even her hair appeared thick and luxurious and fanned her face in a way that made her look even more attractive.

Leaning over quietly, so as not to startle her, he breathed in her scent before getting a single word out of his mouth. It was a fragrance that turned him on even more than he already was. The aroma seemed entrenched into her skin and he was tempted to take his tongue and lick a portion of her bare neck to see if perhaps he could sample a taste of it.

Stone shook his head. Since when had he developed a fetish for a woman's skin? He enjoyed the art of kissing, like most men, but wanting to taste, nibble and devour a woman all over had never been something that interested him.

Until now.

He pushed the thought to the back of his mind, deciding it was too dangerous to even go there; he leaned closer and whispered softly in her ear, "The plane has leveled off so you can let go of me now."

She snapped open her eyes and quickly turned her head to meet his gaze. A part of him suddenly wished she hadn't done that. He found himself staring into the most beautiful set of brown eyes he had ever seen. They were perfect for the rest of her features and something in their dark depths made his body almost jerk in the seat.

She was simply gorgeous, although in truth there wasn't anything simple about it. She literally took his breath away. And, speaking of breath, he watched as she drew in a long, shaky one before glancing down at her left hand. She immediately snatched it off his thigh.

Awareness flashed in her eyes and total embarrassment appeared on her face. "Oh, oh, I'm so sorry. I didn't mean to touch you. I thought my hand was on the armrest. I—I didn't mean to act so improperly."

When Stone saw the degree of distress on her face he decided to assure her that he would survive. The last thing he wanted was for her to come unglued and get all flustered on him. And he really liked her accent. It was totally different from his Southern drawl and had the unmistakable inflection of a northeasterner. She was definitely someone from one of those New England States.

"Hey, no harm's done," he tried to say casually. "My name is Stone Westmoreland," he said, introducing himself and presenting his hand to her.

She still looked embarrassed when she took it and said, "And I'm Madison Winters."

He smiled. "Nice meeting you, Madison. Is this your first flight?"

She shook her head when he released her hand. "Nice meeting you, too, and no, this isn't my first flight, but I have a definite fear of flying. I try using other means of transportation whenever I can, but in this particular situation time is of the essence."

He nodded. "And where are you from?" he couldn't help but ask, her accent affecting him just as much as her touch had. Just listening to how she pronounced her words was a total turn-on.

"I'm from Boston. I was born and raised there."

He nodded again. "I'm from the Atlanta area," he decided to say when moments passed and she hadn't taken the liberty to ask. Whether it was from shyness or disinterest, he wasn't sure. But as far as he was concerned it didn't matter if she wasn't interested in him. He was definitely interested in her.

"I love visiting Atlanta," she said moments later. "I took my class on a field trip there once."

He raised a brow. "Your class?"

She smiled and his stomach flipped. "Yes, I'm a teacher. I teach music to sixth graders."

Stone smiled, surprised. He would never have figured her to be the artsy type. He remembered taking band when he was about eleven and learning to play the clarinet. His band teacher had looked nothing like her. "Must be interesting."

Her smile widened. "It is and I enjoy what I do."

He chuckled. "Yes, in this day and time it's good when a person can enjoy their work."

She stared at him for a second then asked, "And what type of work do you do?"

He hesitated before answering. As a bestselling author he used a pseudonym to ensure his privacy, but for some reason he felt comfortable being truthful with her. "I'm a fiction writer."

A smile tilted her lips. "Oh, how wonderful. Sorry, but I don't recall ever reading any of your books. What exactly do you write about?"

Stone chuckled. "I write action-thriller novels under the pseudonym of Rock Mason."

She blinked and then gasped. "You're Rock Mason? *The* Rock Mason?"

He smiled, glad that she had at least heard of Rock Mason. "Yes."

"Oh, my gosh! My mother has read every single book you've written. She is an avid fan of yours."

His smile widened. "What about you? Have you read any of my books?"

She gazed at him with regret. "No, I usually don't have time to read for pleasure, but from what I understand you're a gifted author."

"Thanks."

"A few of my girlfriends are in book clubs and they select your books to read and discuss whenever they hit the bookstores. You have quite a following in Boston. Have you ever visited there?"

"Yes, I did a book signing in Boston a couple of years ago and thought it was a beautiful city."

Madison beamed. "It is. I love Boston and can't imagine myself living anywhere else. I even attended Boston University because I didn't want to leave home."

At that moment they were interrupted as the flight attendant stopped to serve them drinks and a snack.

"So are you headed for Montana on business?" Stone asked. He remembered her saying something earlier about needing to get there rather quickly. He watched as she took a bite of her muffin and immediately felt his libido register the single crumb that clung to the side of her mouth. If that wasn't bad enough, she took a long sip of coffee and closed her eyes. Seconds later, as if the coffee was the best she'd ever tasted, she reopened her eyes. He saw the play of emotions across her face as she thought about his question.

"No, my visit to Montana is strictly personal." Then she studied him for a moment as if making a decision about something and said, "I'm going to Montana to find my mother."

Stone lifted a brow. "Oh? Is she missing?"

Madison leaned back against her seat, seemingly frustrated. "Yes. She and a couple of other women from Boston flew to Montana two weeks ago to tour Yellowstone National Park." She looked down and studied her coffee before adding in a low voice, "All the other women returned except my mother."

He heard the deep concern in her voice. "Have you heard from her?"

She nodded her head. "Yes. She left a message on my answering machine letting me know that she had decided to extend her vacation another two weeks."

A part of Madison wondered why she was disclosing such information to Stone, a virtual stranger. The only reason she could come up with was that she needed to talk to someone and Stone Westmoreland seemed like a nice enough guy to listen. Besides, she needed an unbiased ear.

"She left a message that she's extending her vacation yet you're going to Montana to look for her anyway?"

Stone's question, and the way he had asked it, let her know he didn't understand. "Yes, because there's a man involved."

He nodded slowly. "Oh, I see."

Frankly, he really didn't see at all and evidently his expression revealed as much because she then said, "You might not think there's reason for concern, Mr. West-moreland, but—"

"Stone. Please call me Stone."

She smiled. "All right." Then she started explaining herself again. "There is good reason for my concern, Stone. My mother hasn't done anything like this before."

He nodded again. "So you think that perhaps there has been some sort of foul play?"

She shook her head, denying that possibility. "No, I think it has something to do with her going through some sort of midlife crisis. She turned fifty a couple of months ago, and until that time she was completely normal."

Stone took a sip of his coffee. He remembered what happened when his mother turned fifty. She decided that she wanted to go back to school and start working outside of the home. His father almost had a fit because he was one of those traditional men who believed a woman's work was in the home raising kids. But his mother had made up her mind about what she wanted to do and nothing was going to stop her. Since his baby sister, Delaney, had gone off to college and there weren't any kids left at home to raise, his father had finally given in.

He shifted his thoughts to Madison's mother. Personally, he saw nothing abnormal with a woman disappearing in the wilds of Montana with a man, if that's what she wanted to do. However, from the worried expression on Madison's face, she evidently thought otherwise.

"So what do you plan on doing when you find her?" he asked curiously. After all, she was still the daughter and her mother was still the mother. He had learned from experience that parents felt they could do whatever pleased them without any interference from their children. At least that had always been the case with his mother and father, and he thought they were the greatest parents in the world.

"I'm going to try and talk some sense into her, of course," Madison said, her lips tightening in determination. "My father died of a heart attack over ten years ago, and my mother has been a widow since that time. She is the most staid, levelheaded and sensible person you could ever meet."

She sighed deeply then added, "Taking off with a man she doesn't know, whom she only met one night at dinner, doesn't make sense and it's so unlike her."

Stone's action-thriller mind went to work. "And you're positive she went off with this man willingly?"

He watched a clearly frustrated Madison take another sip of her coffee before answering. "Yes, there were witnesses, including the ladies who accompanied her on the trip. They said she simply packed one morning and announced that the guy was coming for her and she would be spending the rest of the time with him and to let me know she had decided to extend her trip. Of course I couldn't believe it and had all but called in the FBI before I got her phone call. Unfortunately, I wasn't at home when she called so we didn't talk, but her message clearly said that she was all right and was extending her vacation another two weeks and not to worry about her. But of course I'm worried."

Stone thought that was pretty evident. "Can she take additional time off from her job like that?" he asked, curious with everything Madison was telling him.

"Yes. My mother retired as a hospital administrator last year and owns a day-care center for the elderly. She has an excellent staff. Over the past couple of months she's been spending less time at the office and doing a lot of charity work in the community. She's really big into that."

Stone leaned back in his seat. "Do you have an idea where you plan to look? Montana is a huge place."

"I've made reservations at this dude ranch outside of Bozeman called the Silver Arrow. Have you ever heard of it?"

Stone smiled. Yes, he had. In fact, the Silver Arrow Dude Ranch was only a short distance from Durango's place. He was rather pleased that he and Madison would be in close proximity to each other. "I know exactly where it is. In fact, it's not far from where I'll be staying. The two of us will practically be neighbors."

She smiled like the thought of that pleased her. Or maybe it was wishful thinking on his part, Stone thought as his gaze centered on her lips.

"I've made plans for a tour guide to take me up into the mountains after I'm settled," she said, breaking into his thoughts.

Stone lifted a brow. "Up into the mountains?"

"Yes, that's where the man has taken my mother."

He paused in the act of taking a bite of his muffin. "This man took your mother up into the mountains?" At her nod he then asked, "Why?"

"Because that's where he lives."

After chewing a morsel of the muffin, Stone inquired, "The guy actually lives in the mountains?" He took a swallow of coffee, thinking he'd always thought his uncle Corey was the only man brave enough to forgo civilization and live high up in the mountains. While he worked as a park ranger, Corey Westmoreland stayed in the lowlands, making the trip into the mountains on his days off.

"Yes, according to the information I was able to find, he lives on this huge mountain," Madison said, interrupting his thoughts. "The man is a retired park ranger. I don't have his full name but I understand he's well known in those parts and goes by Carl, Cole, Cord or something like that."

A portion of Stone's coffee went down the wrong pipe and he began coughing to clear his throat.

"Stone, are you all right?" Madison asked in concern.

Stone looked at her, not sure if he was all right or

not. The man she had just described sounded a lot like his uncle Corey.

But a woman on Corey's mountain?

He cleared this throat thoroughly before asking his next question. He met her gaze, hoping he had not heard her correctly. "Are you saying that some guy who is a retired park ranger and who owns a ranch high up in the mountains is the person your mother ran off with?"

After wiping her mouth with a napkin, Madison nodded her head. "Yes. Can you imagine anything so ridiculous?"

No. In all honesty I can't, if we're talking about the same person. Stone thought about what she had told him. He then considered everything he knew about his uncle, especially how he felt about a woman ever setting foot on his beloved mountain.

He then answered Madison as honestly as he knew how. "No, I can't imagine anything so ridiculous."

She must have talked the man to death, Madison thought, glancing over at Stone a short while later. Conversation between them had dwindled off and he was leaning back in his seat, his head tipped back against the headrest, his eyes closed either in sleep or deep thought.

She couldn't help but take this opportunity to examine him.

If a man could be described as beautiful, it would be him. He was more handsome than any man had a right to be. She could easily tell that he had broad shoulders and although he was sitting down there was no doubt in her mind that he probably had pretty lean hips. But what captivated her most about him were his dark almond-shaped eyes and she wished they weren't closed so she could gaze into them some more.

They were as dark as midnight and, when he had looked at her, it was as if he could see everything, right deep into her very soul. Then there was his neatly trimmed curly black hair that was cut low, his high cheekbones and his beautifully full lips that had almost melted her in her seat when he had smiled. And the healthy texture of his chestnut skin tempted her to touch it to see if it was really soft as cotton.

For the first time, her mind was not focused on the fact that she was on a plane, but on the fact that she was sitting next to the most gorgeous man she had ever seen. Ordinarily, she would be the last person to notice a man after what Cedric had done to her a couple of years ago. Finding out the man you were about to marry was having an affair was painful to say the least. Since then she had decided that no man was worth the trouble. Some people were just meant to be alone.

She settled back in her seat, frowning as she wondered if the reason her mother had taken off with a man was because she had been tired of living alone. Abby Winters had been widowed for over ten years, and Madison knew her father's death had not been easy on her. She'd also known, even though her mother had refused to discuss it, that her parents had not had a happy marriage. All it had taken was a weekend spent in the home of a high school friend, whose parents were still very much in love, to notice things she didn't see at home. Her father had never kissed her mother before leaving for work, nor had they exchanged funny-looking smiles across the dinner table when they thought no one was watching.

Her parents had been highly educated people: Harvard graduates. Somehow over the years they had become absorbed in their individual careers. Although there was no doubt in her mind that they had loved her, it was clearly obvious that at some point they had stopped loving each other.

It seemed they had pretty much accepted a loveless marriage. Even after her father's death, her mother still didn't date, although Madison knew several men had asked her out once or twice.

That's what made Abby Winters' actions now so baffling and unacceptable. What was it about the man that had captured her mother's interest enough to do something as outrageous as going off with him to his mountain? As she had told Stone, her mother was the most rational person she knew, so it had to be some sort of midlife crisis. There was no other explanation for it.

And what would she say to her mother when she saw her? That was a question for which she had no answer. The only thing she knew for certain was that she was determined to talk some sense into her. Fifty-year-old women just did not run off with men they didn't know.

Madison shook her head. She was twenty-five and she would never take up with some man she didn't know, even someone as good looking as Stone. She quickly glanced over at him and had to admit that taking off with him was definitely a tempting thought.

A *very* tempting thought.

She pushed the thought aside, thinking that one Winters woman acting impulsive and irrational was enough.

* * *

What if the man Madison Winters had described was really Uncle Corey?

With his eyes closed, that question continued to plague Stone's mind. At the moment he was pretending to be asleep, not wanting Madison to see his inner turmoil. Since the plane was at an altitude where he could use a mobile phone, he considered calling Durango to find out if Corey had abducted the woman. Durango, who was also a park ranger, had moved to Montana to attend college and joined the profession that their uncle had loved so much.

Durango had lived with Corey until he had saved up enough to purchase his own land. But calling Durango was not an option, not with Madison sitting next to him. Although she would try not to eavesdrop, there was no way she would not overhear his every word. He had no choice but to wait until the plane landed to question Durango. He hoped like hell that he was wrong and there was another retired park ranger who lived high in the mountains and whose name began with the letter C.

Stone breathed in slowly. Madison's scent was getting to him again. If he were completely honest he would admit that his blood had begun stirring the moment she had sat next to him on the flight. He had tried ignoring her by concentrating on the activities outside the plane window as the airline crew prepared for takeoff, and had pretty much dismissed her from his mind until she had touched him.

Aroused him was a much better word.

He sighed deeply. This would definitely be one flight he would not forget in a long time. He couldn't help but open his eyes and glance over at her. Her eyes were closed, her lips were parted and she was breathing at an even pace. Unlike before, she was now resting peacefully and had somehow taken her mind off her fear of flying, and a part of him felt good about that. He didn't want to dwell on the protective instincts he was developing for her. Perhaps he felt this way because she reminded him of his baby sister, Delaney.

A lazy smile touched his lips. As the only girl constantly surrounded by five older brothers and six older male cousins, Delaney had been overprotected most of her life. But after graduating from medical school she had pulled a fast one on everyone and had sneaked away to a secluded cabin in the North Carolina mountains for rest and relaxation, only to discover the mountain retreat was already occupied. A visiting desert sheikh, who'd had the same idea about rest and relaxation, had been ensconced in the cabin when she'd arrived. During the course of their "vacation," the two fell in love and now his baby sister was a princess living in the Middle East.

Delaney was presently in the States with her family to finish her residency at a hospital in Kentucky. He enjoyed seeing his one-year-old nephew Ari and had to admit that his sister's husband, Sheikh Jamal Ari Yasir, had grown on him and his brothers, and now he was as welcome a sight as Delaney. Stone knew Jamal loved his sister immensely.

He looked around the plane, wishing there was some way he could walk around and stretch his stiff muscles, but knew that would mean waking Madison to reach the aisle, and he didn't want to do that for fear she would start talking again about the man who could be his uncle. Until he got some answers from Durango, the last thing he wanted to do was come across as if he were deceiving her.

He glanced over at her once more and admired her beauty. To his way of thinking, Madison Winters was a woman no man in his right mind would want to deceive.

Chapter 2

The landing was smooth and as the plane taxied up to the terminal, Madison breathed a sigh of relief to be back on the ground. She unbuckled her seat belt and watched as the other passengers wasted little time getting out of their seats and gathering their belongings from the overhead compartments. Some people were moving quickly to catch connecting flights, while others appeared eager to be reunited with the loved ones waiting for them.

"Do you need help getting anything?"

She turned and met Stone's gaze. His voice was low, deep and seductive, and reminded her of the husky baritone of the singer Barry White. The rhythm of her heart increased.

"No, I can manage, but thanks for asking. If you don't mind, I'll wait until the plane empties before getting off. If you need to get by I can move out of your way."

"No, I'm in no hurry, either. I doubt my cousin is here to pick me up since he's never on time." He smiled. "But then he just might surprise me this time."

His smile did funny things to her insides, Madison thought, glancing around to see how many people were left to get off the plane. The best thing to do would be to get as far away from Stone Westmoreland as soon as she could. The man messed with her ability to think straight and, for the moment, finding her mother needed her full concentration.

"Do you have transportation to the Silver Arrow ranch?"

Again she met his gaze. "Yes. I was told they would be sending someone for me."

Stone nodded. "Too bad. I was going to offer you a ride. I'm sure Durango wouldn't mind dropping you off since it's on the way."

Madison lifted a brow. "Durango?"

Stone smiled. "Yes, my cousin Durango. He's a park ranger at Yellowstone National Park."

Stone watched her eyes grow wide. "A park ranger? Then there's a chance he might know the man my mother took off with," she said excitedly.

Durango might know him better than you think, Stone wanted to say but didn't. Although the man she had described sounded a lot like Corey, it was still hard for Stone to believe that his uncle had actually taken a woman to his mountain. Stone never knew the full story why Corey had written off any kind of permanent relationship with a woman, he only knew that he had. "Yes, there is that possibility," Stone finally said.

"Then, if you don't mind, I'd like to ask him about it."

"No, I don't mind." Stone only hoped that he would get the chance to speak to Durango first.

"The way is clear to go now."

Madison's words recaptured his attention. He watched as she stood and eased out into the aisle. Opening the overhead compartment, she pulled out an overnight bag, a brand he recognized immediately as being Louis Vuitton. He smiled, remembering that he had given his sister Delaney a Louis Vuitton purse as a graduation present when she had earned her medical degree. He had been amazed at how much the item had cost, but when he had seen how happy the gift had made Delaney, the amount he'd spent had been well worth it.

Delaney had once explained that you could tell just how polished and classy a woman was by the purse she carried. If that was the case, Madison Winters was one hell of a polished and classy woman because she was sporting a Louis Vuitton purse, as well. He stood up and followed her into the aisle.

Madison looked ahead and thought the aisle of the plane seemed a hundred miles long. When they had to stop abruptly for the line of people moving slowly ahead of them, Stone automatically placed his hands at her waist to keep her from losing her balance.

She turned and gazed over her shoulder at him. "Thanks, Stone."

"My pleasure."

She smiled thinking it wasn't his pleasure alone. She felt his hard, solid chest pressed against her back and, when he placed his hands on her waist, she was acutely aware of the strength in his touch. He was a tall man. She wasn't conscious of just how tall until he stood up.

He towered over her and when she tilted her head back
to thank him, he met her gaze. The look in his eyes
nearly took her breath away.

Although he wasn't wearing a wedding ring, there
was no way a man who looked this good could be unat-
tached, she thought. A probing query entered her mind.
He'd said his cousin Durango would be picking him up.
Would there be a special lady waiting for him, as well?
In her opinion, Stone Westmoreland had a magnetic,
compelling charm that made him an irresistible force
to reckon with.

When they left the plane, the two of them walked
side by side through the ramp corridor toward the arrival
area. "So, how long do you plan to stay in Montana?"
Stone asked.

Madison could tell he had shortened his stride to stay
level with her. She glanced over at him, met his gaze
and tried to ignore the way her breasts tingled against
the fabric of her blouse. "I'll stay until I find my mother
and talk to her. I'm hoping it won't take long. According
to Mr. Jamison, who owns the Silver Arrow, the cabin
where my mother is staying is not far, but since it's
located in the mountains getting there will be difficult.
He's arranging for someone to take me by car as far as
possible, then the rest will be done on horseback."

Stone lifted a brow and scrutinized her with an odd
stare. "You ride?"

Madison's lips curved into a smile. "Yes. Growing
up I took riding lessons. I'm sure climbing up a mountain will be far more challenging than just prancing a
mare around a riding track, but I think I'll be able to
manage."

Stone wasn't so sure. She seemed too refined and

delicate to sit on a horse for a trip into the rugged mountains.

"That's something I don't understand."

Her words interrupted his thoughts. "What?"

"How my mother got up the mountain. I don't think she's ever ridden a horse. My dad tried getting her to take riding lessons when I took mine but she refused."

Stone nodded. "They probably rode double. Although it might be strenuous, it's possible on a good, strong horse," he said. He could just imagine Madison sitting behind him on horseback. He took a deep, calming breath as he thought about her arms wrapped around him when she hung on to him, and the feel of her breasts pressed against his back while her scent filled his nostrils.

He winced. He had to stop thinking about her like this. He was in Montana to research a book, not to get involved in a serious affair or a nonserious one for that matter. However, he had to admit that the thought of it, especially with Madison as a partner, was a damn good one.

Together they walked to the area where they needed to claim their luggage. Stone scanned the crowd for Durango and wasn't surprised when he didn't see him. He assisted Madison in pulling her luggage off the conveyor belt before getting his bags.

"Thanks for making my flight enjoyable. Because of you I was able to take my mind off my fear of flying."

He decided not to say that, on the same note, thanks to her, he was reminded just how long it had been since he'd had a woman. "Do you see the person who's supposed to be picking you up?" he asked glancing around.

"No. Maybe I should call. Will you excuse me while I use that courtesy phone over there?"

"Sure."

Stone watched her walk to the phone. In a tailored pantsuit that fit her body to perfection, she looked totally out of place in Bozeman, Montana. All the other women were wearing jeans and shirts, and she was dressed like she was attending a high priority business meeting somewhere. He appreciated the sway of her hips when she walked and how her hair brushed against her shoulders with every step she took.

"You can't be left alone one minute before you're checking out a woman, Stone. Even one who has 'city girl' written all over her."

Stone switched his attention from Madison to the man who had suddenly appeared by his side: his cousin Durango. "I sat by her on the plane from Atlanta. She's nice."

Durango chuckled as a wide grin covered his face. "All women are nice."

Stone shook his head. Everyone in the family knew that, like his brother Storm, Durango was a ladies' man, a player of the first degree and, like Stone and their uncle Corey, Durango had no intention of ever settling down. And speaking of Corey....

"When was the last time you saw Uncle Corey?" Stone decided to cut to the chase and ask. He knew that Durango kept up with their uncle's comings and goings. If there was some woman on Corey's mountain, Durango would know about it.

The grin suddenly disappeared from Durango's face; not a good sign as far as Stone was concerned. "Funny you should ask," Durango said frowning. "I haven't seen him for a week and I know for a fact he has a woman up there on his mountain."

That wasn't what Stone wanted to hear. "Are you sure?"

"Yes, I'm sure. I saw her myself when they were passing through. She's a nice-looking woman, probably in her late forties and talks with one of those northern accents. They've been up on that mountain for almost a week now and Corey won't answer the phone or return my calls. It makes me wonder what's going on up there and how this woman got such special privileges. I couldn't believe he broke his long-standing rule about a woman on his mountain."

Stone leaned back against the railing. His mind was reeling and he needed to make sure he had heard everything Durango was telling him correctly. "You're saying that Corey actually has a woman on his mountain?"

"Yes, and she's not a long-lost relative, either, because I asked. Besides, it was obvious she wasn't related by the way they were acting. He couldn't wait to leave my place to head into the mountains and it doesn't appear he's bringing her down anytime soon."

Stone rubbed a hand down his face. "And you're sure you don't know who she is?"

Durango's frown deepened. "No, I don't know who she is, Stone, other than the fact he was calling her Abby. But you better believe that this Abby woman has hooked him in good, and I mean real good."

When the crowd standing directly behind Durango shifted, Stone noticed that Madison had finished her call and had walked up. From the expression on her face it was obvious that she had pretty much overheard most of what Durango had said.

Aw hell!

Durango noticed that Stone's gaze was fixed on something behind him and turned around. He smiled when he looked into the face of the woman Stone had been checking out earlier. He grinned. No wonder his cousin was taken with the woman, she was definitely a looker. Too bad Stone had met her first, because she was definitely someone who would have interested him.

He started to speak and introduce himself, since it seemed Stone had suddenly lost his voice. But something made him pause. Durango had dealt with enough women to know when they weren't happy about something and it was obvious this woman was angry, royally pissed off. And her words stopped him dead in his tracks.

"I believe the woman the two of you are discussing is my mother."

It wasn't hard to tell the two men were related, Madison thought, glancing up at them. Both were tall, extremely handsome and well built. Then there were the similarities in their facial features that also proved a family connection. They possessed the same close-cropped curly black hair, chestnut coloring, dark intense eyes and generous, well-defined mouths.

And both of them could wear a pair of jeans and a chambray shirt like nobody's business.

Madison inwardly admitted that, had she met the other man before Stone, she probably would have felt the same attraction to him, the same pull. However, she thought there was a gentleness and tenderness in Stone's eyes that she didn't easily see in the other man's.

She could tell her statement took the other man by surprise but when she glanced over at Stone, it was obvious that what she'd said hadn't surprised him, which meant he had known or at least suspected the identity of her mother's abductor all along.

She lifted a brow and leveled a pointed gaze at Stone. She had trusted him enough to discuss her mother with him openly, because she had needed someone to talk to, and talking to him had calmed her fears of flying and had also helped her to think through her mother's situation. If Stone had suspected the people she had been talking about were his uncle and her mother, why hadn't he said something?

Stone read the questions in Madison's eyes. "I didn't know, Madison, or at least I wasn't a hundred percent certain," he said in a low and calm voice. "And although I thought there was a possibility the man was my uncle Corey, I didn't want to upset you any more than you already were by adding my speculations."

Madison released a deep sigh. His reason for not telling her did make sense. "All right," she said softly. "So, what do we do now?"

Durango lifted a confused brow and looked at Stone and then back at Madison. "Why should we do anything? When they're ready they'll come back down the mountain."

Stone stifled a grin at the angry look Madison gave Durango. His cousin, the player, didn't have a snowball's chance in hell of winning this particular woman over. He doubted Madison got upset about anything or with anyone too often, but he could tell Durango was making her break her record. Durango had a rather rough way of dealing with women. He wasn't used to the soft and gentle approach. Yet the way women were still drawn to him defied logic.

"This is my cousin, Durango Westmoreland, Madison," Stone decided to say when silence, annoyance and irritation settled between Durango and Madison.

"And when Durango gives himself time to think logically, I'm sure he'll understand your concern for your mother's well-being. And although Durango and I both know that our uncle Corey would never do anything to harm your mother, we can certainly understand your desire to see for yourself that she's fine."

Stone watched a slow smile touched Durango's lips. From childhood they had always been able to read between the lines of each other's words. Stone was letting Durango know, in a subtle way, that he wanted him on his best behavior and to clean up his act.

"I apologize if what I said upset you, Madison," Durango said, offering her his hand in a firm handshake. "I wasn't aware that you thought your mother was in harm's way. If that's the case, we'll certainly do whatever needs to be done to arrest your fears. And let me be the first to welcome you to Montana."

Stone rolled his eyes. No one, he thought, could go from being a pain in the ass to irresistibly charming in a blink of an eye like Durango. Stone watched the warmth return to Madison's eyes and she smiled. Although that smile wasn't directed at him, a riot of emotions clamored through him nonetheless.

"Now that we have all that settled," he decided to speak up and say, "how about the three of us going somewhere to talk? Durango, you mentioned that you had met Madison's mother when Uncle Corey made a stop at your place."

A smile was plastered on Durango's face when he said, "Yes, and I even talked to her for a few minutes while Corey was loading up on supplies. I could tell she was a real classy, well-bred lady."

Madison nodded. She appreciated his comments although her mother's actions were showing another side of her. "Stone is right. I'd like to get to the Silver Arrow and unpack and freshen up, but as soon as I can, I'd like to meet with you and ask you a few more questions."

Durango quickly glanced over at Stone and Stone deciphered the message in his eyes. There were some things Madison was probably better off not knowing about her mother and their uncle.

Stone nodded and Durango caught his drift and returned his attention to Madison and said, "Sure, that will be fine, Madison. Is someone coming to pick you up from the Silver Arrow or can I give you a lift?"

"I don't want to put you to any trouble, Mr. Westmoreland."

Durango grinned again. "Just call me Durango and there's no trouble. The Silver Arrow is on the way to my ranch and is nicely situated between Bozeman and Yellowstone, and only a stone's throw away from the Wyoming line."

Madison nodded. "Thanks, I'll be glad to take you up on your offer. The man who answered the phone at the Silver Arrow said the guy who usually picks up his guests was ill and he was trying to find a replacement."

Durango reached out to take the luggage out of her hand. "Then consider it done."

Madison sat in the vehicle's back seat. Although she hated being in Montana, she couldn't overlook the beauty of this beautiful June day, as well as the vast country surrounding her. It was magnificent and left her utterly speechless. The Rocky Mountains were all around and the meadows were drenched with wildflowers: Red Indian Paintbrush and an assortment of other flowering plants. She had always heard about the beauty of being under a Montana sky and now she was experiencing it firsthand.

They were traveling down a two-lane stretch of highway; she knew they were a stone's throw away from Yellowstone National Park and hoped that she could tour the park before returning to Boston.

At the airport, after Stone and Durango had helped with her luggage, they had walked out to where Durango's SUV was parked in a "no parking zone" with its caution lights flashing. She smiled when she saw he was driving a nice, sleek, shiny black Dodge Durango.

Stone leaned over and whispered in her ear that Durango owned a Dodge Durango because he was conceited enough to think Dodge had named the vehicle after him. Durango, she knew, had heard Stone's comment and had merely laughed it off, and she could immediately feel the closeness between the two men.

"So how long do you think you're going to stay in Montana after meeting with your mother, Madison?" Stone asked, glancing at her over his shoulder. It was easy to see how captivated she was with the beauty of the land surrounding them. Earlier, she had said that she would probably only be in Montana long enough to talk to her mother, but he knew that Montana had a way of growing on you. And he had to admit that there was something about Madison that was growing on him. It was obvious that she had some real concerns about her mother and more than anything he wanted to help her resolve them.

He watched as she switched her gaze from the scenery to him. "I know what I said earlier, but now I'm not sure. I had planned to leave as soon as I had talked to my mother but I might decide to hang around awhile. This place is beautiful," she said, taking a quick glance out of the window again.

She turned back to him to add, "Since school is out for the summer I can enjoy myself. I seldom take vacations during the summer months. Usually I give private music lessons, so this is a really nice break, although I wish it was a planned trip rather than an unplanned one."

Stone really didn't care about the reason she was in Montana, he was just glad that she was. He hoped things worked out between her and her mother but it seemed that Madison had never heard of anyone acting out of character. He had a feeling that, in the world she was used to, things went according to plan and as expected.

He smiled inwardly. In that case, his family would take some getting used to if she ever met them. His father had two brothers. Of the three siblings, their uncle Corey was the only single one. Never having been married and the youngest of the three, he had been a surrogate father to his eleven nephews and one niece.

Corey had left Atlanta to attend Montana State University and fell in love with the land. Once he had a job as a park ranger with Yellowstone National Park, he made the state his permanent home. By the time he retired a year ago, he had been president of the Association of National Park Rangers for the past five years and had accumulated a vast amount of land.

"Well, if you decide to stick around I'd like to show

you the sights. I spent a lot of time here as a kid while visiting my uncle Corey and know my way around pretty well."

A smile touched the corners of Madison's mouth. "Thanks. I might take you up on that." She then asked quietly, "Just what type of person is your uncle Corey? I know Durango said he was harmless and trustworthy, but I'm trying to come to grips with what there is about him that made my mother act so unlike herself."

Stone glanced over at Durango and saw the smile that tilted his cousin's lips; he was grateful that Durango, for once, had the decency to keep quiet. The rumor that Uncle Corey could make even the First Lady stop being a lady was something Madison didn't need to know. Chances were, if she asked anyone working at the Silver Arrow about Corey they would gladly enlighten her since his reputation was legendary.

Stone didn't really know what he could tell her; her mother being on his uncle's mountain didn't make much sense to him, either. He couldn't wait to get Durango alone to get the full story.

"I guess there are times when things happen that defy logic, Madison, and it appears this is the case with your mother and Uncle Corey. Just like your mother's actions are unusual, his actions are unusual, too. For as long as I've known him, which has been for all of my thirty-three years, he's been pretty much of a loner; preferring not to marry and spending most of his time when he wasn't at Yellowstone up on his mountain. And he's always had a rule about taking women up there."

Madison lifted a brow. "And what rule is that?"

Stone smiled. "That it would never happen. Other than female family members, there has never been a woman on his mountain. There must have been something about your mother to make him change his way of thinking about that."

A thought crossed Stone's mind. "Is there a chance that my uncle and your mother knew each other before?"

Madison frowned. That thought had crossed her mind but she didn't see how that could be. "I guess anything is possible. That would certainly explain things somewhat if it were true. But I don't see how that could be possible unless your uncle had visited Boston. My parents dated all through high school and college, and married right after graduation. I was born two years later." She decided not to mention the unhappy marriage her parents had shared even though they had tried to pretend otherwise.

"Then there could be another reason for their madness," Stone said softly, reclaiming her attention, casting a sideways glance.

She looked at him, squinting against the sun that shone through the vehicle window. "And what reason is that?"

"Instant attraction."

Stone watched as Madison immediately parted her lips to refute such a thing was possible, then she closed them tight. She had to know that such a thing was possible because the two of them had experienced that same attraction on the plane, so to deny such a thing existed would be dishonest.

Moments later she said, "I'm sure that's possible but can it be that powerful to make a levelheaded person become impulsive and irrational?"

Stone chuckled. "Trust me, Madison, I've seen it happen." One day he would prove his point by telling her about his two brothers who'd recently married. He didn't count his sister's marriage as anything unusual, since Delaney had always looked at things through rose-colored eyes, which was the main reason he and his brothers had been so overprotective of her during her dating years.

But his brothers Dare and Thorn had been dead set against marrying anytime soon, if ever. He clearly understood why Dare had wed since Shelly had been Dare's true love. When she had returned to town after having been gone ten years, and with a son Dare hadn't known existed, it had been understandable that the two would get back together and make a home for their child. But a sense of obligation had nothing to do with Dare's marriage to Shelly. His brother loved Shelly, plain and simple.

Now there hadn't been anything plain and simple about Thorn's marriage to Tara. Thorn was the last Westmoreland anyone expected to marry and he was a prime example of what instant attraction could do to you if you weren't careful.

"Well, I can't imagine anything like that happening with my mother," Madison said defiantly, recapturing Stone's attention. "Does your uncle have a phone up on his mountain?"

Stone nodded his head. "Yes."

"Then I need the number. I want to call my mother and let her know I'm on my way up there."

Durango, who had been quiet all this time, ended his silence with a chuckle. "You might have a problem reaching them," he said, not taking his eyes off the road.

"Why?" Madison asked curiously. "Are the phone lines down or something?"

"No, but I've tried calling Uncle Corey for the past several days to remind him that Stone was coming for a visit and he's not answering his phone."

Madison arched a dark brow. "He's not answering his phone? But—but what if something has happened to them and they can't get to the phone. What if—"

"They don't want to be disturbed, Madison?" Stone suggested. He saw her eyes shift from the back of Durango's head over to him. He could tell from her expression that his comment had conjured up numerous possibilities in her mind, but there was no hope for it. At some point she needed to accept that her mother had decided to extend her vacation by two weeks because she had wanted to, and not because she had been forced to. As far as Stone was concerned, the same held true with Madison's mother being on that mountain. It didn't seem that his uncle had forced the woman, so chances were she was just where she wanted to be. Sooner or later Madison would have to realize that.

She didn't answer his question. Instead she turned back to the car window and looked out at the scenery again. Stone inhaled deeply and turned back around in his seat. At least he had her thinking and for the moment perhaps that was the best thing.

Chapter 3

What if Mom doesn't want to be disturbed, like Stone suggested?

That thought ran through Madison's mind as she studied the mountains and the ripened green pastures they passed. She couldn't help but think of all the things she knew about her mother.

The two of them were close and always had been, but there were some things a mother didn't share with a daughter and Madison was smart enough to know that. It came as no surprise that she had never thought of her mother as a sensual being. To her, she was simply Mom, although she had always thought her mother was a very beautiful woman.

Stone's comment was forcing her to see her mother through different eyes. One thing she knew for certain was that, since her father's death, her mother hadn't shown any interest in a man, and Madison had never given any thought as to whether that was a good thing or not. Usually, when Abby Winters went to social functions, she attended with Ron Carmichael, a widower who had been her father's business partner, or she would attend with some other family friend.

Although both Durango and Stone had been too polite to state the obvious, it seemed pretty clear that her mother and their uncle Corey were on his mountain engaging in some sort of an illicit affair. And if that was the case, Madison was determined to find out how Corey Westmoreland had tempted her mother to behave in such a manner.

She also knew that, although neither man had voiced it, they probably thought she had taken things a little too far in coming after her mother, and especially when she'd been told her mother was fine. But a part of her had to see for herself. She had to talk to her mother.

And she had to understand, or at least try to understand. What had possessed her mother to do what she did? She had to believe there had to be a good reason.

She licked her lips as they suddenly felt dry. When Stone had talked about instant attraction, she had known just what he'd meant. From the moment she had opened her eyes on the plane to gaze into the dark depths of his, she had been attracted to him in a way she had never experienced before. And she was still attracted to him. Every time he looked at her, she felt a funny feeling inside that started in her breastbone and quickly moved down her body to settle right smack in the center between her legs. She was drawn to Stone. It was Stone who had her breathing fast just thinking how she had touched him intimately on the plane without knowing it. She felt a sudden tingling in her hand when she thought about just where it had been. And the first time he had spoken to her, she had immediately become mesmerized by the sound of his voice.

She sighed deeply. Considering her current state, she needed to get to the Silver Arrow, check into her cabin and pull herself together as soon as possible. She had to remember that she was here for one reason and for one reason only. It had nothing to do with Stone and everything to do with her mother.

But…once the issue of her mother's state of mind was resolved, she couldn't help but think of all the very tempting possibilities.

"You and Durango didn't have to help with my luggage, Stone," Madison said as she watched him place the last piece next to her bed. Once they had arrived at the Silver Arrow, the two men had been adamant about helping her instead of letting the ranch hands do it.

The ranch consisted of numerous rustic cabins that were located some distance away from the main house for privacy. Guy Jamison, the owner, had said he would give her a tour of the ranch once she got settled. He also told her the time dinner would be served and said he was waiting to hear back from the man who'd agreed to be her tour guide up to the mountains.

The cabin she had been given was tucked beneath a cluster of trees and appeared more secluded than the others. Durango bid her goodbye and left after helping Stone with her bags. He went to wait outside in the SUV.

She glanced around, trying to get her mind off Stone and how good he looked standing in the middle of the room. In an attempt not to notice him, she let her gaze float across the décor and furnishings of the cabin. There was a dark oak bureau, dressing table and two nightstands on either side of the biggest bed she had ever seen. It appeared larger than king size and the printed covers made it look very welcoming and comfortable. She also took note of the matching curtains at the windows and frontier-printed rugs on the floor.

"Would you like to join me and Durango for dinner later?"

Madison met Stone's gaze. The attraction that had been there from the beginning was overcharging the room, blazing the distance between them and making her heart pound faster in her chest. Should she have dinner with him? He had indicated they wouldn't be alone since Durango would be joining them. And what if Durango wasn't joining them? Should she hesitate in accepting his offer just because he turned her on? But then she had more questions for Durango about her mother and Corey Westmoreland, and he'd said she could come over to his place.

She took a deep breath, deciding to be upfront with Stone since she couldn't deny the obvious. "The only reason I'm here is because of my mother, Stone, and when I resolve that issue, I'll decide if I want anything out of this trip for myself. Chances are I won't and will return to Boston as soon as I can."

He nodded, understanding what she was saying. "All right," he said and slowly crossed the distance separating them. "If that speech was to let me know you need time to figure things out, that's fine. Take all the time you need."

He needed time to figure things out, as well. Why did she turn him on like no other woman he knew and why at that very moment was the need to taste her about to make him lose his mind? In the past, his writing had always taken center stage in his life. He had lived more or less through his characters, knowing their fears, conflicts and deep-rooted and often chilling adventures. Transferring his thoughts from his mind to paper had been all consuming and the need to block off everything and anyone had been essential. His only goal had been to deliver, on every occasion, what readers expected from a Rock Mason book and he, without exception, had happily obliged them. The last thing he had to spare while working on a book was time for a woman, and in the past that was something he understood and accepted. But he knew he would be hard pressed to understand and accept anything about this situation with Madison Winters other than the fact that he wanted her. Pure and simple.

"Can I leave you with something to think about?" he asked quietly. The afternoon light that was flowing in through the only window in the cabin was casting a shadow on her features, but instead of dimming her allure, the light brought Madison's beauty even more into focus. He swallowed hard, steeling his resolve, only to discover that when it came to this woman he didn't have any.

Madison met Stone's gaze, holding it tightly. Intensely. She wondered what he was giving her time to think about. Did he have words of wisdom to share or was there something else? Her mind began whirling at all the possibilities and, heaven help her, but a part of her wished there was something else. She contemplated him for a long moment, wondering how she should respond if what he had in mind was the latter. Any physical contact, no matter how casual, wasn't a good idea since they had just met that day. Then she remembered that the first phase of physical contact had taken place the moment she had touched him on the plane, although the contact hadn't been intentional. But still, contact had been made and she hadn't been the same since.

And she could be honest enough with herself to admit that her mind had been made up about Stone the moment she had stepped off the plane with him. There was something about him that denoted a sense of honor, something rarely seen in a man these days.

He was the silent type with the word sexy oozing out of every pore on his body. She had never met a man like him before and doubted that she would again. For some reason she felt she could trust him, although blindly placing her trust in a man had been precisely how her heart had been broken two years ago. But with Stone she felt safe.

"Yes, you can leave me with something to think about," she finally said softly, after gathering her courage for whatever was to come. She didn't have long to wait to find out.

He reached out and cupped her chin in his hand, letting her know his intent and giving her every opportunity to put a stop to what he was about to do if that was what she wanted. When she didn't move or say anything, but continued to meet his gaze, while her breathing became just as erratic as his, he lowered his head to hers.

Madison felt the pull of her insides the moment their mouths touched, and immediately she felt the heat of his skin as his jeans-clad thigh brushed against her when he brought her closer into his arms. And when he settled his hands at her hips, and with it came the deep, compelling sizzle of desire, she thought she was certainly going to lose it.

Nothing prepared her for the onslaught of emotions that rammed through her when her lips parted and he entered her mouth and proceeded to kiss her in a way she had never been kissed before. It was a gentle kiss. It was tender. But on the flip side, it contained a hunger that made the pressure she felt in her chest too intense, almost unbearable.

And when he deepened the kiss, capturing her tongue with his, she was grateful that he had the mind to hold her tighter because she would surely have melted to the floor. She savored the hot sweetness of his mouth as he carried her to a level where sophistication, poise and what was proper had no place. As their tongues mingled, dueled and mated, feelings and emotions she had never felt before crashed into her, smothering her in a sexuality she hadn't known existed.

And when he finally broke the kiss, she drew in a long shuddering breath and gazed up at him. His eyes were intense and she knew that she and Stone had shared more than just a kiss. They had also shared an understanding. What was happening between them was probably no different than what his uncle and her mother had experienced.

Instant attraction.

The kind that hit two people from the first so you were compelled to do the unthinkable and act on it.

She sighed deeply and unconsciously licked her lips, tasting the dampness, a lingering reminder of his taste. Sharp coils of desire raced through her and she knew that Stone Westmoreland was a dangerous man. He was dangerous to her common sense. Although she needed to talk to Durango, she couldn't do it today. She needed time to clear her mind and think straight. At the moment the only thing she could think about was romancing Stone. In less than twenty-four hours he had unearthed another side of her, a side even she hadn't known existed and the thought of that frightened her somewhat.

"I don't think joining you and Durango this evening for dinner would be a good idea, Stone," she decided to say.

No matter how desperately she needed to know about her mother and their uncle, she also needed space from this man who caused emotions to grip her that were so foreign and unfamiliar. "I want to get settled in here first and think about a few things. Is there any way we can meet tomorrow, possibly before noon? I'd like to try and contact my mother to let her know that I'm here."

Stone held her gaze. "Tomorrow's fine, Madison. Just tell the lady at the front desk to phone Durango's ranch. They have the number and I'll be glad to come and pick you up."

"All right."

He stared at her for a few minutes then, without saying anything else, he turned and walked out of the door.

Pushing back from the kitchen table, Stone stood to help Durango clear the dishes. "I tell you, Stone, it was the strangest thing seeing Uncle Corey act that way, like a love-smitten twenty-year-old. And I didn't want to say anything in front of Madison, but her mother wasn't acting any better, although it would be clear to anyone that she was a lady with a lot of class."

Stone shook his head. "Well, Madison is determined to find answers. I think I gave her food for thought earlier and she's pretty much accepted the idea that her mother and Uncle Corey are involved in an affair, but she still needs to understand why."

Durango raised a brow as he leaned against the table. "What's there to understand? Lust is lust."

Stone rolled his eyes upward. Durango definitely had a way with words. "Well, with her mother being such a classy, well-bred lady and all, lust as you see it is something Madison just can't seem to understand."

Durango grinned. "Then I guess it's going to be up to you to explain it all to her. Now if you need my help in—"

"Don't even think about it," Stone responded quickly in a growl.

Durango chuckled. "Hey, I was just kidding. Besides, you know how I feel about city women anyway." Even with the laughter in his voice, his words echoed with bitterness.

Unfortunately Stone did know how he felt. "Need help with the dishes?" he asked after walking across the kitchen and placing them on the counter.

"Nope, that's what dishwashers are for. If you want we can try reaching Uncle Corey again, but take my word for it, it'll be a waste of time. He and his lady friend aren't accepting calls. I truly believe they turned the damn thing off."

Stone decided to try calling anyway and hung up later when he didn't get an answer. He shook his head emphatically. "You would think Madison's mother would have tried to reach her daughter."

Durango raised a brow. "I thought she had. Didn't

Madison say on the drive over to the Silver Arrow that her mother had called to say she was fine and was extending her vacation for two weeks?"

"Yes, but she left the message on the answering machine. I'd think she would have made a point to talk to Madison directly to allay her fears."

Durango raised his eyes heavenward. "And I'd think—which is probably the same way Madison's mother is thinking—that at fifty years of age she doesn't have to check in with anyone, not even a daughter, especially if she's assured her daughter that she's okay." He grabbed an apple out of the basket and bit into it like he hadn't just eaten dinner. "Do you know what I think, Stone?"

Stone shrugged, almost too afraid to ask. "No, Durango, what do you think?"

"I think the reason Madison is so busy sticking her nose into her mother's love life…or lust life, is because she doesn't have one of her own."

A hint of a smile played at the corners of Stone's lips. "She doesn't have what? A love life or a lust life?"

"Neither of either. And I think that's where you need to step in."

Stone crossed his arms over his chest and met his cousin's direct gaze. "And do what exactly?"

Durango smiled. "Give the lady a taste of both."

Stone snorted. Only someone like Durango who had a jaded perception of love and marriage would think that way. Although Stone didn't have plans to ever settle down and marry, he did believe in love. His parents' marriage was a prime example of it, so was his sister Delaney's and his brothers Dare's and Thorn's marriages.

"I think I'm going to spend a few hours in your hot tub if you don't mind," he said to Durango.

"By all means, help yourself."

Less than twenty minutes later, Stone was sitting comfortably in the hot tub on Durango's outside deck. A good portion of Durango's land was the site of natural hot springs and the first thing he had done after building the ranch had been to take advantage of that fact and erect his own private hot tub. It was large enough to hold at least five people and the heat of the water felt good as it stimulated Stone's muscles.

He closed his eyes and immediately had thoughts of Madison. Maybe Durango was right about her failure to take her mother's words at face value that she was okay. But in just the short amount of time he had gotten to know Madison he could tell she was a person who cared deeply about those she loved. She probably couldn't help being a consummate worrier. And then maybe Durango was right again. Perhaps Madison needed something or someone in her life to occupy her time so she could stop worrying about her mother.

Stone inhaled deeply. For all he knew she might very well have someone already, some man back in Boston. He immediately pushed that thought from his mind. Madison Winters was not the type of woman who would belong to one man and willingly kiss another. And she had kissed him. Boy, had she kissed him. And he had definitely kissed her. The effects of their kiss still lingered with him. Even now he could still taste her. Durango's beef stew hadn't been strong enough to eradicate her taste from his mouth.

"Hey, Stone, you just got a call."

Stone cocked one eye open and looked at Durango

who was standing a few feet away with a cold bottle of beer in his hand. "Who was it?"

"Your city girl."

Stone quickly opened both eyes and leaned forward, knowing just whom Durango was talking about. "Did she say what she wanted?"

Durango leaned against the door with a smirky grin on his face. "No, but I got the distinct impression that she wanted you."

Madison nervously paced her cabin as she waited for Stone to return her call. Deciding she had walked the floor enough, she dropped down into the nearest chair as she recounted in her mind what Frank, the husband of a good friend of hers who owned an investigative firm, had shared with her less than an hour ago. In addition to that, she couldn't help but replay back in her mind the communication she had picked up from her mother when Madison called her apartment in Boston to replay her messages.

She jumped when she heard a knock at her door and wondered who it might be. It was late and she would think most of the guests and workers at the ranch had pretty much retired for the night. She had to remember this wasn't Boston and that she was practically alone in an area where the population was sparse.

She eased her way to the door. "Who is it?"

"It's me, Madison. Stone."

She let out a sigh of relief when she heard the familiar sound of Stone's voice and quickly opened the door. "Stone, I was waiting for your call. I didn't expect you to come over here," she said, taking a step back to let him in. She was glad that, although she had showered earlier, she had slipped into a long, flowing caftan that was suitable for accepting company.

Stone entered and closed the door behind him. "Durango said you sounded upset when you called so I thought I'd come over right away." His gaze took in her features. They appeared tense and worried. "What's wrong, Madison?"

She inhaled deeply and nervously rubbed her hands together. "I don't know where to start."

Stone studied her for a moment, concerned. "Start anywhere you like. How about if we take a seat over there and you can tell me what's going on," he suggested in a calming voice.

She nodded and crossed the room to sit on the edge of the bed while he sat across from her in a wingback chair. "All right, now tell me what's wrong," he said, his tone soothing.

Madison folded her hands in her lap. A part of her was grateful to Stone for coming instead of calling, although she hadn't expected him to. She lifted her chin and met his gaze; again, like before, she felt that powerful current pass through them and wondered if he'd felt it, too.

She put the thought of the sexual chemistry that was sizzling between them to the back of her mind and started talking. "I called my apartment in Boston to retrieve my phone messages and discovered that my mother had called and left another one."

Stone lifted a dark brow. "Really? And what did she say?"

Madison sighed. "She said she regretted that we keep missing each other but that she wanted to let me know she was doing fine and…"

Stone waited for her to finish and when she seemed hesitant to do so he prodded. "And?"

Madison inhaled deeply once again before saying, "And she plans to extend her trip by an additional two weeks."

For a moment there was not a sound in the room, just this long pregnant silence. Then Stone slowly nodded as he continued to study her. He could tell the message had been upsetting to Madison. "Well, at least you know that she's okay."

Madison shook her head and Stone watch as her hair swirled around her shoulders with the movement. "No, I don't know that, Stone. I'm more worried about her than ever. There's something else I think you should know."

Stone gazed across the few feet separating them. "What?"

Madison slowly stood then nervously paced the room a few times before coming back to stand in front of Stone. "I know that you and Durango tried to reassure me that your uncle is a decent man—honest, trustworthy and safe—but I had to be sure. I had to find out everything I could about him to help me understand why my mother is behaving the way she is. A friend of mine, another teacher at the school where I work, well, her husband owns an investigation firm. After you left here today, I contacted him and gave him your uncle's name."

Stone sat back in the chair, his gaze locked with hers as he rubbed his chin. "And?"

Madison swallowed nervously. "And, according to Frank, when he entered your uncle's name into the database, he discovered another investigative firm, one that's located somewhere in Texas, was checking out your uncle's past, as well. For some reason it seems that I'm not the only one who wants information about him."

Stone frowned and sat up straight in his chair. Anger suddenly lined his features. "Are you trying to accuse my uncle of—"

"No! I'm not accusing him of anything. Even Frank indicated that he's clean and doesn't have a criminal record or anything. I just thought it was strange and felt that you should know."

Stone stared at Madison for a long moment then stood in front of her. "I don't know what interest another investigative company has in my uncle but, whatever the reason, it has nothing to do with his character, Madison. Corey Westmoreland is one of the finest men I know. I admit he can be somewhat ornery at times and set in his ways, but I would and do trust him with my life."

Madison heard the defensive anger in Stone's voice although he tried to control it. She crossed her arms over her chest and gazed up at him. "I wasn't insinuating that he wasn't a—"

"Weren't you? I also think that until you talk to your mother and see her for yourself to make sure she's not up there with some crazy mountain man, you won't have a moment of peace."

Unable to help himself, Stone reached out and brushed a strand of hair back from her face. There were tension lines around her eyes and the mouth he had kissed earlier that day was strained, agitated and on edge. "And I intend to give you that peace. I will take you up Corey's Mountain myself."

His words had an immediate effect on Madison and she released her arms from across her chest. Her heart began beating a mile a minute. "You will?" she asked in a rush.

"Yes. I would head up there first thing in the morning, but unfortunately you don't have the proper attire to make such a trip. We need to take care of that as well as getting the supplies we'll need. If all that works out then we can leave the day after tomorrow, bright and early. We'll take a truck as far as Martin Quinns' ranch, then borrow a couple of his horses to go the rest of the way on up."

Madison tried to mask her relief. She hated admitting it but Stone was right. She wouldn't have a moment of peace until she saw and talked to her mother herself. "I'll make sure I get all the things I need."

Stone nodded. "I'm going to make sure you get all the things you need, too. I'll be picking you up in the morning to drive you into town and take you to the general store. We should be able to purchase everything we'll need from there."

Madison nodded. Uncertain what to say next she knew of the one thing that she *had* to say. "Thank you, Stone."

Her heart lurched in her chest when she saw that her words of thanks had not softened the lines around his eyes. He was still upset with her for what she'd insinuated about his uncle.

"Don't mention it. I'll see you in the morning." And without saying anything else, he crossed the room and walked out the door.

Chapter 4

Whoever said you can take the girl out of the city but you can't take the city out of the girl must have known a woman like Madison Winters, Stone thought, as he sat silently in the chair with his long legs stretched out in front of him and watched her move around the cabin packing for their trip.

That morning they had gone to the general store to purchase the items they would need. Getting her prepared for their excursion had taken up more time than he figured it would. When he had inventoried what she'd brought with her from Boston, he hadn't been surprised to discover her stylish clothing—mostly with designer labels—included nothing that would be durable enough to travel up into the mountains. When they'd driven into town she had agreed with his suggestion that she buy several pairs of jeans, T-shirts, flannel shirts, a couple of sweaters, a wool jacket, heavy-duty socks and, most important, good hiking boots. He had also strongly suggested that she buy a wide-brimmed hat. He'd explained to her that the days would be hot and the nights would be cold.

He had taken care of the other things such as the food they would need, the sleeping bags they would use, as well as the rental of the truck that would carry them as far as the Quinns' ranch.

Stone's lips broke into an innately male smile as he continued to watch her. She was definitely a gorgeous woman but, more than that, he found her downright fascinating. He would even go so far as to say that she intrigued him, especially now when she was frowning while glancing down at herself, as if the thought of wearing jeans and a flannel shirt was nothing she would ever get used to.

Hell, it was something he doubted he would get used to, either. He had seen plenty of women in jeans in his lifetime but none, and he meant none, could wear them like they'd been exclusively designed just for their bodies. Another man might say that she was built and had everything in all the right places, but the writer in him would go further than that and say she was...*a summer pleasure and a fall treasure whose beauty was as breathtaking and captivating as a cluster of tulips and daffodils under a spectacular Montana sky.*

"Do you think I packed enough, Stone?"

Her words intruded on his musings and he glanced at the bed. To be quite honest she had packed too much, but he knew that was the norm for any woman. Somehow they would manage even if it meant leaving some of it at the Quinns' ranch once they got there. The back of a horse could handle only so much on what would be a treacherous climb up the mountain.

"No, you're fine," he said coming to his feet. "I contacted Martin Quinn and he's expecting us by noon tomorrow. We'll sleep overnight at his place then head up the mountain right after breakfast. If our timing is right, we won't have to spend but one night out under the stars."

Madison raised a brow. "It will take us two days to get to your uncle's ranch?"

"Yes, by horseback. At some point during the daylight hours it will be too hot to travel and we'll need to give the horses periodic breaks."

Madison nodded. She then cleared her throat. "Stone, I want to thank you for—"

"You've thanked me already," he said, picking up the Stetson that he had purchased that day off the table.

"Yes, I know, but I also know that taking me to your uncle's place is intruding into your writing time."

He looked at her and the liquid heat that had started flowing through his bloodstream from the moment he had met her was still there. "No, you're not," he said, forcing himself to ignore how good she smelled. "I had planned to go visit Uncle Corey anyway while I was here, so now is just as good a time as any."

"Oh, I see."

Stone doubted that she saw anything. If she did she would have second thoughts of them spending so much time together over the next three days. If she really had her eyes wide-open she would see that he wanted her with a passion so thick he could cut it with a knife. The clean scent of the mountains had nothing on her. She had a fragrance all her own and it was one that reminded him of everything a woman was supposed to be. She was more than just a city girl. She was sensuality on legs and a gorgeous pair of them at that.

He couldn't believe it had only been yesterday when he had first looked into eyes that were so mesmerizing they had taken his breath away. And since then, undercurrents of sensual tension had surrounded them whenever they were together, leaving them no slack but a whole lot of close encounters of the lush kind. He had never been this incredibly aware of a woman in his life.

"Well, I guess that's it until tomorrow morning."

Her words cut into his thoughts, reminding him that he had stood to leave yet hadn't moved an inch. "Yes, I think that's about it except for your attitude about things."

She lifted her chin just a bit. "What do you mean?"

He rather liked to see whenever she became irritated about something. She became even sexier. "I mean," he began slowly, deciding that no matter how sexy she got when she was mad, he didn't want to get her pissed off too much. "Before we head up toward Uncle Corey's mountain, you need to come to terms with what we might find when we get there, Madison."

He watched as she averted her eyes from his briefly and he knew she understood exactly what he meant. She tilted her head and their gazes connected again. "I hear what you're saying but I don't know if I can, Stone. She's my mother," she said quietly.

Stone held her gaze intently. Logical thinking—which he knew she wasn't exemplifying at the moment—dictated that he have something to say to that. So he did.

"She's also a full-grown woman who's old enough to make her own decisions."

She sighed and he could just feel the varied emotions tumbling through her. "But she's never done anything like this before."

"There's a first time for everything." He of all people should know that. Until yesterday, no woman had taken hold of his senses the way she had. He wasn't exactly happy about it and in some ways he found it downright disturbing. But he was mature enough to accept it as the way things happen sometimes between a man and a woman. Unlike his brother Thorn who liked challenges, he was one of those men who tried looking at things logically without complications and definitely without a whole lot of fuss. He accepted things easily and knew how to roll with the flow.

Madison was a very desirable woman and he was a hot-blooded male. He had conceded from the first that getting together with her would be like pouring kerosene on a fire. The end result—total combustion. The only problem with that picture was that, no matter how hot they could burn up the sheets, on some things he had made up his mind with no chance of changing it. Getting involved in a permanent relationship with a woman was one of them. It wouldn't happen.

Seeing the look of uncertainty on her face, he knew she was a long way from accepting the possibility that her mother and his uncle were lovers. As strange as it seemed, he had come to terms with it and eventually she would have to do the same. "I suggest that you get a good night's sleep," he said, moving toward the door. He intended to open it and walk out without looking back.

But he couldn't.

He turned and reached out and pulled her to him, encircling her waist and resting her head on his chest. Some inner part of him just knew that she needed to be held in his embrace. And that same inner part of him also knew that she needed a kiss, as well.

A tenderness fed by a burning flame of desire raced through him, making his heartbeat quicken and his body go hard. She must have felt his arousal and lifted her head. Their gazes locked. Words weren't needed, sexual chemistry had a language all its own and it was speaking to them loud and clear.

She parted her lips on a sigh and he lowered his head and captured the very essence of that moan with his mouth. The taste of her was tempting, and he immediately thought of silken sheets, burning candles and soft music. He thought of touching her all over, loving her with his mouth and his hands until she groaned out his name, then placing her beneath him, entering her, thrusting in and out in the same rhythm he was using at that very moment on her mouth. All during the previous night he'd had a hard time sleeping because his body had silently yearned for her. And he knew tonight, tomorrow night and all of the nights after that wouldn't be any different.

After a long moment, he broke off the kiss and rested his forehead against hers. Kissing her was exhausting as well as stimulating. He could have continued kissing her forever if he hadn't needed to breathe.

"Stone?"

He inhaled and tried to get his body to relax, but her scent filled his nostrils making regaining his calm downright difficult. "Yeah?"

"This isn't good, is it?"

He chuckled against her ear. "You don't hear me complaining, Madison."

"You know what I mean."

Yes, he knew exactly what she meant. "If I go along with your way of thinking, that we should place our full concentration on your mother and Uncle Corey and not on each other, then I would have to agree that it isn't good because the timing is lousy. But if I adhere to my own thoughts, that I feel whatever is going on between my uncle and your mother is their business and that you and I should place our full concentration on each other, then I would say it is good."

He said the words while a barrage of emotions raced through him. They were emotions he wasn't used to dealing with. A part of him suddenly felt disoriented. Totally confused. Fully aware.

The woman he held in his arms was as intoxicating as the most potent brand of whiskey and she had his senses reeling and his body heated. "I'm going to leave the decision as to how we should handle things up to you, Madison. I suggest you sleep on it and let me know what you decide in the morning."

Leaning down, he kissed her again; this kiss was tender but just as passionate as the one before. He pulled back and released her, opened the door and walked out into the cool Montana night.

Clinging to the strength of the decisions she had made overnight, Madison opened the door for Stone the next morning. The eyes that met hers were sharp, direct and she immediately felt herself wavering on one decision in particular as she inwardly asked herself: *how can I stand behind my decision to make sure that nothing happens between us?*

Of the two decisions she'd made, that had been the hardest one and, as she glanced at the strong, vital and sexy man standing in the doorway, she knew it would be the hardest one to keep. Stone wasn't a man any woman could ignore and being alone with him for the next few days would definitely test her resolve. If she were smart she would put any thoughts of a relationship between them out of her mind completely. She had never been involved in any sort of casual affair before and wasn't sure that type of relationship would suit her. But then she had to remember that she had thought her relationship with Cedric had been anything but casual and look where it had gotten her.

"You're earlier than I expected," she somehow found her voice to say. In the predawn light that encompassed him, she searched his eyes for any signs of decisions that he himself might have made and only saw the heated look of desire that had been there from the very first. And she knew if she was ever undisciplined enough to risk all and take a chance, this man would and could introduce her to passion of the hottest kind.

He was standing before her so utterly handsome in his jeans, flannel shirt, boots and Stetson. He looked nothing like an action-thriller author but everything like a rugged cowboy who made the unspoiled land surrounding Montana's Rocky Mountains his home. But she knew there was something else about him that was holding her interest. It was what she saw beyond the clothes. It was the man himself. There was a depth to him that was greater than any man she'd ever met. There was a self-confidence about him that had nothing to do with arrogance and a kindness that had nothing to do with a sense of duty. He did things out of the generosity of his heart and concern for others and not for show. And she felt loyalty to him. He would be true to whatever woman he claimed as his. Cedric could certainly have taken a few lessons from Stone Westmoreland.

He smiled. "I thought we could grab something to eat on the way," he said, interrupting her thoughts. She sighed, grateful that he had. She could have stood there and stacked up all his strong points all day.

She offered him a smile. A part of her was tempted to offer a lot more. He had just that sort of effect on her. "All right. I just need to grab my luggage."

"I'll get it," he said, entering her cabin, immediately filling the space with his heat and making her totally aware of him, even more than she had been before. She watched as he glanced over at the luggage she had neatly lined up next to her bed. Then he looked at her and she heard him swear under his breath before moving—not toward the luggage but toward her.

"I don't know what decisions you made about us," he said in a low, husky voice. "But I thought of you all last night and I swore that as soon as I saw you this morning I would do something."

"What?" she asked, trying to ignore the seductive scent of his aftershave as well as the intense beating of her heart.

"Taste you."

Madison's breath caught and, before she could release a sigh, Stone captured her mouth in his. As soon as their tongues touched she knew she would remember every sweet and tantalizing thing about his kiss. Especially the way his tongue was dueling with hers, staking a claim she didn't want him to have but one he was taking anyway as he tried kissing the taste right out of her mouth. His tongue was dominating, it was bold and it left no doubt in her mind that when it came to kissing, Stone was an ace, a master, a perfectionist. She placed her arms around his neck, more to stop from melting at his feet than for support. He had a way of making her feel sexy, feminine and desirable; something Cedric had never done.

Moments later, when he broke off the kiss and slowly lifted his head to look down at her, she couldn't help asking, "Got enough?"

"Not by a long shot," he said hotly against her moist lips. Then he leaned down and kissed her again and Madison quickly decided, what the heck. Once she had told him of her decision about them he wouldn't be kissing her again anytime soon, so she would gladly take what she could for now.

Her common sense tried kicking in—although it didn't have the punch to force her to pull from his arms just yet. Her practical side was reminding her that she'd only met Stone two days ago. Her passionate side countered that bit of logic with the fact that in those two days she probably knew him a lot better than she'd known Cedric in the years they had dated. Stone was everything her former fiancé was not—including one hell of a kisser.

Desire surged through her and she knew if she didn't pull back now the unthinkable might happen. But then a rebel part of her that barely ever surfaced hinted that the unthinkable in this case just might be something she should do.

She didn't have much time to think about it further

when Stone lifted his mouth again and she, regretfully, released her arms from around his neck and took a step back, putting space between them.

"I guess I better grab that luggage so we can leave," he said, keeping his gaze glued to her face.

"That's a good idea and I don't think there should be any more physical contact between us until we talk," she said softly, trying to hold on to the resolve she'd had that morning. The same resolve his kiss had almost swiped from her.

She watched as he arched a dark brow. "You've made decisions?"

Her gaze held on to his. "Yes."

He nodded then walked across the room for her luggage.

"Tell me about yourself, Stone, and I would love hearing about all of your books."

Stone briefly glanced across the seat of the truck and met Madison's inquiring gaze. They had been on the road for over an hour already and she'd yet to tell him of any decisions she'd made. Even when they had stopped at a café for breakfast she hadn't brought their relationship up. Instead she had talked about how beautiful the land was, how much she had enjoyed teaching last year and about a trip to Paris she had taken last month. She was stalling. He knew it and knew that she knew it, as well.

"Do you want to know about Stone Westmoreland or about Rock Mason?"

A bemused frown touched her face. "Aren't they one and the same?"

"No. To the people I know I'm Stone Westmoreland.

To my readers, the majority of whom don't know me, I'm Rock Mason—a name I made up to protect my privacy. I should correct that and say it's a name my sister Delaney came up with. At the time she was eighteen and thought it sounded cool."

She nodded. "And which one of those individuals are you now?"

"Stone."

She nodded again. And although she had made her mind up not to go there, she couldn't help but ask. The need to know was too strong. "And each of the times you kissed me, who were you?"

He glanced over at her. "Stone." He then pulled off the road, stopped the car and turned to her. "Maybe I need to explain things, Madison. I don't have a split personality. I'm merely saying that a lot of people read a book a person writes and assume they know that individual just because of the words he or she puts on paper. But there's more to me than what is between the pages of my novels. I write to entertain. I enjoy doing so and it pays the bills in a real nice way. Whenever I finish a book I feel a sense of accomplishment and achievement. But when all is said and done, I'm still a normal human being—a man who has strong values and convictions about certain things. I'm a man who's proud to be an African-American and I'm someone who loves his family. I have my work and I have my privacy. For my work I am Rock Mason and for my private life I am Stone. I consider you as part of my private life." With that said he started the car and pulled back on the main road.

Madison blew out a breath. The very thought that he considered her part of his life at all made her heart pound and parts of her feel soft and gooey inside. "So tell me something about the private life of Stone Westmoreland."

Her request drew his brows together as he remembered the last time a woman had asked him that. Noreen Baker, an entertainment reporter who'd wanted to do an interview on him for *Today's Man* magazine. The woman had been attractive but pushy as hell. He hadn't liked her style and had decided when she'd tried delving into his personal life that he hadn't liked her. But she was determined not to be deterred and had decided one way or another she would get her story.

She never got her story and found out the hard way that, although on any given day he was typically pretty nice and easygoing, when pissed off he could be hell to deal with. Instead of giving her the exclusive she had desired, he had agreed to let someone else do a story on him.

"I'm thirty-three—closer to thirty-four with a birthday coming up in August—single, and have never been married and don't plan on ever getting married."

Madison lifted a brow. "Why?"

"It's the accountability factor. I love being single. I like coming and going whenever I please and, with being a writer, I need the freedom of going places to do research, book signings, to clear my mind, relax and to be just plain lazy when I want to. I'm not responsible for anyone other than myself and I like it that way." He decided not to tell her that another reason he planned to stay single was that he saw marriage as giving up control of his life and giving more time to a wife than to his writing.

Madison nodded. "So there's not a special person in your life?"

"No." But then he thought she was special and he had pretty much accepted that she was in his life...at least at the present time.

"What about your immediate family?"

"My parents are still living and doing well. My father works with the construction company my grandfather started years ago. He's a twin."

Madison had shifted her body in the seat to search her pockets for a piece of chewing gum and glanced over at Stone. "Who's a twin?"

"My father. As well as my two brothers, Chase and Storm, and my cousins, Ian and Quade. They are Durango's brothers."

"Are they all identical twins?" she asked fascinated. She'd never heard of so many multiple births in one family before.

"No, everyone is fraternal, thank God. I can't imagine two of Storm. He can be a handful and considers himself a ladies' man."

Madison smiled, hearing the affection in his voice. "How many brothers do you have?"

"Four brothers and one sister. Delaney, who we call Laney, is the baby."

Madison frowned. "Delaney Westmoreland? Now where have I heard that name before?"

Stone chuckled. "Probably read about her. *People* magazine did a spread on her almost a year and a half ago when she married a prince from the Middle East by the name of Jamal Ari Yasir."

A huge smile touched Madison's face. "That's right, I remember reading that article. *Essence* magazine did an article on her, as well. Wow! I remember reading it during…"

Stone glanced over at her to see why she hadn't finished what she was about to say. Her smile was no longer there. "During what?"

She met his gaze briefly before he returned it to the road. "During the time I broke up with my fiancé. It was good reading something as warm, loving and special as the story about your sister and her prince; especially after finding out what a toad my own fiancé was."

"What did he do?"

Madison glanced down at her hands that were folded in her lap before glancing over at Stone. His eyes were on the road but she knew that she had his complete attention and was waiting for her response. "I found out right before our wedding that he'd been having an affair. He came up with a lot of reasons why he did it, but none were acceptable."

"Hell, I should hope not," Stone said with more than a hint of anger in his voice. "The man was a fool."

"And she was a model."

Stone lifted a brow. "Who?"

"The woman he was sleeping with. He said that that justified his behavior. He believed he was actually using her so as not to wear me down. He wanted to preserve me for later."

A dark frown covered Stone's face. "He actually said that?"

"Yes. Cedric was quite a character."

Stone didn't want to get too personal, but he couldn't help asking, "So the two of you never, ahh, never slept together?"

Instead of looking over at him he watched as she

quickly glanced out the window. "Yes, we did, but just twice during the two years we were together."

Stone shook his head. "Like I said before, he was a fool."

Madison leaned back comfortably in her seat. She was glad Stone felt that way. Cedric had tried to convince her that just because he'd been involved in one affair was no reason to call off their wedding. A model, he'd tried to explain, was every man's fantasy girl. That didn't mean he had loved her less, it only meant he was fulfilling one of his fantasies. She guessed fulfillment of fantasies came before fidelity.

"Tell me some more about you, Stone," she said, not wanting to think anymore about Cedric and the pain he had caused her.

She listened for the next few miles while Stone continued to tell her about his family. He talked about his brother Dare who was a sheriff and Chase who owned a restaurant in downtown Atlanta. Once again she was surprised to discover that he had another well-known sibling—Thorn Westmoreland, the motorcycle builder and racer who had won the big bike race in Daytona earlier that year.

"I've seen your brother's bikes and they're beautiful. He's very skillful."

"Yes, he is," he said. "He got married last month and is in the process of teaching his wife how to handle a bike."

By the time they had reached the Quinns' ranch, Madison felt she knew a good bit about Stone. He had openly shared things about himself and the people he cared about. She knew he never, ever wanted to marry but was proud that his parents' marriage had lasted for such a long time. And he was genuinely happy for his sister and brothers and their marriages.

When they pulled the truck up in front of the sprawling ranch house, Madison caught her breath. It was breathtaking and like nothing she had ever seen before. "This place is beautiful," she said when Stone opened the truck door for her to get out.

He laughed. "If you think this place leaves you gasping for air, just wait until you see Uncle Corey's place. Now that place is a work of art."

Madison couldn't wait to see it. Nor could she wait to see her mother. Stone must have read the look in her eyes because he gently squeezed her hand in his, giving her assurance. "She's fine and you'll see her soon enough."

She nodded. Thankful. Before she could say anything a woman, who appeared to be in her middle fifties, came out the front door of the house with a huge smile on her face. She was beautiful and it was quite obvious she was Native American. Her dark eyes were huge in her angular face. She had high cheekbones and long, straight black hair that flowed down her back. "Why, if it isn't Stone Westmoreland. Martin said you were coming and I decided to cook an apple pie for the occasion. I'll share if you autograph a few books for me."

Stone laughed as he swept the woman off her feet into his arms for a hug. "Anything for you, Mrs. Quinn. And you know how much I love your apple pie." When he had placed her back on her feet he turned her around so he could introduce her to Madison.

"Madison, this is Morning Star Quinn, Martin's wife. They are good friends of my uncle Corey and their son McKinnon is Durango's best friend."

Madison smiled. It was easy to see that the woman had Stone's affection and respect. She offered Morning Star Quinn her hand to shake, liking her on the spot. She seemed like such a vibrant person who blended in well with her surroundings. "It's nice meeting you."

"It's nice meeting you, as well. And I've prepared a place for the two of you to stay overnight. I understand you are on your way up to see Corey."

Stone nodded. "Yes. Mr. Quinn mentioned when I spoke with him on the phone yesterday that the two of you haven't seen Uncle Corey in a while."

Morning Star Quinn shook her head. "It's been weeks. He's missed the Thursday night poker game for almost three weeks now, and you know for your uncle that's unusual. But we know he's all right."

"How do you know that for certain?" Madison couldn't help but ask.

Morning Star Quinn raised a curious brow as if wondering why she was interested then smiled at her and responded. "He came down off the mountain a couple of days ago to use the phone. It seems something is wrong with his telephone, which is the reason no one has heard from him. Martin and I had gone to town so we didn't get a chance to see him, but McKinnon was here and had a chance to talk to him. He assured us that Corey was fine."

Mrs. Quinn then switched her gaze to Stone. "McKinnon also said he had a woman with him; a very nice-looking woman at that. Of course that surprised all of us because you know how Corey feels about a woman being on his mountain."

Stone shook his head, smiling. "Yes, I know. In fact that's one of the reasons we're going up to see him."

Tapping her finger to her bottom lip, Morning Star Quinn gazed thoughtfully at Stone. "Then you know her? You know who this woman is?"

Madison knew that, out of consideration for her mother's reputation, Stone would not say. But she knew that Morning Star Quinn was a person that she could be honest with; and was a person that she *wanted* to be honest with. "Yes, we know who she is," Madison finally answered. "The woman up there on the mountain with Corey Westmoreland is my mother."

Chapter 5

Nothing, Madison thought as she walked outside on the huge porch, could be more beautiful than a night under a Montana sky. Even in darkness she could see the outlines of the Rockies looming in the background and was starkly amazed at just how vastly different this place was from Boston.

She turned when she heard the door open behind her and wasn't surprised to see it was Stone. She smiled as she took a couple of minutes to calm the rapid beating of her heart. The more time she spent with him, the more she appreciated him as a man...a very considerate and caring man. Even now she could feel the warmth of his eyes touching her.

Earlier he had helped her unload her luggage and had placed it in the bedroom that Mrs. Quinn had given her to use. Then later, after she had gotten settled, he had come for her when Martin Quinn and his son McKinnon had come home. She had blinked twice when she saw McKinnon. The man was simply gorgeous and had inherited his mother's golden complexion. After introductions had been made, Stone had asked her to take a walk with him to show her around the Quinns' ranch before dinnertime.

On their stroll, he had shared stories with her about how, while growing up, he and his brothers and cousins would visit this area every summer to spend time with their Uncle Corey. It was a guy thing, which meant Delaney was never included in those summer retreats. She usually came to Montana during her school's spring breaks. Stone also shared with her the little escapades the eleven Westmoreland boys and McKinnon and his three brothers had gotten into. He had made her smile, chuckle and even laugh a few times, and for a little while she had forgotten the reason she had come to Montana in the first place. At dinner she had met Morning Star and Martin's other three sons, who were younger than McKinnon, but who had also inherited their mother's Blackfoot coloring, instead of the light complexion of their Caucasian father.

"You okay?" Stone asked quietly, coming to stand beside her.

She tipped her head to look up at him. When he placed his arms around her shoulders as if to ward off the chill in the air, she became very aware of how male he was. And the nice thing about it was that he didn't flaunt it. In fact he seemed totally unaware of the sensuality oozing from him. "Yes, I'm fine. Dinner was wonderful, wasn't it?"

"Yes. Mrs. Quinn always knew how to cook and her apple pie has always been my favorite," he answered.

Madison grinned when she remembered the number of slices he'd eaten and said, "Yeah, I could tell." She then thought of something. "They didn't say a lot about your uncle at dinner." She felt his fingers inch upward to caress the side of her neck, sending a glimmer of heat through her.

"There wasn't much to say. They know the man Uncle Corey is and know that your mother isn't in any danger."

She shot him a quick look. "I know she isn't in any danger with him, Stone. I just don't understand what's going on. And I'm beginning to understand a bit about instant attraction if that's what it was, but still I have to talk to her anyway."

"I understand," he said, giving her shoulders a quick squeeze.

A part of Madison wondered if he did understand when there were times when she didn't.

"Tell me about your parents, Madison."

His question caught her off guard. "My parents?"

"Yes. What sort of marriage did they have?"

She frowned, not sure why he was asking and whether or not she was willing to disclose any details of her parents' relationship as she had seen it. But this was Stone. He had stopped being a stranger to her that first day on the plane and she figured there must be a reason that he wanted to know. "It was nothing like the Quinns' marriage, that's for sure," she said in a rush.

The sound of his chuckle filled the night air. "It wasn't?"

She leaned back and looked up at him as she thought of the two adults with four grown sons. Even with visitors sitting at the dinner table with their sons, they still exchanged smiles filled with over thirty years of intimacies. "No, it wasn't. Is your parents' marriage like theirs?"

Stone looked down at her and she could actually see the smile that touched both corners of his mouth. "Umm, pretty much. I'm proud of the fact that my parents have shared a long marriage, but even prouder that they are still very much in love after nearly forty years."

He shifted his body to lean against the porch rail and took her with him, letting her hip rest along the strength of his. "They claim it was love at first sight after meeting one weekend at a church function. Within two weeks they were married."

He decided not to tell her that his parents had predicted that their six children would also find love that way—at first sight. So far Delaney claimed that's how it had been for her and Jamal, although realizing it had been the tough part for her, as well as for Jamal. And everyone knew the moment Dare had gotten zapped. Stone and Shelly were friends in high school and working on a project together when Dare had come home unexpectedly from college and walked into the living room. He had taken one look at the sixteen-year-old Shelly Brockman and fallen in love with her then and there.

Then there was Thorn. Tara had been his challenge, as well as the love of his life from the moment she had stormed out of their sister Delaney's kitchen one night to give the unsuspecting Thorn hell about something. She had taken him aback and had also taken his heart in that same minute. Again, love at first sight.

He released a deep sigh. That may have been the way

things had happened for his sister and two brothers but it wouldn't happen that way for him. He wouldn't let it.

"Your parents like touching, Stone?"

Madison's question interrupted Stone's thoughts and he couldn't help but chuckle again when he thought of the many times he'd seen his father playfully pat his mother on her behind. "Yes, and they also occasionally kiss in front of us. Always have. We're used to it. Nothing real passionate but enough to let anyone know that they still love each other. I'm sure they leave the heavy-duty hanky-panky stuff in the bedroom," he said grinning, not at all bothered by the fact that his parents might still have an active sex life. He pulled Madison closer to him. "Didn't your parents ever touch?"

After a brief moment she shrugged. "I'd never seen them touch. And I'd never thought anything about it until I went away for the weekend to spend some time at a friend's house. Her parents were like the Quinns... and probably a lot like your parents. It was easy to see they loved and respected each other and it suddenly hit me what was missing at my house, between my parents. Then I started watching them closely and I began to realize that, although they liked and respected each other, they were two people who were not in love but locked in a marriage anyway."

Stone lifted a brow. "Why would they stay married if they didn't love each other?"

She sighed deeply. "I can think of several reasons. Me for one. They would have stayed together just for me. I know in my heart that my parents loved me. I was my daddy's girl and my mother's daughter. I had a great relationship with them both. My father's death was hard on me."

Silence stretched between them; then she said, "Another reason they would have possibly stayed together is for religious reasons. They were both devout Catholics who didn't believe in divorce. It was til-death-do-you-part."

Stone nodded, taking in everything she'd said. "Didn't you say that your father has been dead for ten years?"

"Yes, he died when I was fifteen."

"And during that time, since his death, your mother has never been romantically involved with anyone?"

"No."

"Don't you think that's odd?"

She heaved a sigh. "I never thought about it before. I always assumed she just wanted to bury herself in her work after my father's death. I never assumed she was lonely and in need of companionship."

"Well, that might be the reason she took off with Uncle Corey. There are some things a man or woman can't control at times. Passion. Especially if they haven't shared it with anyone in a while. Hormones are known to get the best of you if you aren't careful."

Madison wondered if he was speaking from experience? She hadn't slept with anyone since Cedric and she definitely didn't feel like she was missing out on anything. He had been her first lover and she really didn't care if he was her last.

But then, standing so close to Stone with the feel of his warm breath on her cheek, she knew she had to rethink that declaration. Anytime he had held her in his arms against his broad chest, her temperature had had a tendency to go up a notch. And whenever she had leaned into his aroused body while they kissed, it always amazed her that he had wanted her. And she would have to admit she had spent the last couple of nights in bed wondering how it would feel if he were to make love to her; for him to climb on top of her and—

"Are you cold, Madison?"

She was jerked out of her racy thoughts. She cleared her throat. "No, why do you ask?"

"Because you were shivering a few moments ago."

"Oh." She met his gaze when he looked down at her. She hoped he didn't have a clue as to why she had been trembling.

"What about you and your fiancé?" Stone asked, pulling her closer so that her cheek rested on his shoulder.

"What about us?"

"I know you said the two of you weren't intimate often, but did you do a lot of touching?"

She sighed deeply. There was an inner urgency within her to share with Stone how things had been with her and Cedric. She'd already told him that they had slept together only a couple of times but now he needed to hear the rest.

"Cedric and I didn't do a whole lot of anything, Stone. I mentioned earlier today that we were intimate two times, but even then it wasn't for enjoyment. It was done only to make sure we were compatible."

Stone shook his head, not sure he'd heard her right. *They'd been intimate a couple of times not for enjoyment but just to make sure they were compatible?* Now he had heard it all. How in the world could you be compatible without enjoyment? "What about passion?"

She shrugged. "What about it?"

Nothing, if you have to ask, he thought. But then he decided that he needed to appease his curiosity anyway.

"Weren't there ever times when the two of you lost control?"

She chuckled as if the thought of his question was ridiculous. "No, and to be quite honest, I never experienced real physical attraction until I met you."

Damn, Stone thought. He wished she hadn't told him that mainly because it was the same way with him. He, too, had never experienced real physical attraction until he had met her. Oh, sure, he'd felt lust for a woman before but for some reason the attraction with Madison was totally different. He thought about her during some of the oddest times and, whenever he did, unexplainable warmth would flood his insides. He never, ever remembered actually hungering for a woman until he had met her. And now she was a constant craving and that didn't bode well.

After a few moments, he said, "I guess we're going to have to come up with some ground rules once we leave here and head up into the mountains."

It took Madison a moment to realize what he meant. But she decided to pretend otherwise and ask just to make sure. "Ground rules?"

"Yes, about us, Madison. About this attraction we can both honestly admit that we have for each other. About these hormones of mine that don't want to behave worth a damn. And about the fact you haven't told me what decisions you've made."

Madison forced a lump down her throat. She quickly remembered the decisions she had made overnight; the ones she'd been determined to stick to when she'd woken that morning. She knew that doing things her way was for the best.

She released a long, resigned sigh and said, "I think

we should only concentrate on the situation with your uncle and my mother. At the present time my mind isn't free to dwell on anything else. I'm not sure how you may feel about it but I prefer that any thoughts about anything between us be placed on the back burner to be analyzed and discussed later, after I see my mother."

Stone shook his head. Back burner, hell! Did she think things would be that easy? Did she actually think two people could turn off sexual chemistry like it flowed from a faucet or tuck it away like an agenda item to be looked at and discussed later? Didn't she realize how difficult it would be for them once they were alone together in the mountains, in constant close proximity to each other?

No, he quickly concluded. She didn't know. She didn't have a clue because, from what he'd gathered tonight from their conversation, her parents had not been passionate beings. And, to make matters worse, her fiancé had been a damn poor excuse for a man. Instead of introducing the woman he was engaged to marry to fiery passion and red-hot desire, the bastard had been too busy doing it with a model.

A part of Stone was glad he had discovered the reason behind Madison's irrational thoughts on the situation involving his uncle and her mother. She couldn't see passion and desire for what they were if she had never experienced them before. It was obvious that she had never felt toe-curling, scream-til-your-throat-becomes-raw passion. Those sensations were something everyone should experience at some point in their lives. He couldn't imagine anything worse than having to suppress your desires—especially for a long period of time.

He quickly made a decision. He would introduce

Madison to the pleasures of sex. She would soon discover that the attraction between them was something neither of them could ignore. He wanted to show her what it meant to have uncontrollable hormones zap the very sense out of you. He wouldn't do anything in particular, just sit back and let nature take its course and, considering everything, he had all the confidence in the world that it would.

Stone Westmoreland was convinced that by the time they reached his uncle's cabin, his city girl would have a clear understanding of how easy it was for a person to lose control to passion of the strongest, most potent kind.

"And you're sure that's the way you want things?" he asked after a long moment of silence.

"Yes. It will be for the best."

He nodded as a slow smile touched his lips. What Madison didn't know was that the best was yet to come. He would give her a summer night in the mountains that she would remember for a long time.

The next morning Stone glanced over at Madison as she sat patiently on her horse. He actually envied the animal's back. He would just love to have her sitting on him with her legs flanking him on both sides while she rode him to sweet oblivion.

He had not gotten much sleep last night, thinking of her and their trip up into the mountains together. He hadn't changed his mind. Before they reached his uncle's place he intended to have taught his city girl a few things. She would see how it was to deal with a real flesh-and-blood man. A man who appreciated everything a woman stood for.

He glanced up at the sky. The sun hadn't quite come up yet which meant it was a good time to start their trip. He could hardly wait. Anticipation was eating away at him, fueling his desire for her even more. "You okay?" he decided to ask her.

She smiled over at him. "Yes, I'll be fine just as long as you're not expecting an experienced cowgirl. I can do okay with a horse but, like I told you, even with the lessons I took, I'm not much of a rider."

He nodded. All that would be changing. She might not be much of a rider now but by the time they reached his uncle's cabin she would be pretty proficient at it. He would definitely teach her how to ride an animal of the two-legged kind.

"Do you think we will come across any wild animals?"

Her question made him stop what he was doing with his saddle and glance over at her. A smile tilted his lips. "You mean which kind of wild animals do you hope that we won't encounter?"

She chuckled and the sound made his stomach clench in desire. It was such a sexy sound and was like a caress to his already sensitized flesh. "Yeah, that's it."

He took the time to get on his horse before answering her. "Namely bears, wolves and mountain lions."

"Oh."

He grinned over at her when he saw the look of fear that appeared in her eyes. "Don't worry. The path I plan to take is one that's well used and most wild animals know to avoid it." He decided not to tell her that he would be taking another route that would delay their arrival at his uncle Corey's ranch by a full day. Madison Winters needed an education in wildlife of the human kind.

But first he had to get his libido under control, which

wasn't easy. She looked so desirable sitting on the horse with her face tipped up to the sun. She had pulled her hair back in a ponytail and was wearing the big wide-brimmed hat on her head. But still, he could see her beautiful dark skin glowing in the predawn light. She was a natural beauty and he wondered how he would be able to keep his hands off her until she made the first move. And she would make the first move. He would see to it. He would lay temptation at her feet, then wait for her to act on it.

"Ready?" he asked, looking over at her.

"Yes."

"Okay then, let's go." They started at a slow pace since he wanted her to get the feel of the animal beneath her. He wanted her to be aware of everything around her: the way the sun was beginning to rise over the mountains, the rustle of the wind through the trees, and the sound of pine needles snapping under their horses' feet. And he wanted to make sure she was aware of him, the man who wanted her.

If she wasn't aware of it now, she would definitely be aware of it later.

They rode in silence for the first few hours, only engaging in conversation when he pointed out something of interest to her. He liked the way she appreciated her surroundings. She might be a city girl, but it was apparent she was enjoying embarking on their journey.

"Thirsty?" he asked, wondering if the ride had taken a toll on her yet. The sun had come up fully now and the heat of it was beaming down on them. He was grateful he was wearing his hat and that she had followed his suggestion and had worn hers.

"Yes, I'm thirsty."

"How about a drink of water?"

"That would be nice," she said, as he brought the horses to a stop.

"Just sit tight while I get the canteen. Mr. Quinn told me before we left that during this past year he and McKinnon built a cabin that's located halfway to Corey's place. They use it when he and his sons go hunting in these parts. He said that we could use it if we liked. So if we make it there before nightfall, we won't have to sleep outside after all."

He idly stroked the back of his horse, wishing it were Madison's body. He then added, "And there's a place up ahead where we can camp for a while and eat lunch. If we continue at this pace, we should be able to make it there before it gets much hotter."

The look on Madison's face indicated that she hoped they would. He grinned. She was being a real trooper. A lot of women would be whining and complaining by now. He remembered the first time his father had decided to take Delaney camping with him and his brothers. He shook his head at the memory. That had been the first and the last time.

He got off his horse and, after making sure both of their mounts' reins were securely tied to a nearby tree, he went to her saddlebag and pulled out the canteen, then walked over and handed it to her.

She quickly took it from him. "Thanks."

He watched as she opened the top and tipped the canteen up to her mouth. Some of the water missed her lips and drizzled down her chin. He was tempted to lap it up with his tongue. He had thought about tasting her that way a lot lately and intended to get his chance real soon.

He continued to watch her, getting turned on just from seeing how her throat moved as the cool liquid flowed down it. His eyes were so focused on her throat that he didn't notice that she had stopped drinking.

"Stone, you can have this back now."

He blinked. "Oh," he said, reaching for the canteen.

"Thanks again. The water was delicious."

"You're welcome. It's natural spring water," he said, thinking that she was delicious, too. Instead of putting the canteen away, he pulled the top back off and began drinking some of the water, deliberately tasting where her mouth had been.

When he finished he licked his lips, liking the hint of a taste of her that he had gotten from the canteen. He glanced up to see her watching him. She didn't say anything but just continued to look at him. And he looked at her. Then he felt it, that deep, hard throb in his gut that made him want to snatch her off the back of the horse and tumble with her in the grass. His body was already hot and was beginning to get hotter, in need of physical contact with her.

He saw how her cheeks darkened and he saw the moment desire filled her eyes. He also saw how fast the pulse was beating in her neck and the way she took out her tongue to moisten her already damp lips. His gaze slowly dropped to her blouse and saw how the nipples of her breasts were straining against the material. Her breathing, as well as his, was erratic. He heard it. He felt it. He wanted to taste it.

"You had enough?" he forced his gaze back to her eyes, as he tried like hell to get his thoughts and mind, and especially his body, back under control.

"Enough of what?" she asked, her voice soft, somewhat husky and definitely sensual. Her gaze was still holding his.

"Water."

She blinked and he saw that her features relayed both her confusion, as well as her longing for something she didn't quite understand yet. But she would in time. He would see to it. "Yes, I had enough," she said, after drawing in a deep breath.

He smiled. She hadn't had enough of anything yet. After putting her canteen back in her saddlebag he went around and got back on his horse. He leaned over and handed her reins to her. "Come on," he said huskily. "Let's continue our ride."

Chapter 6

Up until a half hour ago Madison thought she was hungry, but now something was affecting her appetite... or rather someone.

Stone Westmoreland.

She tilted her head as she watched him. He was standing some distance away tending to the horses. She was sitting on a stump eating one of the sandwiches Mrs. Quinn had packed for them and drinking a cold can of cola, while her eyes were glued to Stone.

She was attracted to him. There was no use denying it since that fact had already been established a few days ago. But what she couldn't understand was why she couldn't get past it. Why did a part of her want to act on it?

It seemed that although her mind was definitely on him, his mind was on the horses. He hadn't looked her way since they had stopped for lunch. She should have been grateful, but she couldn't deny being bothered by the fact that he could dismiss her so easily. But then, hadn't she laid out the ground rules last night? And hadn't those ground rules included a statement that anything developing between them was to be placed on the back burner? Evidently he had taken her at her word and intended to adhere to it.

She let out a deep sigh and the sound must have caught his attention. He lifted his eyes to hers, holding it for several long moments, saying nothing but looking at her. She met his gaze without flinching while desire stirred in her stomach, hot, thick, the likes of which she'd never experienced before. Without a sound, without a touch, and over the distance of twenty feet, she actually felt the heat of his gaze as tiny shocks of warmth began inching all the way up her spine to flow through her body. She even felt heat forming between her legs. Especially between her legs. And the appetite forming in her stomach had nothing to do with regular food. She continued to look at him while trying to cling to her composure, her resolve and her sanity.

Her throat tightened when he began walking toward her and the heat surging through her got hotter. She had never appreciated a Western shirt and tight jeans on a man until she had met him. She couldn't imagine his tall, muscled body wearing anything else...unless it was nothing at all.

Her breath caught. She wished she could strike that thought from her mind, call it back, and not think about it. But the deed was done. That wicked thought went right along with the dreams she'd been having about him lately. The man exuded raw sex appeal without trying and she was fully aware of him, more so than she needed to be.

"You okay?"

Madison shook her head. Not sure words would come out of her mouth even if she wanted them to, but she forced herself to speak anyway. "Yes, I'm fine, Stone."

He nodded as he continued to look at her. "Can I use some of that?" he asked indicating the small bottle of liquid hand sanitizer she had brought along.

"Sure, help yourself."

She watched as he uncapped the small bottle and poured some in his palm and then began rubbing his hands together in slow motion. She immediately thought of him rubbing those same hands all over her…in slow motion. She glanced at her soda can wondering if there was something inside it other than soda that was making her dizzy with such wanton thoughts.

"This is a beautiful spot, isn't it?"

His question got her attention. She shifted her gaze away from his hands to take in the beauty of their surroundings. "Yes, it is. I wish I had thought to bring a camera along."

He lifted a brow. "I'm surprised that you didn't."

She was surprised, too. "I had other things on my mind." And those *other things,* she told herself, were what she should be concentrating on and not on Stone. She continued to watch him as he recapped the hand sanitizer and placed it back in her gear. Then he walked over to his saddlebag to pull out his own sandwich and drink. She sighed. Maybe if she got him talking about his uncle she just might be able to clear her mind of hot, steamy thoughts. She figured it was worth a try.

"Do you have any idea who in Texas is trying to locate your uncle, Stone?" she asked, after she had finished off the last of her sandwich.

He walked back over to her and sat down on the stump beside her. "No, I have no idea. I mentioned it to Durango and he didn't have a clue, either. We decided to turn it over to Quade and let him solve the mystery."

Madison lifted a brow. "Who?"

Stone smiled. "Quade. He's one of Durango's brothers—the one I mentioned was a twin. He used to be a secret service agent. Now he works for the government in some behind-the-scenes capacity. We don't have a clue exactly what he does. We see him when we see him and don't ask questions when we do. But we know how to contact him if we ever need him and usually within seventy-two hours we'll hear back from him."

Madison nodded. "And you think he can find out what's going on?"

"He'll find out."

Madison sat quietly for a moment thinking that Stone seemed pretty sure of his cousin's abilities. Her thoughts then shifted back to the man her mother had run off with. "Tell me about Corey Westmoreland," she said, feeling the need to know as much about him as she could since she would be coming face-to-face with him soon.

Stone glanced over at her after taking a sip of his soda. "Exactly what do you want to know?"

She shrugged. "What I'm really curious about is why everyone thinks it's strange for him to have a woman on his mountain."

Stone's lips lifted into a smile. "Mainly because as long as I can remember Uncle Corey claimed it would never happen. He's been involved with women before but none of them have ever been granted access to this mountain. He's always drawn the line as to how much of his life he's been willing to share with them."

Madison mulled this over for a second then said, "Yet he brought my mother here?"

"Yes, and that's what has me, Durango and the Quinns baffled."

Madison let out a deep sigh. "Now I'm beginning to wonder if perhaps they did know each other before."

Stone stared at her. "There is that possibility, but if I were you I wouldn't try to figure it out. Tomorrow you'll see them for yourself and can ask all the questions you want."

He reached across the distance and caught one of her hands in his and squeezed it gently. "But don't feel bad if she doesn't want to give you any answers. Maybe it's time for you to let your mother enjoy her life, Madison. After all, it's her life to live, isn't it?"

Although a frown appeared on Madison's face, she didn't say anything. Nor did she withdraw her hand from Stone's. All along he had given her food for thought and all along her mind had refused to accept what was becoming obvious.

"So when I see Corey Westmoreland, what should I expect?"

When he didn't answer right away, Madison assumed he was getting his thoughts together. "What you should expect is a fifty-four-year-old man who's been like a second father to his niece and eleven nephews. He's a man who believes in family, honor, respect and love for nature. For as long as I've known him, he has pre-ferred solitude in some things and a vast amount of companionship in others. He won't hesitate to let you know how he feels on any subject and deeply respects the opinion of others."

A smile touched the corners of Stone's lips when he added, "And I learned early in life that he's also a man with eyes in the back of his head. You can't ever pull anything over on him."

The affection Madison heard in Stone's voice caused her to think just how different Corey Westmoreland was from her father. Her father had been an only child. He did have a cousin who'd also lived in Boston, but the two had never had a close relationship, so she hadn't developed a close relationship with that cousin's children who were all around her age.

Her father had been born in the city, raised in the city and lived in the city. They'd never owned a pet while she was growing up and the thought of leaving the city to go camping wasn't anything he would have been interested in doing. And Larry Winters had preferred socializing to solitude, especially when it benefited him. He'd been a financial adviser. He would often host lavish parties for his clients with her mother acting as hostess. She remembered her father being excited each and every time they'd given a party, but now as she thought about it, her mother hadn't particularly cared for entertaining. She had merely accepted it as part of her role as the wife of a successful businessman. She tried to think of one single thing her parents had in common and couldn't think of anything. Last night Stone had asked her why two people who possibly didn't love each other would stay together. Now her question was why had they gotten married in the first place?

She came out of her reverie when Stone removed his

hand from hers. She sat quietly and watched him finish off the rest of his sandwich and down the last of his soda. He then glanced over at her and studied her as if she was going to be his dessert. Visibly feeling the heat of his gaze and not able to sit and take it any longer, she stood and glanced around.

Stone studied Madison for a long moment then asked, "How are you holding up so far?"

She shrugged. "I'm fine. Usually I have an over-abundance of energy. It takes a lot to wear me out."

Stone's gaze drifted down the length of her body. He would definitely remember that later. He watched as she picked up her hat and placed it back on her head.

"Don't you think we should move on if we plan to make it to that cabin before nightfall?" she asked.

He stood and flashed her a slow, sexy grin. "Yeah, Miss Winters, I think that you're right."

The cabin was not what either Stone or Madison had expected. What they assumed they would find was a small one-room structure. But what Martin Quinn and McKinnon had built in the clearing—nestled between large pine trees with a breathtaking view of the mountains and valleys for a backdrop, as well as a beautiful stream running at the back of it—was a cabin large enough to be used as a home away from home.

Stone and Madison took a quick tour of the place. The outside of the cabin featured an inviting wraparound porch. Inside, there was a huge living room with a fireplace, two bedrooms connected by a large single bathroom, and an eat-in kitchen with an enormous window that overlooked the stream out back. It didn't take long for Stone to discover that they would have electricity once he fired up the generator and the linen closets had fresh sheets and coverings for the bed.

Stone sighed, grateful that they had made it to the cabin before nightfall. They still had a few hours of daylight left and he would use the time to feed and care for the horses and start the generator.

He glanced over at Madison who was silently standing beside him. Like him her gaze was on the two bedrooms and he could swear he'd heard her deep sigh of relief.

"I've got a few things to do outside," he said, breaking the silence between them.

She nodded. "Okay, and I can work to get the fireplace going. I have a feeling it's going to be rather cold tonight."

Stone met her gaze, deciding not to tell her that he would be more than happy to provide her with all the heat she would need. "All right, I'll be back later."

It was a full hour or so before Stone returned. Madison had taken advantage of his absence to take a shower. He inhaled the soft, seductive and arousing scent of her the moment he walked into the cabin and came to a dead stop when she walked out of the bedroom.

She had changed into a pair of sweatpants with a tank top, something she must have found more comfortable than jeans. No matter what the woman put on her body, it looked elegant as hell on her. Madison Winters was definitely one class act. Her hair was no longer pulled back in a ponytail but its silky, luxurious strands flowed in sexy disarray about her shoulders. He growled deep in his throat, resisting the urge to cross the room and pull her into his arms and get a real good taste of her, something he'd been dying to do all day.

She glanced up and saw him staring at her. She stared back at him for a moment without saying anything, then a nervous smile touched the corners of her lips. "Although I was tempted, I didn't use up all the hot water. There's plenty left if you want to go ahead and take your bath."

"That sounds rather nice," he said, his voice sounding hoarse. He wanted to take a bath and soak his tired, aching muscles but something had him rooted in place and he couldn't seem to move from that spot.

He continued to stare at her while his insides ached, throbbed. A long period of silence suspended every sound, except for his breathing…and hers. They both jumped when a piece of burning log crackled in the fireplace. Stone shifted his gaze from hers to the fire. "It feels real good in here. Thanks for getting the fire started," he said, although his mind was on another type of fire altogether.

She shrugged. "It was the least I could do while you were outside taking care of the horses and getting the generator started. And I took the liberty to unpack dinner. Mrs. Quinn sent a container of beef stew for us to eat. It's warming now."

Stone nodded and sniffed the air. There was the faint smell of the stew. He hadn't picked up on it when he'd come inside. The only scent his nostrils had caught had been of her. "Smells good."

"It should be ready by the time you have finished your bath."

He nodded. "All right. I guess I'd better get to it then." Seconds passed and he still didn't move. He continued to look at her. Absorb everything about her.

"Stone?"

He blinked. "Yes?"

"Your bath."

A slow smile touched his lips. "Oh, yeah. I'll be back in a minute." He crossed the floor into the other bedroom and closed the door.

As soon as Stone pulled the door shut behind him, he leaned against it and hooked his fingers into the belt loops of his jeans as he tried to get his body under control. He felt blood surge through his body, making him swell in one particular area. He needed to get out of his jeans real quick-like or the force of his arousal that was straining against his zipper would kill him or at least injure him for life.

Part of his plan had been to lay temptation at Madison's feet but she was unknowingly laying it at his. He'd thought with all the chores he'd had to do outside that he would have worked off some of his nervous energy. But as soon as he'd seen her, the only thing he'd managed to do was to work up an oversize case of sexual need.

A prickle of unease made its way up his spine. For Madison to be someone who knew nothing about passion, she definitely looked like a woman who could deliver. And he had a feeling that that delivery would be so much to his liking that he might start getting crazy ideas about wanting to keep her around.

He closed his eyes and clenched his jaw tight. The last thing he needed was to think of any woman in permanent terms. And he refused to let a beautiful, proper-talking, brown-eyed, delectable-smelling city woman come into his life and change things. All he needed to do was remember that episode with Durango a few years ago to screw his head back on tight. The first time his womanizing cousin had let his guard down and fallen for a city woman, he'd been left with scars for life.

But then Stone knew Madison was nothing like the woman who had ripped out Durango's heart. Madison Winters wasn't like any woman he knew. He'd been so hell-bent on introducing her to sexual pleasures that he'd outright forgotten how long it had been for him. He hadn't slept with a woman in over a year after practically shutting off his social life to complete his last book. And the last few women he had been involved with had been downright bores. The need for physical intimacy was tugging at his insides, making him feel things he normally didn't feel; making him want something he usually didn't think twice about doing without.

But still, when all was said and done, no matter what torture he was going through, the woman in the other room was his main concern. Her needs outweighed his and more than anything she needed to understand how it felt to be driven to lose control, to act impulsively and to be spontaneous. She deserved to experience reckless pleasure and uncontrollable passion at least once. And as he moved away from the door and walked toward the connecting bathroom, he knew he wanted that one time to be with him.

Madison placed her hand on her forehead, feeling her skin and wondering why she was beginning to feel so hot. But deep down she knew the reason why. Anytime she was within close proximity to Stone, her temperature went up a few degrees. There was no way she could deny that she wanted him. And hearing the sound of the bath running and knowing that he was in the bathroom naked and wet wasn't helping matters.

Ninety-six hours was the equivalent of four days. That's how long she had known him and here she was thinking all kinds of naughty thoughts. There were still some things about Storm Westmoreland that she didn't know, but she felt certain there was a fair amount that she did know. She had a feeling that the same description he had given his uncle earlier that day could also be used to describe him.

During the ride up the mountain he talked about his family and she knew he was close to them and that all the Westmorelands had a special relationship. And she knew that he also had a love and deep appreciation for nature. That was evident when he had pointed out various plants and trees, as well as telling her about the different types of wildlife that was found in these parts. And she had a feeling there were times in his life— possibly while working on one of his novels—that he sought solitude more often than others. But at the same time he would feel comfortable in any type of social gathering if that was where he wanted to belong.

And she knew that although he would be the last person to brag about his work, she'd heard her girlfriends say countless times that he was an excellent storyteller. She even remembered one of her friends staying overnight at her place after reading one of his thriller-chiller novels, because she was frightened. That was one of the reasons Madison had decided never to read his books. She lived alone in her apartment and the last thing she needed was to start looking over her shoulder or waking up during the night at the slightest sound.

Madison had discovered after reading the newspaper at breakfast yesterday morning that Stone's latest book, *Whispers of a Stalker,* was still on the *New York Times*

bestseller list even after twelve weeks. During the ride
today, Stone had also shared with her information about
his involvement on a national level with the Teach the
People to Read program—a program aimed at fighting
illiteracy.

Another thing she believed with all her heart was
that he was someone who could be trusted. She had felt
comfortable with him from the first and the thought of
them alone in this cabin, miles from civilization, didn't
bother her.

Yes, she decided to admit, it *did* bother her, especially
when it stirred something inside her each and every time
he looked at her with promises of untold pleasures in
his eyes. Pleasures she'd never had before.

She walked to the window and looked out. It was
dark and everything around them appeared black and
still. She had actually seen a bald eagle fly overhead,
but she might have missed the experience if Stone hadn't
pointed it out to her.

"What are you thinking about, Madison?"

Madison quickly spun around, holding shaking fingers to her chest. She hadn't heard Stone approach. In
fact she had been listening to the sound of the water
running during his bath and wondered at what point
he'd turned it off.

He was standing in the middle of the kitchen wearing another pair of jeans and a T-shirt with the words,
The Rolling Stone, boldly displayed across his large,
muscular chest. His hair was damp and she felt like
crossing the distance separating them and rubbing her
hand over his head. And that wasn't the only thing she
wanted to rub her hands over, she thought as he held
her gaze. His eyes blazed with a deep heat. She may not

be experienced in some things, but she could definitely recognize sexual desire in a man; especially this man. It had been in his gaze the first time his eyes had met hers.

"So, you want to keep whatever it was you were thinking a secret?" he asked with a rueful smile.

Madison sighed, turned back to the window. "I was just thinking how quiet things seem outside and yet I know there are plenty of animals out there that make this area their home. In a way I feel as if we are invading their territory."

She felt the heat of him when he came to stand beside her. "Invasion is fine as long as we don't do anything to destroy their natural environment."

She nodded and turned and almost collided with him. She hadn't been aware that he had been standing so close.

"There's something else I've discovered about invasions," he said, holding her gaze.

Madison knew her control was about to be tested. "What?"

"It can make some people rather uncomfortable. Like right now. I am invading your space, aren't I?"

Madison nodded. Yes, he was invading her space but she didn't feel uncomfortable or threatened by it. Instead she felt an incredible magnetism, an intrinsic sensual pull to him.

"Madison?"

She inhaled, pulling air into her lungs before answering, "Yes, but I don't mind sharing my space with you, Stone. Are you ready for dinner?"

She watched as a smile curved his sensuous lips. "I'm ready for a lot a things."

She didn't want to read between the lines but did so anyway. Visions of just what those other things might be danced around in her head. She tried holding on to the decisions she had made yesterday morning about their relationship and discovered she was having a hard time doing so. She cleared her throat. "I'll put the food on the table."

Without giving him a chance to say anything else, she walked off toward the kitchen cabinets to take down a couple of bowls.

"The stew's good, isn't it?"

The sound of Stone's husky voice drifted across the table and was as intimate as a caress. Madison glanced up from eating her stew and met his gaze. A part of her shivered inside from the visual contact. More than once she had caught him staring at her, and against her will her body had responded, each and every time.

Common sense demanded that she fight her interest in him, but it was hard to dredge up will power or common sense around a man like Stone. "Yes, it's delicious," she said trying not to feel the warmth that was spreading through her belly.

Stone pushed his bowl aside, licking his lips. "Too bad we don't have anything for dessert."

Madison swallowed, eyeing his lips with interest. Oh, she could think of a few things she had definitely developed a sweet tooth for over the last few days. His kisses topped the list. "Yes, it is, isn't it?" she decided it was safer to say.

"I'll help you with dishes," Stone said, getting to his feet.

Madison considered his offer and quickly decided that

it wouldn't be a good idea. Earlier she'd told him that she didn't mind him in her space but at the moment she needed him out of it to get her mind focused. "There's no need. I only have a few items to take care of anyway."

"You sure?" he asked.

"Yes, I'm positive. I'd think you'd want to retire early. Today has to have been an exhausting one for you."

Stone's throaty chuckle swirled over her like a sensual mist, absorbing her, snarling her and making desire ripple through her. "No, usually I have an overabundance of energy. It takes a lot to wear me out."

She recognized his words as similar to ones she'd spoken earlier that day. She came to her feet and gathered their dishes off the table. Deep down she was aware of the electrical tension that was beginning to short circuit in her body; however, she was determined not to go up in smoke.

She walked over to the kitchen sink, feeling the heat of Stone's stare; she tried hard to ignore it. His very presence and the scent of him taunted her with the unknown and, although her back was to him, she was aware of every move he made and every breath he took.

Her pulse rate increased when she heard him get up from the table and cross the room to stand less than two feet behind her, and for a few moments he stood silently, not saying anything, not doing anything. Then he took another step, reducing the distance separating them and she quickly turned around.

Their gazes collided. His was so intense the force of it ripped through her, sending a sharp sexual longing to her belly, between her legs and to her breasts, making her nipples harden in immediate response.

Then she felt herself moving, taking a step forward

and reaching out to drape her arms around his neck. She heard the growl he made, deep in his throat, just moments, mere seconds, before he claimed her mouth with a kiss that seduced any resistance she may have had out of her.

The heated, yet gentle thrust of his tongue as it slipped between her lips had her whimpering in pleasure, and he toyed and teased with her tongue while sharing his taste and the intensity of his hunger. She was trying hard to understand what was happening to her. Then she decided, why bother. Who could possibly understand how Stone was making her feel? Who could understand why her heart was beating five times its normal rate and how the heat of him was branding her all over, especially in the area between her legs to the point that she felt her panties getting wet. And when he pressed his body up against her, bringing her closer and letting her feel the magnitude and strength of his arousal, she emitted a soft moan. He was stoking a flame within her and she was a willing victim. She didn't want to dwell on the decisions she had made yesterday morning. The only thing she wanted to think about was how he was making her feel.

She felt him pulling his mouth away and thought, *no, not yet* and tightened her arms around him, keeping their mouths locked, as her tongue became the aggressor, doing what his had done to her earlier. She licked the insides of his mouth from point A to point Z, exploring, tasting, consuming as much of him as she could, but still feeling it wasn't enough. Her body had broken free of any restraints and was raging with an intense sexual need that only he could fill.

He broke free from their kiss and she whimpered in

protest until she felt him lift her top and his mouth latch onto one of her nipples. She had forgotten she hadn't worn a bra and the touch of his tongue to her breast, sucking, flicking and licking was like he was getting the dessert he talked about earlier. She moaned deep in her throat as coils of sexual need tightened deep within her.

He pulled back slightly and she felt herself being lifted effortlessly into his arms. "I want you," he whispered, his voice hot next to her ear.

She wanted him, too, and reached out and pulled his mouth back down to hers. Tonight they were in a cabin deep in the wilderness and succumbing to the call of the wild. She felt out of control with him and knew whatever he wanted to do she wanted to do, too. Never in her life had she wanted or needed a man with this much intensity. She hadn't known such a thing was possible.

He lifted his mouth from hers and she felt herself being carried swiftly out of the kitchen and straight into one of the bedrooms, the one he had planned to use. He placed her on the bed and immediately went to her clothes, pulling the top over her head and easing her sweatpants down her legs.

Heat soared through her as he removed her panties and she knew he was aware just how wet they were. But he didn't say anything, merely tossed them aside. His gaze was still on her, penetrating and compelling. Then he reached out and skimmed his hand across her femininity, as if using his fingers to test her readiness and the degree of her need. She groaned, threw her head back and opened her legs to give him access and he took it.

"Damn, you're hot and wet," he murmured hoarsely

against her ear as his tongue moved over her face to lick the perspiration off her throat and he worked his way up to her chin. He inched his way farther upward and his tongue parted her lips, seeking her taste once again.

But after a moment, that wasn't enough for him. His mouth began moving lower like he was obsessively hungry for her. His tongue worked its way past her breasts and down her chest to her navel, torturing every inch of her in the process. Then he reached the very essence of her heat and used his mouth and tongue to drive her mad in a very intimate French kiss.

She screamed as her body shook with a force that had her digging her fingers into his shoulders to stop the room from spinning, the earth from shaking and her body from splintering in two. The feel of his mouth on her touched off an explosion but still he wouldn't let up. It was as if he was determined to have it all and, in the process, give her everything. Her body was thrown into an orgasm of gigantic proportions that had her nearly sobbing in pleasure and before she could recover from that first orgasm, his mouth and tongue was busy sending her whirling into a second as he once again pushed her over the edge.

Moments later, while she lay there trying to learn how to breathe all over again, he stood back away from the bed and began removing his shirt. She barely had enough strength to prop her elbows on the bed to watch him, studying how well defined his chest was and how a thin line of dark hair led a path downward, past the waistband of his jeans.

She continued to watch, fascinated, and knew at that moment she had never seen a more perfectly made male body. She could stare all day and not tire of seeing it.

She held her breath as he slowly eased down his zipper. Then he pulled off his jeans and briefs, letting her see all of him. Her gaze immediately went to his shaft—thick, large and hard, protruding like a statue from the bed of dark curls that surrounded it. She almost swallowed her tongue.

"I want you," he said huskily, coming back to join her on the bed after putting on the condom he had taken from the pocket of his jeans. "Come here, baby, and let me show you how much."

She eagerly went into his arms and felt her body shudder when her bare skin made contact with his. He took her into his arms and kissed her again. It was as if she hadn't had two orgasms already. Her body was getting aroused all over again. The ache began throbbing between her legs and she knew it would take more than his mouth and tongue this time to satisfy what ailed her there.

He evidently knew it, too. She heard his low groan as he eased her back against the pillows. "I want it all. I want to give you something you've never had before," he whispered huskily in her ear.

She opened her mouth to tell him that he'd already given her something she hadn't ever had before, twice. But he kissed her, silencing her words, drugging her senses and stirring up a need within her that demanded more. Their gazes held, locked and she became ensnarled by the heat in his eyes.

Stone inhaled deeply as he struggled to maintain control. He couldn't last much longer without getting inside of her, needing to be there as much as he needed his next breath. He had tasted her and now he wanted to mate with her, become a part of her, thrust deep and stay forever if there was any way that he could. He moved his body over hers, not breaking eye contact.

"Let me ease inside," he whispered huskily, and she shifted her body to accommodate his request. Then he leaned forward, captured her mouth and kissed her again, wanting to convey without words just how he felt. He rotated the lower part of his body, letting his shaft caress her, seek her out and he found her wet, slick and hot.

He lifted his mouth as his hands gripped her hips. When she began closing her eyes he knew he wanted her to look at him, he wanted to see the expression on her face the moment their bodies joined. "Open your eyes. Look at me, Madison. I want to see you when you take me in."

Her gaze held his and her fingers began stroking his shoulders as she parted her legs for him. Not able, nor willing to hold back any longer Stone eased inside of her. He sucked in a deep breath and his hands held her hips in a firm grip as he continued going as deep as he could, feeling the muscles of her body clench him, take him, claim him.

And then he established a rhythm, slow and easy; the fast and hard thrusting in and out in an urgency that enveloped them. He groaned deep in his throat as he gave her all of him and took all of her in the process. He felt the tremors that began radiating through her body when he increased his rhythmic pace, stroking her, as well as himself into an explosion. He threw his head back and felt the muscles in his neck strain, and when she screamed his name, he lifted her hips to lock her legs around him to share in the orgasm that was overtaking her.

He growled out her name between clenched teeth

and when the shudders began wracking her body, he felt it; something he had never felt before. Passion yes. Satiated hunger—that, too. But there was something else he felt and when he buried his face against her neck, he pushed out of his mind whatever it was. The only thing he wanted at that moment was to share in the aftereffects of such a beautiful mating.

He shifted his weight off her and pulled her into his arms. He somehow found the strength to lean up and look at her. A smile, a deep, satisfied smile, drifted across her lips and the gaze holding his was filled with joy and wonder. Utter satisfaction. And he knew they had shared something special and unique. They had shared passion of the most unbridled and the richest kind, and he knew that before they left this cabin they would do so again, and again and again....

Chapter 7

Stone lay propped up on his elbow as he gazed down at the sleeping woman beside him in the bed. What Madison had said yesterday had been true. She possessed an overabundance of energy and it took a lot to wear her out.

He couldn't help but smile when he thought of the number of times they had made love during the night; her body taking him in, clenching him, satisfying him and demanding from him all that he could give. And he had given a lot; all he had and they had made love until exhaustion had wracked their bodies. It was only then that she had fallen asleep in his arms, her limbs entwined with his. He'd managed to get some sleep in, as well, but now he was wide-awake and fully aroused. He wanted her again. He glanced down at their bodies, seemingly joined at the hips and liked what he saw. He liked it too much.

Taking a deep breath, full realization hit him and he accepted that he had shared something with Madison that he had never shared with any other woman. A lot of himself. No, he had shared *all* of himself. For her he had let his guard down.

His gaze dropped back down to her and latched on to her bare breasts. This attraction he had for her was nothing but lust, he tried convincing himself, but then he remembered how he felt emotionally, each and every time she had screamed out his name while swept up in the throes of ecstasy. Okay, he admitted he would always remember last night, but he refused to get hung up on it and start reading more into it than was there. He had wanted to introduce her to passion, and he had. No big deal. He had wanted to show her how two level-headed individuals could suddenly become overtaken with desire, a desire so consuming that it could stir uncontrollable passion between them. And he'd done that, too. The only thing left was for them to find her mother and Uncle Corey.

He frowned when he thought what would probably happen after that. Once Madison saw her mother and was reassured that she was fine, she'd probably return to Boston. He, on the other hand, would go back to Durango's place and do what he'd intended to do from the beginning. He would get a little R and R before starting work on his next book.

Why did the thought of them going their separate ways begin to gnaw on his insides? Why did the thought of her sharing her newfound passion with another man bother the hell out of him? He had made love to other women and never felt troubled by the thought of them sleeping with someone else after their relationship ended. In fact, he'd always been grateful that his ex-lovers wanted to move on.

He inhaled deeply. He needed distance from Madison to think straight and to get his head back on right. She was making him feel things no other woman had made him feel and he didn't like it worth a damn.

Easing from her side, he slipped out of bed and quickly pulled on his jeans, not bothering to put on his briefs or a shirt. He didn't want her to wake up for fear that he wouldn't know how he would handle things.

Before walking out of the bedroom he glanced back and wished that he hadn't. His gaze roamed over her. She was curled on her side with a satiated smile on her lips while she slept. She looked like a woman made for passion and every muscle in his body ached to make love to her again.

He forced his gaze away as a thickness settled in his throat at the same time as one formed in his midsection. Stone slowly shook his head. He needed distance and he needed it now. Quickly walking out of the room, he closed the door behind him.

Madison stirred awake and squinted her eyes against the bright sunlight that was coming in through the window. She stretched and immediately felt the soreness in muscles she hadn't used in a long time. She smiled. She had definitely used them last night.

Pulling herself up in bed she glanced around, wondering where Stone had gone. She knew they had planned to get an early start to reach his uncle's place before nightfall but now she felt downright lazy. She didn't want to do anything but stay in bed and wait for his return.

She drew in a shuddering breath when she remembered

all the things they had done the night before. He had
introduced her to passion of the most sensual kind. She
had felt emotions and had done things with Stone that
she had never felt or done with her former fiancé. A
blushing heat stole into her features when she thought
how Stone had touched her all over, tasted her all over,
made love to her all over. Even now his scent was
drenched into her skin. Her nostrils were filled with
the aroma of him: manly, robust and sexy.

What was there about Stone Westmoreland that had
made her throw caution to the wind and do what she'd
done? What was there about him that made her eager to
do it again?

When moments passed and Stone didn't return to
bed, and she didn't hear any movement or sound from
the opposite side of the bedroom door, she wondered
where he had gone and decided to find out. What was he
thinking this morning? Did he regret what they'd done?
Did he think she assumed that now that they'd made love
she expected something from him? She remembered
distinctly him saying that he wasn't the marrying kind.
He believed strongly in the institution but also believed
that marriage wasn't for him. He had no plans ever to
settle down. He had told her that he liked his life just
the way it was. He enjoyed the freedom of coming and
going whenever he pleased and not being responsible
for anyone but himself. He didn't want any worries, no
bothers and definitely no wife.

She sighed deeply as she slipped out of bed. She
glanced around for the clothes she had discarded the
night before and decided that, instead of putting them
back on, she would slip into Stone's shirt. It hit her

midthigh and she liked the way it looked on her because it symbolized that she was his and he was hers.

She shook her head, wondering where that thought had come from and decided not to think that way again. Stone wasn't looking for a serious relationship and neither was she. Opening the door she knew she had to pull herself together before seeing him. The last thing she needed was to put more into her relationship with him than was really there.

Madison searched the house and found no sign of Stone. She stepped outside onto the porch. Then she saw him. He was in the distance, shirtless and riding without a saddle. Instead, a blanket covered the animal's back.

She leaned against the column post and watched him. He had told her that he knew how to handle a horse and she'd seen firsthand how well he did so on their trek up the mountains. He had explained that his uncle had made sure his eleven nephews and one niece learned how to ride and had taken the time to teach each one of them how to handle a horse when they came to visit. She had to admit that those lessons had paid off. It was evident that Stone was a skilled horseman. He even shared with her that he owned a horse that was stabled at Highpoint Manor, a place where he could go and enjoy the Georgia Mountains on horseback. From Atlanta it would take him less than two hours to reach the Blue Ridge Mountains where he would get on the back of his horse for an excursion into the wilderness.

Something made him look her way and her breath caught when he saw her. He trotted the horse over to her, coming to a stop by the porch. "Good morning, Madison."

"Good morning, Stone."

Some part of her felt she should be embarrassed after how she'd acted last night and everything they had done together. But she felt no shame. In fact she wasn't even feeling self-conscious that she was standing before him wearing his shirt without a stitch of clothing underneath. It seemed that all her proper Boston upbringing had gone back up North without her, leaving her doing and thinking all sorts of naughty things.

She tipped her head back to look at him. He was sitting on the horse looking sexier than any man had a right to look. Their gazes locked, held and she felt a quickening in her stomach. She also felt a stirring heat between her legs and as he continued to gaze down at her, she saw the color of his eyes darken as desire flooded their depths.

"Come ride with me," he said throatily. His voice was so husky it sent a sensuous chill down her spine.

Without asking where they were going or bothering to bring to his attention the fact that she wasn't appropriately dressed to go riding, she accepted the hand he reached out to her. He leaned over and, with one smooth sweep, gathered her into his arms. However, instead of placing her on the horse behind him, he placed her in front of him turning her to face him. When she lifted a brow in surprise, he said, "You're beautiful and I can't help but want to look at you this morning."

Madison smiled, touched by his comment. "But how will you see to lead the horse with me blocking your view?"

A grin touched the corners of his mouth. "You won't be blocking it. Besides, I get the feeling this horse has been up here several times and knows his way around. I pretty much let him lead the way."

Madison nodded, then held on as Stone urged the horse into a trot. When they got a little distance from the cabin he slowed the horse down to a walking pace. At first she had felt uncomfortable facing him while sitting on the back of a horse, especially with the way he was looking at her, but another feeling was taking over. It didn't help matters when the horse came to a complete stop and began nibbling on the grass. Stone decided to use that time to nibble on her. He leaned forward and captured her lips, kissing her with an intensity that set her body on fire. She encircled his neck with her arms for support while enjoying their kiss.

"Aren't you afraid that we're going to fall off this horse?" she asked him when he pulled his mouth away moments later.

"No. It's just like anything else you ride," he responded, his tone breathy and hot. "You have to keep your balance."

She wondered how a person could keep their balance when their mind was spinning. Stone's kiss had rocked her world and she was dizzy from the impact. He had stroked her tongue with his, causing the heat that was already settled inside of her to go up another degree.

"You look good in my shirt," he said, before reaching out and undoing the top button. Then the second and third.

"Stone, what are you doing?" she asked in a startled gasp, barely getting the words out when he had eased buttons four and five free. She brought her hands up to cover his.

"Undressing you."

Madison could clearly see that. She glanced around. "But, but, we're outside in the open."

"Yes, but we're also alone. No one is here but you, me and this horse, and he's too busy filling his stomach to worry about what we're doing."

"Yes, but—"

That was as far as she got when Stone recaptured her mouth and at the same moment gently slid off the horse with her in his arms, snagging the blanket in the process.

When he ended the kiss and placed her on her feet, she met his gaze and he thought about how different she was from all the other women he had been with. With Madison, he had no control and he wondered if she knew just how seductive she was. He had a feeling that she didn't have a clue.

Stone had left her alone in the cabin because he'd needed distance to think, but all he'd done while out riding was think about her. He couldn't erase from his mind how she had made him feel when she had run her hands over him, sending shock waves of pleasure through his body. Nor could he forget how she had smiled at him after they had both reached their pleasure, snuggling closer to him, resting her head against his chest and going to sleep in his arms like it was just where she wanted to be. Just where she belonged.

With that memory firmly imbedded in his mind, he reached up and began stroking her hair, needing to touch her, to feel connected. He watched with penetrating attentiveness as her breathing quickened, her eyes darkened and her lips parted.

He gently cupped the back of her neck and drew her closer to his face. Bringing her lips just inches from his, he whispered, "I want to make love to you, here, under the Montana sky."

He watched as her eyes drifted closed and when she reopened them, the eyes that looked at him were filled with desire, as well as uncertainty. He wanted to keep the former and remove the latter. He reached for her hand and began slowly stroking her wrist in a slow seductive motion and watched as the uncertainty in her gaze faded.

"I want to make love to you under the Montana sky, too," she whispered when only desire shone in the depths of her dark eyes. Her voice was so low he could barely hear the words.

Stone drew in a sharp intake of breath as the intensity of just how much he wanted Madison hit him. Taking her hand in his, he led her through a path that was shrouded with lush green prairie grass. When he found what he thought was the perfect spot, he spread the blanket on the ground, sat down and pulled her on to his lap.

His mouth captured hers and with a shaking hand, he removed his shirt from her body. Moments later, he pulled back and stood to remove his jeans; taking a condom pack from the pocket before tossing them aside. His hand continued to shake as he sheathed himself.

He is a beautiful man, Madison thought as she watched what Stone was doing. A sheen of perspiration covered his chest; a chest she knew was broad and muscular. Then there were those strong thighs, firm buttocks and the huge erection that promised more of what they'd shared last night.

She inhaled deeply. A slow throbbing ache had started low and deep in her stomach, inching its way through every part of her body. She actually felt a climax building and Stone hadn't done anything but kiss her... but the look in his eyes promised everything. And she wanted it all.

She wanted Stone Westmoreland.

She didn't want to think about the implications of what that might mean. At the moment she couldn't give herself that luxury. The only thoughts she wanted flowing through her mind were intimate ones. She forced the lump in her throat away, as a little voice in the back of her mind whispered, *live for the moment. Enjoy this time with him to the fullest.*

After Stone finished putting on the condom he paused as his gaze held Madison's. Last night while making love, he had never felt so connected, so joined, so linked to a woman. It was as if they had formed a kinship, an unshakable attachment, a special bond that he couldn't dismiss even if he wanted to.

Maybe it was pure insanity on his part to think that way. In that case, he might as well call himself crazy because the thoughts were in his head and there wasn't a damn thing he could do about them now. He would have to figure things out later because what he wanted more than anything, even more than his next breath, was the woman who was sitting on the blanket watching every move he made with so much desire in her eyes, it only made his body harder.

He let out a deep breath and wondered how he could have gone through life for thirty-three years and not known of her existence. She was beautiful, exquisite and, for now, right this minute, she was his.

His.

He swallowed deeply, knowing he had to say something and that he needed to choose his words carefully. He wanted her to know, he *had* to let her know, that this wasn't just another coupling for him. What they shared all through last night, as well as what they were about to share now were special to him and totally out of sync with how he usually did things. He wanted her to know she had touched him in a way that no woman had done before.

When he moved his mouth to say the words, Madison leaned forward, reached out and placed her fingers to his lips. She wasn't ready to hear what he had to say, especially if it was something that would break the romantic spell between them. She didn't want to hear him stress once again the kind of man that he was. She knew that he was not looking for a serious involvement and she respected that, but neither of them could turn their backs on the passion that was now raging between them. Right now, all she wanted to think about—all she cared about—was that this wonderful man had given her a real taste of passion, something she had never experienced before. He'd also shown her how it felt to fall for someone.

And she had fallen helplessly and hopelessly in love with Stone Westmoreland.

He pulled her fingers from his lips and leaned forward, brushing those same lips against hers before letting the fullness of his mouth settle over hers, kissing her with an intensity that sent heat soaring through her veins. The same wanting, longing and desire that she had encountered from the moment she'd met him took over and she pulled him down to her, determined to make this morning a repeat of last night.

He broke off the kiss and his hands and mouth went to

work to drive her insanely out of her mind. She twisted and moaned beneath him sighing his name and reaching out to capture in her hands that part of him she wanted so badly.

When she held his thick arousal in her hand she folded her fingers around him, squeezing him in her palm. She looked up, met his gaze and asked, "Ready?"

The heat from his gaze nearly scorched her insides and when he smiled she became entrenched in passion so intense she could barely breathe. "Ready," he replied.

She let go and the solid length of him probed her feminine folds as he rolled his hips, finding the rhythm he intended for them to share. Sweat appeared on his forehead and she knew he was just as over the edge as she was, just as hungry for this.

Lowering his head, he captured her mouth, sought out her tongue at the same exact moment that he entered her, swallowing the moan that came from deep in her throat. He lifted her hips and wrapped her legs around him as he went deeper. She felt all of him, every single inch of his intimate flesh. He thrust back and forth inside her as he deepened the kiss they were sharing.

Stone released her mouth when a growl erupted deep in his throat. Sensations spiraled through him. He increased their rhythm and his body began moving faster, his thrusts became harder and went deeper. All of him worked tirelessly to satisfy this woman he was making love with and when he felt her body begin shuddering in an orgasm that made her cry out, he knew he had again succeeded.

He threw his head back as his thrusts quickened even more and he knew that, for as long as he lived, he would have memories of the time he had made love to her under a Montana sky. When he felt her body explode in another climax, he was there with her and continued to pump into her until he had nothing left to give.

"Stone!"

"Madison!"

Everything transformed into one sensuously dizzy moment and he captured her mouth, needing to be joined with her from the top all the way to the bottom. And she returned his kiss the same way he was giving it to her, responding to every delicious stroke of his tongue.

Moments later, Stone slid from her body and gathered her into his arms to hold her as she slumped against him. She tucked her face into the warmth of his neck, and he couldn't help but wonder just how he would handle things when she returned to Boston.

"Are you sure that you won't mind staying here another night?"

Madison looked across the kitchen table at Stone. They had made love once again after returning to the cabin and drifted off to sleep. Hunger had awakened them a few hours later and after dressing—or half-dressing, since she had put his shirt back on and he was wearing only his jeans—they had stumbled into the kitchen. For two people who prided themselves on possessing endless energy, they were definitely wearing each other out.

Surprisingly, the kitchen cupboards weren't bare. There were a number of cans of soup and they decided to share some tomato soup.

"Yes, I'm sure, as long as we have something to eat."

She smiled. "Besides, it would be dangerous to travel if we were to leave now. Soon it will be dark."

Stone nodded then reached across the table and captured her hand in his. "Do you regret that we didn't head out first thing this morning as we'd planned?"

She met his gaze. "No."

They went back to bed and made love again and later, after dressing fully, they decided to take a walk around the cabin. "Have you prepared yourself for tomorrow?" Stone asked, holding her hand as they walked along the stream.

Madison glanced up at him. A beautiful sunset was emerging before them and she had a beautiful man to share it with.

"No, I've been so caught up in what we've been doing that I haven't had a chance to really think about it. And maybe that's a good thing."

"Why?"

"Because sharing this time with you has opened my eyes to a lot of things. I hate to think of my parents' love life, but what if my mother never experienced anything as rich and profound as the passion we've shared in the whole time she was married to my father?"

Stone hugged her tighter to him. "Maybe your parents were passionately in love at one point." But he knew what she meant. He also knew that his uncle had a way with women and he couldn't help but wonder if perhaps, when he saw Abby Winters, he had detected untapped passion in her in the same way Stone had detected it in Madison.

"But I plan to do as you suggested, Stone."

Her words intruded on his thoughts and he glanced down at her. "What is that?"

"Keep an open mind about things and not be judgmental."

He nodded. "I'm sure your mother would appreciate that. She'll probably be surprised as hell to see you. The last thing she needs is for you to become the parent and make her feel like a naughty child."

Madison sighed deeply. "Do you think I made a mistake by even coming?"

He put his hand on her wrist to stop them from walking any farther, knowing he had to be honest with her. "At first I did, but now I know it's just your nature. You were concerned about her. I think she will understand that."

Madison hoped so. The closer the time came to seeing her mother, the more she began to feel nervous about her motives in pursuing her. What right did she have to interfere in her mother's life? Her mother was a fifty-year-old woman and if she was going through a midlife crisis then it was her business. She shook her head. Her mother was the only family she had so anything her mother was going through was both of their businesses. She would just have to adjust her way of thinking about things and practice understanding. And thanks to the man standing in front of her, she believed that she could. Stone had shown her the true meaning of passion and the pleasures of making love. And he had also introduced her to the joys of loving and Madison now knew that she truly loved him.

Once things were settled with her mother, she would leave immediately for Boston. The memories she would have of the time she and Stone had spent together would keep her warm on those lonely nights when she would long to have him naked in bed beside her; those times when she would yearn for her dreams of him to become reality. Already the thought of leaving him caused pain to pierce her heart, but she would survive... she had no other choice.

Chapter 8

Wow! That was the one word that immediately came to Madison's mind when they reached the top of the mountain where Corey Westmoreland lived.

Coming to Montana had certainly opened her eyes to the beauty of an area she had never visited before. Seeing the spacious and sprawling ranch house in the distance, set among a stand of pine trees and beneath the beautiful Montana blue sky, forced a breathless sigh to escape from her lips.

"Why would one man need a place so huge?" she turned and asked Stone.

His mouth twitched into a grin. "Mainly because of his family, especially his nephews. When it became evident that the number of male Westmorelands was increasing and this place would be their summer home, Uncle Corey decided he needed lots of space and a huge food budget."

Madison blinked. "You mean, while growing up, all eleven of you would visit at the same time?"

Stone chuckled. "Yeah, we would all be here at the same time. But you'd better believe that, although everyone thought Uncle Corey was nuts for having all of us here, they knew him well enough to know that he would keep us in line and keep us busy. He did and we loved it. My fondest childhood memories were of the times I spent here. That's why me and my four brothers and six cousins have such a close relationship. Each summer we did some serious male bonding and learned how to get along with each other. Once in a while, we'd let Delaney come with us during the summer, but she preferred coming during her spring breaks."

Madison nodded. "Your uncle must really like kids."

Stone's smile wavered some. "He does. It's unfortunate that he never married and had any of his own."

She gazed at him. "Do you like kids?"

He cast her a sideways glance. "Yes. Why do you ask?"

"Because I think it's unfortunate that in a few years you're going to find yourself in the same situation as your uncle."

He held her gaze for a long moment, then said in a low voice, "Yeah, I guess you're right. Come on. Chances are Uncle Corey knows we're coming."

Madison lifted her brow as the horses moved forward at a slow pace with Stone traveling slightly ahead. "How will he know that?"

Stone turned and looked back at her and the chuckle that poured from his lips seemed to echo in the wind. "Because Uncle Corey knows the moment anyone sets foot on his mountain. He may not know it's us who's coming but he knows that somebody is on his property."

And as if to prove how well Stone knew his uncle, Madison watched as the front door of the huge ranch house swung open and a bear of a man—who looked to stand at least six-five—stepped out onto the wraparound porch. He was wearing a Stetson on his head and peered at them as if trying to make out the identity of his trespassers. When moments passed and it became obvious that he'd figured out that at least one of them was his nephew, he smiled, tugged at the brim of his Stetson and stepped off the porch to come and meet them.

When he came closer the first thing Madison saw was that he was definitely a Westmoreland. Upon first meeting Durango she had immediately known that he and Stone were related and the same held true for Corey Westmoreland. He had the same dark eyes, the same forehead, chin and full lips.

The next thing she noticed was that, at fifty-four, he was a very good-looking man. Like his two nephews, he was magnificent. When he removed his hat she saw that his dark hair had streaks of gray at the temple, making him seem distinguished, as well as handsome. And he appeared to be in excellent physical shape. This was definitely a man who could still grab female interest and she could see why her mother had evidently found him attractive and irresistible.

As soon as Corey reached them Stone brought his bay to a stop and was off his horse in a flash, engulfing his uncle in a huge embrace. "Well, my word Stone, it's good seeing you. I almost forgot Durango had mentioned that you would be visiting these parts. The phone's been down for a couple of weeks and I've been cut off from civilization."

Corey Westmoreland then turned his attention to Madison who was still sitting on the back of her horse staring at him. He tipped his hat to her. "Howdy, ma'am," he said walking over and offering her his hand in a friendly handshake. "Welcome to Corey's Mountain, and who might you be?"

Madison saw the look of amusement in Corey Westmoreland's dark eyes and knew he had immediately jumped to the conclusion that she was there because of Stone and that the two of them were lovers. She could give him credit for being partly right.

She accepted his assistance when he reached up to help her off her horse and knew the exact moment that Stone came to stand beside her. "Hello, Mr. Westmoreland, I'm Madison Winters and I've come to see my mother."

There was complete silence for a few moments, then Madison watched as the look in Corey Westmoreland's eyes became tender and, when he spoke, his tone of voice matched that look. "So you're Madison? I've heard a lot about you. Abby will be glad to see you."

Madison nodded as she tried reading signs in the older man's features that indicated otherwise. "She doesn't know I'm coming."

He chuckled. "That won't mean a thing. She hoped you had gotten the messages she'd left so you wouldn't worry. With the phones being down, she couldn't leave any more. I'm hoping Liam will be feeling well enough to do the repairs."

Madison lifted a brow. "Liam?"

"Yes, he's another rancher who lives on the opposite

mountain. He's also the area's repair man and electrician." Corey Westmoreland put his hat back on. "But enough about that. I'm sure you're eager to see your mama."

"Yes, I am." Madison glanced around. "Is she still here?" She watched as the man's mouth lit into a huge smile.

"Yes, she's here. Go on up to the house and open the door and go right on in. When I walked out she was in the middle of preparing dinner."

Madison blinked. "Dinner? My mother is actually cooking?"

"Yes."

Madison frowned. She couldn't remember the last time her mother had cooked. She turned to Stone. "Are you coming?"

He shook his head. "I'll be in later. I need to talk to Uncle Corey about something."

She nodded. Although she knew he probably did need to talk to his uncle, she also knew that he was hanging back to give her and her mother time alone. "All right." And without saying anything else, she walked the short distance to the house alone, wondering what she would say to her mother when she saw her.

Madison opened the door and cautiously walked inside the impressive house. She heard the sound of a woman humming and immediately knew it was her mother's voice. Quickly glancing around she scanned her surroundings. The inside of Corey's ranch house was just as huge as the outside. The heavy furnishings were made of rich, supple leather and were durable and made to last forever. The place looked neat and well-lived-in and several vases of fresh flowers denoted a feminine touch.

"Dinner's almost ready, Corey. I think a soak in the hot tub would be nice afterwards, what do you think?"

Madison swallowed as the sound of her mother's voice reached her. Evidently she had heard the door open and assumed it was Corey Westmoreland returning. Sighing deeply, Madison crossed the living room to the kitchen and came to a stop in the doorway. Her mother, the prim-and-proper Abby Winters, was bending over checking something in the oven. She was wearing a pair of jeans, a short top, was barefoot and had her hair untied and flowing down her back. Her mother had always been weight conscious and had a nice figure; the outfit she was wearing clearly showed just how nice that figure was.

Madison blinked, not sure if this sexy looking creature in Corey Westmoreland's kitchen was actually her mother. She looked more like a woman in her thirties than someone who had turned fifty earlier that year. And Madison found it hard to believe that the woman who normally wore conservative business suits, high-heeled pumps and her hair up in a bun was the same person standing less than ten feet away from her.

"Mom?"

Abby Winters snatched her head up and met Madison's uncertain gaze. She blinked, as if making sure she was really seeing her daughter, and then a huge smile touched both corners of her lips and she quickly crossed the room. "Maddy, what are you doing here?" she asked, mere seconds before engulfing Madison in a colossal hug.

"I wanted to make sure you were all right," Madison said when her mother finally released her.

Her mother lifted a worried brow. "Didn't you get my messages saying I was extending my trip?"

"Yes, but I had to see for myself that you were okay."

Abby pulled her daughter back to her. "Oh, sweetheart, I'm sorry that you were worried about me, but I'm fine."

Madison sighed. What she needed to hear was a little more than that, but before she could open her mouth to say anything, she heard the front door open and Stone and Corey Westmoreland walked in. She watched the expression on her mother's face when she looked up and saw Stone's uncle. If there was any doubt in Madison's mind, it vanished with the look the two of them exchanged. It was a good thing they were already in the kitchen because she could certainly feel the heat simmering between them. It was quite obvious that her mother and Corey Westmoreland had a thing going on.

Madison cleared her throat. "Mom, this is Stone, Mr. Westmoreland's nephew and my friend. Stone, this is my mother, Abby Winters."

She saw Stone blink and knew the prim-and-proper picture she had painted of her mother was definitely not the one Stone was seeing. He took a step forward and took Abby's hand in a warm handshake. "Nice meeting you, Ms. Winters."

Abby Winters' smiled warmly. "And it's nice meeting you, Stone. Corey speaks highly of you and I've read every book you've written. You're a gifted author."

"Thank you."

"And please call me Abby." She glanced back at Madison. "How do the two of you know each other?"

"We met on the plane flying out here," Stone said before Madison could respond.

Abby's smile widened. "Oh, how nice. I'm glad that Madison had some company for the flight. I know how much she detests flying."

The room got quiet and then Abby spoke again. "Corey and I were just about to have dinner. He can show you where the two of you can stay and then we'll sit down and eat. I'm sure you must be hungry."

Madison was more curious as to what was going on between her mother and Corey Westmoreland than she was hungry, but decided she and her mother would talk later. That was a definite. "That's fine."

Sighing deeply, she and Stone followed Corey Westmoreland out of the kitchen.

"So you have no idea who's trying to find you, Uncle Corey?" Stone asked later as he stood with his uncle on the porch. Dinner had been wonderful. For someone who Madison thought couldn't cook, her mother had prepared a delicious feast. Madison and her mother were inside doing dishes and no doubt Madison was grilling her mother on her relationship with Corey. As yet, his uncle had not explained anything to him. Corey acted like it was an everyday occurrence for Stone to show up on his mountain and find a woman cooking and serving as hostess as if she had permanent residence there.

Corey leaned against a column post. "No, I don't know a living soul who would be looking for me," he said shaking his head in confusion. "You said Quade is checking things out?"

"Yes. Durango contacted him."

Corey nodded. "Then there's nothing for me to do but wait until I hear from him." He then looked over at his nephew. "Madison is a pretty thing. She reminds me of Abby when she was young."

Stone turned and gazed at his uncle. "You knew Abby Winters before?"

Corey chuckled as if amused. "Of course. Do you think we just met yesterday?"

Stone shook his head as if to clear his brain. "Hell, Uncle Corey, I didn't know what to think and Madison is even more confused."

Corey nodded again. "I'm sure Abby will explain things to her."

Stone crossed his arms over his chest. "How about if you explain things to me."

A few moments later, Corey sighed deeply. "All right. Let's take a walk."

The two of them walked down a path that Stone remembered well. It was the way to the natural spring that was on his uncle's property. He remembered how he and his brothers and cousins had spent many hours in it having lots of fun. The sun had gone down but it wasn't completely dark yet. The scent of pine filled the air.

"Abby and I met when I was in my last year at Montana State. She had come with her parents to visit Yellowstone as a graduation gift before starting college. I was working part-time at the park and will never forget the day I saw her. She was barely eighteen and I thought I had died and gone to heaven. When I finally got the chance to talk to her without her parents around, I knew she was the person I had fallen in love with and someone I would never forget." Corey smiled. "And she felt the same way. It was love at first sight and the attraction between us was spontaneous."

The smile then vanished from Corey's face. "It was also forbidden love because she was about to become engaged to another man, someone attending Harvard. He was a man her well-to-do family had picked out for her, one of those affairs where two families get together and decide their kids will marry. And no matter how we felt about each other I knew Abby wouldn't change her mind. She was raised not to defy her parents. Besides, I was not in a position to ask her to stay with me. Her fiancé's family had money and I barely had a job. When she left I never saw her again and she took my heart with her. I knew then that I would never marry, because the one woman I wanted was lost to me forever."

Stone nodded, wondering how he would feel if the one woman he wanted was lost to him forever. "There was never another woman over the years that you grew to love?"

Corey shook his head. "No. There was one woman I took up with a year or two later, when I worked for a while as a ranger in the Tennessee Mountains. I tried to make things work with her, but couldn't. We stayed together for almost a year but she knew my heart belonged to someone else. And one day she just took off and I haven't seen her since."

Stone nodded again. "So when you saw Abby three weeks ago, that was the first time the two of you had seen each other in over thirty-two years?"

Corey smiled. "Yes, and we recognized each other immediately and the spark was still there. And after a few hours of conversations—she told me her life story and I told her mine—we decided to do what we couldn't do then, all those years ago. Steal away and be alone. After talking to her it was plain to see she had lived a lonely life just like I had, and we felt we owed it to each other to start enjoying life to the fullest and to be happy. She's only been here three weeks but Abby has brought nothing but joy and happiness to my life, Stone. I can't imagine my life without her now and she's assured me that she feels the same way."

Stone stopped walking and stared at his uncle. "What are you saying?"

A huge grin spread across Corey Westmoreland's face. "I've asked Abby to marry me and she's accepted."

Madison stared at her mother in shock. "Marriage? You and Corey Westmoreland?"

Abby smiled at her only child as she handed her a dish to dry. "Yes. He asked and I accepted. Corey and I met and fell in love the year before I entered Harvard. My parents had already decided my future was with your father and I was the obedient daughter who wouldn't defy their plans."

Madison continued to stare at her mother. "So I assumed right. You and Dad never loved each other."

Abby reached out and took her daughter's hand in hers, knowing that Madison was probably confused by a lot of things. "In a way, your father and I did love each other but not the way I loved Corey. As long as your father was alive, I was determined to make our marriage work, and I did. I was faithful to your father, Madison, and I was a good wife."

Madison knew that was true. "So you came out

here hoping that you'd run into Corey Westmoreland again?"

Abby smiled as she shook her head. "No. For all I knew Corey had gotten on with his life and was married with a bunch of kids. I knew he had wanted to become a park ranger, but I didn't even know if he still lived in this area. Imagine my shock when I went out to dinner that night and he walked into the restaurant. He looked at me and I looked at him and it was as if the years hadn't mattered. I knew then that I still loved him and I also knew that the most joyous part of my life was the summer I met him."

Her hand tightened on Madison's. "But that doesn't mean your father didn't bring me joy. It means that with Corey I can be someone I could never be with your father."

In a way Madison understood. During the past two days, she had behaved in ways with Stone that she had never behaved with Cedric. "So when is the wedding?"

"In a few months. We decided to wait until after his nephew Thorn's next race. That way Corey can make the announcement to all of his family at one time. The entire Westmoreland family always attends Thorn's races."

Madison sighed deeply. "What about you? What about your life back in Boston?"

Abby smiled. "I plan to keep Abby's Manor since there's definitely a need for day-care facilities for the elderly. And it will continue to be managed the same way it's being managed now. Everything else I can tie up rather quickly. My friends, if they are truly my friends and love me, they will want me to be happy. I haven't been involved with anyone since your father's death over ten years ago. I'm hoping everyone will understand my need to be with him."

She then stared for a long moment at her daughter. "What about you, Madison? You are the person who concerns me the most. Do you understand?"

Madison met her mother's gaze. Yes, she understood how it felt to want to be happy, mainly because she also knew how it felt to be in love. As unusual as it seemed, her mother still loved Corey Westmoreland after all these years. Their love had been strong enough to withstand more than thirty years of separation. She knew her mother was waiting for her answer. She also knew that her response was important to her. Abby Winters had been right. The people who truly loved her would understand her need to be happy.

Madison reached out and hugged her mother. "Yes, Mom, I understand and I'm happy for you. If marrying Corey Westmoreland makes you happy, then I am happy."

Abby's arms tightened around her daughter. "Thank you, sweetheart."

Stone Westmoreland glanced at the clock on the nightstand next to the bed. It was after midnight and he couldn't sleep. He had Madison on his mind. She and her mother had joined him and Uncle Corey on the porch and she had congratulated his uncle on his upcoming marriage to her mother and had even gone a step further and hugged Uncle Corey and welcomed him to the family. Uncle Corey had done likewise and welcomed her to his. Then Madison had indicated to all that she was tired and would be going to bed early. He of all people knew of her overabundance of energy and figured that it wasn't exhaustion that had made her escape to her room. She was trying to come to terms with her mother's marriage announcement.

Getting out of bed he slipped into his jeans. Quietly opening the door he entered the darkened hallway. He had walked this hallway many times and knew his way around, even in the dark. The room Madison had been given was only a couple of doors from his. He wondered how she felt knowing his uncle and her mother were probably sharing a bed tonight. He doubted they would change their routine because of their unexpected guests, especially since they intended to marry.

He opened the door and quietly slipped into Madison's bedroom. As soon as he entered and closed the door behind him, he saw her. She was standing across the room gazing out of the window. From where he stood he saw she was wearing a nightgown and the light from the moon that shone through the window silhouetted how the sleepwear sensuously draped her figure.

He breathed in deeply. As much as he wanted her, he hadn't come to her for that. He wanted to hold her in his arms because whether she admitted it or not, she *was* having a problem coming to terms with her mother's upcoming marriage to his uncle.

"Madison." He whispered the name softly and she quickly turned around.

"Stone?"

Without answering, he quickly crossed the room and pulled her into his arms and kissed her, needing the taste of her and wanting to give her the taste of him. Her response made him deepen the kiss and when his tongue took control of hers, the soft moans that flowed from deep within her throat nearly pushed him over the edge.

He gently broke off the kiss. "You were quiet after dinner. Are you all right?"

She nodded against his chest and his arms around her tightened. "They are happy together, Madison," he said, trying to reassure her.

She pulled back from him and glanced up. "I know that, Stone, and that's what's so sad. They went all those years loving each other but not being able to be together."

Stone nodded. "Yeah, my uncle told me."

Madison sighed. "They fell in love from the first. According to Mom, she fell in love with your uncle the first time she saw him although she knew her life was destined to be with someone else."

Stone stared down at her for a moment then asked, "And how do you feel about that, Madison?"

She knew why he was asking. The man her mother had married instead of Corey Westmoreland had been her father. "My heart aches for the three of them. What if there was someone who my father would have preferred to love? I think it's ridiculous for parents to plan their children's future that way. I won't ever do that to my kids."

Stone had been rubbing her back. He suddenly paused. "Kids? You plan to have kids?"

She looked up at him and smiled. "Yes, one day."

He nodded. That meant she also planned on getting married one day. Hellfire. He sure didn't like the thought of that. "You need to get into bed and try and get some sleep."

He saw awareness flash in her eyes when she suddenly

realized he wasn't wearing a shirt. "I'll only get into bed if you get in with me."

He shook his head. "With your mother and Uncle Corey at the end of the hall, I don't think that's a good idea." He didn't want to bring up the fact that he doubted he could lie beside her for any period of time without wanting to make love to her, and their lovemaking tended to be rather noisy.

"Please. I promise to behave. Just stay with me for a little while."

He looked down at her and knew she had no intention of behaving. He would stay but would somehow dredge up enough control to behave for the both of them. "All right, into bed you go. I'll stay with you for a little while."

"Thanks, Stone."

He walked her over to the bed and pushed the covers aside. She slid in and he slid in beside her and pulled her into his arms. She automatically shifted her body in a spoon position against him and he knew she felt his arousal through his jeans. "Wouldn't you be more comfortable if you were to take off your pants?" she asked in a soft voice.

He tightened his arms around her. "Go to sleep, Madison," he growled in her ear.

"Are you sure you want me to do that?"

"Yes, I'm sure. Now go to sleep." He knew he didn't want her to do that but under the circumstances he had no choice. He hadn't missed the looks his uncle had given him at dinner. Corey and Abby were curious about his relationship with Madison. Although they hadn't asked anything, they had gone quiet when Madison had innocently mentioned they had stayed at the Quinns' cabin for two days.

A few hours later, the only sounds Stone heard were Madison's soft even breathing and a coyote that was howling in the distance. He leaned over and kissed her lips then slipped from the bed to return to his room. Before opening the door he glanced back over to look at her and knew that, if he had been in his uncle's shoes thirty some years ago and Madison had been her mother, there was no way he would have let her go and marry another man.

There was no way on God's green earth that he would have allowed that to happen.

Chapter 9

The next two weeks flew by and Madison's heart swelled each and every time she saw her mother and Corey Westmoreland interacting together. It was quite obvious the two were in love and were making up for lost time. She had never seen her mother smile so much and it seemed that Corey had brought out a totally different woman in Abby Winters. Her mother enjoyed cooking, baking and thought nothing of helping Corey do chores around the ranch.

The days of the prim-and-proper Abby Winters were over—but not completely. She still set the table like she was expecting guests for dinner and occasionally Madison would hear classical music on the disc player. Madison liked the change in her mother and more and more she was accepting Corey's role in her life.

Madison then thought about her own love life or lack of it. Stone still came to her room every night and held

her until she went off to sleep. In respect for her mother
and his uncle, he refused to make love to her although
she always tried tempting him into doing so.

She had looked forward to today. Her mother and
Corey had mentioned a few days ago that they would
be gone from the ranch most of the day to visit another
rancher who lived on the other side of the mountain.
That meant that she and Stone would have the entire
house to themselves and she intended to make good use
of it.

She was aware that it had been hard for him to keep
his hands off her and it had been just as hard for her to
keep her hands off him. All it took was a look across
the table into his dark eyes to see the longing and desire,
and to know what he was thinking and feel the sexual
currents that radiated from his gaze.

He stayed away from the house most of the day helping his uncle do various chores around the ranch. Corey
had decided that, with Stone there, now was a good time
to start constructing a new barn. When Stone came in
each afternoon he would take a bath before dinner and
usually retired to his room to work on his book after
sitting and talking with everyone for a while. But no
matter how tired he was, he always came to her room
every night to spend time with her. They would sometimes sit and talk for hours. He would tell her about the
book he was working on and the scenes he had plotted
that day. Once or twice he even read some of them to
her and she was amazed how his mind worked to come
up with some of the stuff he'd written.

Madison sighed with disappointment as she sat at
the kitchen table and looked out. It seemed that she and
Stone wouldn't have the ranch to themselves today after

all. Corey had announced at breakfast that he and Abby had changed their minds and would visit the Monroes another time. She had glanced across the table and seen the same disappointment in Stone's eyes that she knew had been in hers.

"It's a beautiful day for a picnic, don't you think?"

She glanced around and met her mother's smiling face, then shrugged her shoulders. "I suppose so."

"Then why don't you find Stone and suggest that the two of you go to Cedar Canyon? You can take the SUV and not worry about traveling by horseback. It's simply beautiful and there's a lake so you may want to take your bathing suit with you."

Madison perked up. The picnic sounded nice, but… "I don't have a bathing suit."

Abby chuckled. "You can certainly borrow one of mine. That's one of the first things Corey made sure I had when I came here. With so many hot springs and lakes around, it would be a waste not to have one."

Madison glanced back out of the window. She saw Stone in the distance standing next to the corral gate as he watched his uncle rope a calf. "Stone may be too busy to want to take off like that."

Abby chuckled again. "Oh, I don't know. Something tells me that he'll like the idea."

Stone definitely liked the idea and when Madison suggested it he didn't waste any time going into the house to shower and change. He was dying to be alone with her away from the ranch. And the way he was driving the truck indicated that he was in a rush to get to their destination.

"We will get there in one piece won't we, Stone?"

He glanced over at Madison and even though she was smiling, she was hinting that he slow down. He had made a couple of sharp turns around several curves. "Sorry. I guess I'm kind of eager to get there."

She gave him an innocent look. "Why? Are you hungry? Is what's in that picnic basket tempting you?"

He met her gaze and decided to be completely honest. "Yes, I'm hungry but my hunger has nothing to do with what's in that damn basket. You're what's tempting me. Aren't you?" He watched the smile that spread across her lips; lips he was dying to kiss. He had noticed each and every time she had inched her skirt up her legs, although he should have been keeping his eyes on the road.

"Yes. I just wanted to make sure you wanted me," she said grinning.

He brought the car to a screeching stop. Taking a deep breath, he turned to face her. "I want you, Madison, don't doubt that. I want you so bad that I ache. I want you so bad that if I don't get inside of you real soon, I might embarrass myself."

She glanced down at his midsection and nodded when she saw what he meant. "Then I guess we'd better be on our way again, because I wouldn't want that to happen."

"No."

She lifted a brow. "No?"

"No, I don't think I can wait now."

Her brow lifted when she saw he was unbuttoning his shirt. He removed it and tossed it in the back seat of the SUV. She swallowed hard. She had seen him shirtless numerous times but still her midsection filled with heat each and every time she saw him that way. And she didn't want to think about how turned on she got whenever she saw him naked.

"Uhh, would you like to tell me what's going on here?" she said in a low voice. Desire was making it almost impossible for her to speak.

His smile widened into a grin. It was a smile so hot she felt heat center between her legs in reaction to it. "We're what's going on. And the one thing I really like about this SUV is that it's very roomy. My brother Dare owns one and he let my brother Storm borrow it when his car was in the shop. He later wished that he hadn't. Storm discovered just how roomy it was when he used it to go out on a date."

Stone chuckled as he shook his head. "Needless to say, Dare learned his lesson when he found a pair of women's panties under the seat the next day and he swore never to let Storm borrow his truck again."

Madison grinned. "Sounds like your brother Storm is quite a character."

"Yeah, for some reason the women think so and around Atlanta he's known as 'The Perfect Storm.' Of course none of us think there's anything perfect about him but evidently the women do. I don't know who's worse, him or Durango."

After unzipping his jeans, he lifted his hips to pull them off. Madison, he noticed, was watching him intently. "Instead of paying so much attention to me, you might want to start stripping."

She blinked in pure innocence. "Surely you're not suggesting that I get naked?"

"Yeah, that's exactly what I'm suggesting since seeing you naked is definitely one of my fantasies today. I want you naked and stretched out beneath me. Then I want to get inside you and stroke you until you can't take any more," he whispered huskily across the cab of the vehicle.

Madison swallowed. Her heart began pounding. The heat between her legs broke out into a flame. She began burning everywhere, but especially there. "Okay, you've convinced me to cooperate," she said, lifting her skirt and pulling down her panties. She held the strap of black lace up in her hand. "I need to make sure I put these back on. I don't want your uncle to find these in his truck like your brother Dare found those in his."

Stone reached out and plucked them out of her hand and stuffed them in the pocket of his jeans before pulling out a pack of condoms. "I'll try to remember to give them back to you," he said grinning. He then tossed his jeans in the back seat to join his shirt. He glanced over at her. "Need help removing that skirt and blouse?"

Madison smiled. "No thanks. I think I can manage."

"All right." And he got an eyeful while he saw her doing so. He was glad she hadn't needed his help. In his present state he might have been tempted to rip her clothes right off her. His breath caught when he saw she hadn't worn a bra and, when she removed her top, her breasts spilled free and his shaft reacted by getting even harder.

Madison glanced over at Stone. God, she wanted him. Bad. All his talk about wanting her and needing to get inside of her and stroking her had set her on fire. And she didn't feel a moment of embarrassment sitting with him naked in the truck. She was beginning to discover that with Stone she could be prim and proper and she could also be bad and naughty. She felt him ease the bench-seat back and the SUV became roomier.

She licked her lips when she gazed down at him—especially a certain part of him. "And you're sure no one will surprise us and come along?" There was a husky tone to her voice that even she didn't recognize.

"Yeah, I'm sure. I'd never risk exposing you like that. I intend to be the only man ever to see you naked."

She opened her mouth to tell him that sounded pretty much like a declaration that he intended to be with her for a while, but before she could get the words out he had captured her mouth in his and pulled her across the seat to him.

His kiss reflected all the want and desire he'd claimed he had for her; all that he'd been holding back for the past weeks. Now he was letting go and the moan that erupted deep in her throat was letting him know that she appreciated it.

She had missed this, a chance to moan and groan to her heart's delight without having to worry about anyone hearing her. But she knew that Stone had something else in store for her, too. Today he intended to make her scream.

In a smooth and swift move, he had her on her back and the leather felt warm against her naked back and his body felt hot to her naked front. And then there was that hard part of him that was insistently probing trying to get inside of her. She decided the least she could do—since she was more than eager for this pleasure—was to help him along. She reached out and held him in her hand. He felt hot, hard and thick.

"Take it home, baby."

Stone's words, whispered in a deep, husky tone, sent

sensuous chills all through her body and she adjusted her body when he lifted her hips to place her legs on his shoulders. She guided him home and when he entered her and went deep, his growl of pleasure mingled with her sigh of contentment.

He gazed down at her and the look of desire in his eyes touched her in a way she had never been touched. He smiled and so did she. "I know this vehicle is roomy, now let's see how sturdy it is."

Before she could figure out what he meant he began thrusting inside of her at a rhythm that had her groaning and moaning. The seat rocked and she thought she felt the entire truck shake as his body melded into hers over and over again.

"I can't get enough of you, Madison," he groaned throatily as he continued to mate with her, stunned by the degree of wanting and desire he had for her. His jaw clenched and he hissed through his teeth when he felt her muscles tighten around him mercilessly. He reacted by thrusting into her even more. He felt her body shudder and when she let out a scream that was loud enough to send the wildlife scattering for miles, he threw his head back as his own body exploded. At that very moment he thought that he had to be stone crazy, especially when he felt another orgasm rip through her.

"Damn!" Never had he felt such a mind-blowing experience. It was a wonder the truck hadn't flipped over. The windows had definitely gotten steamy.

Moments later they collapsed in each other's arms. Stone raised his head to gaze down at the woman still beneath him; the woman he was still intimately connected to; the woman he wanted again already. And he knew without a doubt that he wasn't stone crazy, but he was stone in love.

"So how was the picnic?" Corey asked as he sat down to the kitchen table for dinner.

"It was nice," Madison quickly said, glancing across the table to Stone. She was glad he didn't lift his head to look at her because if he'd done so, it would definitely have given something away. After making love in the truck a second time, they had continued on to Cedar Canyon. They spread a blanket next to the lake and ate the delicious snack her mother had packed for them. Then they had undressed and made love again on the blanket before going swimming. Then they had made love several more times before coming back to the ranch. To say the picnic had been nice was putting it mildly.

After dinner the four of them were sitting on the porch listening to Corey talk about the progress he and Stone were making on the barn, when one of the dogs barked. Corey glanced in the distance and saw riders approaching.

"Looks like we have visitors," he said, standing. He used his hand as a shield as he squinted the brilliance of the evening sun from his eyes. A smile touched his lips when he said, "It looks like Quade and Durango, and they have two other men with them."

Everyone watched the riders approach. Madison blinked when she saw the men, surprised that Corey didn't recognize the other two since it was crystal clear all of them were Westmorelands. The four could pass for brothers. She glanced over at Stone, but he was looking at the other two men intently, as well. The four riders dismounted and walked toward the porch.

"Durango, Quade, good seeing you," Corey said, grabbing his nephews in bear hugs. He then turned to the other two men. "I'm Corey Westmoreland and welcome to Corey's Mountain." He then frowned, as if seeing them had him confused. He stared at them for a second. "Do I know you two? Damn, I hate staring, but the two of you look a hell of a lot like my nephews here."

Quade Westmoreland cleared his throat. "There's a reason for that Uncle Corey."

Corey glanced over at Quade and lifted a brow. "There is?"

"Yes," Durango said quietly. "I'm sure Stone told you that someone was looking for you."

Corey nodded. "Yeah, that's what I heard. So what has that to do with these two?"

When everyone went silent, Corey crossed his arms over his chest. "Okay, what the hell is going on?"

One of the men, the taller of the two, spoke up. "Do you remember a Carolyn Roberts?"

Corey's arms dropped to his sides. "Yes, I remember Carolyn. Why? What is she to you?"

The other man, who was just as tall as Corey, then spoke. "She was our mother."

"Was?" Corey asked softly.

"Yes, she died six months ago."

Corey shook his head sadly as he remembered the woman he'd dated a full year before they'd gone their separate ways, never to see each other again. "I'm sorry to hear that and you have my condolences. Your mother was a good woman."

"And she told us just moments before she died that you were a good man," the taller of the two said.

Corey sighed deeply. "I appreciate her thinking that way."

"That's not all Mrs. Roberts told them, Uncle Corey. I think you need to hear the rest of it," Quade Westmoreland said.

After glancing over at his nephew, Corey turned to the men. "All right. What else did she tell you?"

The two men looked from one to the other before the taller answered. "She also told us that we were your sons."

It was evident that the two men's statement had shaken Corey, Madison thought. But then all you had to do was to look at the other three Westmoreland nephews to know their claim was true. Quade was a good-looking man and reminded her a lot of Stone. He was quiet and didn't say much, but when he spoke people listened. And there was a dangerous look about him like he enjoyed living on the edge and wouldn't hesitate to take anything into his own hands if the need arose. Then there were the other two men, who until a few minutes ago were virtual strangers. The only names they'd given were their first ones, Clint and Cole. They said they would explain everything once they were seated at the table where they could talk.

Now it seemed everyone was ready. Her mother, being the ever-gracious and proper hostess, had made coffee and served Danishes when the men declined dinner. Abby was now seated beside Corey and, understanding her mother's presence but thinking this was a family matter and her presence wasn't warranted, Madison was about to leave to go to her room when Stone grabbed her arm and almost tugged her down in his lap. "Stay," he said so close to her lips she thought he was going to kiss her.

She glanced over at his cousin Quade who smiled mysteriously. She looked at Stone and nodded, "All right," and sat down in the chair beside him.

"Now, will the two of you start from the beginning?" Corey Westmoreland asked Clint and Cole.

Clint, the taller of the two men, began speaking. "Twenty-nine years ago Carolyn gave birth to triplets and—"

"Triplets!" Corey exclaimed, nearly coming out of his seat.

Clint nodded. "Yes."

Corey shook his head. "Multiple births run in this family, but…hell, I didn't even know she was pregnant."

"Yes, she said she left without telling you after the two of you broke up. She moved to Beaumont, Texas, where an aunt and uncle lived. She showed up on their doorstep and fabricated the story that she had married a man who'd been a rodeo bronco and that he'd gotten killed while competing. She claimed that man's name was Corey Westmoreland and she was the widowed Carolyn Westmoreland. She'd even obtained false papers to prove it. We can only assume she did that because she was twenty-four and her aunt and uncle, her only relatives, were deeply religious. They wouldn't look down on her if she told them she was married instead of a girl having a child out of wedlock."

A few moments later Clint continued. "Anyway, she found out she was having triplets and, since she was using the Westmoreland name, the three of us were born as Westmorelands and no questions were asked. We were raised believing our father had died before we were born and never thought any differently until Mom called us in just seconds before she passed away and told us the truth."

Cole took up the story. "She said our father was Corey Westmoreland but he wasn't dead like she'd told us over the years. She said she didn't know where you were and would leave it up to us to find you. She told us to tell you, when we did find you, that she was sorry for not letting you know about us. If she had told you about her pregnancy she thought you would have done the honorable thing and married her, although she knew you didn't love her and that your heart still belonged to another. We promised her just seconds before her eyes closed that we would do what we could to find you and deliver that message. I believe that she was able to die in peace after that."

For a long moment no one at the table said anything and Madison felt the exact moment Stone took her hand in his and held it like the story had touched him deeply. She understood. It had touched her, as well.

Corey Westmoreland cleared his throat but everyone could see the tears that misted his eyes. "I thank her for wanting me to know the truth after all these years." He then cleared his throat again. "You said there were triplets. Does that mean there's a third one of you?"

A smile touched Clint's lips. "Yes, I'm technically the oldest, Cole's in the middle and Casey is the last."

Corey Westmoreland swallowed deeply. "I have three sons?"

Clint chuckled as he shook his head. "No, you have two sons. Casey is a girl and, just so you know, the reason she's not here is because she's having a hard time dealing with all of this. She and Mom were close and for years she thought you were dead and now to discover you're alive and that Mom kept it from us has her going through some changes right now."

Once again there was silence at the table and then Stone spoke. "Damn, another Westmoreland girl, and we thought Delaney was the only one." He turned and smiled at the two men, his newfound cousins. "Delaney is my sister and we thought she was the only female in the Westmoreland family in this generation. Did the two of you catch hell being big brothers to Casey as much as my four brothers and six cousins caught hell looking out for Delaney?"

Clint and Cole exchanged huge grins. "Hell wasn't all we caught being brothers to Casey. Wait until you meet her, then you'll understand why."

Madison cuddled closer into Stone's embrace as they lay in bed together. "In a way, today's event had a happy ending to a rather sad beginning. At least Clint and Cole got to meet Corey and Corey found out he had two sons and a daughter."

"Umm," Stone said, placing a kiss on Madison's lips. "Uncle Corey is going to make history in the Westmoreland family. He'll become a father and a groom within months of each other. He was so excited that he picked up the phone to call everyone but then remembered the phone was dead. I can't wait until the family gets the news." He chuckled. "And when Clint and Cole told Uncle Corey what they did for a living, he was as proud as could be." Both Clint and Cole were Texas Rangers. According to the brothers, Casey owned a clothing store in Beaumont.

Less than an hour later, when Madison had fallen asleep, Stone slipped out of her bedroom and ran smack into Durango. Durango placed his arms across his chest and had a smirk on his face. "Making late-night visits, I see."

Stone frowned. "You see too much, Durango. Why aren't you in bed like everyone else?"

"Because, Cuz, I was looking for you. When you weren't in your room I assumed you had gone outside to take a dip in the hot spring. Evidently I was wrong."

Stone glared at him. "Evidently. Now why were you looking for me?"

Durango reached into his pocket and pulled out an envelope. "To give you this. I almost forgot because of the excitement. This telegram came for you a few days ago. I assume it might be important."

Stone took the envelope from Durango, tore it open and scanned the contents. "Damn!"

Durango lifted a brow. "Bad news?"

Stone shook his head. "It's from my agent. I sold another book and the offer is eight figures and a Hollywood studio has bought an option on it. He wants me in New York in two days to announce everything at the Harlem Book Fair."

Durango smiled. "Hey, Stone, that's wonderful news and I'd think announcing the deal at that book fair would be good publicity."

"Yeah, but I don't want to go anywhere right now."

Durango lifted a dark brow in confusion. "Why not?" When Stone didn't respond he said. "Oh, I see."

Stone frowned. "And just what do you see, Durango?"

"I see that a city girl has wrapped herself around your heart like one wrapped herself around mine a few years ago. Take my advice and be careful about falling in love. Heartache is one hell of a pain to bear."

Stone sighed deeply as he met his cousin's gaze. "Your advice comes too late, Durango. I think I'm already there." Without saying anything else, he walked off.

Stone glanced at his watch as he waited for Madison to come to breakfast the next morning. He would be leaving with Durango and Quade when they left in less than an hour. Clint and Cole would be staying awhile to spend time with Corey and Abby.

"Stone? Mom said you wanted to see me."

Stone glanced up and smiled when he saw Madison enter the room. She was dressed in a pair of jeans and a Western shirt and looked feminine as hell. He took her hand in his. "Durango gave me a telegram last night. My agent wants me in New York for an important media announcement regarding a recent book deal. I need to leave for New York as soon as possible."

Madison's features filled with disappointment. "Oh." Then, after taking a deep breath, she met his gaze and said, "I'm going to miss you."

He pulled her into his arms. "I'm going to miss you, too. I'll be back as soon as it's over. Will you be here when I return?"

She met his gaze. "I'm not sure, Stone, I—"

"Please stay until I get back, Madison. You haven't been to Yellowstone and I'd like to take you there."

She smiled. "I think I'd like that."

Not caring who might walk up on them at any moment, he pulled her into his arms and kissed her deeply, needing to take the taste of her with him and wanting to leave the taste of him with her. He planned for them to have a long talk about their future when he returned.

"I'll be back as soon as I can," he whispered against her moist lips.

She nodded. "I'll be counting the days."

He pulled her closer into his arms. "So will I."

Chapter 10

At any other time Stone would have enjoyed attending a gala thrown in his honor, but at this moment he didn't appreciate that his agent, Weldon Harris, had planned the surprise event. Even the media had been invited and he cringed when he saw that the one reporter he detested, Noreen Baker, was among the crowd.

He was even more mad that what was supposed to have been a weekend affair in New York had stretched into a full week including unscheduled interviews and parties that his agent had arranged for him to attend. He hated that his uncle's phone still wasn't working. He had no way to let Madison know why he hadn't returned to the mountains.

He saw Noreen Baker glance his way and knew an encounter with her was the last thing he wanted. He turned to make his escape, but when she called out to him, he decided it would be rude not to acknowledge her. He sighed deeply when she approached.

"Congratulations on your achievements. You must be proud of yourself."

"I am," he said curtly, deciding not to engage in small talk.

She glanced around. "And I must say that this is a real nice party for the prolific Rock Mason."

"I'm glad you like it, Noreen. Now if you will ex—"

"Are you still trying to be a recluse?"

He had turned around to leave but her question ticked him off. "I've never tried to be a recluse. If you would catch me when I'm doing my Teach the People to Read functions you would know that. Instead you prefer attending those affairs that promote dirt instead of positive functions."

Noreen looked at him and smiled. "How about telling me something that's positive?"

"Try doing an article on the Teach the People to Read program."

"No, I want to do an article about you. After the announcement a few days ago, you are definitely big news and being young, single and rich, you will be in demand with the ladies. Any love interests? What about marriage plans?"

Stone immediately thought about Madison. He would gladly announce to the world that she was the woman he loved and the one woman he wanted to marry, but information like that in this particular barracuda's hands might be hurtful to Madison. Noreen would never give her a moment's rest in the process of fishing for a story.

She would camp outside Madison's home if it meant getting a scoop.

"How can I consider marriage when there's no special woman in my life?"

Noreen's lips quirked. "What about a special man?"

Stone narrowed his eyes. "You've kept up with my past history long enough to know better than to ask that."

"Okay, so that was a cheap shot and I admit it. So are you telling me that there's no woman that Rock Mason is interested in at the moment? There is no woman you would consider marrying?"

Stone frowned. "I think I've made myself clear on several occasions that Rock Mason enjoys the freedom of being a bachelor too much."

"Is that why you've agreed to do that four-month promotional tour in Europe?"

Stone frowned again, wondering how news of that got leaked to the press. He hadn't made a decision on whether or not he would go on that damn tour and he had told his agent that. A lot depended on Madison. He would only go if she went with him. He had no intention of leaving the woman he loved behind.

He met Noreen's curious gaze and said, "No comment. Now if you will excuse me, there's someone over there that I need to see." Stone then walked off.

Three days later Stone was in his hotel room, finally packing to return to Montana. He had spoken with his family in Atlanta several times over the past week. They had heard from Quade and were excited that there were now three additional Westmorelands. He had also spoken with Durango who indicated that he hadn't seen or spoken to Corey since he'd left.

Stone was anxious to get back to Madison. He missed her like hell. He glanced over at the television when he heard his name and stopped what he was doing as Noreen Baker's face appeared on the screen during a segment of *Entertainment Tonight*. He crossed the room to turn up the volume.

"As we reported last week, national bestselling author Rock Mason accepted an eight-figure deal from Hammond Publishers and with it came movie options, as well as a four-month book tour in Europe. I spoke with Rock a few nights ago at a New York bash given in his honor and he squashed any rumors that he is romantically involved with anyone, and went on to assure me that he still prefers bedding women to wedding them. He also plans to leave for Europe in a few weeks. So any of you women out there who're holding out for the attention of Mr. Money Maker himself, don't waste your time. Rock Mason is as hard as they come when the discussion of marriage comes up and he intends to maintain his bachelor status for quite a while."

Stone switched off the television, shaking his head. Of course, as usual, Noreen had reported only part of the truth. At the moment he hadn't made a decision about Europe. And of course she had put her own spin on what she had gleaned from their conversation.

He crossed the room to finish packing. The cab would be arriving shortly to take him to the airport. Right now the only thing on his mind was getting back to Madison.

Hundreds of miles away, Madison was also packing. She had watched *Entertainment Tonight* and had heard everything the reporter had said. Stone had been gone for ten days and she hadn't heard from him. Although the phone lines were down, if he had wanted to contact her he could have sent her a letter or something. The postal plane delivered mail to the residents in the area at least twice a week.

He still prefers bedding women to wedding them...

She closed her eyes, fighting back tears. Why had she allowed things to get serious with Stone when he had told her from the very beginning what his feelings were on the subject of marriage? He didn't want to be accountable for anyone but himself and he was going to prove it by taking off to Europe for the next four months. Any pain she was suffering was nobody's fault but her own so she couldn't feel betrayed in any way. He had been totally upfront and truthful with her. She had been the one to assume she had meant something to him and that each time they'd made love it meant more than just having sex. She had actually thought that—

"You're leaving?"

She turned at the sound of her mother's voice. After meeting her mother's gaze and nodding, she continued packing. Her mother and Corey had been in the living room with her when *ET* had come on and had also heard everything the reporter had said.

"Running away won't solve anything, Madison. You told Stone you would be here when he returned and—"

"What makes you think he's going to return, Mom? You heard what that lady said. He's made plans to do a book tour in Europe. I made a mistake and put too much stock into what I thought he and I were sharing. End of story."

Abby crossed the room and took her daughter's hand

in hers. "It's never the end of the story when you love someone. The end of the story only comes when the two of you are together."

Madison pulled her hand from her mother. "That may have worked for you and Corey, but then the two of you love each other and deserve a happy ending. I know how I feel about Stone but at no time did he ever tell me that he loved me, and at no time did he lead me to believe we had a future together. I made a mistake by assuming too much. I never expected to fall in love with him so quickly and so hard, Mom, but I did. Even now I don't regret loving him. The only thing I regret is that he doesn't love me back, but I'll get over it. I'm a survivor, and someway, somehow, I'll eventually forget him."

Abby reached out and pulled Madison into her arms. She knew that now was not a good time to tell her daughter that she knew from firsthand experience a woman could never truly forget the man she loved. She'd been there, had tried doing that and it hadn't worked.

She sighed as she released Madison and stepped back. "So, when do you plan to leave?"

"In the morning. I've already talked to Corey and he said the postal plane will arrive tomorrow with the mail and he's sure they won't mind giving me a lift down the mountain and back to the Silver Arrow ranch. When I get back to Boston I'm going to contact the Institute about helping to provide students with summer lessons."

Abby reached out and stroked her daughter's cheek gently, feeling her pain. For her to even think about getting on a small plane showed how desperate she was to leave. "I had hoped you would stay with Corey and me for a while, at least until the end of the summer."

Madison nodded. She had hoped that, too, but knew the best thing for her was to return to Boston. School would start soon and she would go and get prepared for that. "I'll be back in December for you and Corey's wedding."

Even thinking about that brought her pain, knowing Stone would probably be there for the wedding, too. He would just have returned from Europe. "Besides, you did say you're coming home for a while in September to take care of business matters."

Abby smiled. "And when I do, we'll have to do a play or something. Definitely a concert."

Madison smiled through her tears. "That would be nice, Mom. That will really be nice."

"What do you mean she's not here?"

Corey Westmoreland crossed his arms over his chest and met his nephew's glare. "I mean just what I said. She's not here. Did you actually expect her to stick around after what she heard on that television show?"

Stone frowned. "What television show?"

Corey's frown matched Stone's. "The one where that reporter announced to the whole world that you preferred sleeping with women instead of marrying them. I guess Madison felt she fell within that category."

Frustration racked Stone's body and he rubbed his hand down his face. "How could she think something like that?"

Corey leaned back against the porch's column post. "Why wouldn't she think something like that? Have you ever told her anything different?"

Stone inhaled deeply. "No."

"Well, then. She acted just like any woman would act considering the circumstances. And that reporter also mentioned you had agreed to do some European tour and I guess Madison figured if you were planning to do that then she didn't mean a damn thing to you."

Stone met his uncle's stare. "Madison means everything to me. I love her so much I ache."

Corey rubbed his chin as he eyed his nephew. "And what about all that talk you've done over the years about wanting to have your freedom, seeking adventure and not being responsible for anyone but yourself? Not to mention your fear of losing control of your life?"

"My views on all that changed when I fell in love with Madison."

For the longest moment neither man spoke, then Stone said. "There's no need for me to unpack since I'm leaving as soon as I can grab something to eat."

"Where're you going?"

Stone felt his pocket where he'd placed the diamond ring that he had purchased before leaving New York. "I'm going after Madison."

Stone saw her the moment she came out of the Hoffman Music Institute and began walking down the sidewalk. Abby had told him that, since Madison lived only a few blocks from her school, she preferred walking to work on nice days instead of driving. Besides, on any given day, parking in downtown Boston was known to be limited, as well as expensive.

Today was a fair day. The wind was brisk but the sun overhead added a ray of beauty to the city on the Charles; the city that was the origin of the American Revolution and where buildings, parks, fields and churches echoed the city's patriotic past. He remembered Madison once saying how much she loved Boston and he would gladly make this place his home if that's where she wanted to be. He would move anywhere just as long as they were together.

His heart swelled with love when he continued to watch as she came to Downtown Crossing with its brick streets. He wondered if she intended to go into Macy's and decided that now was the time to make his presence known. He hurriedly crossed the street when she stopped to admire the fruit on display at a sidewalk produce stand.

"Madison?"

Madison quickly glanced up. She pressed her hand to her chest and for a moment she forgot to breathe, she was so startled at seeing Stone. "Stone, what are you doing here?" she asked, amazed at how good he looked. It hadn't been quite two weeks since she had seen him last; twelve days exactly if you were counting and she had been unable not to do so. Seeing him reminded her how wrapped up in him she had gotten and how quickly. He was casually dressed in a pair of khaki pants and a polo shirt and she was hard pressed not to let her gaze travel the full length of him.

He was looking at her with an intensity that made her flesh tingle and a shiver moved down her spine. "You said you would stay at Uncle Corey's until I returned," he said, in a deep, husky voice that only added to her dilemma.

She licked her lips nervously and, when she remembered all the things that the reporter had said, she immediately decided that she didn't owe him an explanation, just like he didn't owe her one. "I decided to return home since Mom was okay," she said, as she went back to studying the fruit.

"I think we need to talk," he said and she looked back at him and wished she hadn't. She studied his features. There was a stubble of beard that darkened his chin and tired lines were etched under his eyes. He looked downright exhausted.

"When was the last time you had a good night's sleep?" she asked, as she continued to stare at him for a long moment. She wondered if his lack of sleep was due to all the partying he had done while in New York.

He shrugged. "Not since trying to get back to you. I was too wired up to sleep on the plane from New York to Montana and then when I arrived at Uncle Corey's and found you'd gone, I immediately left again and flew here."

She lifted an arched brow. "Why?"

"Because I have to talk to you."

She sighed. "Where are your things?"

"I checked into a hotel." He glanced around. "Is there someplace we can go and talk?"

Madison swallowed immediately. She had a feeling she knew what he had to say and thought that the last place she wanted him was in her home where she would always have memories of him being there. But it was the closest place and the least she could do was offer him a cup of coffee. "Yes, my condo is not far from here if you'd like to go there."

"Sure."

They walked side by side on the brick streets with little or no conversation between them. Occasionally, she would point out a historical landmark or some other

note of interest. Moments later when she stopped in front
of the elegant Ritz-Carlton Towers he met her gaze. "I
live in the Residences, a portion of the tower that has
private condos," she said, after saying hello to the door-
man. "The entrance is through a private lobby that is
separate from the hotel."

He nodded as he followed her inside to the lavishly
styled lobby that led to a private elevator. "How long
have you lived here?" he asked as they stepped onto the
elevator.

"Ever since I finished college at twenty-one. My
father left me a trust fund and I decided to invest a part
of it in a place that I knew would increase in value. It's
located within walking distance from my job and I like
the ultimate amenity of having the hotel as an extension
of my home. We use the same hotel staff and any pack-
ages, dry cleaning and other deliveries I get are held
until I get home. I have access to all the restaurants in
the hotel, as well as all the hotel's facilities like their
spa and pool." She smiled. "And on those days that I
come home too tired to cook, I can even order room
service."

Stone liked what he saw the moment he walked into
her condo. It was spacious and elegantly decorated. He
could tell the furniture was expensive and added soothing warmth to the interior of the room. "I have one
bedroom, one and a half baths, a living room with a
fireplace, a kitchen and a library, and it's just the size I
need," she said, crossing the room to open the blinds.
The floor-to-ceiling window provided a breathtaking
view of Boston.

His attention was drawn to the beautiful white piano
in the middle of her living room. She saw where his

gaze had gone and said, "That was the last Christmas gift my father gave me before he died. And for me, at fifteen, it was like a dream come true. Sauter pianos are renowned for their outstanding sound, fine touch and unique expressiveness." She brushed some curls back from her face and added, "And as you can also see, it's pleasing to the eye. There's not a day that goes by that I don't admire it whenever I look at it. It's brought me hours of joy."

He nodded. "Do you play it often?"

"Yes. Playing the piano relaxes me." She decided not to tell him that when she had returned from Montana two days ago, it had been the sound of the music she had played on her piano that had brought solace to her aching heart. "If you'd like to have a seat, I'll fix us a cup of coffee."

"Thanks, I'd appreciate it." He watched her leave the room. He had played out in his mind what he was going to say to her and now that the time had come for him to say it, he wondered if he would have trouble getting the words out. He was a master at putting words down on paper but now that it was a matter of the heart, he was at a loss for words. He needed to let her know just how much he loved her and how much she meant to him and that, more than anything, he wanted her in his life. Loving her was more than a stone cold surrender. It was a lifeline he needed to make his life complete.

He sat down on the sofa, liking the softness of the leather. The entire room had her scent and he was engulfed in the pleasantly sweet fragrance of her. He leaned his head back and decided to close his eyes for a second. He could hear her moving around in the kitchen and in the distance he could hear the sound of boats tooting their horns as they passed in the harbor and the faint sound of an airplane that flew overhead. But his mind tuned out everything as he slowly drifted into a deep sleep.

"I forgot to ask how you want your—"

Madison stopped talking in midsentence when she saw that Stone had literally passed out on her sofa. Quickly walking over to the linen closet she pulled out a blanket and crossed the room back to him. She touched his shoulder. "Stone, you're tired," she said softly. "Go ahead and stretch out on my sofa and rest for a moment."

Glazed, tired eyes stared at her. "But we need to talk, Madison," he said in a voice that was heavy with sleep and weighty with exhaustion.

"And we *will* talk," she said softly, quietly. "As soon as you wake up from your nap. Okay?"

He nodded as he stretched out on her sofa. She placed the blanket over him and moments later his even breathing filled the room. She sighed. He was intent on talking to her and she didn't want to think about what he had to say. He probably thought, considering the affair they'd shared, that he owed her the courtesy of letting her know that things were over between them and he was moving on.

She didn't want to think about it and decided to take a shower and relax and try to forget he was there until he woke up and made his presence known. But as she looked down at him she realized that, even if he didn't make a sound, she would know that Stone was within reaching distance and for her that was not good. It was not good at all.

* * *

Stone slowly opened his eyes as soft music drifted around him. He immediately recognized it as a piece by Bach. When Delaney had been around eight or nine, she had taken music lessons for a short time and he distinctly remembered that same classical number as being one she had relentlessly hammered on the piano as she prepared for her first recital. He slowly sat upright and gradually stood, folding up the blanket Madison had placed over him.

He sighed deeply. He had come all this way to talk to her and instead he had passed out on her. He stretched his muscles then decided to go look for her. He needed to let her know how he felt about her and hoped she felt the same way about him.

Stone found her standing on a balcony that extended from her bedroom. She had changed out of the slacks and silk shirt she'd been wearing to a long flowing skirt and a matching top. She was standing barefoot, leaning against the rail with a glass of wine in her hand as she looked at the city below. He was sure he'd been quiet, that he hadn't made a sound, but still she turned and looked straight at him. Their gaze held for several moments and when a small smile touched her lips, his stomach tightened in response to that smile. "How was your nap?" she asked.

He covered the distance separating them and came to stand beside her. "I didn't mean to pass out on you like that."

"You were tired."

"Yes, I guess I was."

"And you're probably hungry. I can order room ser—"

"We need to talk, Madison."

She turned back to look out over the city. "You know you really didn't have to come, Stone. I understood how things were from the beginning so you don't owe me an explanation."

Stone lifted a brow, wondering what she was talking about. "I don't?"

She turned and met his gaze. "No, you don't. You never misled me or implied that anything serious was developing between us. In fact you were very honest from the beginning in letting me know how much you enjoyed your freedom and that you never planned to marry." She inhaled deeply. "So you're free to go."

He gazed at her for a moment as if enthralled by all she had said, and then asked, "I'm free to go where?"

She shrugged. "Back to New York, Montana, on your European book tour or anywhere you want to go. I guess you figured that, with your uncle marrying my mom, we should end things between us in a proper way so there won't be any hard feelings and I just want to assure you that there won't be. No matter what, Stone, I will always consider you my friend."

Stone took the glass of wine from her hand after suddenly deciding that he was the one who needed a drink. He looked at the glass and made sure that he placed his mouth on the exact spot that showed the imprint of her lips. The white wine tasted good and felt bubbly as it flowed down his throat. He emptied the glass then set it on the table next to where they were standing. He then met Madison's curious gaze. "So you think that's the reason I'm here? To bring our intimate association to a proper close?" he asked, managing a soft smile.

She met his gaze. "Isn't it?"

Her question, asked in a quiet, soft voice, stirred something deep inside Stone and he regretted more than ever that he had never told her that he loved her. She needed to know that. She needed to know that each and every time he had made love to her had meant more to him than just satisfying overzealous hormones. Yes, he had taken her with a hunger that had almost bordered on obsession, and he had always been acutely aware of everything physical about her. But he had also been aware of her emotional side. That had been what had first touched his heart. Her love and concern for the people she cared about.

Knowing he needed to get her out of the vicinity of her bedroom, he took her hand in his. "Come on. Let's go into the living room and talk."

He led her through the bedroom and into the living room. When she started to sit beside him on the sofa, he pulled her into his arms and placed her in his lap. He smiled at the look of surprise that lit her features.

"Now then, I think I need to get a few things straight up front," he said.

She lifted a brow. "Such as?"

"The reason I'm here and the reason I hadn't gotten any sleep in over forty-eight hours. First let me start off by saying I'm not going back to New York or Montana, and I'm sure as hell not going on some European book tour—unless you go to all of those places with me."

Madison blinked, confused. "I don't understand."

Stone chuckled. "Evidently. And in a way it's entirely my fault. I failed to make something clear to you each time that we made love."

He saw how her throat tightened when she swallowed. "What?"

He met her gaze and held on to it, locked it with his. "That I love you."

She pulled back and stared at him in disbelief. "But, but, I—I didn't know," she said, her words coming out in a stream of astonished puffs of air.

He skimmed a fingertip across her lips. "That's why I'm here, Madison, to let you know. I think I fell in love with you the moment I saw you on the airplane, although it took me a while to come to terms with it. I should have told you before I left for New York, but I was in a rush to leave and decided to wait and tell you when I got back. The trip took longer than I expected. I watched that television show, just as you did, but I didn't think when you heard what the reporter said that you would believe it had anything to do with my relationship with you. When she interviewed me I didn't want to mention you or tell her how I felt about you, mainly because I wanted to keep things between us private. Besides, I wasn't sure how you felt about me since we hadn't talked."

He leaned over and replaced his fingers with his lips and brushed a kiss across her mouth. "And I still don't know. I've told you how I feel about you, but you've yet to say how you feel about me."

Madison snuggled closer into Stone's arms and reached up and placed her arms around his neck. The same happiness that shone in her heart was reflected in her eyes. "I love you, Stone Westmoreland, with all my heart. I think I fell in love with you the first moment I looked into your eyes on the airplane, too. And I was so embarrassed when I realized where my hand had been and how close I came to touching a certain part of you. But now I know it went there for a reason," she said, shifting her body and reaching down to actually touch him.

She smiled upon realizing how hard he was and what that meant. "I didn't know at the time that that part of you, all of you, was destined to be mine and I feel like the luckiest and the happiest woman in the world."

Stone groaned out her name as he captured her mouth and deepened the kiss when she sank into him, returning his kiss the way he had taught her to do, enjoying the passion that would always be there between them. Moments later he pulled back and cupped her face in his hands.

"Will you marry me, Madison? Will you agree to spend the rest of your life with me and be my soul mate? I know how much you love Boston and that you don't ever want to leave and that's fine. We can make our primary home here and—"

Madison quickly touched her mouth to his to cut off his words. "Yes, I'll marry you, Stone. I love you and my home will always be wherever you are. I know how much you like to travel and now, after visiting Montana and seeing so much beauty there, I see what I've been missing by not traveling. Now I want to go to those places with you."

Her words touched him and he reached out, pulled her back into his arms and again kissed her, long and deep. When he lifted his head, he stood up with her in his arms. "I love you," he told her again as he carried her into the bedroom. He gently placed her on the bed and stood back. He then reached into his pocket and pulled out a small white velvet box.

"I bought this for you while in New York. I had every intention of asking you to marry me when I got back to Montana." He leaned forward and handed her the box.

With tears misting her eyes, Madison nervously opened it to find a beautiful diamond engagement ring. It was so lovely that it took her breath away. She gazed back at Stone. "I—I don't know what to say."

Stone chuckled. "Baby, you've already said everything I wanted to hear. The only thing left is for us to set the date. I don't want to seem like I'm rushing things, but I want us to get married as soon as possible.... I'll understand if you prefer to wait until next June and have a huge wedding here."

Madison shook her head. "No, I had planned a big wedding with Cedric and I don't want that for us. We don't need it. We can go before the justice of the peace and I'd be happy. I just want to be your wife."

Stone's smile widened. "And more than anything, I want to be your husband. Before leaving Montana, Uncle Corey suggested the Westmorelands get-together at his place the second week in August. He wants everyone to meet Abby, as well as his sons and daughter. I know that's only six weeks from now but what do you think of us having a wedding then, there on Corey's mountain?" he asked, taking the ring and placing it on her finger. He liked the way it looked. He could tell that she liked the way it looked, too. She held her hand out in front of her and kept peeking at it, smiling.

She then glanced up at him. "I think August will be a wonderful time. When do you leave for Europe?"

He shook his head. "I haven't agreed to that book tour, Madison. Everything hinges on what you want to do. I know how much you like teaching and—"

She leaned up and placed a finger to his lips. "Yes,

I've always enjoyed teaching because that's what I limited myself to do. I appreciated those nights when you came into my bedroom at Corey's and shared your writing with me. And, because of it, I now have a burning desire to do something I've always wanted to do but was never brave enough to try."

"What?"

A wishful thought flashed across her face. "Compose my own music. I once shared a few pieces I'd composed with a friend at school and she told me how good she thought they were and that it was something I should do. And I think I will."

He pulled her into his arms. "I think that's a wonderful idea and is one that I wholeheartedly support." He nuzzled her neck, liking her scent and thinking he would never get enough of it.

Madison looped her arms around his neck and pulled him down on the bed with her and he kissed her slowly, deeply and began removing her clothes. When he had her completely naked, he sat back on his haunches and stared at her, a deep look of love in his eyes.

"It's your turn, Stone. Take off your clothes," she said softly, pulling at his shirt.

He stood, appearing more than happy to oblige. She watched as he removed every stitch of clothing and, when he rejoined her on the bed, she reached out and ran her finger down his chest. "This is nice," she said, leaning forward and flicking her tongue across his hardened nipples.

When she felt his shudder, Madison felt confident, loved and, thanks to Stone, passionate. She moved her hand lower and let her fingers travel past his waist and stroke that part of him she had almost touched on the plane. She heard his breathing increase and felt his body harden even more beneath her hand. He also felt hot and ready.

"You want me," she said softly, marveling at how much he did.

"Yes, and I'll always want you." He gently pushed her back on the bed to touch her everywhere, kiss her everywhere, taste her everywhere; and when she couldn't take any more and was thrashing about beneath him, he covered her mouth with his the same moment that he parted her legs, lifted her hips and eased inside of her. She shifted her body to welcome him and, with one quick thrust, he was bedded deep inside her.

He held himself still in that position as his mouth mated relentlessly with hers, filled with emotions of every kind. And when her muscles began clenching his heated flesh, he slowly began moving, establishing a rhythm that would bring them both pleasure.

Moments later when they both went spiraling off the edge, lost in passion of the richest kind, Stone knew his parents' prediction of love at first sight had been right. Loving Madison was something he would look forward to doing for the rest of his life.

Epilogue

When Stone and Madison returned to Montana they discovered that Corey and Abby had decided not to wait for a Christmas wedding but wanted to marry sooner. So the four of them—Corey, Abby, Stone and Madison—decided to have a double wedding on Corey's Mountain in August. Martin Quinn, a former judge, agreed to perform the ceremony.

Now the day of the wedding had arrived and, as Madison glanced around, she knew that only Abby Winters-Westmoreland could bring such style, grace and elegance to the rugged mountains of Montana for the mother-and-daughter wedding. Almost everyone had arrived by plane on the airstrip that several ranchers in the area shared. Her mother had even had a band flown in for the affair, as well as a well-known catering company from Boston. Every time she glanced over at her mother and Corey she saw just how happy they were together. It had taken thirty-two years but they were finally together and she knew it was meant to be this way.

"Ready?"

Madison glanced up at her husband of less than an hour and knew it was time to meet the rest of his siblings and cousins. She had met his parents, his sister Delaney, her husband Prince Jamal Ari Yasir and their son Ari last night. Almost everyone else had arrived an hour or two before the wedding was to take place, so she hadn't had the chance to meet them beforehand.

"Yes, I'm ready," she said, inhaling deeply.

Stone leaned down and kissed her lips; then, taking her hand in his, he led her over to an area where a group stood talking. A couple of people she recognized, but others she did not.

First he introduced her to his married brothers, Dare and Thorn, and their wives, Shelly and Tara. Madison could immediately feel the love flowing between the couples and hoped that her and Stone's marriage would be just as strong and loving.

Stone then introduced her to his brother, the one he said the ladies called "The Perfect Storm." She could see why. He was drop-dead gorgeous and she had a strong feeling that he knew it. Then she met Storm's fraternal twin, Chase, and he was just as gorgeous. In fact she was discovering that all the male Westmorelands were good-looking men.

Next came the cousins: Jared, Spencer, Ian, Quade and Reggie. She had already met Quade and Durango, and Durango pulled her into his arms and gave her an astounding, welcome-to-the-family kiss on her lips and said he liked her even if she was a city girl. She gave

Stone a questioning look and the response in his eyes indicated that he would explain things later.

She then got the chance to see the newest Westmoreland cousins again, Clint and Cole, as well as the daughter Corey Westmoreland never knew he had: Casey.

Casey Westmoreland was shockingly beautiful and Madison thought it amusing to see how all the single men present who weren't Westmorelands were giving her their undivided attention. Now she understood what Clint and Cole had meant when they'd insinuated that it hadn't been easy being Casey's brothers.

After all the introductions were made, Stone pulled Madison into his arms. They would be leaving the mountain in a few hours to spend a week in San Francisco. Her mother and Corey were headed in the opposite direction to spend a week in Jamaica.

Madison had never been to the Bay area and Stone, who'd been there several times, had planned a special honeymoon there for them.

They would be leaving the country within the month for Stone's four-month European book tour. They would return just weeks before Christmas and had decided to make Atlanta their primary home.

"I can't wait to get you all to myself," Stone whispered to his wife moments later, when her mother had indicated it was time to cut the cake and to take more pictures.

"I can't wait to get you all to myself, too," Madison said smiling and meaning every word. She had a surprise for him. She had composed a song just for him. And she knew as she gazed lovingly at her husband that it was a song that would stay in her heart forever.

* * * * *

RIDING THE STORM

Chapter 1

"Jayla? What are you doing in New Orleans?"

A gasp of surprise and recognition slipped from Jayla Cole's lips when she quickly turned around. Her gaze immediately connected with that of the tall, dark and dangerously handsome man towering over her as they stood in the lobby of the Sheraton Hotel in the beautiful French Quarter.

There stood Storm Westmoreland. The man had the reputation of being able to talk the panties off any woman who caught his interest. According to what she'd heard, even though Storm sported a clean-cut, all-American-kind-of-a-guy image, he was a master at providing pleasure without promises of forever. The word was that he had the uncanny ability to turn any female's fantasy into reality and had created many memories that were too incredible to forget. Many women considered him the "Perfect Storm."

He was also a man who, for ten years, had avoided her like the plague.

"I arrived in town a couple of days ago to attend the International Organization for Business Communicators convention," she heard herself saying, while trying not to be captivated by the deep darkness of his eyes, the sensual fullness of his lips or the diamond stud he wore in his left ear. And if all that weren't bad enough, there was his skin tone that was the color of semi-sweet chocolate, hair that was cut low and neatly trimmed on his head and the sexiest pair of dimples.

He was dressed in a pair of khakis and a pullover shirt that accentuated his solid frame. His chest was broad and his butt was as tight as she remembered. He always looked good in anything he wore. Her heart accelerated at the memory of her mischievous teenage years when she'd once caught him off guard by boldly brushing up against him. She had thought she'd died and gone to heaven that day. And just like then, Storm was still more than just handsome—he was drop-dead, make-you-want-to-scream, gorgeous.

"What about you?" she decided to ask. "What are you doing in New Orleans?"

"I was here for the International Association of Fire Captains meeting."

She nodded, doing a remarkable job of switching her attention from his strong male features to his words. "I read about your promotion in the newspapers. Dad would have been proud of you, Storm."

"Thanks."

She saw the sadness that immediately appeared in his eyes and understood why. He hadn't gotten over her father's death, either. In fact, the last time she had seen

Storm had been at her father's funeral six months ago. He did, however, on occasion call to see how she was doing. Adam Cole had been Storm's first fire captain when he had joined the squad at twenty, over twelve years ago. Her father always thought of Storm as the son he'd never had.

She would never forget the first time her dad had brought him to dinner when she was sixteen. Storm had made quite an impression on her. Not caring that there was a six-year difference in their ages, she'd had a big-time crush on him and would never forget how she had gone out of her way to make him notice her. But no matter how much she'd tried, he never did. And now as she thought back, some of her tactics had been rather outrageous as well as embarrassing. Thank goodness Storm had taken all of her antics in stride and had rebuffed her advances in a genteel way. Now, at twenty-six, she was ten years older and wiser, and she could admit something she had refused to admit then. The man was not her type and was totally out of her league.

"So, how long will you be in The Big Easy?" he asked, breaking once again into her thoughts.

"I'll be here for the rest of the week. The conference ended today, but I've made plans to stick around until Sunday to take in the sights. I haven't been to New Orleans in over five years."

He smiled and it was a smile that made her insides feel jittery. "I was here a couple of years ago and totally enjoyed myself," he said.

She couldn't help wondering if he'd come with a woman or if he'd made the trip with his brothers. Everyone who'd lived in the Atlanta area for an extended period of time was familiar with the Westmoreland brothers—Dare, Thorn, Stone, Chase and Storm. Their only sister, Delaney, who was the youngest of the siblings, had made news a couple years ago when she married a desert sheikh from the Middle East.

Dare Westmoreland was a sheriff in a suburb of Atlanta called College Park; Thorn was well-known nationally for the motorcycles he raced and built; Stone, who wrote under the pen name of Rock Mason, was a national bestselling author of action-thriller novels and Chase, Storm's fraternal twin, owned a soul-food restaurant in downtown Atlanta.

"So how long do you plan on staying?" she asked.

"My meeting ended today. Like you, I plan on staying until Sunday to take in the sights and to eat my fill of Cajun food."

His words had sounded so husky and sexy she could actually feel her throat tighten.

"How would you like to join me for dinner?"

Jayla blinked, not sure she had heard him correctly. "Excuse me?"

He gave her what had to be his Perfect Storm sexy smile. "I said how would you like to join me for dinner? I haven't seen you since Adam's funeral, and although we've talked briefly on the phone a couple of times since then, I'd love to sit and chat with you to see how you've been doing."

A part of her flinched inside. His words reminded her of the promise he had made to her father before he'd died—that if she ever needed anything, he would be there for her. She didn't relish the thought of another domineering man in her life, especially one who reminded her so much of her father. The reason Storm and Adam Cole had gotten along so well was because they'd thought a lot alike.

"Thanks for the offer, but I've already made plans for later," she said, lying through her teeth.

It seemed that turning down his offer didn't faze him one bit. He merely shrugged his shoulders before checking his watch. "All right, but if you change your mind give me a call. I'm in Room 536."

"Thanks, I'll do that."

He looked at her and smiled. "It was good seeing you again, Jayla, and if you ever need anything don't hesitate to call me."

If he really believed she would call him, then he didn't know her at all, Jayla quickly thought. Her father may have thought of Storm as a son, but she'd never considered him a brother. In her mind, he had been the guy who could make her all hot and bothered; the guy who was the perfect figment of a teenage girl's imagination. He had been real, bigger than life and for two solid years before leaving Atlanta to attend college, he had been the one person who had consumed all of her thoughts.

When she returned home four years ago, she had still found him totally irresistible, but it didn't take long to realize that he still wouldn't give her the time of day.

"And it was good seeing you again, too, Storm. Just in case we don't run into each other again while we're here, I hope you have a safe trip back to Atlanta," she said, hoping she sounded a lot more excited than she actually felt.

"And I ditto that for you," he said. He surprised her when he grasped her fingers and held them firmly. She'd shivered for a second before she could stop herself. His touch had been like a shock. She couldn't help noticing how strong his hand was, and his gaze was deep and intent.

She remembered another time their gazes had connected in such a way. It had been last year, when the men at the fire station had given her father a surprise birthday party. She distinctively remembered Storm standing across the room talking to someone and then suddenly turning, locking his gaze with hers as if he were actually seeing her for the first time. The episode had been brief, but earth-tilting for her nonetheless.

"Your father was a very special man, Jayla, and he meant a lot to me," he said softly before releasing his grip and taking a step back.

She nodded, putting how intense Storm's nearness made her feel to the back of her mind while holding back the tears that always flooded her eyes whenever she thought of losing her father to pancreatic cancer. He had died within three months of the condition being diagnosed.

Although while growing up she had thought he was too authoritative at times, he had been a loving father. "And you meant a lot to him, as well, Storm," she said, through the tightness in her throat. "You were the son he never had."

She watched him inhale deeply and knew that her words had touched him.

"Promise that if you ever need anything that you'll call me."

She sighed, knowing she would have to lie to him for a second time that day. "I will, Storm."

Evidently satisfied with her answer, he turned and walked away. She watched, transfixed, trying to ignore how the solid muscles of his body yielded beneath the material of his shirt and pants. The last thought that came into her mind before he stepped into the elevator was that he certainly did have a great-looking butt.

When the elevator door swooshed shut, Storm leaned back against the back wall to get his bearings. Seeing Jayla Cole had had one hell of an effect on him. She had been cute and adorable at sixteen, but over the years she had grown into the most breathtaking creature he'd ever set his eyes on.

"Jayla." He said her name softly, drawing out the sound with a deep, husky sigh. He would never forget the time Adam had invited him to dinner to celebrate Jayla's return to Atlanta from college. It was supposed to have been a very simple and quiet affair and had ended up being far from it. He had walked into the house and felt as if someone had punched him in the stomach. The air had miraculously been sucked from his lungs.

Jayla had become a woman, a very beautiful and desirable woman, and the only thing that had kept him from adding her to his To Do list was the deep respect he'd had for her father. But that hadn't kept her from occasionally creeping into his dreams at night or from being the lone person on his Would Definitely Do If I Could list.

He sighed deeply. She had the most luscious pair of whiskey-colored eyes he'd ever seen, medium brown hair that shimmered with strands of golden highlights and skin the color of creamy cocoa. He thought the entire combination went far beyond classic beauty. And he hadn't been able to ignore just how good her body looked in the shorts and tank top she'd been wearing and how great she'd smelled. He hadn't recognized the fragrance and he'd thought he knew them all.

She had actually trembled when he'd reached out and touched her hand. He'd felt it and her responsiveness to his touch had given his body a jump-start. It had taken everything within him to pretend he wasn't affected by her. Since he was thirty-two, he calculated that Jayla was now twenty-six. She was now a full-grown woman. All woman. But still there was something about her that radiated an innocence he'd seldom found in women her age. It was her innocence that confused him most. He was an ace at figuring out women, but there was something about her that left him a bit mystified and he couldn't shake the feeling. But one thing he was certain about—as far as he was concerned, Jayla was still off-limits.

Maybe it had been a blessing that she'd turned down his invitation to dinner. The last thing he needed was to share a meal with her. In fact, spending any amount of time with her would only be asking for trouble, considering his attraction to her. He released a moan, a deep throaty sound, and realized that the only thing that had changed with the situation was that Adam was no longer alive to serve as a buffer and a constant reminder of the one woman he could not have.

"Damn."

Just thinking about Jayla sent a jolt of desire straight from the bottom of his feet to the top of his head, leaving an aching throb in his midsection. Storm rubbed a hand down his face. Nothing had changed. The woman was still too much temptation. She'd been a handful while growing up; Adam had been faced with the challenge of raising his daughter alone after his wife died, when Jayla was ten.

Adam had been a strict father, too strict at times, Storm thought, but he'd wanted to keep his daughter safe and not allow her to get into the kind of trouble other teenagers were getting into. But Adam had also been a loving and caring father and had always placed Jayla first in his life. Storm had always admired the man for that.

Storm's thoughts went back to Jayla and the outfit she was wearing. It hadn't been blatantly sexy, but it had definitely captured his interest. But that was as far as he would allow it to go, he thought with a resigned sigh. Jayla was definitely not his type.

He enjoyed his freedom-loving ways too much and no matter what anyone thought, he knew the main reason he lived a stress-free life was because of his active sex life. In his line of business, you needed an outlet when things got too overbearing. And as long as he was responsible and made sure all his encounters didn't involve any health risks, he would continue to engage in the pleasures of sex.

Okay, so he would admit that he was a man with commitment issues, thanks to Nicole Brown. So what if it had been fifteen years, there were some things a man didn't forget and rejection was one of them.

He and Nicole had dated during his senior year in high school and had even talked about getting married when he finished college. He would never forget the night he had told Nicole that his future plans had changed. He decided that, unlike his brothers, he didn't want to go to college. Instead, he wanted to stay in Atlanta and attend the Firefighters Academy. Nicole hadn't wasted any time in telling him what she thought about his plans. A man without a college education could not provide adequately for a family, she'd told him, and had broken up with him that same night.

He had loved her and her rejection had hurt. It had also taught him a very valuable lesson. Keep your heart to yourself. You could have sex for sex's sake, but love and marriage would never be part of the mix. So what if his uncle Corey, who had pledged to remain a bachelor for life, as well as his older brothers Dare, Thorn and Stone, had all gotten married in less than a year? That didn't mean he or his twin Chase would follow in their footsteps.

His thoughts shifted back to Nicole. He had seen her at a class reunion a few years back and had been grateful things had ended between them when they had. After three marriages, she was still looking for what she considered the perfect man with a good education and plenty of money. She had been surprised to learn that because firefighters made it a point to constantly study to improve their job performance and prepare for promotional exams, he had eventually gone to college, taking classes at night to earn a bachelor's degree in fire science and later a master's degree in public administration.

His thoughts left Nicole and went back to Jayla. He remembered when she had left Atlanta to attend a college in the north. Adam had wanted her to stay closer to home, but had relented and let her go. Adam would keep him updated on how well she was doing in school. He'd always been the proud father and when she had graduated at the top of her class, Adam had taken all the men in his squad out to celebrate. That had been four years ago....

The chiming of the elevator interrupted his reverie. The elevator opened on his floor and Storm stepped out. He had reached the conclusion that, incredible-looking or not, the last woman he would want to become involved with was Jayla Cole. But once again he thought about how she looked downstairs in the lobby. Incredible. Simply incredible...

The next morning, Jayla leaned back in her chair at the hotel restaurant, sipped her orange juice and smiled brightly. The call she had received before leaving her hotel room had made her very happy. Ecstatic was more like it.

The fertility clinic had called to let her know that everything had checked out and they had found a sperm donor whose profile met all of her requirements. There was a possibility they could schedule the procedure in less than a month.

She felt downright giddy at the thought of having a child. Her mother had died when she was ten, and her father's recent death had left her suffering with occasional bouts of loneliness. She had been an only child; she never had a sibling to share that special closeness with and now more than ever she wanted a child to love and to add special meaning to her life.

At first, she had looked at the pool of guys she had dated over the past couple of years, but for the most part they left a lot to be desired—they'd been either too overbearing or too overboring. So she'd decided to try a fertility clinic. After doing a load of research she had moved ahead with the preliminary paper work. Now in less than two months, she would take the first steps in becoming a new mother. A huge smile touched her lips. She couldn't wait to hold her baby in her arms. Her precious little one would have chocolate-colored skin, dark eyes, curvy full lips, cute dimples and…

"Good morning, Jayla. You seem to be in a rather good mood this morning."

Jayla looked up and met Storm's gaze. Although she had decided to avoid him for the remainder of her time in New Orleans, she wasn't upset that they had run into each other again so soon. She was too elated with life to let anything or anyone dampen her spirits today.

"I *am* in a good mood, Storm. I just received some wonderful news," she said smiling brightly. She saw the curiosity in his eyes, but knew he was too well-mannered to ask her for any details. And she had no intention of sharing her plans with him. Her decision to venture into single parenthood was personal and private. She hadn't shared it with anyone, not even Lisa, her best friend from work.

"Mind if I join you?"

Her smile widened. "Yes, have a seat."

She watched as he sat down and noticed his outfit complemented his physique just as it had the day before. He definitely looked good in a pair of cutoff jeans and a T-shirt that said Firefighters Are Hot.

"So what are you having this morning?" he asked, glancing over at her plate.

"Buffet. And everything is delicious."

He nodded. "Umm, I think I'll try it myself."

No sooner had he said the last word, a waiter appeared and Storm informed the man that he would be having the buffet. "I'll be back in a minute," he said standing.

Jayla watched as he made his way across the room to where the buffet was set up. She couldn't help but watch him. She knew there was no way she could feel guilty about being drawn to him, since she had always been attracted to him. And at least she wasn't the only one, she thought, glancing around and seeing that a number of admiring women had turned to check him out. However, it appeared he was more interested in filling his plate than in all the attention he was getting.

Jayla blinked when she suddenly realized something. Storm's features were identical to those she had requested when she'd filled out the questionnaire for the fertility clinic. If the clinic filled her request to the letter, the donor whose sperm she would receive would favor Storm and her baby would almost be his clone.

She shook her head, not believing what she'd subconsciously done. When she blinked again, she noticed that Storm had caught her staring at him, lifted his brow in question and then stared back at her.

Jayla's heart thudded in her chest as she watched as he crossed the room back to her with a plate filled to capacity. "Okay, what'd I do?" he asked sitting down. "You were staring at me like I'd suddenly grown an extra nose or something."

This time, Jayla had to force herself to smile. "No, you're fine. I just couldn't help but notice how much food you were piling on your plate," she said instead of telling him the real reason she'd been staring.

He chuckled. "Hey, I'm a growing boy. All my brothers and I eat like this."

Jayla took another sip of orange juice. She had met his brothers a while back and remembered all four of them being in excellent shape. If they routinely ate that much food, they must also work out…a lot. "Your parents must have had one heck of a grocery bill."

"They did, and while we were growing up my mom didn't work outside of the home, so it was up to my dad to bring home the bacon. And not once did he complain about the amount of money being spent on food. That's the way I want it in my household *if* I ever marry."

Jayla lifted a brow after taking another sip of orange juice. "What?"

"I don't want my wife to work outside of the home."

Jayla gazed at him as she set down her glass. She had heard that very thing from several people who knew him. It was no secret that when Storm Westmoreland married, he would select a domestic diva.

"I have deep admiration and respect for any woman who works inside the home raising her family," she said truthfully.

His features showed signs of surprise. "You do?"

"Yes, raising a family is a full-time job."

He leaned back in his chair and studied her for a moment before asking, "So you would do it? You would be a stay-at-home-mom?"

"No."

He sat up straight. "But you just said that you—"

"Admired women who did it, but that doesn't necessarily mean that I would do it. I believe I can handle a career and motherhood and chose to have both."

"It won't be easy."

Jayla chuckled as she pushed aside her plate. "Nothing about being a parent is easy, Storm, whether you work in the home or outside the home. The most important thing is making sure the child is loved and well taken care of. Now if you will excuse me, I think I will try some of that fruit."

Storm watched as she stood and crossed the room. Wasn't it just yesterday that he had decided to stay away from her because she was too much of a temptation? When he had walked into the restaurant, he had sensed her presence even before he had actually seen her. Then he had glanced around and his gaze had locked in on her sitting alone at a table, drinking her orange juice with a huge smile on her face, completely oblivious to anyone and anything around her. Even now, he couldn't help but wonder what had put her in such a good mood.

He took a sip of his coffee, thinking she evidently didn't want him to know since she hadn't shared whatever it was with him. Electricity shot through him as he continued to watch as she put an assortment of fruit into a bowl. He liked the outfit she was wearing, a fuchsia sundress with spaghetti straps and a pair of flat sandals on her feet. She had gorgeous legs, and her hair flowed around her shoulders, emphasizing her beauty from every angle. She looked the very image of sexiness and at the same time she looked comfortable and ready for the New Orleans heat that was normal for a September day.

"The food in this place is good," she said returning to the table and digging into the different fruits she had brought back with her.

He lifted his dark head and his stomach tightened as he watched her slip a slice of pineapple into her mouth and relish it as if it were the best thing she'd ever eaten. She chewed very slowly while his gaze stayed glued to her mouth, finding the entire ordeal fascinating as well as arousing.

"So, what are you plans for today?"

Her question reeled him back in. He set his fork down and leaned back in his chair. He met her gaze, or at least tried to, without lowering it to her mouth again. "Take in the sights. I checked with the person at the concierge's desk and he suggested I do the Gray Line bus tour."

Jayla smiled brightly. "Hey, he gave me the same suggestion. Do you want to do it together?"

Innocent as it was, he wished she hadn't invited him to join her sightseeing expedition in precisely those words. *Do it together.* A totally different scenario than what she was proposing popped into his head and he was having a hard time getting it out of there. "You sure you don't mind the company?" he asked searching her face. Although he got very few, he recognized a brush-off when he got one and yesterday, after asking her to dinner, she had definitely given him the brush-off.

"No, I'd love the company."

He wondered what had changed her mood. Evidently the news she'd received had turned the snotty Jayla of last night into Miss Congeniality this morning.

"So what do you say, Mr. Fireman? Shall we hit the streets?"

Hitting the sheets was more to his liking, but he immediately reminded himself just who she was and that she was still off-limits. "Sure. I think it would be fun." *As long as we keep things simple,* he wanted to add but didn't.

She chuckled, a low, sexy sound, as she leaned forward. "And that's what I need, Storm, some honest-to-goodness fun."

He looked at her for a moment, then suddenly under-stood. The past six months had to have been hard. She and her father had been extremely close, so no doubt the loneliness was finally getting to her.

A jolt of protectiveness shot through him. Hadn't he promised Adam that he would look after her? Besides, if anyone could show her how to have fun, he could. Because of his attraction to her, over the years he had basically tried to avoid her. Now it seemed that doing so had robbed him of the chance to get to know her better. Maybe it was time that he took the first step to rectify the situation so that a relationship, one of friendship only, could develop between them.

Having fun with a woman without the involvement of sex would be something new for him, but he was willing to try it. Since there was no way the two of them could ever be serious, he saw nothing wrong with letting his guard down and having a good time. "Then I will give you a day of fun, Jayla Cole," he said and meaning every word.

A smile touched the corners of his mouth. "And who knows? You just might surprise yourself and have so much fun, you may not ever want to get serious again."

Chapter 2

A rush of excitement shot through Jayla's bloodstream when the bus made another stop on its tour. This time to board the *Steamboat Natchez* for a cruise along the Mississippi River. So far, she and Storm had taken a carriage ride through the French Quarter, a tour of the swamps and visited a number of magnificently restored mansions and courtyards.

The *Natchez* was a beautiful replica of the steamboats that once cruised the Mississippi. Jayla stood at the railing appreciating the majestic beauty of the river and all the historical landmarks as they navigated its muddy waters. She was very much aware of the man standing beside her. During the boat ride, Storm had kept her amused by telling her interesting tidbits of information about riverboats.

As he talked, she tipped her head and studied him, letting eyes that were hidden behind the dark lenses of her sunglasses roam over him. She enjoyed looking at him as much as she enjoyed listening to him. Soft jazz was flowing through several speakers that were located on the lower deck and the sound of the boat gliding through the water had a relaxing effect on Jayla.

When Storm fell silent for a few moments, Jayla figured she needed to say something to assure him that he had her full attention, which he definitely did. "How do you know so much about riverboats?" she asked, genuinely curious. She watched his lips curve into a smile and a flutter went through her stomach.

"Mainly because of my cousin Ian," he replied as he absently flicked a strand of hair away from her face. "A few years ago, he and some investor friends of his decided to buy a beauty of a riverboat. It's over four hundred feet long and ninety feet high, and equipped with enough staterooms to hold over four hundred passengers."

"Wow! Where does it go?"

Storm leaned back against the rail and placed his hands in the pockets of his shorts. "Ian's riverboat, *The Delta Princess,* departs from Memphis on ten-day excursions along the Mississippi with stops in New Orleans, Baton Rouge, Vicksburg and Natchez. His crew provides first-class service and the food he serves on board is excellent. In the beginning, business was slow, but now he has reservations booked well over a year in advance. It didn't take him long to figure out what would be a drawing card."

Jayla lifted a brow. "What?"

"Gambling. You'd be surprised how many people have money they figure is worth losing if there's a chance that they might win more."

Jayla could believe that. A couple of years ago, she and Lisa had taken a trip to Vegas and had seen first hand just how hungry to win some people were.

When there was another lull in the conversation, she turned away from him to look out over the river once more. It was peaceful, nothing like the tempest that was raging through her at the moment. Storm had kept his word. She'd had more fun today with him than she'd had in a long time. He possessed a fun-loving attitude that had spilled over to her. There were times when he had shared a joke with her that had her laughing so hard she actually thought something inside her body would break. It had felt good to laugh, and she was glad she'd been able to laugh with him.

She tried to think of the last time she had laughed with a man and recalled that it had been with her father. Even during his final days, when she'd known that pain had racked his body, he'd been able to tell a good joke every now and then. She heaved a small sigh. She missed her father so much. Because he had kept such a tight rein on her, she had been a rebellious teen while growing up. It was only when she'd returned from college that she had allowed herself to form that special father-daughter relationship with him.

After his death, at the encouragement of the officials at the hospice facility, she had gone through grief counseling and was glad she had. It had helped to let go and move on. One of the biggest decisions she'd been forced to make was whether to sell her parents' home and move into a smaller place. After much soul-searching, she had made a decision to move. She loved her new home and knew once she had her baby, it wouldn't be as lonely as it was now. She was getting excited again just thinking about it.

"So what are your plans for later?"

Storm's question invaded her thoughts and she tipped her head to look over at him. "My plans for later?"

"Yes. Yesterday, I invited you to join me for dinner and you turned me down, saying you'd already made plans. Today, I'm hoping to ask early enough so that I'll catch you before you make other arrangements."

Jayla sighed. She knew her mind needed a reality check, but she wasn't ready to give it one. Spending the day with Storm had been nice; it had been fun and definitely what she'd needed. But she didn't need to spend her evening with him as well. The only thing the two of them had in common was the fact they both loved and respected her father. That would be the common link they would always share. But spending more time with Storm would only reawaken all those old feelings of attraction she had always had for him.

She took off her sunglasses, met his gaze directly and immediately wished she hadn't. His eyes were dark, so dark you could barely see the pupils. The jolt that passed through her was so startling she had to remind herself to breathe.

"I was wondering when you were going to stop hiding behind these," he said, taking the sunglasses out of her hand when she was about to put them back on. He gave her a cocky smile. "But I didn't mind you checking me out."

Jayla couldn't hide the blush that darkened her cheeks. Nor could she resist easing her lips into a smile. So he'd known she had been looking him over. "I guess

216*Riding the Storm*

it probably gets rather annoying to you after a while, doesn't it?"

He arched a brow. "What?"

"Women constantly checking you out."

He smiled again. "Not really. Usually I beat them to the punch and check them out, so by the time they decide they're interested, I know whether or not I am."

A grin tilted the corners of Jayla's lips. "Umm, such arrogance." She took her sunglasses from him and put them back on, preferring her shield.

"Instead of arrogance, I see it as not wasting time," he said simply. "I guess you can say I weed out those who won't make the cut."

Jayla sighed deeply and struggled with good judgment as to whether to ask her next question. Although she may have struggled with it, curiosity got the best of her. She couldn't help but ask, "So, did I make the cut?"

For a moment, she thought he would not answer. Then he leaned forward, pulled off her sunglasses and met her gaze. "With flying colors, Jayla Cole. I'm a hot-blooded man and would be telling a lie if I said I didn't find you attractive. But then, on the other hand, I have to respect who you'll always be to me."

"Adam's daughter?"

"Yes."

Jayla had to resist grinding her teeth in frustration. She doubted he realized that he'd hit a sore spot with her. Not because she was Adam Cole's daughter, but because being her father's daughter had been the reason Storm had always kept his distance from her. A part of her had gotten over his rejection years ago, but still, it downright infuriated her that he had labeled her as "hands off" because of his relationship with her father.

She watched as he pointedly checked his watch, as if to signal their topic of conversation was now over. "You never did say whether or not you had plans for later."

Jayla almost reached out to snatch her sunglasses from his hand again, then changed her mind. Instead, she decided to have a little fun with him. She stepped close to him, reached out and took hold of the front of his shirt. "Why, Storm? What do you have in mind for later?" she asked, in a very suggestive tone of voice.

She watched as he studied her features with a well-practiced eye before he said, "Dinner."

She pressed a little closer to him. "Dinner? That's it?"

He glanced around. There were only a handful of people about. Most had gone up on deck to listen to the live jazz band that was performing. His gaze returned to hers. "Yes, that's it. Unless…"

She lifted a brow. "Unless what?" she asked, then watched as his mouth curved into a smile. A very sexy smile.

"Unless you want me to toss you into the river to cool off."

Jayla blinked. His smile was gone and the dark eyes staring at her were serious. She stared back, willing him to get the message she was sending with her eyes. His words had ticked her off. "Do you think I need to cool off, Storm?"

The smile that returned to his lips came slow, but it came nonetheless. "I think you need to behave, brat," he said, playfully tweaking her nose.

She frowned. Those were the same words he had spoken to her ten years earlier when she had made that pass at him. She knew he'd been as right then as he was now, but, dammit, it really annoyed her that he was still using her father as an excuse to keep her at arm's length. A part of her knew it was ludicrous for her to be upset, especially when she should probably be grateful, considering his "wham, bam, thank you, ma'am" reputation.

His Don Juan exploits were legendary. Even so, a part of her hated his refusal to acknowledge she was not a child any longer. She was a full-grown woman and it was up to her to decide whom she was interested in and whom she wanted a relationship with. After all, pretty soon she would be a woman with the responsibility of raising a child alone.

"So, what about dinner, Jayla?"

Time seemed to stop as Jayla considered her options. On the one hand, having dinner with him was a really bad idea. She sure didn't need someone like Storm in her life, especially with her plans with the fertility clinic and her future as a single mom a definite go. That's what the rational part of her brain was trying to get through to her. On the other hand, there was that irrational part, the one that resented him for being all knowing and too damn caring. That part of her head said that one little dinner would do no harm. She knew she should leave well enough alone, but part of her just couldn't.

She met his gaze. "I'll think about it." And without saying anything else, she took her sunglasses from his hand and walked away.

Storm shook his head as he watched Jayla stroll across the deck. She'd had a lot of nerve asking if she made the cut, as if she hadn't felt the sparks that had flown between them yesterday as well as most of the morning. Fortunately for him, it was an attraction that he could control. But he had to admit that when she had pretended to come on to him a few moments ago, he had almost broken out in a sweat.

He remembered her teen years. During that time Adam had described her as headstrong, free-spirited and an independent thinker. It seemed not much about her had changed.

Storm watched as she moved around the tables that were filled to capacity with an assortment of food and knew he had to rethink his relationship with her. A lot about Jayla *had* changed and he was looking his fill, taking all those changes in at that very moment.

He couldn't remember the last time any woman had gotten his attention the way Jayla had. She didn't know how close she'd come to getting a kiss from him when she had molded her body to his. His gaze had latched on to her lips. They had looked so soft that he'd wanted to find out for himself just how soft and kissable they were.

He sighed. Her ploy had been no more than teasing, but his body was still reeling from the effects. However, no matter what, he had to keep her best interests at heart, even if she didn't know what her best interests were and even if it killed him.

Why couldn't he keep his eyes off her? Hadn't he decided she was off-limits? He glanced away and tried to focus on the beauty of the river as the riverboat continued to move through it. It was a beautiful September day and he had to admit he was enjoying Jayla's company. She had a knack for making him want to see her smile, hear her laugh; he could honestly say he had relished his time with her more than he had any woman in a long time.

He wondered if she was romantically involved with anyone. He recalled Adam mentioning once that he felt she was too nitpicky when it came to men and that she would never meet the "perfect man" that met her satisfaction. That conversation has taken place years ago and Storm couldn't help wondering if her attitude had changed. Had she found someone? Something or someone had definitely had her smiling when he'd first seen her at breakfast that morning. All she'd said was that she had just received some wonderful news, news she hadn't bothered sharing with him. Did the news have anything to do with a lover?

"Storm, don't you want something to eat?"

The sound of her voice grabbed his attention and he glanced back over to her, met her gaze and had to swallow. The hue of her eyes seemed to pull him to her. And he didn't want to think about her mouth, a mouth that now contained a pulse-stopping smile. It seems the feathers he had ruffled earlier were now all smoothed. When he didn't answer quickly enough, she quirked a brow and asked, "Well, do you?"

He fought the urge to tell her yes, that he was hungry, but what he wanted had nothing to do with food. Instead of saying anything, he strolled over to join her at the table and took the plate she offered him. "Yes. Thanks."

"You're welcome. You might want to try these, they're good," she said popping a Cajun cheese ball into her mouth.

Storm's breath hitched. He watched her chew, seeing her mouth barely moving. He quickly decided it wouldn't be that way if they were to kiss. He definitely intended to get a lot of movement out of that mouth. He continued to stare at her mouth for a moment and then sighed. Thinking about kissing her was not the way to go. He needed to concentrate on sharing a platonic relationship with her and nothing more,

"If you eat enough of these, there might not have to be a *later.*"

Her words reclaimed his attention. "Excuse me?"

She smiled. "I said if you eat enough of these you might be able to forgo dinner later. They're so delicious."

His first instinct was to tell her that to him, food was like sex—he rarely got enough of it. But he decided telling her that wasn't a good idea. After they had both filled their plates, they walked up the steps to the upper deck where tables and chairs were located.

His attention shifted to claiming a table close to the rails so they could continue to enjoy the view of the river while they ate. When they were both seated, he turned his attention back to her. Her hair was blowing in the midday breeze and he stared at the magnitude of her beauty once again. While his attention was on her, her attention was on her food. Most people who came to New Orleans appreciated its culinary excellence and he could tell by the way she was enjoying her bowl of seafood gumbo that she was enjoying the cuisine, too.

Instead of concentrating on his food, Storm was becoming obsessed with a question. When he realized that he wasn't going to be able to eat before he got an answer, he decided to come out and ask her the one question that was gnawing at him.

"So, are you seeing anyone seriously, Jayla?"

He watched her lift her head and met his gaze. She smiled. "No, I've given up on men."

Storm frowned. Her answer was not what he had expected. "Why?"

She leaned back in her chair. "Because there're too many out there like you."

He leaned forward, lifting a dark brow. "And how am I?"

"The 'love them and leave them' type."

He couldn't dispute her words since he was definitely that. But still, there was something about hearing it from her that just didn't sit well with him. "Not all men are like me. I'm sure there are some who'd love to get serious with one woman and make a commitment."

She tipped her head back and grinned. "Really? Any recommendations?"

His frown deepened. There was no way he would ever introduce her to any of his friends. Most of them were players, just like him, and his only unmarried brother was too involved with his restaurant to indulge in a serious relationship. His thoughts then fell on his six male cousins, eight now if you counted the most recent additions to the Westmoreland family—the two sons his uncle Corey hadn't known about until recently. But still, he wouldn't dare introduce her to any of them either. If she was off-limits to him, then she was off-limits to them, as well.

"No," he decided to answer. "There aren't any I can recommend. Where have you been looking?"

She chuckled as she went back to her gumbo. "Nowhere lately, since I'm no longer interested. But when I was interested I tried everywhere—bars, clubs, blind dates and I even used the Internet."

Storm's mouth fell open. "The Internet?"

She smiled at the look of shock on his face. "Yes, the Internet and I have to admit that I thought I had gotten a very promising prospect...until I actually met him. He was at least fifteen years older than the picture he had on the Web site made him seem and instead of having two hands, it seemed he had a dozen. I had to almost deck him a few times for trying to touch me in places that he shouldn't."

Storm's hands trembled in anger at the thought that she had done something so foolish as to place herself in that situation. No wonder Adam had asked him to look out for her. Now he regretted that he hadn't done a better job at it. He could imagine any man wanting to touch her body, since it was so tempting, but wanting to touch her and actually doing it were two different things. "Don't ever date anyone off the Internet again," he all but snarled.

Jayla grinned. "Why, Storm, if I didn't know better, I'd think you were jealous," she said playfully.

Storm wasn't in a playful mood. "Jealous, hell. I'm just trying to look out for you. What if that guy would have placed you in a situation you couldn't get out of?"

Jayla raised her gaze upward. "Jeez, give me the benefit of having common sense, Storm. We met in a public place and—"

"He was groping you in a public place?"

She took a sip of her drink and then said, "We were dancing."

Storm took a deep, calming breath as he tried reeling in his anger. "I hope you learned a lesson."

"I did, and there's another reason I've given up on men."

He raised a brow. "Yeah, what's that?"

Her eyes turned serious. "Most are too controlling, which is something I definitely don't need after having Adam Cole for a father. I didn't start dating until I was seventeen, and I wasn't allowed to do sleepovers at my friends' homes."

Storm frowned. "There was nothing wrong with your father wanting to protect you, Jayla. I'm sure it wasn't easy for a single man to raise a daughter, especially one as spirited and defiant as I'd heard you could be at times."

Jayla shrugged. "Well, whatever. You wanted to know the reasons I'd given up on men and I've just told you why I don't date anymore. I figured what the hell, why bother. Men are too much trouble."

The eyes that were gazing up at him were big, round, sexy and serious. He shook his head. To tell the truth, he'd often thought women were too much trouble, too, but at no time had he considered giving them up. "I don't think you should write men off completely."

The jazz band that had taken a break earlier started back up again and conversation between him and Jayla ended. While she became absorbed in the musicians, he sat back and studied her for a long time. Being concerned about his late mentor's bratty daughter meant he was a good friend and not a jealous suitor as she'd claimed. He never cared enough about a woman to become jealous and Jayla Cole was no exception...or was she?

Jayla sipped her drink and half listened to the musicians who were performing a very jazzy tune. Of course she had recognized Storm's concern as a protective gesture but still, she couldn't resist ribbing him about being jealous.

He was so easy to tease. Charming, gorgeous and sexy as sin. But what she'd told him had been the truth. She had basically written men off. That's why she had decided to use the fertility clinic instead of a live donor.

She had made up in her mind that marriage wasn't for her. She enjoyed her independence too much to have to answer to anyone, and men had a way looking at their wives as possessions instead of partners, a lover for life, his other half and his soul mate. Her time and concentration would be focused on having her baby and raising it. Then later, if she did meet someone who met her qualifications, he would have to take the total package—her and her child.

She glanced over at Storm and saw his full attention was focused on the musicians. There was a dark scowl on his face and she wondered if he was still thinking about her and the Internet man.

Running into him in New Orleans was definitely an unexpected treat. She decided to enjoy the opportunity while it lasted. So far, their day together had been so much fun…at least for half the time. The other half of their time together she'd been too busy fighting her attraction to him to really enjoy herself. He was no different from the other men she had dated—possibly even worse—but that didn't stop that slow sizzle from moving through her body whenever he looked at her.

A part of her couldn't help but wonder if all the things she'd heard about him were fact or myth.

"The riverboat has returned to dock, Jayla."

His words, spoken low and in a husky tone, intruded into her thoughts. She glanced around and saw that the riverboat had returned to the Toulouse Street Wharf. "We returned sooner than I thought we would," she said, forcing down the lump of disappointment that suddenly appeared in her throat.

"We've been cruising the Mississippi for over three hours," he said, returning the irrepressible smile that had recently vanished from his lips. "Don't you think it's time we got back?"

She shrugged, wondering if he'd gotten bored with her already. Without saying a word, she stood and began gathering up the debris from their meal. He reached out and stopped her. She looked up and met his gaze.

"I'm not one of those men who expects a woman to clean up after him."

She opened her mouth to speak, but the words wouldn't come out. His hand was still on hers, holding it immobile, and she could feel the sensuous heat from his touch all the way down to her toes. She pressed her lips together to fight back the moan that threatened to escape. How could he overpower her senses in such a way that she couldn't think straight?

Frowning, she blew out an aggravated breath as she pulled her hand from his and resumed what she was doing. "I don't consider it as cleaning up after you, Storm. It's an old habit. Whenever Dad and I ate together, I always cleared the table afterward. We had a deal. He cooked and I cleaned."

"Really?" he asked, studying her intently as his lips quirked into a smile. "And why was that? Can't you cook?"

She glanced up at him and the deep dimples in

his cheeks did things to her insides that were totally beyond her comprehension. She figured it would have been a lot easier for her to understand if she wasn't a twenty-six-year-old virgin. While in college she'd *almost* gone all the way with a senior guy by the name of Tyrone Pembrooke. But his roommate had returned unexpectedly, interrupting things. For her, it had been fortunate since she'd later discovered he had made a bet with his fraternity brothers that he would get into her panties in a week's time. She had almost learned too late that the name the senior guys had given the freshman girls was *fresh meat*.

"Yes, I can cook," she finally answered Storm. "Dad loved home cooking. He thought food wasn't worth eating if it wasn't made from scratch. He just couldn't get into those little microwave dinners that I was an expert at preparing."

Storm chuckled as he helped her gather up the remaining items off the table. "Hey, I can understand your father's pain since I like home-cooked food, too."

They walked over to the garbage container and tossed in their trash. "You cook for yourself every day?" Jayla asked as they headed toward the lower deck to depart.

"No. Since my shifts run twenty-four on and forty-eight off, I eat at the station when I'm working and the days I'm off I eat at Chase's Place, my brother's restaurant."

She nodded, remembering that his twin brother, Chase Westmoreland, owned a restaurant in downtown Atlanta. It was a really popular place; she had been to it several times and always found the food delicious. She glanced down at her watch. "When we get back to the hotel, it will be nap time for me."

"Umm, not for me. There's still more for me to see. I think I'll go check out that club on Bourbon Street that's located right next to the drugstore. I hear they have good entertainment."

Jayla lifted a brow. She knew exactly what club he was referring to, since a group of the guys who'd also attended the convention had visited there. And if what she'd heard about it was true, its only entertainment was of the striptease kind. She frowned wondering why the thought of Storm watching women bare all bothered her. Why did men fail to realize that there was more to a woman than what was underneath her clothes?

"Well, I hope you enjoy yourself," she said. Her tone had been more curt than she had intended.

"Oh, trust me, I will."

And she knew, just as clearly as he'd said it, that he would.

Chapter 3

Storm was having a lousy time, but when he glanced over at his cousin Ian, it was evident that he was enjoying himself. Ian had contacted him last night and told him that *The Delta Princess* would be making a stop in New Orleans and suggested they meet for drinks at this club.

A few seconds later, Ian must have felt him staring and looked over at him. "What's the matter with you, Storm?"

Storm decided to be honest. "I'm bored."

Ian lifted a brow. "How can you be bored looking at women take off their clothes?"

He shrugged. "It all looks basically the same."

A smile curved the corners of Ian's lips. "Well, yeah, I would hope so."

Storm couldn't help but return the smile. He and Ian were first cousins—their fathers were brothers. While growing up, they had always been close. They were the same age and one thing they'd always had in common was their appreciation of the opposite sex. Storm wasn't surprised that his cousin thought the fact that his lack of interest in women stripping naked was strange.

"Okay, who is she?"

Storm looked confused. "Who's who?"

"The woman who's ruined your interest in other women."

Storm frowned. He glared at Ian. "Where on earth did you get a crazy idea like that from? No one has ruined my interest in other women."

Ian met his glare. "And I say you're lying."

Storm released a frustrated sigh. Ian was damn lucky he hadn't hauled off and hit him. But that was his brother Thorn's style. Thorn was known for his moody, ready-to-knock-the-hell-out-of-you temperament. At least, that had been his attitude until he'd gotten married. Now Tara had unruffled Thorn's feathers and the last few times he'd seen him, Thorn had actually been easygoing. Marriage had certainly made a happy man out of Thorn, as well as his brothers Dare and Stone. Storm found it downright sickening. He'd also been curious as to why his brothers were smiling all the time. As far as he was concerned, they weren't getting anything at home that he wasn't getting out there in the streets.

Or were they?

"I can't believe you just sat there calmly after I called you a liar, so it must be true," Ian said, taking another sip of his beer.

Storm rolled his eyes. "I just don't feel like knocking the hell out of you right now Ian, so back off." What he preferred not to let his cousin know was that he had pretty much hit on the truth. For the time being, Jayla *had* ruined him for other women and he couldn't understand why. He certainly hadn't ever been intimate with her and he never ever intended to be. And yet, here he was bored to death at the sight of these half-clad dancers, while the thought of Jayla taking off her clothes made him break into a sweat.

"Want another drink, cuz?"

He glanced over at Ian. What he wanted was to go back to the hotel and call Jayla to see what she was doing. "No, I'll pass. When will you be back in Atlanta?"

Ian leaned back in his chair and smiled. "In a few weeks. I promised Tara I'd be in town for that charity ball she's working on. Why?"

"I'll check you out then." Storm stood and tossed a couple of bills on the table. "I'll let Uncle James and Aunt Sarah know you're doing okay."

Ian nodded. "And for heaven's sake if Mom asks if I was with a woman when you saw me, please say yes. With your brothers getting married, she's starting to look at us kind of funny."

Storm grinned. His mother was beginning to look at him and Chase kind of funny, too. He glanced around the room before turning his attention back to Ian. "I guess I can tell her that and not feel guilty about lying, since this place is full of women. I'll just leave out the part that the woman you were seeing was naked."

Ian chuckled. "Thanks, I'd appreciate that."

Storm turned to leave.

"Hey, Storm?"

Storm turned back around. "Yeah?"

Ian met his gaze directly. "I know it's just a temporary

thing, man, but whomever she is I hope she's worth all the hell you're going through."

Storm frowned, opened his mouth to give his cousin a blazing retort that no woman was putting him through hell, changed his mind and turned and walked out of the club.

Jayla heard the phone ring when she had finished toweling herself off and slipped into the plush hotel bathrobe. She quickly left the bathroom and picked up the phone on the fourth ring. "Hello?"

"How was your nap?"

Jayla frowned. The last thing Storm needed to know was that she hadn't been able to sleep, thanks to thoughts of him being surrounded by naked women. Each time she'd tried closing her eyes, she saw women, taking off their clothes, heaving their breasts in his face, skimming panties down their legs and giving him an eyeful of all their treasures. She'd even heard there were some women who were bold enough to sit naked in a man's lap if he tipped her well enough.

"My nap was fantastic," she lied. "How was the entertainment at the club?" she asked then wished that she hadn't.

"It was definitely interesting."

Jayla's frown deepened. A part of her wanted to slam the phone down, but she had too much pride to do so. Besides, she took great care of herself and thought she looked rather decent, in or out of her clothes. As far as she was concerned, there was nothing those women who'd stripped off their clothes had on her other than that none of them was Adam Cole's daughter.

"I called to see if you're free later."

She rolled her eyes upward. So they were back to that again. "Dinner, you mean?"

"Yes."

In her present frame of mind, he was the last person she wanted to see. It was on the tip of her tongue to suggest he invite one of the "ladies" from the club to dine with him. But she thought better of making the suggestion, since he might very well do it. "I think I'll pass on dinner. I'm not hungry."

"Well, I am, so how about keeping me company?"

She lifted a brow. "Keep you company?"

"Yeah, I enjoy being with you."

Jayla dropped down on the bed, feeling ridiculously pleased by his admission. Although she knew that she shouldn't read too much into his words, she suddenly felt confident, cocky and in control. "Well, I hope you know that my company is going to cost you," she said, breaking the silence between them.

"In what way?"

She rubbed her fingers over the smooth wood-grain texture of the nightstand next to the bed. "I'm not hungry for anything heavy, but I'd love to have a slice of K-Paul's mouthwatering strawberry cheesecake."

She could hear him chuckle on the other end. "K-Paul's Louisiana Kitchen? I've heard of the place, but have never eaten there. I'm going to take your word that I won't be disappointed," he said.

She grinned. "Trust me, you won't be."

"How long will it take for you to get ready?"

"I just got out of the shower so it won't take me long to slip into something."

* * *

It was close to forty-five minutes before Jayla appeared in the lobby.

But the moment she walked off the elevator, Storm knew she had been well worth the wait. His chest grew tight as he watched her walk toward him, thinking she looked absolutely incredible.

He'd known he was in trouble when she had mentioned on the phone that she had just gotten out of the shower. Immediately, visions of her naked had swam his mind, which was a lot better than any live scene he had witnessed at that club earlier.

Common sense told him to pull himself together and remember who she was. But at the moment, all his senses, common or otherwise, were being shot to hell with every step she took toward him. He stood practically unmoving as he watched her, enraptured, while hot desire surged through his bloodstream.

She was dressed in a short dress that totally flowed over her figure, emphasizing the gorgeous shape of her body as well as her long beautiful legs. His gaze lowered slightly to those legs. It had been hard to keep his eyes off them this morning, and it seemed this evening wouldn't be any different. She had the kind of legs any man would just love to caress and have wrapped around him.

He drew in a deep breath, not wanting to think such thoughts but discovering he was hard-pressed to stop them from coming. Whether he liked it or not, he was undeniably attracted to Jayla Cole.

"Sorry I kept you waiting," Jayla said when she came to a stop in front of Storm.

"You were worth the wait. Ready to go?"

"Yes."

They took a cab over to the restaurant and Storm was glad he'd gotten the hotel to make reservations for him. The place was packed. "Something smells delicious," he whispered to Jayla as a waiter showed them to their table.

"Everything in here is delicious," she said smiling.

Including you, Storm was tempted to say. He wondered how he could assume that when he'd never tasted her, but he just knew that she would taste delicious.

The waiter presented them with menus. "Just coffee for me now and I'll wait for later to order dessert," she said handing the menu back to their waiter.

Storm glanced over at her. "Since you're familiar with this place, what do you suggest?"

Jayla caressed her upper lip with the tip of her tongue as if in deep thought. "Umm, I'll have to recommend Chef Paul's Duck & Shrimp Dulac. I had it the last time I was here and it was totally magnificent."

Storm nodded and returned the menu to the waiter. "Then that's what I'll have and I'd like a bottle of sparkling mineral water."

"Great choice, sir," the waiter said before walking off.

Storm leaned back in his chair. "So, do you return to work on Monday?"

Jayla shook her head. "No, I won't officially return to work until a week from Monday. Then on Tuesday of that same week, I have a meeting with a Dr. Tara Westmoreland. Is she a family member of yours?"

Storm smiled. "Yes, Tara is my sister-in-law. She and my brother Thorn tied the knot a few months back. Why would you need to meet with Tara? She's a pediatrician and you don't have a child."

Not yet, Jayla thought to herself. "The reason I'm meeting with Dr. Westmoreland is for business reasons—in fact, we're doing lunch. The company I work for, Sala Industries, is picking up the tab for the caterers the night that the Kids' World calendar is unveiled at a charity ball, and Dr. Westmoreland is on the committee. It will be a huge event, and we expect well over a thousand people to attend."

"I understand the ball will be next month," he said, after the waiter had returned with their drinks.

"Yes, the second weekend in October, in fact. And I understand your brother Thorn is Mr. July."

"Yes, he is." Storm couldn't forget how Tara had been given the unlucky task of persuading Thorn to pose as Mr. July. Doing so hadn't been easy, but things had worked out in the end, including Thorn's realizing that he loved Tara and the two of them getting married. Kids' World was a foundation that gave terminally ill children the chance to make their ultimate dream—a visit to any place in the world—come true. All proceeds for the foundation came from money raised through numerous charity events.

"I understand the calendar turned out wonderfully and the sale of them will be a huge success," Jayla said smiling, interrupting his thoughts. She gazed across the table at him for a second, then said. "Tell me about your family."

Storm raised a brow after taking a sip of his water. "Why?"

She smiled. "Because I was an only child and whenever you mention your siblings or your cousins I can tell you all share a special closeness. It was lonely growing up without sisters or brothers and I've already made up my mind to have a large family."

Storm chuckled. "How large?"

"At least two, possibly three, maybe even four."

Storm nodded. He wanted a large family as well. "The Westmoreland family is a big one and we're all very close. It started out with my grandparents who had three sons, one of which was my father. My parents had six kids, all boys until Delaney came along. Dare is the oldest, then Thorn, Stone, Chase and me. As you know, Chase is my twin brother. My father's twin brother's name is James and he and his wife Sarah also had six kids, but all of them were boys—Jared, Spencer, Durango, Ian, Quade and Reggie. My father's youngest brother, Uncle Corey, never married, so it was assumed he'd never fathered any kids, but we discovered differently a few months ago."

Jayla placed her coffee cup down, curious. "Really?"

"His sons, who never knew he was their father, just like he never knew he had sons, had an investigator track him down. Uncle Corey is a retired park ranger in Montana and that's where they found him."

Jayla was fascinated with the story Storm was sharing with her. "But how did he not know that he was a father?"

"It seems a former girlfriend found out she was pregnant after they'd broken up and never bothered telling him. Unknown to Uncle Corey, the woman gave birth to triplets."

"Triplets?"

"Yes, triplets. Multiple births are common in our

family. Like me and Chase, Ian and Quade, and my father and Uncle James are fraternal twins."

Jayla inhaled, trying to absorb all this. "And your uncle's former girlfriend had triplets?"

"Yes, the first in the Westmoreland family. It seems that she told them their father had died when they were born and only revealed the truth on her deathbed. Although Uncle Corey never married the woman, she had moved out west to Texas and had taken his last name, so fortunately, her kids were born as Westmorelands."

"So your Uncle Corey has three sons he didn't know a thing about?"

"No, two sons and one daughter." He shook his head, chuckling. "And all this time we all thought Delaney was the only girl in the Westmoreland family in two generations. Last month Uncle Corey suprised us and got married!"

They suspended conversation when the waiter brought out Storm's food. Storm surprised Jayla when he handed her a fork. "There's too much here for one person. Share it with me."

She glanced at his plate. He did have a lot and it looked delicious. "Umm, maybe, I'll just take a few bites," she said taking the fork from him.

"Help yourself."

And she did. The picture of them sharing a meal played out a rather cozy and intimate scene in her mind, one she tried to ignore. She licked her lips after they had finished. The food had tasted great. "Now you're going to have to help me eat that cheesecake."

"Hey, I can handle it."

His words triggered a flutter in the pit of her stomach. There was no doubt in her mind that Storm

Westmoreland could handle anything. And he did. They finished off the strawberry cheesecake in no time.

Storm checked his watch after he signed the check for their bill. "It's still early. How would you like to go dancing?"

His words echoed through Jayla's mind. She knew the smart thing to do would be to tell him no, but for some reason, she didn't want to think smart. She didn't want to think at all. She was in the company of a very handsome man and she was in no hurry for them to part ways.

She met his gaze. "I'd love going dancing with you, Storm."

The club that had come highly recommend from one of the waiters at K-Paul's was dark, rather small, and crowded. Storm and Jayla were lucky to find an empty table inside Café Basil, which had a reputation of being the undisputed king of nightlife in the French Quarter.

Storm doubted that another couple could fit on the dance floor. Already, the place was jam-packed, but he was determined that they would squeeze in somehow. There was no way he would leave this place tonight without molding Jayla's body to his and holding her in his arms.

He glanced across the table at her, barely able to make out her features in the dimly lit room. Her body was swaying to the sound of the jazz band that was playing and as he watched her, he had to restrain the emotions that were pulsing inside of him.

He had been with numerous women before and each one had met his specific qualifications—whatever they'd been at the time. And every single one of them had known the score. He promised nothing other than a good time in bed. He wasn't interested in satisfying emotional needs, just physical ones. But there was something about Jayla that was pulling at him. The pull was definitely sexual, but there was something about it that was emotional, too.

And Storm Westmoreland didn't do anything with women that hinted of the emotional so why was he here, bursting at the seams to take Jayla into his arms on that dance floor?

Before he could ponder that question, the tune that was playing stopped and another started. Some of the dancers went back to their seats, clearing the way for others to take their turn. "This is our number," he said to Jayla, standing and reaching out for her hand.

She smiled and placed her hand in his. Immediately, he felt a tug in his gut that he tried ignoring as he led her onto the dance floor. He took a deep breath, then exhaled slowly the moment she came into his arms and molded her body to his.

"I like holding you," he said truthfully into her ear moments later, wanting her to hear his words over the sound of the band.

She leaned back and searched his face a moment before asking, "Do you?"

"Hmm…"

She smiled and he thought it was the most beautiful smile he'd ever seen on a woman and felt good that his words had brought a smile to her lips. Speaking of lips…

His gaze shifted to her mouth and he couldn't help

but take in their proximity to his. All he had to do was inch a little closer and—

"You smell good, Storm."

He inhaled deeply and slowly shook his head. She could say the damnedest things at times. They should be concentrating on small talk that was socially acceptable for platonic friends and not the sultry murmurings of lovers. "Thanks, but you shouldn't say that to me."

"Why not? If you can tell me that you like holding me, then I should be able to tell you that I think you smell good."

His hands were around her waist, holding her tight, and her arms were draped about his neck. The music playing was slow and their bodies were barely moving. He knew it and she knew it, as well. He was also certain that she was aware that he was aroused. With her body so close to his, there was no way that she didn't know it.

He wanted her to feel all of him and pulled her closer into his arms. Automatically, she placed her head against his chest and he closed his eyes as they swayed to the sound of the music. If she thought he smelled good, then he thought likewise about her. The scent of her perfume was intoxicating, seductive and a total turn-on. Moments later, the music faded and they stopped dancing, but he refused to release her. He needed to continue to hold her in his arms.

Jayla lifted her face and met Storm's gaze. The look in his eyes was intense and purely sexual. "I should try and continue to fight this," he said as if the words were being forced from him. She could clearly understand what he meant.

She did. "Don't fight it," she said softly.

He narrowed his eyes at her. "You're not helping matters, Jayla." His words were a low growl in her ear.

She narrowed her eyes right back at him. "Why should I?"

He stared at her for a long time. Then he glanced around. It seemed they were the center of attention. He looked back at her. "But you deserve more than just—"

"A one-night stand? Shouldn't I be the one to make that decision, Storm? I'm twenty-six-years old. I work and pay my own bills. I'm a woman, not a child, and it's time you realized that."

He stared at her for a long moment, then said, "I just did." He tightened his hand on hers and tugged her along with him out of the club.

"Where are we going?" Jayla asked, almost out of breath as she tried keeping up with Storm's long strides as he tried hailing a cab.

"Back to the hotel."

A few moments later, Storm cursed. There were few cabs around and the ones he saw were already occupied. He glanced across the street and saw a parked horse-drawn coach. Evidently, someone had used it for a wedding and it reminded him of the coach that might be used as a prop in *Cinderella*. "Come on," he said, keeping a firm hold on Jayla's hand.

They quickly crossed the street and approached the driver, who was holding the reins to keep the horses from prancing. "We need a ride back to the Sheraton Hotel on Canal," Storm said, nearly out of breath.

The old man raised a bushy brow. "My rates are by the hour."

"Fine, just get us there quick and in one piece."

The driver nodded his head, indicating that he understood. Storm then turned and opened the carriage door. When Jayla lifted her leg to climb inside, Storm swept her into his arms and placed her inside on the seat. He then climbed in and shut the door.

As the coach lurched forward, anticipation and sexual desire the likes he had never known before gripped him and he could think of only one thing that could relax him.

He paused, wondering if he had lost his mind and then quickly decided that he had. There wasn't a damn thing he could do about it. He would worry about the consequences of his actions tomorrow. He was too far gone tonight.

He glanced over at Jayla where she sat on the other side of the seat. The interior lighting provided him with barely enough illumination to see her features, but he heard her breathing and it was coming out as erratic as his own.

"Come here, Jayla."

She met his gaze before sliding across the seat to him. He curved his hand about her neck and drew her to him. Leaning forward, he captured the lips he had been dying to taste for over ten years. He took possession and staked his claim. He couldn't help himself.

He felt the shiver that flowed from her body to his when she surrendered her tongue to his. He took his time to savor what she offered, relentlessly mating his mouth with hers as he tried to satisfy what seemed to be an endless hunger. Her taste was like a drug and he felt himself getting addicted to it as his controls were pushed to the limit, wanting more and determined to get it. He lapped up every moan she made while glorying in the feel of her kissing him back.

He deepened the kiss and she proved that she could handle him, tongue for tongue, lick for lick, stroke for stroke. It seemed that he had also tapped a hunger inside of her that she hadn't fed in a while. He intensified the kiss, knowing she wanted him as much as he wanted her.

They felt a jolt when the coach came to a stop and they broke off the kiss, pulling apart. He glanced out the window, then glanced back at her. They were at the hotel. Would she change her mind or would they finish what they'd started?

Knowing the decision was hers, he leaned over and placed a kiss on her lips. "What do you want, Jayla?" he asked, his breath hot and ragged against her ear. He hoped and prayed that she wanted the same thing that he did.

He watched as a smile touched her lips. She then reached out to run her hand down his chest, past his waist to settle firmly on his arousal that was pressing hard through his pants.

He swallowed hard, almost forgetting to breathe. His mind was suddenly filled with scenes of all the things he wanted to do to her.

She met his gaze and in a soft voice whispered, "I want you to make love to me, Storm."

Chapter 4

Storm's knuckles gently brushed across Jayla's cheeks just moments before his mouth descended on hers. The words she'd just spoken were what he wanted to hear, and at that moment he needed to taste her again.

He was swamped with conflicting emotions. A part of him wanted to pull back, unable to forget she was Adam's daughter, but then another part of him accepted and acknowledged what she'd said was true. She was old enough to make her own decisions. Even Adam had pretty much conceded that before he'd died.

He slowly, reluctantly, broke off the kiss and took a deep breath. Her eyes glinted with intense desire and he was suddenly filled with a dangerously high degree of anticipation to give her everything she wanted and needed. Without saying a word, he took her hand. Together, they got out of the coach and went into the hotel. The walk across the lobby to the elevator seemed endless, and all Storm could think about was what he would do to her once they were alone. That short dress she was wearing had driven him crazy all night. More than once, his gaze had been drawn to her bare legs, legs he wanted wrapped around him while they made love.

"My room or yours?" he asked, moments before the elevator door swooshed open before them.

Their eyes met and held. "Whichever one is closest," she said as desire continued to flicker in her eyes.

"That would be yours."

They stepped into the elevator and after the door closed behind them, he leaned against the wall. They were alone and he tightened his hands by his sides. The temptation to pull her into his arms and devour her mouth again was unbearable, and when she swept the tip of her tongue nervously across her top lip, his stomach clenched and he swore beneath his breath.

"I want you so damn much," he had to say. The scent of her perfume was soft and seductive.

"And I want you, too, Storm."

That statement didn't help matters, either. He had wanted to pull her into his arms the moment the elevator came to a stop on her floor, but taking a deep breath, he held the door as she stepped out off the car before him. Holding hands, they walked silently down the corridor to her hotel room. Intense sexual need was closing in on him. He had to admit he'd never wanted a woman this badly.

When they reached her room, he leaned against the wall as Jayla opened her purse, pulled out her key and inserted it into the lock. She opened the door with ease and walked into the room. He didn't waste any time following and closing the door behind them. She flipped a switch that brought a soft glow of light to the room, then turned slowly to him, meeting his gaze.

They didn't say anything for a brief moment; then he reached out and pulled her into his arms. His mind told him to take things slowly but the moment he touched her and desire swept through his body, he threw the thought of taking things slowly out the window. The only thing he could think of was lifting her short dress and becoming enfolded in her feminine heat.

He tightened his arms around her as his mouth greedily devoured hers and his chest expanded with the solid feel of her breasts pressing against it. His tongue again made a claim on her mouth while his hands skimmed across her backside, making him intensely aware of just how shapely she was. He deepened the kiss and a hoarse sound of pleasure erupted from his throat. Moments later, he broke off the kiss and pulled back. He wanted her with an intensity that bordered on desperation.

"You sure?" he asked, wanting to make certain she knew exactly what she was getting into.

"I'm positive," she said, drawing up close to him.

"Hell, I hope so." He pulled her back to him and his mouth came down on hers with a ferociousness that he didn't know he possessed. Fed by the raging storm that had erupted within him, his mouth plundered hers, sweeping her breath away and tasting the sweet, deep and delicious taste that was distinctively hers. He felt the tremor that passed through her and it increased his need to make love to her to the point where his veins throbbed.

Storm lifted his head just long enough to reach out and whip the short dress over Jayla's head, leaving her standing before him clad in a silky black camisole. He

suddenly became dizzy with the sight of her standing
before him, lush and sexy. Her scent was seductive
and the pale lighting in the room traced a faint glow
across her dark skin. His temperature went up another
notch and he knew at that moment what he was about to
share with Jayla went way beyond his regular routine of
"wham-bam, thank you, ma'am." And for a mere second,
that thought bothered him. But like everything else that
was out of the norm for him tonight, he placed it on
the back burner. He'd deal with his confusing thoughts
tomorrow.

He reached out and pulled her back to him, capturing
her mouth at the same time he picked her up in his
arms and walked toward the bed. He placed her in the
center of it and tumbled down beside her, his hands
immediately going to her camisole to remove it from
her body.

He sucked in air through clenched teeth when he
pulled back and looked down at her, completely naked.
At that moment he felt an unbearable desire to feel his
mouth on her skin. Leaning toward her, his tongue
traced a path down her neck to her breasts, where it
stopped and drew a hard, budding nipple into his mouth
and feasted, licking, sucking.

He felt her tremble again and heard the purring sound
that came from deep within her throat. She wanted more
and was letting him know it. He took his hand and ran
it across the flat of her stomach, moving lower until
he found the moist heat of her. He touched her there,
glorying in her dampness. Deftly, expertly, his fingers
went to work.

Jayla felt her breath rushing in and out of her lungs.
Although there was light in the room and her eyes were

open, she felt her world was on the edge of blackness. She felt light-headed, dizzy, dazed, and she was feeling things that she'd never felt before. Storm's fingers were driving her out of her mind, and what his mouth was doing to her breasts was pure torture. Her body felt hot, on fire, in need of something it had never had before, but something it desperately needed.

She groaned deep in her throat. It was either that or scream out loud. So she clamped her mouth shut, but couldn't stop from releasing a sound that was alien to her ears. At the moment, nothing mattered but the feel of Storm's mouth and hands on her.

"I can't wait any longer," she heard him say, as he eased away from her. She watched as he stood next to the bed and quickly removed his shirt, almost tearing off the buttons in the process. Then he wasted no time in removing his pants and briefs. She continued to watch him when, with the expertise of a man who had done it many times before, he ripped the condom from the packet he had taken from his pant pockets and slid it over his erection.

She blinked at the size of him and before she could form the words to let him know of her virginal state, he had returned to the bed, pulled her into his arms and captured her mouth with his, once again giving in to the thirst of her desire, a desire that only he could quench. Want and need spiraled through her, making blood pump fast and furious through her veins. It seemed his mouth and hands were everywhere. Her insides were churning, her stomach was spinning and her brain had turn to mush. She didn't know what was driving him, but whatever the source, it was driving her, too. She felt the tip of his erection pressing against the entrance to her feminine mound in such a way that beckoned her to part her legs for him.

Then he kissed her again, long, hard, as his tongue plowed hers in breath-stealing strokes. She savored all the things he was doing to her, all the ways he was making her feel and wondered if the feelings would ever end, hoping and praying that they wouldn't, yet at the same thing knowing there was something else she needed, something she had to have.

She felt him place his body over hers, felt the strength of his thighs entwining with hers and relished the strong beat of his heart against her breasts. He lifted her hips into his hands.

He broke off their kiss and met her gaze, looked down at her the moment he pushed himself inside of her, with one deep, hard thrust. Her body stiffened and she gasped as a surge of pain ripped through her.

He immediately went still as total disbelief lined his features. "Jayla?"

Her name was a low rumble from deep within his throat. She saw the shock that flared in his eyes and felt the tension coiling within him. A spurt of panic swept through her at the thought that he wouldn't finish what he'd started, so she decided to take action.

"Don't ask," she said, then leaned upward and recaptured his mouth with hers. Her hands clutched at his shoulders and her legs wrapped solidly around him, locking him in place. She felt his resistance and began kissing him in all the ways he had kissed her that night, letting her tongue tangle relentlessly with his. He slowly began moving, easing in and out her, claiming her, taking her, making love to her in a way she always dreamed that lovemaking was supposed to be. The only thought on her mind was the strength of him driving back and forth, rocking her world and sending her over the edge. She knew she would remember every moment of this night for as long as she lived.

A groan eased from Storm's lips as Jayla's body met his, stroke for stroke. His hand reached down and lifted her hips to him for a closer fit, as if they weren't already close enough. She was tight, sensuously so, and his body surged in and out of hers, back and forth, massaging her insides the same way and with the same rhythm that her breasts were massaging his chest.

He had recovered from shock at discovering she'd been a virgin and decided since he was the one initiating her into lovemaking, that he would do it right. And the little whimpering sounds coming from her lips told him that he was definitely making an impact.

"Storm…"

He felt her body jerk at the same time she pressed her head into his shoulder to stifle a scream. The intensity of her climax jolted him, nearly stealing his breath before he followed her in his own release, yanked into the strongest and most mindless orgasm he had ever experienced in his entire life. And it was destined to be the longest…or perhaps he was having multiples, back to back. There was no way to tell since the earth-shattering sensations were hitting him all at once in every form and from every possible angle. The feeling was unique, incredible, out of this world and once in a lifetime. He hadn't expected this and was caught off guard by the magnitude of what was happening to him. He was being hurled into something he had never before experienced.

"Jayla!"

Her name was torn from his lips and he threw his head back as he continued to pump rapidly into her when he felt another climax claim him—his third, possibly a fourth. With a growl that came low from deep within his throat, he leaned down and pressed a kiss to her mouth as his body continued to tumble into oblivion, and he knew what they had shared was nothing short of heaven.

"I did as you requested and didn't ask then, but I'm asking now, Jayla."

Storm's words gave her pause. She let out a deep breath and wondered why he couldn't be one of those men who just accepted things as they were?

She looked up at him and saw the intensity in the depth of his dark eyes. She also saw the impressive shape of his lips and his well-toned, broad chest that was sprinkled with dark curly hair. And it wasn't helping matters that they were both naked in bed, with him leaning on his elbow and looming over her. She closed her eyes and shook her head. The man was too handsome for his own good…or for hers.

"Tell me," he whispered, then leaned down and placed a soft kiss on her bare shoulder. "Tell me why, in this day and age, a twenty-six-year-old woman would still be a virgin."

She met his gaze. "Because women in this day and age have choices," she said slowly, then asked, "Have you ever taken a love compatibility quiz?"

Storm arched his brow. "A what?"

She smiled at the confused look on his face. "A love compatibility quiz. There's a site on the Internet where you can go and take this quiz if you're looking for Mr.

or Miss Right. Well, after a few dates with losers—men who lacked confidence but had plenty of arrogance and who also acted as if it was a foregone conclusion that our date would end in my bed—I decided to take the quiz and my results indicated that my Mr. Right didn't exist."

Storm frowned down at her. Would he ever understand women? "You've been avoiding a serious relationship because of some quiz?"

"Pretty much...yes. I discovered like oil and water, me and relationships don't mix because I have a low tolerance when it comes to men who expect too much too soon."

It took Storm a minute to analyze everything she'd said. "What about those guys you dated off the Internet?"

Jayla released a single, self-deprecating chuckle. "That was my way of trying to prove the quiz wrong. From then on, I never wasted my time going on a guy hunt."

"But...but didn't you date in college?" Storm sputtered. Why hadn't her going off to college assured her returning to town with her hymen no longer intact?

She smiled again, a bit sadly this time. "Yes, but unfortunately, not long after I got there I met a guy name Tyrone Pembroke."

"What happened? He broke your heart?"

She chuckled derisively. "On the contrary. Actually he did me a favor by showing me just what jerks some guys were. He opened my eyes to the games they played, games I wasn't interested in. After Ty, I made it a point not to get serious about any one guy and since I wasn't into casual sex, I never felt pressured into sleeping with anyone."

Storm nodded. "So why now and why with me?"

To Jayla's way of thinking, that was an easy question. "Because of timing. I know you and I like you. I also know your position on relationships. I'm not looking for anything beyond what we shared tonight and neither are you, right?"

Storm held her gaze. "Right." The last thing he needed was a clingy woman who wanted to occupy his time. Still, although he didn't want to feel it, he felt a special connection to Jayla since he had been her first. He couldn't recall ever taking a woman's virginity before.

"Now that I've answered your question, do you think I can get some sleep?" Jayla asked softly. "I'm exhausted."

Storm glanced down at her. Was she dismissing him? "Do you want me to leave?"

She smiled. "Actually…" she began, as she snuggled closer to him. "I was hoping you'd want to stay all night."

A grin spread across Storm's lips. Hell, yeah, he wanted to stay all night. "I think that can be arranged," he told her as he leaned down and placed a kiss on her lips. "Excuse me for a second while I go into the bathroom to take care of something. I'll be right back."

"All right."

There was just enough light in the darkened room to let Jayla admire Storm's nude form as he crossed the room to the bathroom. She inhaled deeply as heated sensations shot through her. He'd been the perfect lover. He was confident, secure in who he was, but not arrogant. She felt tired and yet exhilarated at the same time. Slightly sore, but still smoldering from his lovemaking. Funny how things worked out. Storm was the man she'd been trying to get to notice her since the time she had started noticing boys. She was beginning to believe the cliché that good things came to those who wait. Now timing had not only finally worked for them, it was working against them as well. At any other time, she would have loved to take what she'd shared with Storm tonight to a whole other level, but not now. What she had needed was him out of her system so she could focus on the baby.

Her baby.

"I'm back."

Her nipples peaked in instant response to his words. She watched as he made a casual stroll over to the bed, totally at ease with his naked state. Seeing him that way stirred up desires within her again and she no longer felt as tired as she had earlier.

"Do you want me to prepare you some bath water to soak in for a while before you go off to sleep?" he asked, coming to sit on the side of the bed next to where she lay. "If you don't, you might wake up feeling a lot sorer than you probably do now."

Jayla leaned back against her pillow, seriously doubting that most men were as considerate as Storm was being. She pressed her lips together, liking his suggestion. "You're right, a soak in the tub sounds wonderful."

He smiled as he stood up. "I'll be back when your bath is ready."

"All right."

Again she watched him cross the room, finding it hard to tear her gaze from the sight of him, especially his tight behind. She smiled, feeling downright giddy at the thought that he'd agreed to spend the night with her. She might as well stretch this out for as far as she could because when they returned to Atlanta, things would be different. She would go her way and he would go his. They would both resume a life that had nothing to do with each other. He would go back to being a hero by fighting his fires and saving lives and she would eagerly prepare for the most life-altering experience she'd ever encountered—pregnancy.

"Ready?"

Hearing the sound of his voice, she glanced across the room. A thick surge of desire shot through her veins at the sight of him leaning in the doorway, naked and aroused. If she wasn't ready, he certainly was.

"Yes, I'm ready," she said, barely able to voice the words. She moved to get out of bed and then he was there, sweeping her up into his arms. The heat of his skin seeped through the heat of hers and the feeling was electrifying. She immediately knew the meaning of the words *raging hormones*. Hers were totally out of control. She quickly decided that she needed to get back in control of things.

"I can walk, Storm."

"Yes, but I want to carry you. That's the least I can do."

She clamped her lips tight, deciding not to tell him that he had done quite a lot. He had turned their night into more than a one-night stand. It had become a romantic interlude, one she would remember for the rest of her life.

As he carried her into the bathroom, her breasts tingled from the contact with his skin. And when he leaned down, shifting her in his arms to place her into the bubbly water, sliding her body down his, the sensations that rocketed through her almost took her breath away.

"The water might be a little warmer than what you're used to, but it will be good for your muscles," he said, in a voice that let her know he, too, had been affected by the contact of their bare skin touching.

She nodded as he placed her in the water. He was right. The water was warm, but it immediately felt good to her body. She glanced up at him as he stood beside the tub looking down at her. She tried to keep her attention on the top part of his body and not the lower part. "You seem to be good at this, Westmoreland. Is this how you treat all your virgins?"

He chuckled and his gaze captured hers. "Believe it or not, I've never done a virgin before."

She lifted a brow. "Never?"

His smile widened. "No. never. You're my first, just like I was your first."

Jayla watched as his features shifted into a serious expression as if he had to really think about what he'd just said for a moment. "Do you need my help?" he asked her.

She shook her head. "No, I can manage. Thanks."

He nodded. "Call me when you're ready to get out."

She smiled. "Storm, really, I can manage things."

"Yeah, I know you can but I want you to call me anyway." Then he left, closing the door behind him.

* * *

Storm poured himself a glass of ice water and tipped it to his mouth, wishing it was something stronger but appreciating the cool liquid as it soothed his dry throat.

He had sworn off having anything to do with Jayla years ago; yet now, after finally making love to her, he was aching so badly for her again that it actually hurt. To make matters worse, the taste of her was still strong on his tongue and, before he could contain himself, he groaned, which was followed by a growl that erupted from deep within his throat. Jayla Cole had no idea just what a desirable and sexy woman she was. Even being a novice at making love, she was every man's fantasy. He could see her attracting the wrong kind of men and felt a heartfelt sense of pride, as well as relief, that she had kept her head on straight and had not been taken in by any of them.

But was he any better? His no-commitment, hands-on-but-hearts-off, no-strings-attached policy left a lot to be desired, but he and Jayla had been struck by that unique kind of passion that had sent her straight into his arms and had propelled him unerringly into her bed.

And he had no regrets.

Frowning, Storm took another huge swallow of water. No woman had ever gotten to him like this. It was time for him to start building a defense to the passion she aroused in him. He pulled on his pants and did his best to reorder his chaotic thoughts and unruly emotions.

He heard a sound and turned around. Jayla was standing in the doorway wearing one of the hotel's complimentary bathrobes. His heart fluttered as he assessed her from head to toe. She looked refreshed.

She looked incredible, blatantly sexy. With a steadying breath, he asked, "Why didn't you call me when you were ready to get out of the tub?"

She smiled and his pulse kicked up a notch. "Because although I was tempted, it wouldn't be a good idea to start becoming dependent on you."

For him, it wasn't an issue of dependency. He'd known she could manage on her own but he had wanted to be there to help her anyway. There was something about her that pulled at his protective instincts…among other things. "Do you feel better?"

"Yes," Jayla said, blowing out a ragged breath as her gaze roamed over him, noticing that he had put his pants back on. What a shame. She was beginning to get used to seeing him naked.

She met his gaze again and couldn't help but notice that his eyes were dark, very dark, and her body's reaction to it was spontaneous. "I, ah, need to get a nightgown out the drawer," she said in a voice that sounded soft and husky even to her ears. She swallowed deeply when he slowly crossed the room to her.

"Have you ever slept in the nude?" he said, reaching out, opening her robe and sliding his hands over her bare skin, beginning with her waist, moving to her hips and then reaching around to cup her bottom.

"Ah, no," she said, barely getting the words out.

He gave her that killer smile. "Would you like to try it? I can't think of anything I'd like better than to have your naked body next to mine all night."

A small purring sound left Jayla's throat when he leaned forward and his tongue licked the area underneath her right ear, then the left. A sensuous shudder ran all through her, and she thought that a woman could definitely become dependent on his kind of treatment. And then she ceased to think at all when he stopped messing around with her ears and shifted his focus, opening his mouth hotly over hers.

Images of how intimate they'd been less than an hour ago flooded her mind. They had been together in bed with him on top of her, their legs entwined, their bodies connected while making love the same way they had done numerous times in her dreams. But this was no dream; it was reality. And the scent of his body heat and the sound of his breathing while he was kissing her did more than stir up her desire; it was stroking her with an intensity that shook her to the core, forging past those emotions she kept tightly guarded.

The thought that Storm was seeping through the barriers she'd set around her emotions disturbed Jayla, but she was too absorbed in the way his tongue was stroking the insides of her mouth to worry about it. This kiss was so full of greed and sensuality that she could feel the air crackling around them, and she was returning with equal vigor everything he was putting into their kiss.

And then slowly, reluctantly, he pulled back and his gaze locked to hers. "So, do we get naked?"

She swallowed. The huskiness in his voice made her want to do a lot more than get naked. "Yes," she managed to get out in a shaky breath.

"Good," he murmured, then reached up and pushed the robe off her shoulders, letting it fall in a heap at her feet. "Let's go back to bed."

Taking her hand into his, he lifted it to his lips and placed a warm kiss against the center of her palm. And then he picked her up in his arms and carried her to the bed. He placed her in the middle and then stood back to remove his pants.

Jayla watched him while thinking that nothing, other than a fire alarm going off, could distract her at that moment. She wanted to see every inch of him again, especially that part that had given her so much pleasure. He kept his gaze on her as he slowly eased down his pants. Then she watched as he pulled a condom packet out of his pants and went through the process of sheathing himself.

When he had finished, he glanced over at her and smiled. "Although I don't plan for us to do anything but sleep, there's nothing wrong with playing it safe."

She sighed and it took a lot of effort to concentrate on his words and not on him. "Umm, yes, that's smart thinking."

He quickly got into the bed, pulled her into his arms and felt her shiver. "You're cold?" he asked in a low, husky voice.

She shook her head. "No, quite the contrary. I'm hot."

He smiled. "I know a way to cool you off," he said, shifting his position to reach down between her legs to slide his fingers back and forth through her feminine curls.

She closed her eyes and moaned as he slowly but thoroughly began stroking a fire within her. "I—I don't think that's helping, Storm," she murmured, barely able to get the words out.

"Sure it is," he whispered close to her ear. "Just relax, feel and enjoy."

And she did.

His fingers literally drove her crazy. The sensation of

his fingertips as they intimately skimmed her feminine folds at a sensuously maddening and erratic pace had her purring and moaning.

She made the mistake of opening her eyes and meeting his gaze. Something she saw in the depths of his eyes took her breath away. Her senses suddenly became filled with an emotion that caused a tightening in her chest at the same time that her body lost control, exploded. The sensations that shot through her made her cry out, call his name and then he was capturing her mouth with his, kissing her deeply while he continued to skim the tip of his fingers between her legs.

Moments later, she felt her body become weak and she could barely reclaim her breath as he cuddled her limp body next to his, holding her tightly. She knew if she wasn't careful, that she was going to fall—

No! She couldn't go there. She couldn't even think such a thing. The only thing she wanted to focus on was how he was making her feel. She had made plans for her future and Storm Westmoreland wasn't a part of those plans. But here, now, at this very moment, he was part of her present and was giving her undiluted pleasure. She could not refuse what he was offering and when they parted in two days, she would always have these memories.

Chapter 5

Storm drew in a long breath as he looked down at the woman asleep in his arms. His chest tightened and he forced back the surge of desire that swept through him. She was an unbelievably beautiful woman.

Bathed in the rays of predawn light that spilled through the hotel's window, Jayla's hair, a glossy medium brown with strands of golden highlight, was spread across the pillow and shone luxuriously against the darkness of her creamy skin.

Sharing a bed with her hadn't been easy. In fact, he doubted that he'd gotten any sleep. While trying to find that perfect sleeping position, she had twisted and turned most of the night. And he had been tormented with each and every move she'd made. At one time, she had lain facing him, with her leg thrown over his, with his arousal pressing against her center.

Then there had been that time when she had shifted

around, placing her back to his chest, her sweet delectable backside right smack up against his groin. More than once during the course of the night he had been tempted to just say, "To hell with it," and ease inside of her. His mind had been filled with numerous possibilities. Instead, he had fought the urge and had wrapped his arms around her waist, pulled her close and thought about the time when he *had* been inside of her.

He would never forget how it felt, the moment he'd realized that she was a virgin. At first he'd been shocked, stunned and then panic had set in. But the notion of ending their lovemaking session had fled his mind when she pulled his mouth down to hers and kissed him with a hunger that he had quickly reciprocated.

And now he wanted her again. If truth were told, he hadn't stopped wanting her but had held back to give her body time to adjust to him. Now he was driven with an undeniable need to bury himself deep within her welcoming warmth again. He glanced over at the clock. It was just past six. He wanted to let her sleep but couldn't. He had to have her. Now.

He leaned over, close to her lips. "Jayla?" he whispered. A few moments later, she purred his name and slowly lifted one drowsy eye. Then she opened the other eye and blinked, as if to bring his face into focus.

"Storm," she murmured in a voice that was muffled with sleep, but to his way of thinking sounded sensuous as hell. Little tendrils of hair had drifted onto her face and graced one of her cheeks. He pushed the hair back from her face before sliding that same hand down the length of her body. Shifting slightly, he wanted her to feel his arousal pressing against the curve of her pelvis.

"I want you," he whispered and wondered if she could hear the urgency in his tone. The need. The desperation. She must have because she inched her lips closer to his for him to take control of her mouth, mate with it.

And he did.

His every muscle, his every nerve, felt sensitized as their tongues tangled with a hunger that was driving him crazy. The sweet, honeyed taste of her consumed his mind, sent a flame through his body and made him quickly lose touch with reality.

"Storm," she said softly, breaking off their kiss as her hands reached down, tentatively searching for him. When she captured him in the warmth of her hands, he thought he had died and gone to heaven. "I want this."

He definitely knew what she was asking for and didn't waste any time rolling her beneath him. He reached down and touched her, finding her hot, wet and ready. Lowering his head he needed to taste her breasts and drew one hardened nipple into his mouth, gently pulling it with his tongue, glorying in the shivers he felt going through her.

And then with her hands still holding him, she placed him at her opening and, slanting her hips upward, began easing him inside her. At this stage of the game, his arousal didn't know the meaning of slow and he pushed deep inside, finding her body still tight, but not as tight as it had been the night before. He stopped to give her time to adjust to him, but her soft moans and the rotation of her hips let him know she didn't want him to stop.

He thrust harder, buried himself to the depth they both wanted, and then he kissed her again, needing the contact to her mouth. And then he began to move inside of her as intense, dizzying, mind-boggling desire consumed him, sending him on a voyage that was out of this world. And Jayla was right there, taking the trip with him, as they flew higher and higher to the place where passion was taking them. A place that was a potent blend of exultation and euphoria, a place where he wanted to think that few people went—at least not to this degree and certainly not this level.

"Wow," he whispered huskily, for lack of a better word, and then he increased his pace, established their rhythm and like finely tuned musical instruments they played together in absolute harmony. Each movement added sensation and increased their pleasure. He dragged in a deep breath, feeling as if he were seconds from toppling over the edge, moments from exploding.

He clamped his hands down on her hips while he mated relentlessly with her. Her feminine muscles began gripping, clutching him with every thrust he took. And when he heard the sharp cry that was torn from her lips and felt her body jolt at the same time she arched her back, then shattered in his arms, he let go and began drowning in his own release.

"Jayla!"

He threw his head back, as something, everything, inside him broke free. If he thought he'd experienced pure, unadulterated ecstasy inside her body before, then this was a pleasure so raw and primitive that he doubted he would ever be able to recover from it. It was as if this was where he belonged, where he was supposed to be.

He quickly banished those thoughts from his mind as they continued to move together. He felt as if every cell within him was electrified, energized as they were propelled even deeper into the sensuous clutches that held them.

And then, before they could recover, it happened again, just as fast and just as potent. They were hurled into another orgasm so powerful that he actually felt the room spin and wondered if he would ever regain his equilibrium. A cry tore from his throat, only to be drowned out by the sound of hers as once again they were plunged into the throes of pure ecstasy.

With a shuddered sigh, he pulled her closer to him, felt himself getting hard all over again and knew this woman was doing more than draining his body. She was draining his very soul and at the moment, he couldn't do a damn thing to stop her.

Jayla couldn't move, so she lay still, feeling sated, exhausted and caught up in the aftereffects of remarkable sex. She stared up at the ceiling as she tried to calm the rhythm of her breathing. She smiled as she forced herself onto her side and faced Storm. He was lying flat on his back with his eyes closed. He, too, took long, deep, steadying breaths. When she saw he was once again aroused, the sight of him sent her senses into a mindless sensuous rush all over again. He was as hard as a rock, seemingly ready for another round. How on earth was that possible?

She sighed deeply. "Everything I've heard about you is true, Storm." She watched as he slowly lifted his eyes, slightly turned his head and looked over at her.

"What have you heard about me?"

Every bone in her body felt as if it had melted, so she chuckled huskily. "That you're perfect in bed. Did you know some women call you, The Perfect Storm?"

Storm frowned. For some reason he didn't want her to think about the other women he'd been with. And he didn't want to think about them, either. The only woman he wanted to think about was her. Instead of answering her question, he leaned over and kissed her deeply, thoroughly, and moments later, when he pulled back, he reached down and touched her intimately. "I didn't mean to be rough."

A huge smile touched the corners of her lips. "You weren't. I got everything I asked for and then some."

"Yeah, but you're new at this."

"And enjoying every minute." She studied him for a moment, then said. "I was curious about you when I was sixteen. You were the first guy I was really interested in."

"Was I?"

"Yes."

Storm held her gaze. He could vividly recall how, whenever he dropped by to visit Adam, her whiskey-colored eyes would seek him out and convey her every youthful emotion. She'd had a crush on him. He had been aware of it and he had a feeling that Adam had been aware of it as well. Storm had known that around her he would have to tread lightly, because she was the boss's daughter who was noticing boys for the first time; but unfortunately, instead of a boy, she had set her sights and budding desires on a man. To make matters worse, she fully intended for him to notice her and he had tried like hell not to.

"Do we stay in bed for the rest of the day or do we get up and do something else?" she asked, interrupting his stroll down memory lane. "Just to let you know, the thought of staying in bed all day doesn't bother me."

Storm couldn't help but laugh. "What have I created here, a monster?"

She lifted a brow. "Like you can talk. I'd say you're up for it," she said, pointing out his aroused state.

"Well, yeah, but some things can't be rushed. Just give me some time, will you."

"Sure, if you think you need it, but from what I understand most men need time to get it up, not down."

One corner of Storm's mouth lifted. He was enjoying this turn in their conversation, but he knew if they didn't get out of bed really soon, their conversation might turn into something else. Forcing himself to move, he slowly sat up. "I guess I need to go back to my room and take a shower." He glanced over at the clock. "Do you want to meet me downstairs for breakfast?"

"Yeah, I'm starving."

He nodded knowingly. "And after breakfast, how about if we do some more sightseeing today?" *Anything to keep them out of their hotel rooms.* "When does your flight leave tomorrow?" he asked. Suddenly, reality of how short their time together would be began to seep in. From the expression on her face he could tell that she felt it, too.

"In the morning, around eight. What about yours?"

"Tomorrow evening, around three."

She nodded. "Too bad we aren't on the same flight," she said quietly.

He'd been thinking the same thing. "Yeah, it's too bad." But then, maybe it was for the best. Too much more of Jayla Cole would go to his head and right to a place he wasn't quite ready for.

He sighed deeply. So much had happened between them in the last forty-eight hours. "Nothing has changed, right Jayla? Neither of us is looking for a serious relationship."

Jayla glanced at him, understanding his need to reestablish ground rules. "Yeah, right, nothing has changed. Trust me, a serious relationship with anyone is the last thing I want or need right now. I'm going to be so busy over the next few months that an involvement of any kind will be the furthest thing from my mind."

He lifted a brow as he slid out of bed. "Oh? What will you be doing?"

Jayla nervously licked her lips. There was no way she could tell him that she would be preparing for motherhood. "There's this project that I'm going to start working on."

"Oh, and what kind of project is it?"

She sighed deeply; he would ask. She decided to brush off his question and forced out a chuckle, saying, "Nothing you'd be interested in, trust me."

He smiled as he studied her for a long moment, then said. "I might surprise you. If you ever need my help, don't hesitate to call."

She smiled. "Thanks for the offer, but I have everything under control."

"All right. I'll be back in a second."

She watched as he walked into the bathroom and closed the door. She rolled over on her stomach and buried her face in his pillow, enjoying his lingering scent. Had she been dreaming or had Storm just offered to help with her project? She felt it was pretty safe to assume that the last thing Storm Westmoreland would want was to be a daddy. Besides, she had no regrets in going solo. A man like him as the father of her child would definitely cramp her style. He'd already stated his belief that a woman couldn't work outside the home *and* raise a family. She didn't envy the woman he would end up marrying, since it was evident that he would be a controlling husband.

She got out of bed, slipped into her robe, walked over to the window and glanced out to watch the impending sunrise. Tomorrow, she and Storm would bring an end to their short affair and she hoped when they returned to Atlanta that they didn't run into each other anytime soon. It would be difficult to see him and not think about the intimacy they had shared here in The Big Easy. There definitely wouldn't be anything easy about that.

Storm slid his hands around Jayla's waist and pulled her snugly against him. "An hour?" he asked with a puzzled lift of his brow. "Are you saying it will take you an entire hour to pick out an outfit for tonight?"

She smiled up at him. "Yes. Already I see a number of things in this dress shop that I want to try on. It has to be just perfect."

"Jayla," he began, but she cut him off.

"Please, Storm. I want a new outfit for tonight."

He studied the excitement in Jayla's face, thinking she was even more beautiful than before, if that were possible. When he had met her for breakfast, he'd told her of the phone call he had received from his cousin Ian. Ian, a good friend of New Orleans's mayor, had been invited to a huge gala being given in the man's honor. Ian had invited Storm as his guest and Storm had gotten the okay to bring Jayla as his date. Instead of going sightseeing as they had originally planned, Jayla had insisted that the first thing she needed to do was go shopping for something to wear that night.

"All right, I guess I can find something to kill time while you shop," he said releasing her. "But I'll be back in an hour, Jayla."

She grinned, nodding. "And I'll have everything I need by then."

A short while later, Storm took his time as he strolled around Jackson Square. It was a beautiful day and a lot of tourists were out and about. He smiled when he thought of how excited Jayla had been when he'd mentioned tonight's affair. He had enjoyed seeing her happy. He was also enjoying her company…almost a little too much. She was definitely someone he liked being with, both in and out of bed. More than once he had to remind himself not to make more of what they were sharing than there was.

It was no big deal that over the past few days, they'd discovered that they enjoyed many of the same things. She liked jazz, and so did he; she enjoyed watching bone-chilling thriller movies and so did he. She was one of the few people who lived in Atlanta whose favorite football team *wasn't* the Atlanta Falcons. His favorite team was the Dallas Cowboys and she was a fan of the Philadelphia Eagles.

It seemed the only thing they didn't agree on was his belief that a woman's place was at home raising her kids and not in an office all day. Jayla insisted that a man who held such traditional views would be too controlling in a marriage. He didn't see himself as wanting to control, but rather he saw himself as someone who wanted to be the sole provider for his family in the purest sense of the word.

He glanced at his watch. He still had over forty-five minutes to go before he went back to that dress shop for

Jayla. Damn, but he missed her already. A warning bell suddenly went off in his head. He'd never admitted to missing a woman before, so why was he doing it now? He sighed deeply, deciding to be honest with himself. The honest truth was he liked having Jayla around and for him that didn't bode well.

He frowned as he continued to walk around Jackson Square, wondering what was there about her that was getting to him and playing games with his mind. They were games he had no desire to play. She knew the score and so did he. Neither of them wanted anything beyond what they were sharing here in New Orleans. Getting together and developing some sort of relationship when they returned to Atlanta was unacceptable, totally out of the question, a definite bad idea.

Then why was he allowing such thoughts to invade his mind?

"You're confused, aren't you?"

Storm turned to the sound of the craggy voice and saw an old woman sitting on the bench less than five feet from where he stood. He lifted a brow. "Excuse me. Did you say something?"

The old woman smiled serenely. "Yes. I said you're confused. Nothing like this has ever happened to you before, has it?"

Storm tilted his head to the side as he studied the woman, wondering if she was operating with a full deck. She was talking as if she knew him. "I think you might have me mixed up with someone else."

"No, I don't," she muttered with a shake of her head. "And I'm not crazy," she said, as if reading his mind. "I'd tell you more if you let me look into your future."

Storm nodded as understanding dawned. The old

woman was a fortune-teller. New Orleans was full of them. He crossed his arms over his chest amused. "And what do you think you can tell me that I don't already know?"

"Oh, you'd be surprised."

Storm didn't think so but decided to humor the old woman. "Okay, then surprise me. What do you have to work with? Tarot cards or a crystal ball?"

The older woman met his gaze and looked at him with a scrutiny that Storm found unnerving. Finally, she responded. "Neither. I'm a palm reader."

Storm nodded. *That figured.* "Okay, how much to read my palm?"

"Twenty dollars."

He sighed as he reached into his pocket and pulled out a twenty-dollar bill while wondering why he was wasting his time. He glanced at his watch. He still had a good thirty minutes left before Jayla was ready and having his palm read was just as good as anything else to pass the time away.

He sat down next to the woman on the bench and stretched out his hand to her. "Okay, what does my palm say?"

He watched as the woman took his hand into her frail one and studied his palm. Moments later, when she lifted her gaze, the intensity in the depth of her dark eyes almost startled him. She smiled sympathetically. "I can see why you're confused."

He frowned. "Meaning what?"

"You are about to make unexpected changes in your life and although you yearn for peace, turbulence is in your future. Keep your sights high, be patient and let destiny take its course."

Storm's frown deepened. He had just gotten a promotion three months ago, so what changes was the woman talking about? He had thought about moving out of his present house and buying a larger one, but what problems could a decision like that bring on? There had to be more.

He lifted his brow. "Is that it?"

She stared at him and sighed deeply. "Trust me, son. That will be enough."

He shook his head, a part of him found the entire thing outright amusing. "Ahh, can you be a little more specific?"

"No, I've told you everything you need to know."

He slowly stood. He couldn't wait until he and his brothers had their next card game so he could tell them about this experience. Knowing them, they would probably find the whole thing hilarious. "Well, it was nice getting my palm read," he said, not knowing what else to say.

She shook her head slowly. "I wish you the best of luck."

Storm looked at the woman. She'd said it like she had truly meant it. "Thanks," he said before walking off, not sure just what he was thanking her for.

"Tell her you like the red one."

He turned back around and lifted a brow. "Excuse me?"

The old woman smiled. "Tell her you like the red one the best."

Storm frowned, not understanding what she meant. He decided it would be best not to ask, so he nodded, turned back around and kept walking. Moments later, when he returned to the dress shop, he saw Jayla standing at the checkout counter waiting for him. His face lit into a smile as he walked over to her. "Did you find anything?"

"Yes," she answered excitedly. "I found two really nice outfits and they're both beautiful. I want you to pick out the one you like the best."

He watched as she turned and grabbed two dresses off the counter, one blue and the other red. Storm blinked twice and his throat suddenly went dry when he remembered what the old woman had said. *Tell her you like the red one*. He stared at the two outfits that Jayla was holding up in front of her.

"Well, which do you like the best, Storm?" she asked, looking from one dress to the other.

"The red one," he replied promptly, feeling somewhat dazed, like he was a participant in *The Twilight Zone*.

Jayla didn't notice his consternation as she handed the red dress to the smiling saleswoman behind the counter. A huge grin touched her lips. "I like the red one best, too."

Later that night, Storm had to admit that he definitely liked the red dress, especially on Jayla. His tongue had nearly fallen out of his mouth the moment she had stepped off the elevator to meet him in the lobby.

Instantaneous. Immediate. A jolt of mind-wrenching desire had shot straight to his groin. There was nothing like an eye-catching, incredulously sexy, tight-fitting dress on a woman who definitely had sleek and delectable curves. Her silver accessories made her look sophisticated, elegant and hot, all at the same time. The dress was short, really short, but then she had legs that transformed the dress from provocative to mind-blowing. Her breasts sat high and looked full, lush and ready to tumble out of the low-cut neckline at any given moment.

"I had a lot of fun tonight, Storm, and I like your cousin Ian."

He glanced at her. They were sitting in the back of a cab on their way back to the hotel. It was dark, but the moonlight, as well as the bright lights from the buildings they passed, provided sufficient light for them to see each other's features clearly. But even if he hadn't been able to see her, he would have definitely been able to smell her. The perfume she was wearing was a luscious, blatantly sensual scent and it was doing downright crazy things to his libido.

"Yeah, and I could tell he liked you," he responded huskily. *Almost a little too much,* he thought. He smiled when he remembered the look on his cousin's face the moment he and Jayla had walked into the party. Ian's expression of appreciation was also shared by most of the other men present. His heart had swelled with pride that she was with him.

And he couldn't forget how Ian had pulled Jayla to him and planted a kiss on her lips when they'd been leaving. He grinned, knowing Ian had intended to give him a dose of his own medicine. Ian had wanted to get a rise out of him, the same way he enjoyed getting a rise out of his brothers whenever he kissed their wives. Now he knew how it felt.

"I can't wait to get to the hotel to get out of these shoes. They are killing my feet."

Storm smiled and was glad that because of the darkness, Jayla couldn't see the heated gleam in his eyes. He couldn't wait to get her back to the hotel to get her out of something else. The sight of her in that dress had nearly driven him mad all night. He couldn't wait to see just what she had or didn't have underneath it.

"Lift your feet into my lap and I'll be glad to give you some temporary relief," he murmured, wanting to touch her any way he could. She didn't waste time taking him up on his offer and she shifted her body to slide her legs across his lap. He knew there was no way she could not feel the hardness of his groin with her legs resting across his thighs.

He went about removing the silver stiletto heels and began massaging her feet. Her panty hose felt smooth and silky to his touch, and the thought that he'd never pampered another woman this way suddenly hit him. He tossed the thought from his mind as he continued to gently and methodically stroke her feet, thinking there was nothing like a great pair of legs and she had a pretty nice pair.

"Umm, I could get used to this. You have gifted hands, Storm."

He smiled. "Anything to make you happy." He thought about what he'd said and shook his head. He wondered what it would take to make a woman like her completely happy.

"We got back too soon," Jayla said, and he glanced out of the cab's window to see they had arrived back at the hotel. He strapped her shoes back on her feet and felt an immediate sense of loss when she pulled her legs out of his lap.

He glanced over at her, determined to remove that disappointment from her voice. He leaned over, pulled her against him and captured her lips. The taste of her was arousing...as if he needed to be aroused more than he already was. In minutes, he had her groaning and liked the sound of it.

"My room or yours?" he whispered softly against her lips.

She stared at his mouth a moment before answering in a voice that increased his heart rate another notch. "I've never been inside a man's hotel room before and since this trip to New Orleans has been a first for me in a lot of ways, let's go to your room tonight."

He kissed her again, devouring her soft lips and thinking he could definitely get used to this.

Jayla awoke when she heard the ringing of the telephone. A quick glance at the clock on the nightstand indicated it was the wake-up call she had ordered. She watched as Storm reached over, picked up the receiver and, without answering, hung it back up. He then met her gaze and for a moment she thought she saw a quick instant of regret in his eyes when he said, "I guess it's time."

"Yeah, it seems that way," she said softly, not wanting to get out of bed and get dressed, although she knew that she should. She needed to go to her room and pack. Her flight was scheduled to leave in a few hours and she had to make sure that she arrived at the airport on time.

Heat spread low in her belly when Storm continued to look at her. Whenever he looked at her, it did things to her. She would remember every moment of last night. She had entered his hotel room and he had closed the door behind them. She had walked into his embrace and the kiss they'd shared had been blazing and within seconds he had removed her dress and panty hose, leaving her wearing only a thong.

She would never forget the way he had looked at her, how he had swept her up into his arms and carried her over to the bed and made love to her as if pleasing her were the most important thing in his life. The lovemaking that they had shared had been simply amazing.

"Do you need help packing?" he asked, looking breathtakingly handsome, sleep-rumpled and delicious. He smiled as he braced himself up on one elbow and looked down at her. He reached out and gently touched the nipples of her breasts. They hardened with his touch and she felt a warmth begin to build between her legs.

She returned his smile, knowing if she were to take him up on his offer she would never finish packing. "Thanks for the offer, but I believe I can manage."

She felt her smile slowly fade away as reality set in. Although she did not regret any of the time she had spent with him, she knew it was about to end. There was no other way, and it would be for the best. She had to shift her focus away from Storm and back to the baby she wanted more than anything. As soon as she got home, she would schedule an appointment with the fertility clinic to get things started. A continuation of Storm in her life would only complicate things and she didn't do well with complications. Besides, she knew there was no Mr. Right for her, especially one by the name of Storm Westmoreland.

So why was it so hard for her to get out of his bed? And why did she want to make love to him again, one last time before she finally walked out the door?

"I enjoyed our time together, Jayla."

His words interrupted her thoughts and she met his

gaze, studied his eyes. "I did, too, and still no regrets, right?"

He reached out and threaded his fingers through her hair. "No regrets. We're adults and we did what we wanted to do."

A smile curved her mouth. "Thank you Storm for showing me how great lovemaking can be."

He looked at her, countered her smile. "You're welcome."

"But life goes on," she decided to say when more than anything she wanted to kiss him.

He nodded. "Yes, life goes on, but it won't be easy. If I were to run into you anytime soon," he said, gently smoothing his fingertips across her cheek, "there's no way I'll see you and not think about that red dress and those killer high heels, not to mention the only thing you were wearing under that dress."

She chuckled. "Shocked you, huh?"

A huge smiled tipped one corner of his mouth. "Yeah, you shocked me. You also pleased me."

Storm decided that what he couldn't tell her was that she was unlike any woman he had ever known. She was someone who could laugh with him, tease him and talk to him just about anything. And the sex had been amazing and there was no way he could let her go without making love to her again. He needed this one last time to seal the memory of their time together into his mind forever.

Forever.

That was a word he had never included in his vocabulary, one he had never associated with a woman. He didn't do forever, and never thought about it. But he had to admit that with Jayla Cole, he thought of things he

had never thought of before. And he was glad for the
time they had spent together. He had learned things
about her that he otherwise might not have known,
such as her passion for strawberry cheesecake and how
she volunteered her spare time at Emory University
Hospital's Cancer Center.

"Storm, I need to get up, get dressed and leave."

He stared at her, feeling a sense of finality and a
part of him felt a sense of loss he'd never experienced
before and one he couldn't explain. And then, suddenly,
he wanted her with an urgency he had never wanted her
or any woman before. Blood rushed through his veins
and he breathed in deeply.

"Storm…"

He looked at her and his breath stopped. He had to
have her again, this one last time. He eased her beneath
him the same moment that he lowered his head and
captured her lips, tasting her, mating his tongue over
and over with hers. She had stamped her mark on him
and now he was going to make sure he stamped his on
her.

For just a little while, he would make her *his*, and
if he lived a hundred years, there would be no regrets.
What he would have were memories to last a lifetime.

And from the way she was returning his kiss he could
tell she wanted those memories, too.

Chapter 6

"So, how was your trip to New Orleans?" Lisa Palmer asked as she sat back in her chair at Jayla's kitchen table.

Jayla looked up and met her best friend's curious stare. "It was fine. Why do you ask?"

"Because I've noticed that since you've been back, you haven't said much about it."

Jayla drew in a deep breath and wished she could ignore Lisa's curious scrutiny. It was just like Lisa to pick up on her reference about the trip. She knew that sooner or later she would have to come clean and tell her friend everything, including her planned trip to the fertility clinic.

"Umm, why do I get the feeling that you're not telling me something?"

Cupping her chin in her palm, Jayla forced a smile. "You're imagining things."

Lisa shook her head. "No, I don't think so." She gazed

at her thoughtfully, then said, "There's something different about you. You look more relaxed and well-rested which can only mean one thing."

Jayla swallowed, wondering if she really had a different look about her. "What?" she asked softly.

Lisa's lips tilted into a deep smile. "That you got plenty of rest this trip, which is a good thing that I didn't go with you. Had I gone I would have worn you out with endless shopping and—"

"I ran into someone."

Lisa lifted a brow. When seconds ticked off and Jayla didn't say anything else, Lisa scooted closer in her chair. "Okay, are you going to keep me in suspense or are you going to tell me?"

Jayla took a sip of her lemonade before responding. "I ran into Storm Westmoreland."

Lisa placed her glass of lemonade down on the table. "Storm Westmoreland? The Perfect Storm?"

Jayla chuckled. "Yes, that Storm."

Lisa stared at her for a moment as she recalled Jayla once telling her about the crush she'd had on Storm Westmoreland at sixteen. And, like most women in the Atlanta area, she also knew about his reputation as a womanizer, and that's what bothered her the most. "What was Storm Westmoreland doing in New Orleans?" she asked, having a feeling there was a lot more to the story.

Jayla chuckled again. "He was attending a conference."

"And...?"

Jayla was quiet for a moment. She knew Lisa had a thousand questions and decided she might as well tell her everything or else she would get grilled to death.

"And we ran into each other and one thing led to another and we ended up having an affair."

She almost grinned when she saw Lisa's jaw drop. She then watched as Lisa picked up her glass and drained it as if it contained something stronger than lemonade.

Lisa then turned her full attention to her. "You're no longer a virgin?" she asked as if her mind were in shock.

Jayla did grin this time. "Nope."

Lisa then slumped back in her chair and pinned her with a look. Jayla was well aware of *that* look. It was a look that said you'd better tell me everything and start from the beginning.

"Like I said," Jayla said, before she was hammered with relentless questions, "Storm and I ran into each other, decided to spend time together and one thing led to another."

"Evidently."

Now it was Jayla who pinned Lisa with a look. "And don't expect me to tell you *everything* because there are some details you're better off not knowing." Her mind was suddenly filled with thoughts of everything she and Storm had done. They had made love so many times she had lost count, and each time had been better than the last.

What she held special was the first time and how, afterward, he had drawn her bath water, gently picked her up into his arms and carried her into the bathroom. But it was the last time they'd made love on the morning she'd left, that stood out in her mind more than the others.

With a loving tenderness that had almost brought tears

to her eyes, he had used his hands and mouth to drive her over the edge, making her body burn out of control for him. And only when she was about to come apart in his arms did he fill her and begin moving back and forth inside her, combining tenderness with compelling need, and sending her escalating into a sharp, shattering orgasm that had taken her breath away and had left her sated, exhausted and spent. And as much as she'd tried to stay awake, she had drifted off to sleep. They both had. When they had awakened, she'd dressed quickly and returned to her room to pack.

He had gone to her room with her to help her pack and the last kiss he had given her before she had walked out of the hotel room door for the airport had been off-the-charts fantastic. She knew that if she never made love to another man, she would always remember having that time with Storm. It had been more than just good, mind-blowing sex. For three days, he had made her feel special, as if knowing he'd been her first had been extraordinary and he was still in awe of the gift she had given him.

"Jayla?"

She jumped when Lisa snapped a finger in front of her face. "What?"

"You haven't answered my question."

Jayla frowned. "What question?"

"Do you have any regrets?"

Jayla immediately shook her head. "No. Twenty-six years was long enough to be a virgin, but I'd never met a man I felt worthy of giving myself to until Storm."

Lisa raised a dark brow. "With Storm's reputation, you thought he was worthy?"

"Yes, because he didn't try to snowball me into doing

it with him. In fact, at first he actually tried resisting my advances. I'm the one who came on to him. And he always behaved like a perfect gentleman, giving me choices and not assuming anything."

Lisa nodded, and then a curious glint shone in her dark eyes. "Is everything we've heard about him true?"

Jayla tried to ignore the heat that was settling between her legs when she thought about just how true it was. When it came to lovemaking, Storm Westmoreland was a practiced and skillful lover. She couldn't help but smile. "Yes, everything we've heard is true."

A silly smirk appeared on Lisa's face and she sat back in her chair. "Damn. Some women have all the luck," she said with envy. She then smiled. "So when will the two of you see each other again?"

Jayla tried to ignore the ache that suddenly settled around her heart, convincing herself it was only indigestion. "We won't be seeing each other again. What we shared was nothing more than a no-strings-attached affair, and since neither of us is into relationships, we decided that when we returned to Atlanta, he would continue to do his thing and I would continue to do mine."

Lisa lifted a brow. "You don't have a 'thing' to do. You basically live a boring life. All you do is go to work and come home, except for those days when you're volunteering at the cancer center."

Jayla knew what Lisa said was true, but in a few weeks all of that would change. She smiled. "Well, I want you to know that my life will no longer be boring. I've decided to take the first step in doing something I've wanted to do for a long time."

"Oh, and what's that?"

"Have a baby."

Jayla watched Lisa's expression. She looked as if someone had just pulled a chair out from under her. Lisa looked at her long and hard before finally saying something. "What do you mean, have a baby?"

"Just what I've said. You of all people know how much I love children."

Lisa shrugged. "Hey, I love them, too, but I'm not planning to have any until Mr. Right comes along and I'm ready to settle down and get married."

Jayla raised her eyes to the ceiling. "Well, yeah, but for some of us there is no Mr. Right, so I've decided not to wait any longer."

Lisa was quiet for a moment as she pinned Jayla with that look again. "Tell me you didn't deliberately try and get pregnant by Storm Westmoreland."

Jayla couldn't help but laugh. Lisa's question was so ridiculous. Storm Westmoreland would be the last man she would want to father her child. He was too controlling. "Trust me, that thought never crossed my mind. Besides, I would never trick any man that way. I made all the necessary arrangements before I left for New Orleans, and I'm going to go to a fertility clinic and have the procedure done."

Lisa quickly held up her hand. "Time out. Back up. What are you talking about?"

Jayla smiled. The expression on Lisa's face was both endearing and maddening. They were as close as sisters and she knew her best friend well enough to know that she would not agree with her decision regarding the fertility clinic. But then, Lisa didn't have any problems finding a Mr. Right since she was already involved in a serious relationship with a wonderful guy. Added to that was the fact that Lisa came from a big family, so she didn't know the meaning of loneliness.

"I'm talking about my decision to have a baby. I've already done the preliminary paperwork and they'd located a potential donor who fits the profile I've requested. All that's left is for me to take another physical, which is scheduled for next Friday. Once it's determined when I'm most fertile during my cycle, I'll be going in to have the procedure done. If I'm not successfully inseminated on the first try, then there will be another try and if necessary, a third or however many times it takes. I'm sure my eggs will eventually be ripe for some donor's sperm," she said smiling.

Lisa, Jayla noticed, wasn't smiling back. In fact, she looked mortified. "Tell me you're joking about this, Jayla."

Jayla sighed deeply. She then worked her bottom lip between her teeth several times, which was something she tended to do when she was bothered by something. Over the years, Lisa may not have agreed with everything she did but had always supported her. Jayla knew because of her friend's traditional beliefs, this would be a hard sell, which was why she had put off telling Lisa about her plans.

She lifted her chin. "No, I'm not joking, Lisa. I've made up my mind about this. You may not agree with what I'm doing, but I really do need you to support me on this. I want a baby more than anything."

"But there are other options, Jayla."

"Yes, and I considered those other options and none will work for me. I want a baby not an involvement with a man who may not be Mr. Right, and I don't have time to wait until I finally get lucky. Times have changed. A woman no longer needs a man to get pregnant or to raise a child, and that's the way I want to do things."

Lisa didn't say anything for a long moment, then she reached across the table and captured Jayla's hand in hers. "Although I can understand some women having the procedure done in certain situations, your case is different, Jayla, and what you plan to do goes against everything I believe in. When it's possible, I think a child should benefit with the presence of both the mother and father in the home. But if you're hell-bent on going through with it, then I'll be there to do whatever you need me to do."

Jayla blinked back the tears in her eyes. "Thanks."

"Hey, Storm, get your mind back on the game, stop daydreaming and throw out a card."

Thorn Westmoreland's words recaptured Storm's attention and he threw out a card then leaned back in his chair and frowned. "I was not daydreaming and my mind *is* on the game," he said throwing out a card.

After another round of bid whist, Stone Westmoreland shook his head. "If your mind is on the game then you're a lousy card player since you just threw out a diamond instead of a heart which means you've reneged." A huge smile tilted the corners of Stone's lips. "But I'm not complaining since that puts me closer to winning."

Storm pushed back his chair and stood, glaring at his four brothers. Apparently they'd found his lack of concentration amusing but he didn't find a damn thing funny about it. "I'm sitting out for a while. I need some fresh air."

While he was walking away he heard his brother Thorn ask the others, "What's wrong with him?"

"Don't know," his brother Dare replied. "He's been acting strange ever since he got back from that conference in New Orleans."

"Maybe the pressures of being a fire captain is getting to him," he heard his brother Chase add. "There's nothing worse than letting a job stress you out."

"Yeah," his other brothers agreed.

Storm shook his head when he opened the door and stepped out on the lanai. His brothers didn't know how wrong they were. His new promotion or work-related stress had nothing to do with the way he'd been acting since returning from New Orleans.

He glanced up and noticed a full moon and the stars in the sky. It was a beautiful night and he was glad he had come outside to appreciate the evening for a little while.

After Thorn and Tara had gotten married, they had moved into Tara's place since it was larger than Thorn's, but only temporarily. They were building their dream home on a parcel of the Westmoreland family homestead, which was located on the outskirts of town. It was a pretty nice area if you liked being out in the boon-docks and cherished your privacy.

Storm shook his head as an image of a woman forced its way into his head. It was the same image he'd been trying like hell to forget the past week. Jayla Cole.

He balled his hands into fists at his sides as he wondered what was wrong with him. He'd had affairs before but none had affected him the way this one had. No woman had ever remained in his thoughts after the affair had ended. He'd known there would be memories, hell, he had counted on savoring them. But he had wanted them safely tucked away until he was ready to revisit them. He hadn't counted on having no control of his own memories.

Visions of Jayla in the red dress were taking him to the cleaners and wringing him out. And then there were those images of the sway of her hips whenever she walked, whether she was in heels or flats. It didn't matter. The woman was sensuality on legs. She was a mouthwatering piece flat on her back as well. All he had to do was close his eyes and he was reliving the evenings filled with their mind-boggling, earth-shattering lovemaking.

She had fired up and completely satisfied a need within him that he hadn't known existed. Each and every time he had taken her to bed they had made incredible love. He could get her so wet, so hot, so ready, and likewise she could get him so hard, so needy, so out-of-his-mind greedy, to the point where getting inside her body was all he could think about; all he wanted.

And then there was the look on her face whenever she came. It was priceless. It was as if the force of what she felt stole her breath and the intensity of it exploded her world into tiny fragments as she tumbled into mindless completion. Seeing that experience on her face would then push him over the edge into the most potent climax he'd ever experienced, usually more than one—back to back.

"Damn," he let out a low growl and wiped a sheen of perspiration from his forehead with his hand. He was used to sexual experiences, but getting seduced by memories was something that he was not used to or comfortable with. Hell, he had even thought about dropping by her house to make sure she was all right. If that didn't beat all. He had never checked up on a woman after the affair ended.

"Storm, are you okay?"

He inhaled deeply when he heard his sister-in-law's voice and quickly decided that although it was dark, it wouldn't be a good idea for him to turn around just yet. There was a glow of light filtering out from the living room and he had gotten hard just thinking about Jayla.

"Storm?"

"Yeah, Tara, I'm fine." Seconds later when he was sure he had gotten his body back under control he turned around and smiled.

Tara Matthews was beautiful and had nearly blown Storm and his brothers away the first time they had seen her at their sister Delaney's apartment in Kentucky. And he might have even considered having a relationship with her, but he'd soon discovered that Tara was a handful. He and his brothers had quickly concluded that the only man who could possibly handle her was their brother Thorn, so they had deemed her Thorn's challenge. Now, a little more than two years later, she was Thorn's wife. But she still held a special place in his heart as well as the hearts of his brothers because in the end though Thorn may have handled her, Tara had proved that she was capable of handling Thorn, which wasn't an easy task.

He met her gaze and saw concern in her eyes. "I was worried about you," she said softly. "When I passed through the dining room and saw you missing, your brothers said you had needed fresh air. I didn't know if you were coming down with something, especially when they'd said you'd been playing badly tonight."

Storm laughed, then gave her a playful grin. "Hell, they claim I play lousy even when I'm winning."

Tara nodded smiling. "So, how was your trip to New Orleans?"

Funny you should ask, he thought as he slumped back against a column post. He sucked in a deep breath when another vision of Jayla floated through his mind. He envisioned his mouth finding her most sensitive areas, especially her ultra-hot spot and tilting her up to his mouth and making her scream.

"Storm?"

"Huh?"

"I asked how was your trip." She took a step closer to him and looked deeply into his eyes. "Are you sure you're okay? Your eyes seemed somewhat dazed."

And my body is hard again but we won't go there, he thought, thinking the best thing to do was go back inside and play cards and hope that this time he could keep his mind on the game. "I'm fine and I had a great time in New Orleans. I even saw Ian while I was there and he mentioned that he would be in town for that charity benefit that you're working on."

A smile touched the corners of Tara's lips. "Really," she said excitedly. "That's the night we'll unveil the charity calendar for Kids' World and everyone will get to see Thorn as Mr. July."

Storm laughed. "I don't think that's the only reason Ian is coming, Tara," he said, thinking that maybe if he kept talking he wouldn't have to worry about visions of Jayla intruding. "The main reason Ian's coming is because you asked him to, but there's another reason."

Tara lifted her brow. "And what reason is that?"

A grin appeared on Storm's face. "He figures there will be a lot of pretty, single women in attendance."

Tara shook her head smiling, finally getting the picture. "Well, I'm sure there will be plenty of single women there since eleven of the men who posed for the calendar are still single. Thorn is the only one who has gotten married since those photos were taken."

Something suddenly pulled at Storm's memory. He remembered Jayla mentioning that she would be meeting Tara for lunch the Tuesday after returning to work. Unless those plans had changed, that meant the two of them would be meeting tomorrow. There was no way he could ask Tara about it without her wondering how he'd known. But if they were to meet tomorrow for lunch and if he knew where, he could unexpectedly drop by and pretend that he'd been in the area. For some reason he wanted to see Jayla again and if they *accidentally* ran into each other, she wouldn't think he had intentionally sought her out…although in essence, he would be doing just that.

"So, Tara, how about if I took you, Madison and Shelly to lunch tomorrow?" he suggested. He knew Dare's wife Shelly hadn't returned from visiting her parents in Florida, Stone's wife Madison would be leaving with Stone tomorrow on a book-signing trip to Kansas City, and if Tara had made other plans for lunch then he would find out soon enough.

"Thanks, Storm, that's really sweet of you, but Shelly and Madison will be out of town and besides I already have a lunch date. I'm meeting with a woman who's working with me on the charity benefit. Her company has agreed to pick up the tab for all the food and drinks that night."

Bingo. He was suddenly beginning to feel pretty good now. Confident. Cocky. Smug. He straightened from leaning against the post. "Oh, that's too bad. Where are you going?"

Tara lifted a brow. "Excuse me?"

He inhaled slowly, knowing he couldn't appear too inquisitive. The last thing he needed was for Tara to get suspicious of anything. "I asked where are you going for lunch? It might be a place where I've eaten before. Perhaps I can tell you whether the food and service are good."

Tara smiled. "Trust me, I know you've eaten at this place plenty of times and can definitely vouch for the food and service being the best. My lunch date left it up to me to select a place and although I haven't told her yet, I'm going to suggest that we have lunch at Chase's Place."

His heart suddenly did a back flip and his mouth curved into a huge smile. Things couldn't have worked out better if he was planning things himself. Tara was taking Jayla to his brother's restaurant, a place where he ate lunch on a regular basis, so it wouldn't seem out of the ordinary if he showed up there tomorrow. "I think that's a wonderful choice."

She shook her head smiling and before she could say anything, Thorn's loud voice roared through the air. "Storm, get back in here if you're in this game, and you better not be out there kissing my wife."

Storm laughed. "He's a jealous kind of fellow, isn't he?" he asked, taking Tara's hand as they walked back inside.

She grinned and he could see her entire face light up with absolute love for his brother. "Yes, but I wouldn't have him any other way."

"Chase's Place?" Jayla asked, making sure she had heard correctly.

"Yes," Tara said brightly on the other end of the phone. "It's a soul-food restaurant that's owned by my brother-in-law Chase Westmoreland, and the food there is wonderful."

Jayla rose from behind her desk, no longer able to sit. She knew the food there was wonderful but at the moment that wasn't what was bothering her. She recalled Storm saying that he routinely ate at his brother's restaurant. She was tempted to suggest they go someplace else but quickly remembered that she had been the one to suggest that Tara select the place for lunch. She sighed deeply. "I've eaten there before and you're right, the food is wonderful."

"And he's promised to take good care of us."

Jayla raised a dark brow. "Who?" She heard Tara chuckle on the other end before answering.

"Chase. He's good at taking care of people. "

"Oh." It was on the tip of Jayla's tongue to say it must run in the family because Chase wasn't the only Westmoreland who was good at taking care of people. She vividly remembered the way Storm had taken care of her, fulfilling and satisfying her every need.

She tried forcing the memories to the back of her mind. "What time do you want us to meet?"

"What about around one-thirty? That way the noonday lunch crowd won't bombard us. But if you think you'll be hungry before then we can—"

"No, one-thirty is fine and I'll meet you there." After ending the call, Jayla sat back at her desk. If she saw Storm again, what was the correct protocol to handle the situation? Women and men had affairs all the time and she was sure that at some point they ran into each other again. Did they act casually, as if nothing had ever happened between them and they were meeting for the first time? Or were they savvy enough to accept that they had shared something intimate with no regrets, moved on and didn't make a big deal about it? She decided the latter would work. It wasn't as if they had been total strangers.

She glanced at her watch. One-thirty was less than five hours away. Although Atlanta was a big town, she and Storm were bound to run into each other sooner or later, but part of her had been hoping it was later. She had expected to see him at the charity benefit, but had figured she would be prepared to see him by then. It was more than a week since they had been together, nine days, if you were counting, and unfortunately, she was.

She closed her eyes and exhaled a deep breath. If she saw him, she would play it cool, take the savvy approach and hope and pray that it worked.

"Is there a reason why you're hanging around here?"

Storm shrugged and shot his twin a beguiling smile. "I like this place."

The expression he read on Chase's face said he knew better, since he only dropped by to eat and rarely hung around to socialize. He usually was too busy pursuing women to visit with his brother for very long. His answering machine had maxed out while he'd been out of town and his phone hadn't stopped ringing since he'd been back. But for some reason, he wasn't interested in returning any of those women's calls.

"Well, if you don't have anything better to do with your time, how about waiting tables?" Chase said, interrupting his thoughts. "One of my waitresses called in sick and we're shorthanded."

Storm glanced at his watch while shaking his head. "Sorry. I like you, Chase, but not that much." He turned and glanced at the entrance to his brother's restaurant and wondered if perhaps Tara and Jayla had changed their minds and decided to go someplace else since it was past lunchtime. No sooner had that possibility crossed his mind, than the door swung open and the two women entered.

His breath caught at the sight of Jayla. Because he was sitting at the far end of the counter, he knew she wouldn't be able to see him but he could definitely see her. She was dressed differently than she'd been in New Orleans. Today, Jayla was Miss Professional in her chic navy blue power suit. She still looked stunning and as sexy as sin. Storm could feel his libido going bonkers. He swung around to Chase. "Hey, I've changed my mind. I will help you out after all."

Chase raised a suspicious brow. "Why the change of heart?"

"Because if a man can't depend on his twin brother in a time of need, then who can he depend on?" Storm asked, giving Chase a boyish grin.

Chase cast a speculative glance over Storm's shoulder and said dryly, "I hope the person you're all fired up at seeing is the woman with Tara and *not* Tara. I would hate for Thorn to kill you."

Storm chuckled. "Relax. I got over Tara a long time ago. I just like getting a rise out of Thorn."

He leaned over the counter and snagged a pencil from Chase's shirt pocket and tucked it behind his ear. He then picked up a pad off the counter. "Who's working the table where they're sitting?"

"Pam."

Storm smiled. "Then tell Pam to take a break or, better yet, tell her to find another table to work. I got that one covered." Before Chase could say anything, Storm stood and headed over to where Tara and Jayla were sitting.

"We made perfect timing," Tara said smiling. "Had we arrived any earlier this place would have been packed." The menus were in a rack on the table and she passed one to Jayla.

Jayla nodded as she opened the menu. She was tempted to glance around but decided not to. Chances were if Storm had been there earlier as a part of the lunch crowd he would have already left.

After they had looked over the menus for a few moments, Tara glanced up, smiled and asked, "So what are you going to get?"

Tara's question recaptured her attention and she couldn't help but return the other woman's smile. Already she'd decided that she liked Tara Westmoreland. They had spoken several times on the phone, but this was the first time they had actually met in person. Jayla thought the woman was simply gorgeous and could quickly see how she had captured the heart of motorcycle tycoon, Thorn Westmoreland.

"Umm," Jayla said smiling as if in deep thought as

she glanced back down at the menu and licked her lips. "Everything looks delicious, but I think I'll get—"

"Good afternoon, ladies, what can I get you?"

Jayla's head snapped up and she blinked upon seeing Storm standing beside their table. "Storm!" Without thinking, she said his name as intense heat settled deep in her stomach.

Storm's mouth curved into a devilish grin, and that grin reminded her of sensations he could easily elicit, tempting her into partaking in any number of passionate indulgences. "I'm not on the menu, Jayla, but if I'm what you want, I can definitely make an exception."

Chapter 7

"I take it the two of you know each other," Tara said curiously as a smile touched her lips. She glanced from Storm to Jayla.

Jayla cleared her throat, wondering how much she should say. Before she could decide on how to respond, Storm spoke up.

"Jayla's father was my first fire captain and was like a second father to me," he said, giving them his killer-watt smile. "So, yes, we know each other."

Jayla swallowed deeply, grateful for Storm's timely and acceptable explanation.

"It's good seeing you again, Jayla."

She smiled. "It's good seeing you, too," she said, meaning every word, although she wished that she didn't.

"And you look good, by the way."

Her smile widened. "Thanks." He looked rather good,

too, she thought. He was dressed in a pair of khaki trousers and a polo shirt. And he smelled good. His cologne could always jump-start her senses. It was a good thing she was already sitting down because she could actually feel her knees weaken. Everything about Storm was a total turn-on—the rippling muscles beneath his shirt, his extraordinary butt, long legs, his too-hot grin and eyes so dark they reminded you of chocolate chips…. Had she forgotten that she had a weakness for chocolate chips just as bad as her weakness for strawberry cheesecake?

She glanced over at Tara and saw that she was still watching them and Jayla decided it wouldn't be a bad idea to go ahead and place her order. She cleared her throat. "I'll have today's special with a glass of iced tea."

"All right." Storm scribbled down Jayla's order, not knowing and not really caring what today's special was. The only thing on his mind was that he was getting the chance to see her again.

He then turned his attention to Tara and smiled. "And what will you have, Mrs. Westmoreland?"

Tara lifted a brow. "An explanation as to why you're waiting on tables."

Storm chuckled. He was busted. Leave it to Tara to ask questions. She'd been hanging around his brother Thorn too long. "Chase was shorthanded so I thought I'd pitch in and help him out."

Tara nodded, but the look she gave let him indicated that she knew there was more to the story than that. He wondered if parts of their conversation last night were coming back to her. "That was kind of you, Storm, and I'll have today's special, as well, with a glass of lemonade."

Storm wrote down her order, then said, "I'll go ahead and bring your drinks." He winked at them and then walked off.

Jayla watched him walk away. When she returned her attention back to Tara she knew the woman had been watching her watch Storm. "Small world, isn't it?" she asked trying to pull herself together before she actually started drooling.

Tara smiled. "Yes, it is a small world," she agreed as she studied Jayla. Storm had been blatantly flirting with the woman, which was nothing surprising. Tara had seen Storm in action many times before. But something was different with the way he had flirted with Jayla; however, at the moment she couldn't put a finger on just what that difference was.

"I'm looking forward to the charity benefit," Jayla was saying, rousing Tara from her musings and reminding her of the reason for their meeting.

"So am I, and the committee appreciates Sala Industries agreeing to be our food and beverage sponsor. Kids' World will benefit greatly from their contribution. The money raised from the calendar will be more than enough to make the children's dreams come true."

Jayla smiled in agreement. "Doesn't it bother you that your husband is Mr. July on that calendar?"

Tara laughed as she remembered how she'd maneuvered Thorn into posing for the calendar. Actually, they had come to an agreement only after Thorn had made her an offer she couldn't refuse. "No, I'm not bothered at all. It will be nice knowing other women will find my husband as sexy as I do."

Jayla nodded. She had seen Thorn Westmoreland before in person and the man was definitely sexy. But she didn't think anyone was sexier than Storm. She couldn't help but glance to where he had gone. He was behind the counter preparing their drinks and, as if he knew she was looking at him, he lifted his head, met her gaze and smiled.

It was a smile that sent shivers all the way through her body. It was also a smile that seemed to say, *I remember everything about those days in New Orleans*. She couldn't help returning his smile as she also remembered everything about their time together.

When she turned her attention back to Tara, Jayla realized that Tara had noticed the silent exchange between her and Storm. "Umm…I, well—" she started to say, feeling somewhat embarrassed that Tara had caught her ogling Storm.

Tara reached across the table and touched her hand. "No need to explain, Jayla. I'm married to a Westmoreland so I understand."

Jayla pulled in a deep breath, wondering how could Tara possibly understand when she didn't understand her feelings for Storm. "It's nothing but simple chemistry," she decided to say to explain.

Tara smiled, thinking of her reaction to Thorn Westmoreland the first time she had seen him. "Happens to the best of us, trust me."

Jayla laughed, suddenly feeling relaxed and thinking that, yes, she really did like Tara Westmoreland.

Chase shook his head as he stared at his brother. "Are you going to stand there all day and stare at that woman with Tara?"

Storm met Chase's gaze and grinned. "I like watching her eat. I love the way her mouth moves."

Chase's gaze followed Storm's and he didn't see anything fascinating about the way she was eating, although he would be the first to admit that she was good-looking. He turned his attention back to Storm. "Who is she?"

"Adam's daughter."

Chase snapped his gaze back to the table where Tara and the woman were sitting. "Are you saying that's Adam Cole's girl, all grown up?"

"Yes."

"Wow. I haven't seen her since she was in high school. He would bring her in here every once in a while for dinner." He let out a low whistle. "Boy, has she changed. She was a cute kid, but now she is definitely a looker. I'd say she is a woman who looks ripe for loving."

Storm turned and glared at his brother as he leaned against the counter and shoved his hands deep into his pants pockets. "I'm going to ignore the fact that you said that."

Chase smiled. "Hey, man, I didn't know things were *that* way with her," he offered by way of apology.

Storm's glare deepened. "And what do you perceive as *that* way?"

Chase's smile widened. Storm was so used to getting a rise out of people that he couldn't recognize when someone was trying to get a rise out of him. "You're interested in her. *That's* obvious."

Storm shrugged. "Of course I'm interested in her. Adam was someone I cared a lot about. He was like a second father to me. He was—"

"We're not talking about Adam, Storm. We're talking about his daughter. Come on and admit it. You're interested in her as a woman and not as Adam's daughter."

Storm frowned. "I'm not going to admit anything."

Chase chuckled. "Then why did you get jealous a few minutes ago?"

Storm blinked, then looked at his twin as if he were stone crazy, definitely had gone off the deep end. "Jealous?" he repeated, wondering how Chase could think such a thing. "The word *jealous* is not in my vocabulary."

Chase studied his brother's face and knew he had pushed him enough for one day, but couldn't resist taking one final dig. "Then it must have been added rather recently. Not only is it now in your vocabulary, you should spell the word with a capital *J*. And I thought the reason you were acting strange had to do with work. The way I see it, that woman sitting over there definitely has her hook in and is reeling you in."

Storm drew in a deep breath, squared his shoulders. The eyes that stared at his twin were hard, ice cold. "You're going to regret the day you said that."

Chase laughed. "And I have a feeling that you're going to regret the day you didn't figure it out for yourself."

Jayla slipped off her pumps as soon as she walked into the house and closed the door behind her. She let out a deep breath. Lunch with Tara Westmoreland had gone well and they had finalized a lot of items for the charity benefit. But what stood out in her mind more than anything was seeing Storm again.

More than once she had glanced his way. The heat in his eyes had ignited a slow, sensual burn within her. Across the distance of the room, he had silently yet expertly aroused her, almost making concentration on her discussion with Tara impossible.

And when he had placed their meals on the table, her eyes had been drawn to his hands and it didn't take much to remember how skilled his fingers were, and how those fingers had known just the right places on her body to touch to drive her crazy. It was only when he had left the restaurant, shortly after serving their lunch, that her mind had become functional. Only then had she been able to zero in on the business that she and Tara had needed to accomplish.

On her drive back to the office, she had to remind herself several times that there was nothing between her and Storm and that any future involvement with him was out of the question. They each had a different agenda. To consider a possible relationship between them would only complicate things. What they had shared in New Orleans, just great sex, was over.

Placing her purse on the counter that separated the kitchen from her dining room, she started sorting through the mail she had retrieved from her mailbox and smiled when she saw a letter from the fertility clinic.

Tearing it open, she quickly scanned the contents and her smile widened. It was a letter reminding her of the physical that was scheduled for the next week and information about the insemination procedure.

Placing the letter in the drawer, she laughed, feeling elated, happy beyond words. She anxiously awaited that day—after the procedure was done—when a doctor would confirm she was pregnant. Although Lisa didn't totally agree with what she planned to do, at least her friend would be there to support her. And, of course, Lisa had agreed to be her child's godmother.

In her heart, Jayla believed things would work out. She had a good friend who would stand by her and she had a good job. And as she had told Lisa, if the artificial insemination didn't work the first time around, she would try a second and, if need be, a third time. She would repeat the procedure as many times as it took to get pregnant whatever the cost. Thanks to the trust fund her father had left for her, as well as the insurance funds that had been left after all the burial expenses had been taken care of, she could afford making her dream of having a baby come true.

She decided to take a shower and relax before fixing dinner. Later, she would find a comfortable spot on her sofa to sit and prop her feet up on her coffee table and enjoy a good book. She tried shaking off the lonely feeling that she suddenly felt. Lisa had a date with her boyfriend Andrew tonight, which meant she wasn't available for a chat.

She tried not to recall that this time nearly a week and a half ago, she had been in New Orleans with Storm. Nor did she want to think about how much she had enjoyed his company. Of course, the time they had spent in bed had been great, but there had been more than that. She had discovered a fun side to Storm. Before New Orleans, she'd always assumed that he was a really serious sort of guy.

She had enjoyed laughing with him, talking to him, dancing with him, sharing food with him and going sightseeing with him. He had been full of surprises in more ways than one. She couldn't help but compare him to the last guy she had dated, Erik Turner. Erik had turned out to be an A-number-one bore and had expected they'd go straight to her bedroom when he'd brought her home from their first date. He had actually gotten pissed off when she'd turned him down.

Frowning, she headed for her bedroom as she remembered how angry she had gotten, too, that night. Angry
for having such high expectations that most men would
treat a woman like a lady, decently respectable and not
assume anything—especially on the first date. Erik had
been included in a long line of disappointments for her,
but he had definitely been the last straw and had been
an eye-opener. That night Jayla realized that she didn't
want to be one of those women who were in such a
frenzy to be involved in a relationship that they failed
to look at the signs that said, "This may not be the best
person for me."

Another pitfall she had avoided, which was the main
reason she had remained a virgin for so long, was the
mistake some women made of equating sex with love.
She'd learned from listening to the women she worked
with, that some women still believed that if a man slept
with her, it meant he loved her. She definitely hadn't
assumed such a thing with her and Storm. It had been
her hormones and not her heart that had been raging out
of control. Storm didn't love her and she didn't love him.
She hadn't expected anything from him and he hadn't
expected anything from her. They had communicated
well both in and out of bed, and the one thing they
understood and agreed upon was that their affair would
be one that led nowhere.

Sighing, she began removing her clothes for her
shower. But as much as she didn't want to think about
it, she couldn't get the memory of Storm and the way
he had looked at her today out of her mind.

Drawing in a deep breath, Storm raised his hand to
knock, then pulled back as he asked himself, for the

umpteenth time, why he was standing in front of Jayla's front door. And no matter how many times he asked the question, the answer always came up the same.

He still wanted her.

Seeing her today had done more harm than good and what Chase had said hadn't helped matters. The notion that Jayla had hooked him was preposterous. Okay, he would admit she was still in his system. He had discovered that a man didn't have sex with a woman at the magnitude that he'd had with Jayla and not have some lingering effects. Lingering effects he could handle; the notion of some woman reeling him in, he could not.

Tonight, and only tonight, he would break his rule of not performing repeats after an affair ended. But he had to make sure that the only thing that was pulling him back to her was the incredible sex they'd shared. Physical he could handle, but anything that bordered on emotional he could not.

Taking another deep breath, he finally raised his hand and knocked on the door. As he waited for her to answer it, he hoped to God that he wasn't making a huge mistake.

He was about to knock again when he heard the sound of her voice on the other side. "Who is it?"

"It's me, Jayla. Storm."

She slowly opened the door and the anticipation of the removal of the solid piece of wood that stood between them sent a shiver of desire up his spine and down to his midsection. When she opened the door enough for him to see her, the sight of her nearly knocked him to his knees like a gale-force wind. It was obvious that she had just gotten out of the shower. Her hair was loose,

flowing around her shoulders, and there were certain
parts of her, not covered by her short bathrobe, that were
still wet. He itched to take the robe off her to see what,
if anything, she was wearing underneath it.

"Storm, what are you doing here?"

Her voice, low in pitch yet high in sensuality, rapidly
joined forces with desire that had already taken over his
body. He was almost afraid to stand there and look at
her. Too much longer and he might be driven to topple
her to the floor and make love to her then and there.

"Storm?"

Claiming that he just happened to be in the neighbor-
hood would sound pretty lame when she lived in North
Atlanta and he resided in the southern part of town.
Believing that honesty was the best policy, he decided
to tell her the truth as his gaze locked on hers. "Seeing
you today made me realize something," he murmured
softly as he leaned in her doorway.

He watched her throat move when she swallowed.
"What?"

"That I didn't get enough of you in New Orleans. I
want you again."

He heard her inhale sharply and the sound triggered
the memory of how her voice would catch just seconds
before she came. His mind was remembering and his
body was, too. He was tempted to pull her close and let
her feel just how hard she was making him. "May I come
in?" he decided to ask when she didn't say anything.

"Storm…"

"I know I shouldn't have come and I'm just as
confused about showing up here as you are," he quickly
said. "But seeing you today *really* did do something to
me, Jayla, and it's something that's never happened to me

before. It was as if my body went on overload and you're the only person who can shut it down. Since returning from New Orleans, I've been constantly reminded of the best sex I've ever had, and tonight I couldn't handle things any longer."

He sighed deeply. There. He'd said it. He'd been honest and upfront with her, although it had nearly killed him to admit such a thing. Even to his ears his predicament sounded almost like an addiction. His blood was pumped up a notch. Every muscle in his body ached at the thought of making love to her again and a part of him knew the look in his eyes was just shy of pleading. He might even go so far as to follow the Temptations' lead and sing out loud, "Ain't Too Proud To Beg."

It was all rather pathetic, but at the moment there wasn't a damn thing he could do about it. Jayla Cole was under his skin…at least temporarily. Just one more time with her should obliterate this madness. At least, that's what he hoped.

He watched her as she tried to make up her mind about him, but patience had never been one of his strong points and he couldn't help asking, "So are you going to let me in?"

Silence filled the air.

Moments later, Jayla sighed deeply. Her mind was in battle over what she *should* do versus what she *wanted* to do. She knew what she should do was send Storm packing after reminding him of their agreement. But what she really wanted to do was give him what she knew they both desired.

Just one more time, she decided. What could possibly be wrong in giving in to an indulgence just one more time? However, more than just once would be a complication she didn't need. Her heart hammered hard in her chest. She knew once he stepped inside and closed the door behind him, that would be the end of it...or the beginning. But as her body began to slowly tremble, her control began slipping. She knew that tonight she needed him just as much as he seemed to need her. He was right. This *was* madness.

"Yes," she finally said, taking a step back. "You can come in."

He entered and closed the door behind him. Locked it. The click sounded rather loud in the now awkward silence between them. That small sound was enough to push her heart into overdrive, making it beat that much faster.

"Thirsty?" she asked, deciding she should at least offer him a drink.

"Yes, very."

She turned toward the kitchen and was surprised when he reached out, gently grabbed her, pulled her close to him and wrapped his arms around her. "This is what I'm thirsty for, Jayla. The taste of you."

When her lips opened on a breathless sigh, his tongue swept into her mouth as if he needed to taste her as much as he needed to breathe. His lips were hot and demanding, and his tongue was making love to her mouth with an intensity that overwhelmed her. Helpless to do anything else, she looped her arms around his neck and held on while the heat of him consumed her, breaching any barrier and snatching away any resistance she might have had.

Too late. He was inside and intended to fill her to capacity in more ways than one.

She pushed good judgment, initial misgivings and any lingering doubts aside. She would deal with them later. Right now, being in Storm's arms this way was most important and demanded her full concentration. And everything about him—his scent, his strength, his very sensuality—permeated her skin, seeped into her blood and sent her senses spinning.

When he tore his mouth away from hers, she drew in a long audible sigh. She looked up at him and the air surrounding them seemed to crackle with ardent awareness. He reached out and traced a slow path down the center of her neck, then slowly pushed aside her robe to reveal what was underneath.

Nothing.

She heard his sharp intake of breath and he pushed the robe off her shoulders to the floor. "A few moments ago, I was thirsty for your mouth, but now I'm starving for this," he said reaching out and stroking her between the legs. "Once I get you in bed, I plan to make love to you all night."

His voice was low, uneven and so sexy that it sent shock waves all through her body. She met his gaze, saw the deep darkening of his eyes and any grip she had on reality slipped, joining her robe on the floor.

"That's a promise I intend to hold you to, Storm Westmoreland," she said on a breathless sigh, just seconds before he swept her into his arms.

Chapter 8

"Which way to your bedroom?"

"Straight ahead and to your right."

Storm didn't waste any time taking her there and immediately placed her naked body in the middle of the bed. He took a step back to look at her. For a moment, he couldn't move, too overwhelmed by her beauty to do anything but to take it all in…and breathe. He ached to make love to her, and sink his body into the wet warmth of hers.

Love her.

Air suddenly left his lungs in a whoosh and he summoned all the strength he could not to fall flat on his face. The thought that he wanted to love her had been unintentional, absolutely ridiculous, outlandish and totally absurd. He only did non-demanding relationships and short-term affairs. He wasn't into strings, especially the attached kind. He suddenly felt a tightening in his chest at the same time that he felt a bizarre quickening around his heart.

Hell! Something was wrong with him. Then, on second thought, maybe nothing was wrong with him. He was merely imagining things. He was aching so badly to be with Jayla again that he wasn't thinking straight. That had to be it. When he got home later tonight, on familiar turf, his mind would be clear. And spending a day at the station tomorrow around the guys would definitely screw his head back on straight.

"Are you going to stand there all night, Storm?"

He blinked, attempting to clear his mind and immediately became entranced with the warmness of Jayla's smile and the teasing heat of intimacy in her eyes. He swallowed deeply and tried to get a grip, but all he got was a harder arousal. "Not if I can help it," he said, suddenly needing to connect with her that instant. He needed to touch her, taste her, mate with her.

Right now.

He yanked his T-shirt over his head and then began fumbling with the fastening of his jeans, and became irritated when the zipper wouldn't slide down fast enough because of the size of his erection. Finally, he was able to tug his jeans down his legs and quickly stepped out of them. He reached down and took a condom packet out of the back pocket of the now discarded garment.

After he took the necessary steps, he looked at her and one corner of his mouth quirked up. "Now to keep that promise."

Simply looking at Storm caused Jayla's blood to pump rapidly through her veins. The look in his eyes said that he would hold nothing back. Her pulse quickened as he slid his body onto the bed. He moved with the grace of a leopard, the prowl of a tiger and the intent of a man who wanted a woman. Overhead, the glow from the ceiling light magnified the broad expanse of his chest. He was perfectly built, his flesh a chocolate brown and every muscle well defined.

When he joined her on the bed she couldn't stop herself from reaching out to touch him. Her fingers trembled as she ran them through the dark, tight curls on his chest, and she smiled when she heard his breathing hitch. Hers did likewise when she felt the hardness of him press against her thigh. Her gaze was drawn to his nipples. They were hard, erect, and she wanted to know the texture of them under her tongue. He had tasted her breasts many times, but she'd never tasted his.

Leaning forward, her mouth opened over a stiff bud and her tongue began sliding around it, tasting it, absorbing it, sucking it. But for her, that wasn't enough. Reaching down she took hold of his hard heated flesh and her thumb and forefinger began caressing the hot tip. This was the first time she had ever tried to bring a man pleasure, to drive him insanely wild with desire with her hands. And from the sounds Storm was making, it seemed she was doing a good job.

When she heard him groan her name, the sound forced from deep within his throat, she lifted her head, but continued to let her hand clutch him, caress him, stroke him. "Umm?" she responded as she moved her mouth upward to take a tiny bite of his neck, branding him.

"You've pushed me too far, Jayla," Storm growled, as the need within him exploded. With one quick flick of his wrist, he tumbled her backward, ignoring her squeal of surprise. But she didn't resist and instead of moving from him, she moved to him, reaching up and looping her arms around his neck as he placed his body over hers, pressing his erection against the heat of her feminine core.

"Gotta get inside," he whispered brokenly as his hand clutched her waist, his thighs held hers in place. Taking her arms from around his neck, he captured her wrists and placed them above her head. He looked down at her, met her gaze at the same time he pushed himself inside of her.

He gasped. The pleasure of being inside of her was almost too much. He tipped his head back and roared an animalistic sound that mirrored the raging need within him. Then he began moving, in and out, straining his muscles, flexing his pelvis, rolling his hips while holding her in a firm grip, rocking her world, just mere seconds away from tumbling his own.

The bed started to shake and the windows seemed to rattle, but the only storm that was raging out of control was him, pelting down torrents of pleasure instead of sheets of rain. He didn't flinch when he felt her fingernails dig deeper into his flesh, but he did groan when he felt her inner muscles squeeze him, clench him, milk him. The woman was becoming a pro at knowing just what it took to splinter his mind and make him explode. No sooner had he thought the word, he felt her body do just that.

"Storm!"

And while she toppled over into oblivion, he continued to move in and out, claiming her as his.

His.

The thought of her belonging to him, and only to him,

pushed him over the edge in a way he had never been pushed before. He thrust deep into her body, burying himself to the hilt, as his own release claimed him, ripped into him—not once, not twice, not even three times. The ongoing sensations that were taking over his body were more than he could stand.

"Jayla!"

And she was right there with him, lifting her hips off the bed, opening wider for him, moving with him, as they drove each other higher and higher on waves of excruciating pleasure.

The first light of dawn began slipping into the windows, fanning across the two naked bodies in bed. Jayla slowly awoke and took a long, deep breath of Storm and the lingering scent of their lovemaking.

It was there, in the air, the scent of her, of them—raw, primitive—the aftermath of her crying out in ecstasy, clutching his shoulders, pushing up her hips while he drove relentlessly into her, going as far as he could go, then tumbling them both over the edge as their releases came simultaneously.

She closed her eyes as panic seized her. What on earth had she done? All she had to do was open her eyes and glance over at Storm who was lying on his side facing her, still sleeping with a contented look on his face, to know what she had done. What she needed to really ask herself was how had it happened and why.

Storm had a reputation of not being a man who looked up a woman for a second helping. Once an affair ended, it was over. If that was the case, then why had he dropped by? What was there about her that had made him come back for more?

Jayla's features slipped into a frown. Although most women would have been ecstatic that Storm had deemed them special enough to grace their bed a second time, to her he was a distraction. And a distraction was the last thing she needed now, especially with her upcoming appointment at the fertility clinic. If he were to find out about her plans, like Lisa he would probably try and talk her out of it. But unlike Lisa, he wouldn't understand her decision, or support her anyway, even if he disagreed with her.

She took a quick glance at him and wondered why it mattered to her that he might not support what she planned to do. Jayla was pretty sure Storm would frown upon the idea of her having a baby by artificial insemination. Like her father, Storm was a traditionalist. He believed in doing things the old-fashioned way. She had to admit that at least in the bedroom she found Storm's old-fashioned, always-remain-a-gentleman ways endearing. Being a gentleman didn't mean he wouldn't engage in some off-the-charts, blow-your-mind hot sex like they had definitely shared last night. It simply meant that he would never try anything that made her feel uncomfortable. Nor would he ever assume anything. The only reason he was still in her bed at the crack of dawn was because he had asked if it was okay for him to stay the night. He hadn't just assumed that it was. If only she could shake his belief that a woman could not manage both a career and motherhood. How primitive was it for someone to think that way in this day and time?

She shook her head as she quietly slipped out of bed thinking Storm had definitely earned his rest. The man had energy that she wished she could bottle. No sooner had they completed one climax, he was going down for another, and somehow he always managed to take her with him. It was as if his orgasms—and the man had plenty—always triggered hers. Multiple orgasms were something she'd read about and at the time, the thought of it happening to anyone seemed too far-fetched to consider. But she was living witness that it was possible. She smiled thinking Storm had spoiled her. She wouldn't know how to act if another man ever made love to her.

Her smile slowly died at the thought of making love to another man. Would she spend the rest of her life comparing every future lover to The Perfect Storm? She shook her head as she made her way into the bathroom for a shower. She was getting in deeper by the minute.

Storm woke slowly to the sound of running water and the scent of jasmine. He smiled, closing his eyes again as visions of what he and Jayla had done played through his mind like a finely tuned piano.

He reopened his eyes, thinking he was just as confused now as he'd been the night before. He wasn't sure why he was here in Jayla's bed instead of his own bed. Then he remembered. He'd had to be with her last night. He had been willing to say or do anything to get back into her bed. Even if it had meant begging.

He glanced at the clock on her nightstand. It was early, but time for him to go. He had to report to the station today to pull a twenty-four-hour shift. He thoroughly enjoyed his new position of fire captain. To move from the ranks of lieutenant had meant many nights and weekends of studying for the fire department's promotional exam. During that time, he had given up a lot of things, including women. And even then, the thought of going without one hadn't bothered him. There hadn't been one single woman that he could name that he had missed making love to during all that time.

He closed his eyes again, not ready to move, not sure that he could if he wanted to. But the thought of Jayla, naked, wet and standing beneath a shower of water suddenly made him go hard, as if his body could do anything else around her.

He sighed deeply and suddenly the features of that old woman, the one who had read his palm in New Orleans, flitted across his mind at the same time the words she had spoken rang through his ears: *You are about to make unexpected changes in your life and although you yearn for peace, turbulence is in your future. Keep your sights high, be patient and let destiny take its course.*

He opened his eyes, quickly sat up and glanced around the room. It was as if the old woman's voice were right there. He shook his head, thinking he was definitely losing it.

He turned when he heard the sound of a door opening and glanced over his shoulder to see Jayla walk out of the bathroom with a towel wrapped tightly around her. She gave him a soft smile that immediately made him go hard…as if he wasn't already. And no matter how much he thought he was crazy this morning, he didn't have one single regret about last night.

"You should have woken me up and I would have joined you in the shower," he said, standing and crossing the room to her.

He watched as her gaze took in his nakedness, as it left his face to slowly roam down his chest, down past his stomach to settle…yeah, right there. He felt his erection get larger, become harder and saw her eyes grow dark with desire and her cheeks become flushed.

"You like being in your natural state, don't you?" she asked, lifting her gaze back to his.

He smiled. "Yes, and I like you being in your natural state, too."

She shook her head and chuckled. "I think we need to talk."

"I'd rather do something else." His smile widened. All she had to do was drop her gaze back to his midsection to know what he had in mind.

She cleared her throat. "Well, unfortunately we both have jobs to go to this morning, right?"

"You would have to remind me of that, wouldn't you?" he asked, pulling her into his arms. "Have dinner with me at Anthony's tomorrow night."

She quickly pulled back. "Dinner?"

He dipped his head and captured an earlobe in his mouth. He'd heard the surprise in her voice. Hell, he was even surprised that he had suggested such a thing. "Yes, dinner. We can talk then, okay?" He knew what she wanted to talk about. She wanted to know why he was not adhering to their agreement. He hoped when he saw her again he would have some answers.

"Storm...I don't think that we—"

He lifted her chin with the tip of his finger so their eyes could meet. "Like you said, we need to talk, Jayla, and we can't do it here or at my place."

She nodded, understanding. At least at Anthony's, there wouldn't be any bedrooms around. "Okay."

Then Storm captured Jayla's mouth in a kiss that he definitely needed. The taste of her was like a drug to which he was addicted. She was a problem that needed a solution, but for now...

Wednesdays had always been referred to as over-the-hump day and it wasn't until today that Jayla actually understood what it meant...at least in terms of her and Storm.

It was almost lunchtime and Jayla was still besieged with constant memories of the night she'd spent with Storm. She glanced around to make sure no one noticed the blush that had to have appeared on her face, even with her dark skin tone.

She was in a room with, of all people, the vice president of the company, as well as the sales and advertising managers for Sala Industries. It was that time of the year when she needed to prepare the annual public relations report that the company distributed to the general public, interest groups and stockholders to make everyone aware of the company's activities and accomplishments the previous year. One of Sala's main goals for the year had been to increase their involvement in community affairs. Being a part of the charity benefit for Kids' World was one of the many projects they had undertaken to do just that.

Jayla had worked for the company since college and up until recently, the job had been the single most important thing in her life outside of her relationship with her father. After his death, she had moved her job up to the number-one spot, which was why she had made a decision to have a baby. She had needed a life outside of work and someone to share that life with her. She smiled, thinking that she had only eight days to go before she went to the fertility clinic for her physical, the first step toward making her dream come true.

She glanced across the conference table and saw Lisa looking at her strangely. She lifted a brow and Lisa surreptitiously lifted one back. Jayla couldn't help but smile. Evidently, Lisa had seen her blush a few times.

As soon as the meeting was over, Lisa pulled her back the moment she was about to walk out the room and whispered, "We need to talk."

Playing dumb she smiled and asked, "What about?"

"Like the fact you sat through most of the meeting like you were zoned out. It's a good thing Mr. McCray didn't notice."

Jayla sobered quickly as she came to her senses. Having erotic flashbacks on her time was one thing, but having them on her employer's time was another. "Sorry."

Lisa laughed. "Hey, girlfriend, don't apologize. I'd trade places with you in a heartbeat. You've been with Storm Westmoreland again haven't you?"

Wondering how Lisa could know such a thing, Jayla asked innocently, "What makes you think that?"

Lisa raised a dark brow. "It's either that or you're reliving some dynamite memories. My guess is that you're reminiscing about the past twenty-four hours."

Jayla sighed as she closed the door so that she and Lisa could have total privacy. She sat back down at the table and Lisa joined her. She met her best friend's curious gaze. "Storm dropped by last night."

Lisa leaned back in her chair and grinned. "That's a first. I heard that once an affair was ended, Storm Westmoreland never looked back. Booty calls are not exactly his style."

Jayla shot her a frown and Lisa held up her hand apologetically. "Sorry. I was just making an observation."

Jayla let out a breath. That was one observation she didn't need. "He wants to take me out tomorrow night. To dinner. At Anthony's."

Lisa smiled. "Real classy place, so what's the problem?"

Jayla returned the smile. Lisa could be so good for her at times. "The problem is what you indicated earlier. Storm is not a man who looks up women from his past. I knew that in New Orleans and he knew that, and it was understood that when we returned to Atlanta we would have no reason to seek the other out."

Lisa nodded. "And he's seeking you out."

"Yes, and I can't let it happen."

Lisa sat up and leaned in closer. "Is it okay for me to ask why?"

Jayla dragged a hand through her hair, and drew in a frustrating breath. "Because it's lousy timing. My life is about to undergo some major changes, Lisa, for Pete's sake. My physical is set for next Friday and soon after that, I plan to get inseminated. The last thing I need is Storm deciding, for whatever reason, that I'm a novelty to him."

"Hey, Jayla, don't sell yourself short. There might be another reason that Storm Westmoreland finds you interesting, other than you being a novelty. The guy might actually like you. I mean really, really *like* you. There's a chance that you've blown him away."

Lisa's comments gave Jayla pause. She thought about that possibility all of two seconds and shook her head. "Impossible. Even if there was a remote chance that was truc, Storm and I could never get serious about each other."

Lisa lifted a brow. "Why?"

Jayla frowned. "He's too much like my father. He would want to keep a tight rein on me. He actually believes a woman should be a stay-at-home mom. I guess he thinks the ideal woman is one he can keep barefoot and pregnant."

Lisa smiled. "Hey, I could do barefoot and pregnant with a man like him," she said, wiggling her eyebrows.

"Well, I can't. I have my life mapped out just the way I want, thank you. I'm having a baby without the complications of a man. The last thing I need is someone dictating how I should live my life and there's no doubt in my mind that Storm would be very domineering."

Lisa's smile widened. "Yeah, but also very sexy."

Jayla raised her gaze to the ceiling. "But I can't think of sexy when all I can see is domineering."

Lisa laughed. "Evidently you could last night if those blushes were any indication. But if you feel that way, you should let him know. It should be simple enough to tell him you aren't interested and to stop coming around."

Jayla nodded. Yes, that should be simple enough and she would tell him tomorrow night at dinner.

Storm walked into Coleman's Florist Shop and glanced at the older woman who was standing behind the counter. Luanne Coleman was considered one of the town's biggest gossips, but he still enjoyed doing business with her. And besides, none of the women he ever ordered flowers for lived in College Park, the suburb of Atlanta where he and the majority of his family resided and where his brother Dare was sheriff.

"Good morning, Ms. Luanne."

She glanced up from looking at the small television screen that was sitting on the counter. Her soaps were on. "Oh, hello, Storm. You want to send the usual?"

He smiled. By the usual, she meant a bouquet of fresh-cut flowers. "No, I want to send something different this time."

He knew that would grab her attention. She stared at him for a long moment, then raised her brow over curious eyes and asked, "Something different?"

"Yes."

She nodded. "All right, what do you have in mind?"

He glanced around. "What do you have that will last a while?"

"I have plenty of live plants and they make beautiful gifts."

Storm nodded. He didn't recall seeing a live plant in Jayla's home and thought one would be perfect, especially in her bedroom for her to look at and remember. "Good. I want you to pick out the biggest and prettiest one, and this is the person I want it delivered to," he said, handing her a slip of paper.

She took it and glanced at the name. She then looked at him and smiled. "How much do you want to spend?"

A huge grin touched his lips. "The cost isn't important. Just add it to my account. And make sure it's delivered this afternoon."

She nodded and smiled as she quickly began writing up his order. "She must be very special."

Storm sighed heavily. There. He had heard someone

else say what he'd been thinking all day, so the only thing he could do was smile and agree. "Yes, she is."

Jayla blinked at the man holding the huge potted plant in front of him. The plant was almost larger than he was. "Are you sure you're at the right address, sir?"

"Yes, I'm positive," the older man said, peeping from behind the bunch of healthy green leaves of a beautiful and lush-looking areca palm. "It's for you."

Jayla nodded as she stepped aside to let the man bring the plant inside, wondering who on earth could have sent it. When the man had placed it down, he turned to leave. "Wait, I need to give you a—"

"The tip's been taken care of," the man said. And then he was gone.

Jayla quickly pulled the card from the plant and read it.

> *Whenever you look at this, think of me.*
> *Storm*

Jayla's heart skipped a beat. No it skipped two, possibly three. She blinked, then sank down on her sofa. Storm had sent her a plant, a beautiful, large, lush green plant and for the first time in a long time, she was at a loss for words.

Chapter 9

"Thanks again for the plant, Storm. It's simply beautiful."

"You're welcome and I'm glad you like it."

"And thanks for bringing me here, tonight. Everything was wonderful."

"You're welcome again."

Then she glanced around Anthony's, the stunning and elegant antebellum mansion that had a reputation of fine service and delicious food. Being here reminded her of New Orleans, and she wondered if perhaps that was the reason Storm had chosen this place.

She glanced back over at Storm and their gazes met. He'd been watching her, something she noticed he'd been doing all evening. He had arrived at her house promptly at seven and since she'd been ready, she had only invited him inside long enough for her to grab her purse and a wrap.

At least, that's what she had assumed.

The moment he had stepped inside her home, he had pulled her into his arms and kissed her, making her realize that although she wished otherwise, there was definitely something going on between them, something that had not ended in New Orleans.

She regarded him with interest and although she knew that she should broach the subject of why they were here, she wasn't ready to do that yet. Tonight was too beautiful to bring up any unpleasantries just yet. "So, how are things going at work?" she asked, after taking another sip of her wine.

In New Orleans, he had told her that he had made the transition from lieutenant to captain rather well, but hadn't gone into much detail. Because her father had been a fire captain for years, she was familiar with all the position entailed. She was well aware that today firefighters needed more training to operate increasingly sophisticated equipment and to deal safely with the greater hazards that were associated with fighting fires in larger, more elaborate structures, as well as wild fires.

In her eyes, all firefighters were heroes, but she knew being a fire captain also required strong leadership qualities. A captain had to possess the ability to establish and maintain discipline and efficiency, as well as direct the activities of the firefighters in his company.

"Work is fine, and how are things at Sala Industries?" he asked rousing her from her musings.

She smiled. "Things are great. In addition to working with Tara on the Kids' World charity benefit, I'm working on another project that involves an environmental agency."

He nodded. "And what about that project you were excited about? How is it going?"

She swallowed, knowing exactly what project he was referring to. She worked her bottom lip between her teeth several times before responding. "I haven't started it yet."

She decided it was time to discuss the reason they were there. They had dodged the subject long enough. She met his eyes and a shiver ran through her when she saw the desire in their dark depths. Wanting to make love with him seemed natural. Too natural. It was a good thing they were in a public place.

Her body continued to stir and an unbearable heat spread through her. Trying to ignore her torment, she considered him for a long moment, then spoke, her voice barely above a whisper. "You said you would explain things tonight, Storm."

I did say that, didn't I? Storm thought as his gaze continued to hold Jayla's. The only problem was that he wasn't any closer to answers today than he had been yesterday. The only thing that he was certain of was that he wanted to continue to see Jayla. He enjoyed being with her, taking her out and having fun with her and wanted to continue to do all those things they had done together in New Orleans. For some reason, she had his number and he was helpless to do anything about it.

"Storm?"

He blinked and realized while he'd been thinking that he had been staring at her like some dimwit. He cleared his throat. "Jayla, is there a possibility for us to start seeing each other?"

It was evident from the look on her face that his question surprised her. "Why?" she asked, regarding him as if the question were totally illogical.

"I like you."

She blinked, then threw him a grin that caught him off guard. "Storm, you like women. I know that much from your reputation."

He didn't like hearing her say that. They weren't talking about other women; they were talking about her. He didn't place her in the same category with those other women he'd dated before. To him, none of them could be compared to Jayla.

He watched as she leaned over the table and, with a curious arch of her brow, whispered, "It's the virginity thing, isn't it?"

Storm nearly stopped breathing. He blinked, not understanding just what she was asking him. Seconds later, it dawned on him just what she'd insinuated and he frowned. "Why would you think something like that?"

She straightened back in her chair and shrugged. "What else could it be? I was your first virgin. You said so yourself. So I'm a novelty to you." She picked up her wine glass to take another sip, smiled, then said, "Trust me, you'll get over it."

His frown deepened. "Tell me something," he said, leaning back in his chair. "When did you figure that out?"

Her smile widened. "What? That I'm a novelty to you or that you'll get over it?"

"That you're a novelty to me."

She licked her lips and Storm felt his gut catch. "The night you showed up at my place. Seeking me out was so unlike how you're known to operate, so I figured there had to be a reason, since any woman can basically please a man in bed. It slowly dawned on me why I was different."

Storm inhaled deeply. He was glad they were sitting at a table in the rear of the restaurant in an area where they were practically alone. He would hate for anyone to overhear their conversation.

He shook his head slowly. Everything she'd said had sounded logical. With one exception. It was so far from the truth that it was pitiful.

He smiled. "First of all, contrary to what you think, Jayla, any woman cannot please a man in bed. When making love to a woman, most men—and women for that matter—experience various degrees of pleasure. On a scale from one to five, with five being the highest, most men will experience at least a three. In some situations, possibly a four, and only if they're extremely lucky, a five."

She lifted a brow. "How did I rate?"

Storm's smile widened. He'd known the curiosity in Jayla would give her the nerve to ask. In fact, he'd hoped that she would. "You rated a ten."

She blinked, then a smile touched the corners of her lips. "A ten?"

He chuckled. "Oh, yes, a ten."

He watched as she thought about it for a second, then she shook her head, perplexed and confused. "But—but how is that possible if a ten isn't on the chart?"

He reached across the table and captured her hand in his. "Because you, Jayla Cole, were off the charts." He watched her smile widen, evidently pleased with herself. Then he added, "And it had nothing to do with you being a virgin, but had everything to do with the fact that you are a very passionate woman."

He tilted his head and said, "It also had a lot to do with the fact that the two of us are good together. We click. When we make love, I feel a connection with you that I've never felt with another woman." What he didn't add was that when he made love to her, he felt as if they were made for each other.

"Wow, that's deep, Storm," she said regarding him seriously.

He sighed as he nodded. "Yeah, it is deep and that's why I'd like for us to continue to see each other."

Jayla inhaled. She would like to continue to see him, too, but she knew that wouldn't be a wise thing to do. In less than a month, she would be getting inseminated and hopefully soon after that, she would become pregnant. The last thing she needed was to get involved with anyone, especially Storm, no matter how tempting the thought was.

"Jayla?"

She met his gaze. "I don't think that would be a good idea, Storm. This new project will take up a lot of my time, and I won't have time for a relationship."

He considered her words. He was still curious as to what kind of project she would be working on. He had asked her about it in New Orleans and she had danced around an answer. The only thing he could come up with was that it involved her job, perhaps a confidential, top-secret assignment. "And there's no way we can work around this project?"

"No."

Her response had been quick. Definite. "When will you start?"

She shrugged. She would have her physical next Friday and then hopefully within three weeks after that, she would go in to have the procedure done. "Possibly within a month."

He met her gaze levelly. "Is there any reason we can't continue to see each other until then?" Slowly, he raised her hand to his lips and kissed it.

Jayla swallowed and knew what she should say. She should tell him yes, there were plenty of reasons why they couldn't continue to see each other for the next month, but for some reason she couldn't get the words out. What Storm had said earlier was true. They were good together. They clicked and they connected. And deep down, a part of her felt she needed this time with him. Afterwards, at least she would have her memories of their time together.

"No, there's no reason," she finally said. "But you will have to promise me something, Storm."

He kissed her hand again before asking. "What?"

"When I say it's over, then it's over. You won't drop by and you won't call."

He shook his head. "I can't agree to that, Jayla. I promised your father that I would periodically check on you and—"

"I'm not talking about that, Storm. I'm taking about you dropping by or calling with the intention of us becoming involved again. You have to promise me when I say it's over, that it will be over. No questions asked."

Storm stared at her for a long moment as emotions tumbled inside of him. They were feelings he didn't understand, but he knew that no matter what, things would never be over between them, project or no project. He would see to it.

"All right," he agreed. "You'll be calling the shots and I'll abide by your wishes."

"Hey, Storm, are you in this game or not?"

Storm glanced over at Thorn and frowned. "Yes, I'm in."

"Well, keep your mind on the game. You're daydreaming again."

Storm's frown deepened. "Yeah, whatever." He glanced across the table at his four brothers who had smirks on their faces. "What's so funny?"

It was the oldest brother, Dare, who answered. "Word's out on the streets that some woman has finally caught the eye of the Storm. I pulled old man Johnson over the other day for running a Stop sign, and he said that he'd heard you were so besotted with some gal that you can't pee straight."

When Storm narrowed his eyes, Dare held up his hand. "Hey, those were Mr. Johnson's words, not mine."

Chase chuckled. "And I've heard that you're sending so many flowers to this woman that the money Coleman Florist is making off you is the reason Mrs. Luanne has that new swing on her front porch."

"And I heard," Stone piped in, as a huge smile touched his lips, "that you've been seen all over Atlanta with her and that she's a beauty. Funny that we haven't met her yet."

Thorn added, "Hey, Storm, what happened to your 'love them and leave them' policy?"

Storm leaned back in his chair thinking that Thorn's

question was a good one, but one he didn't intend to answer.

"I've seen her," Chase said grinning. "She came into the restaurant one day to have lunch with Tara."

"Tara?" Thorn asked, raising a curious brow. "Tara knows her?"

Chase nodded. "Evidently, since they had lunch together that day. However, I don't know if Tara knows that Storm has the hots for her."

"Excuse me, guys," Storm said interrupting his brothers' conversation. "I don't appreciate you discussing my business like I'm not here."

Stone chuckled. "All right, then we'll discuss your business like you're here." He then looked at Chase. "So, is she as good-looking as everyone claims she is?"

Chase grinned. "Yeah. She's Adam's daughter all grown up."

Thorn frowned. "Adam? Adam Cole, Storm's boss who died a few months back?"

"Yep."

Stone glanced over at Storm. A curious glint shone in his eyes. "You're actually seeing Adam Cole's girl?"

Angrily, Storm stood and threw down his cards. "That's it. I'm out of the game."

Dare stared up at his youngest brother. Being the oldest, he had to occasionally bring about peace…and in some situations, order. "Sit back down, Storm, you're getting overheated for nothing. And to be quite honest with you, for all intents and purposes, you've been out of the game since you got here. You haven't been concentrating worth a damn all night."

One of Dare's dark eyebrows lifted. "And what's wrong with us wanting to know about this woman that you're seeing? As your brothers, don't you think we have a right to at least be curious?"

Storm inhaled deeply as he glanced around the table and glared. "I don't appreciate any of you discussing her as if she's like the other women I've dated."

Dare nodded. "If she's not like the other women you've dated, then it's up to you to tell us that. There's nothing wrong with letting us know that you think she's special, instead of trying to keep her a secret," he said in a low voice.

Storm sat back down and glanced around at his brothers. They were staring at him, waiting expectantly. He sighed deeply. "Her name is Jayla Cole and yes, she's Adam's daughter all grown up and we're seeing each other. We're taking things slow, one day at a time, and yes, she's special. Very special."

Stone smiled. "When will we meet her?"

Storm leaned back in his chair. "I'll introduce her to everyone the night of the charity benefit for Kids' World. Her company is a corporate sponsor and she's working closely with Tara to pull things together for that night."

Dare nodded. "And all of us will look forward to meeting her then." He glanced around the table and grinned. "Now let's play cards."

Jayla sat curled up on her sofa and glanced around her living room, thinking the past week had been like a scene from a romance novel. Storm had sent her flowers practically every single day and had wined and dined her to her heart's content.

On Saturday night, they had gone to a laser show on Stone Mountain and then on Sunday evening, he had taken her to a movie. Because he had been at the station all day Monday, she didn't see him again until Tuesday night, when he'd dropped by with Chinese food. They had sat eating at her kitchen table while she had told him about how her day had gone and how things were coming together for this weekend's charity benefit.

They had talked about his day, as well. He had told her that he had been selected to head up the city's fire prevention program for the coming year and that he was excited about that.

She glanced down at the letter she had in her hand, the same letter that had arrived last week from the fertility clinic reminding her of tomorrow's appointment. Seeing it and rereading it had reaffirmed her decision to have the procedure.

She nearly jumped when she heard the phone ring. Thinking that perhaps it was Storm, she placed the letter on the table, then quickly moved across the room to answer it. He had called earlier and said he would be playing cards tonight with his brothers rather late and that he would see her tomorrow. "Yes?" she said, after picking up the phone.

"It's Lisa. How are things going?"

Jayla smiled. Lisa had been out of town most of the week on business. "Everything's going fine. How was your trip?"

"Wonderful. I love Chicago. You know that."

Jayla chuckled. Yes, she did know that. Lisa enjoyed shopping and Chicago was her favorite place to shop.

"So, are you planning to keep your appointment tomorrow?"

Lisa's question immediately silenced Jayla's thoughts. She frowned. "Of course, why wouldn't I?"

"Because from what you told me every time I've called this week, you and Storm have been seeing a lot of each other."

Jayla shrugged. "So? What Storm and I are sharing is short-term. I know that and so does he."

"But it doesn't have to be that way, Jayla. I believe things could last if you gave them a chance."

Jayla rolled her eyes to the ceiling. "Lisa, trust me, they won't. What Storm and I share is physical. I'm enjoying his company and he's enjoying mine. Why does it have to be more than that?"

For a long moment, there was silence. Then Lisa asked softly, "What are you afraid of, Jayla?"

Jayla flinched. "I'm not afraid of anything."

"I think that you are. Storm Westmoreland is everything a woman could want in a man and you are in a good position to be that woman. Why are you willing to turn your back on such a wonderful opportunity?"

Jayla closed her eyes. She could never be the kind of woman Storm wanted. Besides, he wasn't what she wanted, either. At the moment, no man was. She wanted a baby and not a complicated relationship. She'd long ago given up on finding Mr. Right. The "married with children" routine was a fairy tale that might never come true for her. Her biological clock was ticking and she had made the decision to start a family sooner rather than later.

She turned when she heard a knock at the door. "Look Lisa, there's someone at the door. I'll talk with you later. Bye."

After hanging up the phone, she glanced at the clock on the wall, then crossed the living room to the door. It was late, after midnight. The only reason she was still up was because she had taken the morning off for her physical at the fertility clinic. Since her appointment wasn't until nine, that meant she would get to sleep late.

She knew before she got within a foot of the door that her late-night visitor was Storm. That would explain the reason her heart was beating so fast and her senses were getting heated. She tried forcing her conversation with Lisa out of her mind. Her best friend was wrong and she wasn't afraid of anything, especially a serious relationship with Storm. She merely chose not to have one.

"Who is it?"

"Storm."

She quickly opened the door and he stood there, staring at her. His eyes were dark, intense, and she immediately recognized the look in them. Her lips curved into a smile. "Hi."

He returned her smile and the heat infiltrating her senses kicked up another notch. "Hi, yourself. The card game ended and I wasn't ready to go home."

"Oh?"

"I had to see you, Jayla."

A teasing glint shone in Jayla's eyes. "Okay, you see me. So now what?"

He slowly took a couple of steps forward, and she took a couple of steps back. When he was completely inside the house, he closed the door behind him and locked it. He walked the few feet over to her, cupped her shoulders in his hands and pulled her to him, her mouth just inches from his. "Now this," he breathed against her lips.

Then kissed her.

As soon as their mouths touched, Storm felt something hot rush through his bloodstream. The scent of Jayla, as well as the taste of her, was getting to him and the only thing he could think of doing was devouring her, making love to her. Suddenly, some emotion that he'd never felt before flared within him, almost bringing him to his knees, and he finally acknowledged it for what it was.

Love. He loved her.

Storm drew back and stared at her for a quick second before his mouth came back down on hers again. His hands were everywhere as he began removing her clothes, and broke off the kiss just long enough to remove his own. Then he swept her into his arms and carried her into the bedroom.

What should have been a no-brainer had been hard as hell for a staunch bachelor like him to figure out. The reason he had wanted a relationship with Jayla had nothing to do with them being great together in bed, but everything to do with emotions he hadn't been able to recognize until tonight.

He was in love with Jayla Cole. She had caught more than the eye of the Storm. She had captured his heart.

Chapter 10

Anchoring himself above Jayla on his elbows, Storm looked down at her and smiled. Dang, she always looked beautiful after experiencing an orgasm. What more could a man ask for than to be right there to experience each one with her.

He sighed deeply. Now that he knew he loved her, he had to figure out a way to get her to fall in love with him as well. First, he would have to gain her complete trust, and then he had to make sure she clearly understood that he was her Mr. Right and wanted a long-term relationship with her, one that ended in marriage. A smile curved his lips. Yeah, that's what he wanted, Jayla as his wife.

"Why are you smiling?"

He met her gaze. Her eyelids were heavy and her cheeks had a sated flush. Leaning down, he brushed a kiss across her lips. "After what we've just shared, how can you ask me that?"

As usual, everything had been perfect. The way their bodies had come together while a trail of fire had blazed between them. It was a fire he hadn't wanted to put out, but instead had done everything within his power to ignite even further, to make it burn out of control.

And it had.

By the time he had entered, she had been delirious with desire, begging breathlessly for him to make love to her; she'd been a she-cat, clawing his back and nipping his shoulders. And when they had finally come together, she had cried out his name and he had continued to move inside of her, taking them to heights of profound pleasure.

He loved her, he thought in wonder, as he leaned down and murmured her name against her cheek. "Mind if I stay the night?"

He felt her smile against his lips. "Umm, I would be highly disappointed if you didn't," she said softly.

He chuckled. "In that case, I'll stay." He pressed his mouth to hers and kissed her, needing the taste of her again. Moments later, he slowly pulled back and flicked his gaze over her features. Heat immediately surged through his groin. If he didn't get out bed, he would be making love to her all over again, and she needed her rest.

"I'll turn off the lights," he whispered.

"All right, but hurry back."

He grinned as he eased out of bed and slipped into his jeans. And just think he'd assumed that she needed her rest. He glanced at the huge plant that sat in the corner. It was just where he'd wanted it, in her bedroom so she could think of him whenever she saw it.

As he walked out of the bedroom, the image of Jayla's sexy smile when she'd told him to hurry back filled his mind and made him want to do just as she'd requested. When he got to the living room, he leaned down to turn off the lamp near the sofa and his gaze caught sight of a letter lying on the coffee table. It was a letter from a fertility clinic.

Without thinking that he didn't have any right to do so, he picked up the letter and read it. A few seconds later, he sank down on her sofa, not believing what he had just read. He felt stunned. Confused. Jayla had sought out the services of a fertility clinic to get artificially inseminated with some stranger's sperm? Why?

He reread the letter, thinking there must be a mistake but again the contents were the same. She was scheduled to have a physical tomorrow—which actually was today—and then, when it was determined her body would be most fertile, she would go in to have the procedure done.

"You were supposed to hurry back."

Storm stood when Jayla walked out of the bedroom. When she saw the letter in his hand, she quickly crossed the room and snatched it from him. "You had no right to read that, Storm."

He just stared at her as every muscle in his body vibrated. Confusion gave way to anger. "Then how about you telling me what this is all about."

She glared at him. "It's private and personal and doesn't concern you."

"Doesn't concern me? Like hell, it doesn't. If it concerns you, then it concerns me. Are you actually considering having your body inseminated with some man's sperm?"

Jayla tipped her head back; her anger clashed with his. He'd made it sound as if what she planned to do was something filthy and degrading. "It's not what I'm considering doing, it's what I will be doing. I made the decision months ago."

Taken back by Jayla's statement, he wiped a hand down his face as if doing so would erase his anger. When he looked over at her, she was standing with her hands on her hips, glaring at him. A thought suddenly popped into his head. "Wait a minute. Is this the project you've been so excited about lately?"

"Yes."

He shook his head, not believing the conversation they were having. "I understand the need for that procedure in certain situations, but not with you. Why would you even consider doing such a thing, Jayla?"

Her eyes were consumed with fire. "Because I want a baby, that's why! I want a baby more than anything."

Storm was shocked by that revelation. She had once mentioned she wanted to have kids, but she had never given him the idea that she'd been obsessed with having one. "And you want a child to the point where you would actually consider having a baby from someone you don't know?"

"Yes. In fact, I prefer it that way. I want a baby and not the baby's father. I don't want a man coming in my life trying to run things."

"Run things how?"

"Like telling me how to live my life, forcing the issue

of whether I can have a career outside of my home, a man who'd try to control me and keep a tight rein on me."

Of all those things she'd named, Storm recognized only one that he might eventually become guilty of.

"And what's wrong with a man wanting the sole responsibility of taking care of his wife so she won't have to work outside the home?"

Her glare thickened. "For some women, nothing, but I prefer taking care of myself. I don't want to depend on anyone."

Storm frowned and crossed his arms over his chest. "So, for your own selfish reasons, you're willing to deny your child a father?"

"If it means not wasting my time looking for a Mr. Right who doesn't exist, then yes."

Storm tried to keep his anger in check. Why couldn't she see that he was her Mr. Right? He slowly shook his head again. "If you want a baby, then I'll give you *my* baby."

"What!"

"You heard me. I'll be damned if I'll let another man get the woman I love pregnant."

Jayla was shocked at the words he'd spoken. "The woman you love?"

Silence shredded the air and Storm knew he had to get her to understand the depth of how he felt. He crossed the room and with his fingertip, lifted her chin to meet his gaze. "Yes. I love you, Jayla, and if you want a baby, then we'll get married and I'll give you one."

She stared at him as if she didn't believe he'd suggested such a thing. And then she took a step back from him.

"Things wouldn't work between us, Storm. You would want more from a wife than I'm willing to give."

"And what about the fact that I love you?"

She shrugged. "I believe you like sleeping with me, but I find it hard to believe that you really love me, Storm."

She sighed deeply when he didn't say anything but continued to stare at her. "We agreed that we would end things between us whenever I was ready," she finally said to break the silence. "Well, I'm ready. For us to continue seeing each other will only complicate matters."

"Complicate matters like hell!" he said, his voice rising. "I tell you that I love you and that I want to marry you and give you the baby you want, and you're telling me that you don't believe a word of it and to get out of your life? And to top things off, you plan to continue with this crazy scheme to have a baby from a man who not only doesn't love you, but a man *you* don't even know?"

"I don't owe you an explanation for anything I do, Storm. And considering everything, it would be best if you left."

Storm stared at her for a moment, then moved past her to the bedroom. Moments later, fully dressed, he came back into the living room. He stood in front of her and said softly, "I hope that one day you'll take your blinders off. Maybe then you'll recognize your Mr. Right when he comes and stands right in front of you."

He then turned and walked out the door.

When Storm left, Jayla moved around the house trying to convince herself that she was glad they would no longer be seeing each other. The last thing she needed was a man trying to control her life.

After closing things up and turning off the lights, she slipped back into bed, and tried to ignore the scent of Storm that still lingered there. She closed her eyes.

I love you, Jayla...

She opened her eyes, flipped on her back and stared up at the ceiling as she tried to convince herself that she wasn't the one with blinders on, he was. Couldn't he see that what he was feeling wasn't really love but lust? Die-hard bachelors like Storm didn't fall in love in a blink of an eye or after a few rolls between the sheets.

She turned to her side and closed her eyes, trying to force thoughts of Storm from her mind. But she couldn't. Steeling herself, she sighed, knowing the memories of the times they'd spent together were too deep, too ingrained in her memory.

Getting over him wouldn't be easy, but dammit she would try. She would shift her focus elsewhere and appreciate the good things that were happening to her. Everything she'd wanted was falling in place. Tomorrow, she would go to the fertility clinic for her physical and then she would wait eagerly for the day when she would be inseminated.

Storm was not the most important thing to her— having a baby was.

"Hey, Captain, you got a minute?"

Storm glanced up from the stack of papers on his desk. After having a sleepless night, he had gotten up at the crack of dawn to come into the station. Most of his men hadn't arrived yet. Although it wasn't a requirement, he was one of those captains who preferred working the same hours as the firefighters he supervised.

"Sure, Cobb, come on in. What can I do for you?"

Darryl Cobb had recently become a father again. Four months ago, his wife Haley had given birth to their third child. Darryl was a few years younger than Storm and they had known each other since their high school days. He'd also known Darryl's wife, Haley, from high school, as well, and remembered Darryl and Haley dating even back then. Evidently, Haley hadn't had a problem recognizing Darryl as her Mr. Right since the two of them had been married for over ten years now and always seemed happy together.

"I was wondering if I can take a few hours off today. The baby has a doctor's appointment and Haley just called. Her boss called an important meeting for later today."

Storm nodded. Haley was a computer programmer for a financial management company. "That shouldn't be a problem," Storm said, turning to check the activity board. "You're supposed to teach a class on fire prevention at that elementary school today. Do you have a replacement?"

Darryl smiled. "Sure do. Reed has agreed to cover for me."

Storm nodded. The one thing he liked about the men he supervised was that they got along and were quick to help each other out when something unexpected came up. "In that case, your taking a few hours off won't be a problem," he said making a notation on the activity sheet.

He glanced back over at Cobb. "So how has it been going since Haley returned to work?"

Darryl chuckled. "Crazy."

"Then why did she go back?" he asked, then quickly felt he'd been out of line for asking such a question. But from the laugh Cobb gave him, evidently he hadn't been surprised by the question. From Storm's early days as a firefighter, it had been a joke around the station that his views on women working outside the home were unrealistic and so outdated they were pitiful. He'd been told that it would be hard as hell to find a woman who'd agree to do nothing but stay at home, barefoot and pregnant.

"Well, that humongous house we just bought in Stone Mountain was one good reason for her to return to work," Darryl said, still chuckling. "But another reason is that Haley enjoys what she does and I'm not going to ask her to give it up." He looked pointedly at Storm and said, "That's where a lot of men make their mistakes."

Storm raised a brow. "Where?"

Darryl smiled. "In assuming that they are the only ones who have it together. I personally think it's women who really have it together, and we're merely bystanders looking in. Besides, with Haley and me both sharing equally in the raising of our kids, I feel I'm playing just as an important role in their lives as she is, and that's important to me. It has nothing to do with which one of us is bringing home the bacon, but mainly how the both of us are serving the bacon. Together, we're forming a deep, nurturing attachment to our children and are giving them all the love we have, which is a lot. And to me that's the most important thing."

A few moments later after Cobb had left, Storm stood at the window in his office and looked out as he thought about what Darryl had said. Was one of the reasons Jayla hadn't recognized him as her Mr. Right because in her mind he was all wrong?

Had what Nicole done to him all those years ago driven his beliefs that a husband should be sole provider for his wife and family? He would be the first to admit that because of Nicole's rejection, he'd always wanted to prove the point that a man, highly educated or not, could take care of his household. His father had done it and had raised a family on a construction worker's salary.

He thought of his brothers and their wives. Even married to a sheikh, his sister Delaney was still working as a pediatrician and doing one hell of a job raising their son Ari, who was beginning to be a handful. But then her husband Jamal also played an equally important role in raising their son. Then there were his sisters-in-laws, Shelly, Tara and Madison. Although Shelly and Dare were the only ones who had a son, eleven-year-old AJ, Storm was fairly certain that if Tara and Madison were to get pregnant, they wouldn't consider giving up their careers.

He closed his eyes and remembered the scene that had played out in Jayla's living room last night. The woman he loved was planning to let another man get her pregnant only because she was convinced there wasn't a Mr. Right for her. She actually believed there wasn't a man who could and would understand her need to be in control of her life.

He opened his eyes and glanced down at his watch. According to that letter he'd read last night, she had a physical at nine this morning at that fertility clinic. After the physical, it would probably be two to three weeks before the actual procedure could be performed. Hopefully that would give him time to convince Jayla that he really did love her, and that he would satisfy all her needs, including her need to remain independent... to a certain degree. Changing his conventional views wouldn't be something he could do overnight, but it was something he could definitely work on, especially for Jayla.

The most important thing was to show her that he was the right man for her. The only man for her. For the second time since returning from New Orleans, the old fortune teller's words crept into his thoughts.

You should keep your sights high, be patient and let destiny take its course.

He smiled. Perhaps the old woman hadn't been a flake after all and had known exactly what she'd been talking about. Tomorrow was the night of the charity benefit and because of her involvement, he knew Jayla would be there. He would start wooing her with the intensity of a man who had one single goal in his mind.

To win the love of the woman he intended to marry.

"You can go ahead and get dressed, Ms. Cole," the nurse said smiling. "The doctor will return in a few minutes to go over the results of your tests."

"Thanks."

Jayla sighed deeply as she began putting her clothes back on. She'd had a sleepless night and hadn't been as excited about the appointment this morning as much as she'd wanted to be because of thoughts of Storm. And it hadn't helped matters that she'd been crying most of the morning.

She walked over to the mirror in the room and looked at herself. She looked pathetic. Her reflection revealed a woman who was truly drowning in her own misery. And it was a misery well deserved. Even Lisa hadn't given her any slack when she'd called this morning and she'd told her about the argument she'd had with Storm. And when she'd mentioned that Storm had told her that he loved her and wanted to marry her, her best friend had actually gone off on her. But then, what was a best friend for if she couldn't give you hell when you needed it?

The sad thing about it was that everything both Storm and Lisa had said was true. She wouldn't recognize her Mr. Right if he came to stand right in front of her.

She sighed deeply as she slipped back into her panty hose. So what if Storm was one of those men who wanted to take care of his woman? Wasn't it better to have a man who wanted to take care of you than to have a man who expected you to take care of him? And was it so awful that he was a little on the conventional side? She would be the first to admit that she found some of his old-fashioned ways sweet. Besides, if his conventional way of thinking became too much for her, couldn't she just make it her business to modernize him? And so what if he had ways like her father? Adam Cole had been a great parent and a part of her could now say she appreciated her strict upbringing. A couple of the girls she had wanted to hang around with in high school had either gotten pregnant before graduating or had gotten mixed up with drugs.

Upon waking this morning, it had taken several hours of wallowing in self-pity, as well as being forced to listen to Lisa's tirade, before she'd finally taken the blinders off. Storm loved her and he was her Mr. Right and she loved him. She couldn't fight it, nor could she deny the truth any longer. She loved him and had always loved him.

Oh, she understood now why he had kept his distance so many years ago but still, it had been a bitter pill for a young girl to swallow. A part of her had built up an immunity against ever being rejected by him again. But now she was a woman and she wanted what any other woman would want—a man to love her. And that man had offered to marry her and give her the baby she wanted. How blessed could a woman be?

Her feeling of euphoria quickly disintegrated when she remembered she had thrown his words of love back in his face. She had a feeling that Storm was a man who wouldn't take rejection well. What if he never wanted to see her again?

She quickly slipped into her skirt, thinking she had to work fast to correct the mistake she'd made or she would lose him completely. And the first thing she had to do was to cancel her plans to get inseminated. The only man she wanted to father her child was Storm.

She turned when she heard a knock at the door. "Come in." She smiled apologetically when Dr. Susan Millstone walked in. Before the doctor could say anything she quickly said, "I've changed my mind."

After closing the door behind her, Dr. Millstone tilted her head and looked at her. "You've changed your mind?"

"Yes. I've decided not to go through with the artificial insemination procedure after all."

The doctor leaned against the closed door. "May I ask the reason you've changed your mind?"

Jayla smiled. "Yes. The man that I love wants to marry me and give me his child, and I want that, too, more than anything." *And I hope and pray I haven't lost him*, she thought.

Dr. Millstone chuckled as she shook her head. "What you've just said will make what I have to tell you a little easier."

Jayla raised a brow. "Oh?"

"I just went over the results of your physical and it seems you're already pregnant."

The news was so shocking that Jayla dropped into a nearby chair. She looked back up at the doctor, not believing what she'd been told. "I'm pregnant?"

The doctor chuckled again. "Yes. You're almost a month along."

Jayla shook her head, as if trying to keep it from spinning. She was almost a month pregnant! "New Orleans," she said softly, as a smile touched her lips.

"Excuse me?"

She met Dr. Millstone's grin. "I said New Orleans. I got pregnant in New Orleans. But how is that possible when we were careful?"

A smiled played at the corner of Dr. Millstone's mouth. "I deliver a lot of babies whose parents thought they were careful, too. No birth control is one hundred percent."

Jayla chuckled. "Evidently not."

"So, can I assume that you're happy with the news?"

Jayla jumped up as the feeling of euphoria took control of her again. "Yes, I'm happy! I am ecstatic!"

she said, laughing joyously. She just hoped and prayed that Storm would be happy and ecstatic, as well, when she told him that she loved him and was having his baby.

Chapter 11

Everyone who was somebody in Atlanta had turned out for the Kids' World charity benefit. There were politicians, CEOs of major corporations, celebrities and well-known sports figures, all of whom considered Atlanta home.

There was also a sheikh in attendance, the very handsome Prince Jamal Ari Yasir, who was dressed in his native Middle Eastern attire and causing quite a stir among the ladies, single or otherwise. Jayla smiled, knowing the stir was a waste of time and effort since it was well known that Prince Yasir was happily married to the former Delaney Westmoreland, Storm's sister.

Jayla glanced across the room at the group of men standing together laughing and talking. Although Storm hadn't arrived yet, it didn't take much to recognize the men as Westmorelands. Their kinship was clearly evident in their facial features, their height as well as their sex appeal.

She began wondering if perhaps Storm had changed his mind about coming. After leaving the clinic yesterday, she had decided to take the rest of the day off. Too excited to work, she had gone home and called Lisa and invited her to lunch.

She'd barely gotten the words out after Lisa arrived when she burst into tears of happiness. Then she told Lisa of her fears about telling Storm. What if he no longer loved her? What if her rejection had killed his feelings for her?

Lisa, in her usual optimistic way, had assured her that although Storm might be a little angry with her right now, she doubted his love could have died so quickly.

Jayla had wanted to call and ask him to come over, but then she'd remembered he was on duty at the fire station. So, instead of talking to him yesterday, she had walked around the house wondering what she would say when she saw him tonight.

"Everything looks beautiful, doesn't it?"

Jayla turned when she recognized the voice of Tara Westmoreland. Tara was accompanied by three other women whom Jayla didn't immediately recognize. At first, Jayla thought each of the women was beautiful in a unique way. Like Tara, they were smiling and each of their smiles reflected a sincere friendliness. Jayla returned their smiles as Tara made the introductions.

The women were Shelly Westmoreland, who was married to Sheriff Dare Westmoreland; Madison Westmoreland, who was married to Stone Westmoreland; and Storm's sister, Delaney Westmoreland Yasir. Jayla swallowed deeply. All three women, like Tara, were part of the Westmoreland clan. Somehow, Jayla found her voice to respond to Tara's earlier comment. "Yes, everything is beautiful and your committee should be proud of what they've accomplished."

Tara chuckled. "Yes, but your company also played a huge role. The food is wonderful. Everyone is talking about the catering service that is being used. It's quite evident that Sala Industries went out of their way tonight."

"Thanks."

"And I have to say the dress you're wearing looks simply gorgeous on you," the woman who had been introduced as Madison Westmoreland said.

"Thank you," Jayla said smiling, beginning to feel more relaxed.

She and the women launched into a discussion of styles in clothing and movies they'd recently seen when they heard a sudden buzzing from a group of single women standing not far away. A quick glance at the entrance to the ballroom revealed why. Storm and his cousin Ian had walked in and were crossing the ballroom floor to join the other Westmoreland men. Both men looked dashing and handsome dressed in black tuxedos.

Part of Jayla wished Storm would look her way; then, seconds later, she decided maybe it would be best if he didn't when she overheard the conversation between two women standing not far away.

"Hey, I'm going to make it my business to go after 'The Perfect Storm' tonight," the more statuesque of the two said.

The other woman giggled and said, "Storm Westmoreland has a reputation of not doing the same woman twice."

"Yeah, but I heard that just once is all it takes to blow your mind and I definitely intend to have that one time," the statuesque one countered.

A flash of jealousy raced through Jayla, and she started to turn to the woman and tell her that when it came to Storm, hands off. But she couldn't do that. She didn't have the right.

She glanced up when she felt someone gently touch her arm. "I wouldn't worry about what the 'hottie duo' are saying if I were you," Shelly Westmoreland whispered, smiling. "I heard from a very reliable source that Storm has found a special lady and only has eyes for her."

Jayla blinked in surprise at Shelly's words and glanced at the other women standing beside her. They all nodded; evidently, they'd heard the same thing. Was it possible that they knew she and Storm had been seeing each other? And who was this reliable source Shelly Westmoreland was talking about? Had Storm mentioned her to members of his family?

Her heart stopped and she wasn't sure what to say to the four women who were staring at her with such genuine and sincere smiles on their faces. Tears pressed at the corner of her eyes.

"I may have lost him," she whispered, as her mind was suddenly filled with doubt and regret.

Delaney Yasir chuckled and placed an arm around Jayla's shoulder. "I doubt that. My brother hasn't taken his eyes off of you since he arrived."

Hope ran through Jayla. "Really?" She was standing with her back to Storm so she couldn't see him.

Madison Westmoreland grinned. "Yes, really."

"Hey, Storm, you want something to drink?" Jared Westmoreland asked his cousin as he grabbed a glass a wine off the tray of a passing waiter.

"Storm doesn't want anything to drink," Ian said, grinning. "The only thing Storm wants is that woman who's standing over there talking to the Westmoreland women."

Stone Westmoreland lifted a brow and glanced across the room. The woman's back was to them, so he couldn't get a look at her. "You've met her?" he asked in surprise.

Ian chuckled. "Yes, Storm introduced us in New Orleans."

That comment got everyone's attention. Chase stared at Storm. "You took her to New Orleans with you?"

Before Storm could respond, not that he would have anyway, Ian spoke up. "Of course he didn't take her to New Orleans with him," he said, as if the thought of Storm taking any woman out of town with him were ludicrous. "They just happened to be in the same place at the same time. Her father was Storm's old boss, Adam Cole."

Thorn Westmoreland took a slow sip of his drink and said, "Her parentage is old news, Ian, but her being in New Orleans with Storm is definitely something that we didn't know about."

"And something all of you are going to forget you heard," Storm said. The tone of his voice matched the look on his face. Highly irritated. Totally annoyed. Deadly serious. "And I thought I told you guys that I don't like you discussing my business like I'm not here."

Chase gave his twin a dismissive shrug and said, "Yeah, whatever." He then turned his attention back to Ian. "So what else can you tell us about Storm's lady?"

Ian met Storm's gaze and got the message loud and

clear, although it was obvious his brothers hadn't...or they chose no to. Ian grinned and decided to play dumb. "I forget."

Storm smiled. He knew he could count on Ian to keep his secrets, just as Ian knew he could count on him to keep his. Things had always been that way between them. He then turned his attention back to Jayla and wished the crowd would thin out so his view wasn't as blocked, or that she would at least turn around so he could see her. He wanted to look into her eyes to let her know that no matter how much she might want him out of her life, he was there to stay.

Moments later, as if he had willed it to be so, the crowd thinned out and she turned and met his gaze. His heart almost stopped when he saw how radiant she looked. And what made her even more beautiful was the fact that she was wearing that red dress.

His dress.

It was the same one he had picked out for her in New Orleans. He wondered, hoped and prayed that there was a hidden meaning behind her wearing that dress. Could he dare hope she might realize that he was her Mr. Right? Knowing there was only one way to find out, he walked away from the group.

His destination was the woman he loved.

Jayla's breath caught in her throat when she saw Storm heading toward her. She couldn't tell from his expression whether he was glad to see her or not, but one thing was certain—he wasn't going to avoid her. But maybe she was jumping to conclusions. Although he was headed to where she was standing, he might be coming over to say hello to his sister and sisters-in-law since they were standing next to her.

"Here comes Storm Westmoreland," she overheard one of the women from the "hottie duo" say. "And I think he's seen my interest and is coming over to talk to me."

"Fat chance of that happening," Tara whispered. Jayla couldn't help but smile and hoped Tara was right. As Storm got closer, her hope went up a notch when she saw he was still holding her gaze. She sighed deeply when he stopped in front of her.

"Hi, Jayla."

She smiled up at him and tried to keep her heart from pounding erratically in her chest. "Hi, Storm."

It was only then that he released her gaze and glanced at his sister and sisters-in-law. "Good evening, ladies, and, as usual, all of you look beautiful and bestow much pride upon the Westmoreland name."

He glanced back at Jayla. "And you look beautiful, as well, Jayla."

"Thanks." And before she lost her nerve, she asked, "Is there a chance I might speak with you privately for a moment?" The man standing before her looked so irresistibly handsome, so utterly gorgeous that it almost took her breath away.

Her pulse quickened when he stared into her eyes with an intensity that made her shiver. He nodded, then said, "Sure." He shifted his gaze from her to the others and said, "Please excuse us for a minute." After taking her hand in his, Storm led her through the doors and outside into the lobby.

"There're a lot of people here tonight," Storm said, as they continued walking down the elegant and immaculate hallway.

"Yes, there are," Jayla replied. The benefit was being

held in the ballroom of the Atlanta Civic Center and the facility was the perfect place to host such an event. She wondered where Storm was taking her. It was obvious that wherever it was, he wanted them to have privacy.

They stopped walking when they came to a beautiful atrium. All the greenery, flowering plants and the huge waterfall added warmth and even more grace and style to their surroundings. Jayla suddenly felt nervous, not sure of herself, but then she knew she had to say her piece. No matter what, he deserved to know about their baby, but she couldn't tell him that now. If he wanted her back, it had to be because he still loved her and not because he would feel obligated because she was carrying his child.

She cleared her throat. "Storm."

"Jayla."

She smiled when they had spoken at the same time. She glanced at him and his features were expressionless and she had no idea what he was thinking.

"Ladies first," he said, meeting her gaze.

Jayla swallowed. She knew that a lot was at stake here, but she remembered the words her father would often say—*nothing ventured, nothing gained.* She cleared her throat. "I kept my appointment at the clinic this morning."

He contemplated her silently for a moment, and then asked, "Did you?"

She expelled a soft breath, still unable to read him. "Yes, but I've decided not to go through with the procedure." She thought she saw relief flash through his gaze but wasn't sure.

He held her gaze steadily, studied her for a moment. "Why did you change your mind?" he asked.

Jayla swallowed again as she lifted her chin. "Because I realized that you were right and that I did have blinders on. So I took them off and when I did, I could see things a lot clearer."

Tension hummed between them; she felt it. "And what do you see, Jayla?" he asked softly.

She breathed deeply and decided to tell him just what she saw. "I see a tall man who is so strikingly handsome I can barely think straight, who has eyes so dark they remind me of chocolate chips and a voice so sexy it sends shivers down my spine. But most importantly, since taking my blinders off, I can see my Mr. Right standing right in front of me. Now. At this very minute. And I pray that I haven't ruined things, and there's a possibility that he still wants me, because, since taking off my blinders, I've also discovered just how much I love him and just how much I want him in my life."

Jayla held her breath, not knowing what he would say, not knowing if he would accept her words. Then, she saw a slow smile come into his face and spread from corner to corner on his lips. And those lips leaned down and came mere inches from hers and whispered, "I'm glad you quickly came to that conclusion, Jayla Cole, because I love you and there was no way in hell I intended to let you go."

Before she could say anything, he captured her mouth in a kiss. It was a kiss that was so powerful and tender that it immediately brought tears to her eyes. Storm loved her and she loved him and she believed in her heart that everything would be okay. Together, they would make their marriage work because love was the main ingredient and she believed they had plenty of that.

He reluctantly broke off their kiss. "I know you can't leave until everything is over, but I have to get you alone."

Jayla grinned and glanced around. "We're alone now, Storm."

He chuckled. "Yeah, but this place is too public for what I want to do to you." His features then turned serious. "But more importantly, Jayla, we need to talk and come to an understanding about a few things, all right?"

She nodded. "All right. But no matter what, we'll work things out."

He pulled her back into his arms. "Most definitely."

It was well after midnight when Jayla entered Storm's home. The evening had been perfect and a lot of money had been raised for Kids' World, which meant that plenty of terminally ill children's dreams would be coming true. It wasn't hard to guess that the calendars would sell like hotcakes. Over one hundred thousand calendars had been sold, and an order had already been placed for that many more.

And it hadn't come as a surprise to anyone that the single women had gone wild over the twelve men who had posed for the calendar, especially Mr. July, Thorn Westmoreland. However, any women who might have given thought to the possibility that she had a chance with Mr. July, married or not, discovered just how wrong they were when, after receiving the plaque that had been presented to all twelve men, Thorn crossed the room and kissed his wife, proclaiming to all that Tara Westmoreland was all the woman he wanted and needed.

And, Jayla thought as she inwardly smiled, Storm had made a number of declarations himself tonight. That single woman who'd vowed that she would get at least one time with Storm had been brazen enough to approach him while he and Jayla had stood together talking. Storm had smoothly introduced Jayla to the woman as his fiancée. The woman had congratulated them and walked off, thoroughly disappointed.

He had also introduced her to his parents and the rest of his family. She even got to meet the newest additions to the Westmoreland clan, his cousins Clinton, Cole and Casey. She had quickly decided that the Westmoreland family was a very special one and they all stuck together like glue.

"Would you like something to drink, Jayla?"

She turned and watched as Storm closed the door and locked it. "No, thanks." She nervously glanced around and stopped when her gaze came to rest on a framed photograph that sat on his fireplace mantle. It was a photo that the two of them had taken with her father at his last birthday party, the one the men at the fire station had given him. Her father had insisted that she and Storm stand next to each other while he stood in the background. Because of Adam Cole's six-seven height, he appeared to be towering over them. And he was smiling so brightly that she couldn't help wondering if perhaps he'd known about her feelings for Storm and, in his own special way, had given them his blessings that night, because less than five months after that picture was taken, he'd died.

Storm followed her gaze and after a few moments said, "Whenever I look at that picture and really study it, I think that your father was a lot smarter than either of us gave him credit for being."

Jayla nodded. Evidently their thoughts had been on the same page. She inhaled deeply and then met Storm's gaze. "I agree." She broke eye contact with him and continued her study of his home. With earth-toned colors and basic furnishings, it was clearly a bachelor's place. But everything was neat and in order. "Nice place."

"Thanks. A few months ago, I decided to sell it and get a bigger place," he said as his gaze roamed over her from head to toe. "Thanks for wearing that dress. It's my favorite."

Jayla smiled. "That's the reason I wore it. I was trying to give you a sign, or at least make you remember the time we spent together in New Orleans. I figured the only other person who would know I'd worn this dress before was Ian, and I counted on him not noticing."

Storm lifted a brow. He hated to tell her, but Ian had noticed. In fact, every man who'd been present tonight had noticed Jayla Cole in *that* dress. And each and every time he saw a man looking at her, even when trying not to, he was inwardly overjoyed that she belonged to him.

And now with her standing in the middle of his living room, there was nothing he was itching to do more than to take that dress off her because chances were, like before, the only thing underneath that dress was a pair of thongs. But he knew before they could get to the bedroom, there were issues that needed to be resolved between them.

Sighing, he slowly crossed the distance that separated them and took her hand in his. "Come on, let's sit down and talk."

She nodded and then he led her over to the leather sofa and they sat down. "I've done a lot of thinking, Jayla, and you're right. There's nothing wrong with a woman working outside the home if she wants to do so. The reason I was opposed to it was because years ago, while a senior in high school, I thought I was in love with a girl who threw my love back in my face when I told her of my decision not to go to college but to attend the Firefighters Academy instead. She said that a man without a college education could not properly take care of the needs of his family. When she said that, something snapped inside me and I intended to prove her wrong and, with college or not, I wanted to be a man who could sufficiently provide for all of my family's needs."

Jayla nodded. She could see the pride of a man like Storm getting bruised with a woman saying something like that. She sighed, knowing it was time to get rid of her emotional baggage as well.

"Because Dad was so strict on me while I was growing up," she started off by saying, "I had this thing against marrying a man who I thought would try and control me. But now I see that Dad had the right approach in raising me, or no telling how I might have turned out."

She inhaled in a deep breath, then added, "I believe all those times I thought I was looking for Mr. Right I failed miserably because it wasn't time to find my Mr. Right. It wasn't time until I saw you again in New Orleans."

Storm lowered his mouth to hers and the kiss he gave her was filled with so much intensity and passion, Jayla couldn't help the groan that purred from her throat. Nor could she ignore the sudden rush of heat that threatened to consume her entire body as Storm continued to claim her mouth, staking a possession all the way to the darkest recesses of her soul. She kissed him back, putting into the kiss all the love and feeling that he did, claiming his mouth as well and staking her possession.

He pulled back, stood and pulled her into his arms. "Will you marry me, Jayla Cole? Will you love me for better or worse, richer or poorer, in sickness and in health, till death do us part?"

Tears gathered in Jayla's eyes. "Yes! Oh, yes! I love you."

Storm grinned. "And I love you, too." His gazed locked with hers and smiled. "Tell me again what you see."

She smiled up at him, knowing it was time to tell him her other news. "I see my Mr. Right…and," she whispered softly, "I also see the man who is the father of my baby."

Jayla watched Storm's expression and knew the exact moment it dawned on him what she'd said. For a moment, he continued to gaze at her, his dark eyes clouded with uncertainty, hope. "Did you just say what I think you said?" he asked breathlessly.

She smiled. If there was any doubt in her mind that he wanted a baby, their baby, it evaporated when she saw the look of sheer happiness in his eyes. "Yes. After taking my physical, I told the doctor that I had changed my mind about the insemination procedure and she said it was a good thing since I was already pregnant."

Jayla chuckled. "By my calculations, I got pregnant in New Orleans but I still can't figure out how that happened when I know for certain that protection was used every time we made love."

Storm laughed. "Yeah, but a condom can only hold so much, sweetheart. When a man is driven to have multiple—"

Jayla placed a finger to Stone's lips and grinned. "Okay, I get the picture."

He swept her into his arms and chuckled. "I'm glad that you do and I guess you know what your pregnancy means," he said as he moved toward his bedroom.

"What?"

"There's no way we'll have a June wedding, even if you wanted one. We're getting married as soon as possible."

She laughed. "How soon?"

"Tomorrow isn't soon enough for me."

"What about in a month?"

"Umm, that's negotiable," he said as he placed her in the middle of his bed.

When he stood back, Jayla's gaze swept over him. When she saw the magnitude of his arousal, she inhaled deeply. "I have a feeling I might not be able to move in the morning."

He smiled as he began removing his clothes. "I have a feeling you just might be right. And I have a feeling that if you weren't pregnant now, you could very well be in the morning."

Jayla smiled and her gaze met his. "And you're sure you're okay with becoming a father, Storm? It's a lot for a devout bachelor to take on a wife and child at the same time."

His smile widened. "But I won't have an ordinary wife and child," he said coming back to her, completely naked. "They will be extraordinary because they are mine. And I promise to take very good care of them,

Adam's daughter and grandchild, just as I believe he knew that I would."

He leaned over and slowly peeled the dress from Jayla's body. Then he quickly removed her shoes and panty hose. Finally, he removed her thong. "I really like that dress, but I like you naked a lot better."

He then joined her on the bed. "Do you know what is about to happen to you, Jayla?"

She laid a hand against his cheek. "No, tell me," she implored softly, seeing the dark, heated look of desire in his eyes. It was a look that sent sensuous shivers all through her body.

He smiled. "You're about to be taken by *Storm*."

Jayla smiled. She was definitely looking forward to that experience.

Epilogue

A month later

"You may kiss your bride."

As the Westmoreland family looked on in the backyard of his parents' home, Storm smiled as he turned to Jayla and captured her mouth in the kind of kiss that everyone thought should have been saved for later, but one he was determined to bestow upon his bride anyway.

"At least he has his own woman to kiss now," Dare whispered to Thorn.

"It's about damn time," Thorn Westmoreland replied, grinning.

Finally, Storm tore his mouth away from Jayla and smiled. He then leaned over and whispered something in her ear and whatever he said made her blush profusely.

"Umm, I wonder what he said that made her blush

like that, considering the fact she's already pregnant," Stone whispered to Chase.

Chase shrugged. "You know Storm. Nothing about him surprises me."

"Well, hell, I'm still in shock," Jared Westmoreland said, shaking his head. "Storm was the last Westmoreland I thought would marry, and just think, in less than nine months he'll be a daddy."

Jared then chuckled as he glanced at Dare, Thorn, Chase and Stone. "What is it with your side of the family? All of you are tying the knot."

Chase frowned. "Not all of us."

Stone smiled. "Your time is coming, Chase." He then glanced over at his cousins, Ian, Jared, Spencer, Durango, Quade, Reggie, Clint and Cole. "And all of yours."

Durango narrowed his eyes. "Don't try putting a damn curse on us like that old woman put on Storm."

Dare shook his head laughing. "She didn't put a curse on Storm, she merely read his palm. Besides, if it's going to happen, then it's going to happen. The big question is who's next."

He studied his remaining single brother and his eight male cousins. He smiled, having an idea just who the next Westmoreland groom would be, and he couldn't wait to see it happen.

He grinned. "All I have to say is that when it happens, don't fight it. You'll find out later that it will be the best thing to ever happen to you."

Quade Westmoreland frowned. "No disrespect, Sheriff, but go to hell." He turned and walked off, and the other single Westmoreland men did likewise.

Dare laughed and he kept on laughing while thinking there would definitely be another Westmoreland wedding before long. He would bet on it...if he were a betting man.

* * * * *

REQUEST YOUR FREE BOOKS!

2 FREE NOVELS PLUS 2 FREE GIFTS!

KIMANI ROMANCE

Love's ultimate destination!

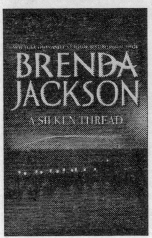